MW00935683

The Road to TIMNATH

Di Ruod Tu Timnat

Sylvia Gilfillian

authorHOUSE®

AuthorHouse™
1663 Liberty Drive
Bloomington, IN 47403
www.authorhouse.com
Phone: 1 (800) 839-8640

Published by AuthorHouse 06/14/2016

ISBN: 978-1-5246-0822-4 (sc)
ISBN: 978-1-5246-0821-7 (e)

Library of Congress Control Number: 2016907736

Print information available on the last page.

This book is printed on acid-free paper.

Author's Note

I started writing this book as the story of Joanie and Jimmy. However, as I went on, new characters introduced themselves into the narrative and I felt compelled to tell their stories.

As I went further into the narrative, I found myself in a language crisis and, as usual, the thorny issue of Jamaicans and our language reared its head. I struggled with this issue over many rewrites. However, I came to my final position after I wrote a paper called *Finding the Authentic Creole Voice in Caribbean Literature* and submitted it as part of the requirement for my MFA degree. This paper led me to the decision to try to cover the entire Jamaican language continuum in this novel. Therefore, **The Road to Timnath** is told from several narrative perspectives and in different voices.

The novel opens and closes with the voice of Audrie Matthews, a Jamaican who has lived abroad for more than twenty years.

She is very passionately and unapologetically Jamaican and speaks the Creole that she took from Jamaica with her.

I have given her the Jamaican Creole language but I have kept an English spelling system for the most part for two major reasons. The first is one of practicality. She controls the narrative for several chapters and I felt that if I used only phonemic spelling, I would literally need to write a translation for non-Jamaican readers. I also wished to imply that she has some level of formal education even though she speaks mostly in the Creole. She lapses into English from time to time, as most Jamaicans like her, do.

There are several older basilectal speakers in the novel, such as, Miss Maudie and Miss Mama. I have tried to represent their speech by spelling some words phonetically. The aim is to make their voices as authentic as possible. However, to make their speech accessible to non-Jamaican readers, I have kept some English spellings. I have also been careful to avoid presenting these women as flat, comic characters. They are, instead, rendered as people who occupy the world as themselves-contradictory at times, funny, but fully realized.

Other characters, such as Miss Birdie and her husband, The Reverend James Whitehead, speak mostly in Jamaican Standard English but resort to a mesolectal variation of the Creole language in their most intimate moments.

I must also point out that *me* and *mi* are pronounced identically in the text when used in Jamaican Creole, the latter being the traditional pronunciation. *We* and *wi* are used in the same way. The differences in spelling are for grammatical purposes, only.

For the reader who expects this novel to be one character's story with various minor characters playing supporting roles, this expectation will not be fulfilled. I have set out to give almost all of the characters an important role in the development of the action and the unfolding of events. While my intent is not boldly didactic, I wish to suggest that, as in real life, it is not always possible for us to identify the heroes and villains of events. Very often, they are one and the same.

I also agonized over whether or not I should allow my characters to use expletives. I simply did not wish to offend some of my greatest supporters and mentors. However, I am a writer and a writer must tell the truth. Some Jamaicans swear and some do not, and although this work is entirely fictional, it is a depiction of a particular culture. I did not see how I could give a full treatment of time, place, setting, action and dialogue, while artificially sanitizing the dialogue. I wish to assure my readers, however, that at no time did I set out to use coarse language purely for its shock value.

Finally, I chose to do a chapter by chapter, non-alphabetized glossary. My intent was to present the unfamiliar words and terms in the order in which they appear in each chapter with the hope that this would make for ease and convenience for the reader.

S.A.G.
2016
New Jersey

In memory of Paulett Elaine Morais
and Landon Sengupta

Epigraph

And she put her widow's garment off from her, and covered her with a veil, and wrapped herself, and sat in an open place, which is by the way to Timnath; for she saw that Shelah was grown, and she was not given unto him to wife.

Genesis 38:14 (KJV)

CHAPTER 1

Audrie Agette Matthews

2003

When chobl tek yu, pikni shot fit yu
When you get into serious trouble, a child's shirt will fit you
When trouble arrives, you will make all possible adjustments, even if they appear ridiculous; we are humbled by misfortune
Fren kill fren and doti waata out faiya
It is possible for a friend to kill a friend and for dirty water to put out a fire
A friend may betray a friend and an enemy may do something good
(Jamaican Proverbs)

Yu ever have so much tings happen to yu *wan* time dat yu feel like yu head *gwaihn buss*? Dat is how me feel dese days. On mi insides, me feel like a *run-weh* train. Me glad, me *bex* and me sad all at di same time. *Muos* days, *A* feel like *sombadi* put a stick up mi *behain* and A *kyan niida si-dong* nor *tan-up* straight.

In June, Jimmy *kaal* me and him was soundin tired and despondent. Him ask me if him kyan come to me *fi* a while. Now, A been waitin well over twenty years fi dis kaal but it still *tek* me like a *staam*. Me *staat* fi cry but me *swala* mi *yai-waata*, quick-quick, and try fi soun real casual and doubtful.

"If yu sure is somting yu *waahn* fi do," me tell him. "A *duohn* waahn no problems *wid* Miss Birdie and yu *granfaada*, because *dem* might feel dat me wait fi dem to raise yu from yu was a *biebi* and as soon as yu *ton* man, me tek yu weh from dem."

"This is not about Mama or Daddy," di *bwai* tell me, soundin forceful and mannish and so much like him faada dat mi belly feel like it was gwaihn *jrap-out*.

"This is about me and something that I need to do, but, if you don't want me to come..."

Me cut him *aaf* before him *kuda* finish and tell him dat A will send di airline ticket to Uncle Nathan, mi husband uncle, and him *shud* not even argue wid me, because him *jos* finish university and me know him no have no money. Him *grii* wid me quick-quick bout di money and me get aaf a di phone and get out mi phone book and staat fi look in a di yellow pages fi travel agencies.

In di two weeks before Jimmy come, me go *chuu* so much confusion dat me had to *taak* to mi supervisor at di hospital. She is di director of nursing and she is a Trinidad *uman*. Like me, she know bout sufferin. She run weh from medical school in a 1976, because her faada wanted was to force her fi married to *wahn uol* man in aada fi annex di man *prapati*. Every time me hear her tell it, me laugh. She seh di dyam man was so uol, him *aredi* a piss *pahn* himself, and her faada and mada plan big wedn behain her back. She was on di next flight to Miami and stayin in a di Y before her parents know what time it was.

Myrna is wan tough uman and *choswordi*, too. She no tek no crap from nobadi and yu kyan chos her wid yu very life. Dat quality haad fi find in a any workplace, because *eniweh tu-moch* uman a wok is always hell to pay. Yu know how we kyan run wi mout. Anyhow, Myrna is not *ongl* mi supervisor but she is mi bes fren in di *wol* wide *worl.*

Well, as me was sayin, di bwai tek me like a staam but me fight mi way chuu di downpour and come out victorious, or so A did tink at di time.

Me ask Myrna fi go wid me to di airport because me really fraid. Me no know how fi meet mi own son because is plenty *waata paas aanda di bridge* since 1980 and di civil war in a Jamaica *wa* no mention in a any history book.

American government was busy in di Caribbean and Latin America in a di 1970s and 80s and we Jamaica and Grenada people have much story to tell. *Laad Gaad!* If muos ordinary Americans did know how much nation on dis eart a *kyari hebi haat* fi wa America government do dem, every *laas* wan a dem wuda ton goodwill ambassador or go a confession fi di *wol-heap* a wickedness wa dem government do in a dem name. Di average American no know dat dem government *farin palisi* often translate into mayhem in a innocent people life. *Aye sa.*

Kansida me, for example. Me never plan fi come to America and me never plan fi run weh *lef* mi wan *pikni*. Some people wuda even seh dat me a hypocrite because if me never come to dis country, me wudn know dat me have more dan *kuoko head* and dat me kuda ton nurse. *Teng* Gaad fi GED and community college. But, if yu ask me fi choose between di life me did have wid mi husband, Junior Whitehead, and di life me have now, me wuda chose di *fors*, hands dong. Yu know how much me lose when gunman mow-dong mi husband because dem tink him was a communist? Dem force me fi run weh from evriting dat me know, fi save mi life.

Yu kyan imagine wa me go chuu fi get to where I am today? Mek me tell yu *sinting*, me hear plenty people a taak bout dem is Christian and me no pay dem no mind. Nowadays, Christian is too often di catchphrase fi anybody who a look fi excuse fi hate people. Is America me come learn dat fi plenty people, Christian and Republican mean di same ting.

But I know I am changed. Yu know dat yu know Jesus when Satan come to yu and tek yu to a high place and show yu all di reasons why yu have a right fi avenge yuself, and yu run him weh from yu wid di wod a Gaad. Is when yu get to a place where two tings suggest *demself* to yu, and di evil look way more enticin and gratifyin, and yu ton weh yu face from it, and deliberately choose di good dat duohn feel good at all.

Dat is when yu know dat yu filled wid di Holy Ghost. Yu filled wid di Holy Ghost when yu speak wid tongues dat taak goodness, even as evil a kaal yu in a voice sweeter dan yu lover.

Me know wa me a taak bout because wan Sunday afternoon me had to mek dat choice, and is not like me get a letter in di mail dat give me a *waanin* ahead a time. Me simply ton aan mi television fi watch an interview program and see dis *baal-head*, pot-belly man a grin him *tiit* dem and a seh how him is retired CIA agent who used to be active in Jamaica and Grenada in di 1980s. Him was taakin bout how him regret wa him do because him duohn believe now, dat America was justified in doin what was done.

Den di man proceed fi taak bout how dem get dem information *rang* and *kil-aaf* wahn innocent, young university professor in a Kingston, because dem mistake him fi *smadi* else.

By di time him a taak bout how di man was a brilliant Rhodes Scholar, mi realize seh is di killin a mi husband di man a chat bout. Me jump up and fling mi wol plate a dinner pahn di television screen. Di rage dat *tek huol* a me mek mi see notn but *daaknis* because when him did a do him *doti deed* dem, *jankro did nyam out him kanshan and tof dry chrash in deh* but now dat him uol and him gut big like *governor washing tub*, him a come confess fi ease him guilty kanshan.

Dat wol night, A never sleep. Me lie dong in a mi bed wid mi cell phone in mi han and a try fi convince miself dat me shudn kaal mi neighbor gun-totin son who always in and out a prison. A was tinkin seriously bout tekin out a contract pahn di man. Him come pahn di television and him provide him name and where him wok, so, me know dat him wudn haad fi find.

Me choose fi do good dat night because me waahn fi see Gaad when me dead. But me kyan tell yu dat di choice never feel good at all. Me had was to taak to Myrna a few times and me still a taak to mi psychiatrist and mi minister, and miself.

Yu *mos a wanda* by now a wa di hell me a run mi mout bout, so, A will try to go back to di beginnin.

MI MADA USED to wash clothes up at di manse in Chalky Hill. She did leave mi faada in Westmoreland and go to stay wid her *breda* and him wife in Trelawny. Yu see, after tirty years of matrimonial obedience, mi mada discover dat mi faada was keepin company wid a fat, young, *coolie gyal* in a di *dischrik.* Mama decide den and dere dat since her pikni dem *gaan paas di worse* and she no have notn more fi give Dada, she wud bes go bout her business. Me hear her tellin wan a mi aunty dem dat she was too uol fi fight over man and since she reach di change-a-life, all of her nature gaan. She add dat if mi faada wanted to staat a new family in him uol age, she wasn about fi *stap* him, but she wudn stay nearby fi play *naana* to him outside pikni dem.

Wan day when him gaan to di sugar estate to work, she pack wi few possession dem and tek me and mi big sister go a Trelawny go live wid mi uncle and him wife. Di main reason Mama finally leave him was because him *bax-dong* mi sister when him ketch her wid her *bwaifren.* Mama seh she prefer fi leave him dan fi chop him up. Believe me, if it was when Mama was in her prime, she wuda did chop him up fi true.

Me staat fi attend a secondary school wan town over from Chalky Hill and when me was on holiday, me go up to di manse go help Mama wid di washin. Miss Maudie was di housekeeper up dere at di time, and if mi memory serve me right, Uncle Nathan did mention dat she still workin dere. Well, it was Miss Maudie who ask Mama fi help wid di washin and she manage fi persuade Miss Birdie fi pay fi di service.

Dat was how me meet Junior, di same summer dat me ton eighteen. Me did jos finish school and was workin at a wholesale supermarket on weekends, but me still help out Mama, when me kud. It was a lot fi her fi manage and she wasn strong. Me never see people who have so much clothes fi wash, every single week. Is like Miss Birdie and Reverend Whitehead change dem clothes *chrii* time a day.

It was on a Friday me meet him and me remember it like yesterday. Me was pinnin di white clothes pahn di line and had a mout full a clothespin. Mama was second-rinsin di bed sheet and pillow case dem in a di washroom, so, she never see when him waak up behain me. Me was alone in a di backyaad and a kansida over mi faada, because we get news dat di young gyal *nyam him out* and gaan lef him. Uncle seh him hear dat Dada *maaga* till him back and belly meet and me did a fret pahn him because *alduoh* him rough, me did still love him.

Me hear di footstep dem and ton roun. Me open mi mout and staat fi *back-weh* from di look-good man weh a waak toward me. Mi knock over di pan full a clothespin at mi foot dem. Di pan begin fi roll weh dong di hill toward di wire fence and him staat run after it and lose him balance. Before me kud seh a wod, di man crash in a di *bag-wire* fence, rip him shirt and scratch-up him han dem.

Him always jokingly tell me afterwards dat me cost him dearly in dignity and blood. Him never *ha fi* tell me who him was, duoh, because him look jos like Reverend Whitehead, ongl younger, *shaata* and a likl *daaka*. Him hair was as curly as mine because mi faada was East Indian and Mama, *St. Elizabeth German* and black. Him yai dem behain di glasses was muddy blue, jos like when sea rough. Di greatest shock to me, duoh, was dat him hair hang dong in shoulder lent dreadlocks.

Me stand right weh me was and watch him carefully as him *git-up* from aaf a di *grong* and *dos-aaf* him behain. Den him waak over to di clothesbasket and reach fi a white kerchief. It *belang* to him faada and me staat fi pull it weh from him and den me ketch miself.

Him dab-dab him scratch-up *han-migl*, wan after di *ada*, but him yai dem never leave mi face. A never look back pahn him, directly, but me know him a watch me. Me did use to man a watch-watch me but none a dem never mek mi haat *gyalop* weh lef me before. Me *swala mi spit* and continue fi pin more clothes pahn di line.

As me waak dong di line, him *fala* me and when me glance pahn him, all me see is tiit. At fors, me feel bex and him *mos a* did see it pahn mi face, because him seh, "Relax, damsel. I mean you no harm. I am just curious that a beautiful *daata* like you round here washing clothes."

By dis time, it look like Mama hear him voice because she come out a di washroom and stan up at di door and a watch we. Me kudn read her expression from weh me was, but A kuda tell from di way she *kimbo,* dat she wasn very pleased.

Mama presence never seem fi *bada* him but before me kuda give him di *hat-wod* wa come to mi mind, Miss Birdie come to di back door and kaal him fi him lunch.

Dat evenin, James John Whitehead, the second, who evribadi kaal Junior, insist on drivin us home, and we was tired so we accept di *aafa.* Me kud tell from di way dat Miss Birdie yai dem a blaze like two fire stick and how she *shub* out her mout till it *lang* like *snook*, dat she never like di idea wan bit but, as him was gwaihn tek Miss Maudie home, she kudn very well object.

Di followin evenin, him come up to mi uncle *yaad* and taak to him man-to-man bout him interest in me. Uncle kaal fi Mama and all chrii a dem si-dong out pahn di verandah and a discuss me as if I had no say in di matter. Me feel a likl bex but at di same time, me feel good, because no man like dat ever look mi way before. A was used to di man dem in mi dischrik in Westmoreland a *hala* all *kain* a *out-a-aada* suggestion to me from me staat fi *buss bres,* but me done decide lang time dat me no waahn notn fi do wid dem. Mi faada seh me too high and mighty and is wan ting uman good fa, but me no pay him no mind wid him *uol-fashan*, coolie ways. Every time me and mi sister visit him Indian relatives, dem always a ask

Dada why him no hurry up and married we aaf before *niega* man *spwail* we.

Mama ask Junior outright what an educated man like him waahn wid a likl gyal who jos finish secondary school, but Junior ongl laugh and tell her dat love have notn to do with *klaas* and education. Uncle tell him dat him have di greatest rispek fi Reverend Whitehead and Miss Birdie and him know seh dem raise him good, but him also know dat Rastaman love fi have plenty uman and fi beat dem.

Junior laugh and laugh when Uncle taak and den him seh, "Some Rastaman beat women and some preacher man beat women. That is something you do because it is in you. I don't even believe in beating children."

Di moment him seh dat, Uncle get goin bout not sparin di rod and *spwailin di chail.* It was a good while before di discussion get back roun to me.

Him come every evenin fi dat week and di family tek to him, especially when him si-dong and eat wid we. By di third evenin, me was no langa nervous roun him and dat weekend, him ask Mama if him kuda tek me fi a *drive out.*

Him kyari me go a Montego Bay go visit some a him fren dem who own a smaal hotel. Dat was how me get an inside view of how rich Jamaica people live. Me feel foolish, duoh, because fi di fors time in a mi life, me had a helper serve me. It was a strange experience because me kuda see seh di helper bex when she see me and me feel out-a-place, like an imposter. Me seh very likl so dat me wudn shame Junior. At dat time, me kudn taak good English like him and when me find out dat weekend dat him was a lecturer at di university in Kingston, me feel more out a mi *dep* dan ever. Di ting bout Junior, duoh, was dat him kyari him position lightly. Is after me begin goin to college here dat me realize seh me did married to a prodigy. Junior had a doctorate in Economics by di time him was twenty-two.

Today, me kyan taak as good as anybody else and when me go to work, me even know how fi twang fi put mi American co-worker dem at ease. Some a dem tend to assume dat if yu have different accent, yu stupid. Me hate when dem come up in a yu face and taak loud to yu like yu deaf. Me chat me *Patwa* because me love it, but me kyan chat di Queen's English if me need to.

Di followin Friday, Junior come dong from town and taak Mama and Uncle into allowin him fi tek me weh fi di weekend. At fors, Mama look fretful but mi uncle wife get in pahn di discussion and tell her dat di man come from good *backgrong* and even if him breed me, him wud mind di chail. Me never like her argument when she tell Mama dat a good *biebi-faada* better dan a *wotlis* husband, but di argument satisfy Mama and she agree fi mek me go.

Dat Saturday night, Junior never jos kiss me and mek me go to mi room. Him tek me by mi han, lead me inside and mek me him uman. Him tek him time wid me and mek me learn what mi body kuda feel and do. A believe dat was when me get pregnant wid Jimmy.

Before Junior, di wan single sexual experience me had was a rape. Dat was what Jamaican man kaal *huol-dong-an-tek*.

It was a cousin who did come from town fi spend holiday wid we. Him was mi auntie granson and him grow up pahn Spanish Town Road. Dada never like him because him seh him too *raw*.

Me and him go tie out Dada goat dem and him drag me in a bush and force himself pahn me. It happen so *faas* and it was over before him kuda fully penetrate me, but dat experience lef me wid a fear fi man and dem *tieli*.

When him git-up aaf a me, me reach fi a stone and buss him *farid* and den me tell him dat me gwaihn mek Dada chop him up. Him run go back go a di house and tell Mama how him no do me notn and me buss him head. Me try fi tell Mama wa him do me, but me mout full-up a spit and me staat fi vomit.

Me staat fi cry and den me run out a di lean-to kitchen and me no stap till me reach di river and me waak all di way out till di waata paas me waist. Me feel di burnin between mi leg dem when di waata touch me. It feel like a fresh cut but me did fraid fi touch dong deh.

Me mek di waata wash weh mi shame and when me go home, Mama have him bag pack and she put him pahn di mail van and send him go back a town.

Dat night wid Junior was notn like dat. Fors, him tek me by mi han and lead me to di room dat him fren dem give we. A was shy and nervous but him pull me up close to him *ches* and whisper in mi *yez*, "Relax, baby girl. I won't do anything to hurt you."

Me kudn look pahn him and mi haat did a beat so haad, me kuda hear it in a mi yez dem. A was afraid but not of him. Me was afraid of dat unknown territory wa dem kaal big man and big uman business. Remember, A was ongl eighteen year uol, and all Mama ever tell me bout sex was dat A wasn to do it, because if me breed, she *naa* mind me two time. Me know fi sure dat if Dada was dere, him wuda did tell Junior dat him ha fi put some money in a him han before him tek me. Fi mi faada did believe seh evriting kuda reduce to di exchange a money.

When me look roun di room, mi yai dem lan pahn a big *pitcha winda* dat tek up *almuos* di entire waal of dat side a di room. Me kuda see di sea and di wave dem a roll up to di shore and a brok-up in a di sand. Still holdin mi han, him waak me over to di winda.

Junior put wan han in a di smaal a mi back and him put di ada to di side a mi head and ton me roun. Him *taala* dan me but not by much. Me stand dere wid mi back to di winda and me feel di cool sea breeze gainst me. Him slide him han from di side a mi head, dong paas mi jaw and yez and me feel him finger begin fi gently outline mi lips. Me look up pahn him and see dat him yai dem a smile and me smile right back at him and den him kiss me.

Him touch me wid *kainness* and him kiss me like me was somting precious and of infinite value and den him waak me back to di bed and begin fi tek-aaf mi clothes, and den, him tek-aaf fi him. When me feel him body finally *kanek* wid me, A was more dan ready and him never tek notn from me dat A never freely give.

Is twenty-chrii years since him gaan and me no *li-dong* wid *aneda* man since den. Is not wan or two man try after me at work. Some even have it fi seh me and Myrna a bull-dagger, but me no pay dem no mind. Maybe if me did get di chance fi see Junior in a him casket and watch dem put him weh in a di grong, den, maybe me kuda did love aneda man. Me no have no good answer fi provide nobadi. Is like dat paat a mi life cut-aaf in mid-sentence and me no know how fi go back go finish it.

On wi way from Montego Bay, Junior seh to me, "Audrie, baby, I have been around and I have traveled some. I have met many women and I have been with a few, but no woman has ever touched me the way you have. There is a purity to you that I have never encountered before and I want to come home to you every day of my life."

While him a taak, him a drive wid wan han and him have di ada wan roun me. Me was half-in and half-out a di passenger seat and me shuda did feel well uncomfortable, but by den, A was so in love wid Junior, dat if him did tell me fi run naked in front a di *kyaar*, me wuda probably did kinsida fi *dwiit*.

Him continue fi taak to me and as mi yez was right up gainst him ches, me a lisn to him haatbeat and how him voice-box a vibrate and me a tink bout all dat we did do in a di bed di night before. What him seh next mek me sit up straight and ton me head fi look pahn him.

Him seh, "I plan to make you my wife and when I come back from Kingston on the weekend, I am taking you to meet Mama and Daddy."

Me remind him seh me know dem aredi, but him insist dat me mos go wid him fi mek it official.

Gaad know, A never waahn fi go up dere to di big, imposin church house pahn di hill, fi meet Miss Birdie, because evribadi in di dischrik know dat she is a haad uman. Goin roun di back fi wash doti clothes was wan ting, but goin dere as Junior uman was not somting me was ready to do. Is bad enough dat Junior come back from university wid him head full a dreadlocks and a taak bout Socialism, but to tek up wid smadi like me wud be more than she kuda tek.

Mi fears prove true when him kyari me go meet dem di nex Saturday. Miss Birdie never even come out come look pahn me and when him tell him faada dat him plan fi married to me, Reverend Whitehead shake him head and tell Junior dat him mekin a big mistake. Dere was notn but kainness in a him yai dem when him taak, but him rejection *hat* mi to mi bone.

JUNIOR TEK ME weh from Chalky Hill and married to me in an Ethiopian Orthodox church in Kingston. Mama come and so did Uncle and him wife and mi sister. Miss Birdie and him faada never show up but Junior fren dem from di *Twelve Tribes Rastafarian Movement* give we a wandaful reception in di Blue Mountains. Di sweetest joy, duoh, was when we come out a di reception and find Uncle Nathan a wait fi we, outside. Him did well bex dat Junior tek him so sudden but him kiss me on both cheeks, tell me dat if him wasn past him prime, him wuda *tiif* me from Junior and den him insist on payin fi wi honeymoon.

Me and Junior go to Grand Cayman fi a wol week and we spen muos a di time in di hotel because a di heat and di dyam sand fly dem. Me never care, duoh, because as Mama wuda seh, mi yai dem did daak and mi belly did full-up a love.

Me had mi biebi seven mont later and few mont after dat, gunman murder Junior on him way home from work. It was on a Saturday night dat it happen. Come to tink of it, is like evriting bad dat ever happen to me, happen pahn a Saturday.

Di biebi was jos about fi ton chrii mont uol and Junior tell me fi leave him wid wi fren Bernadette who live over by Hermitage. Him wanted me to go wid him to a History workshop him was gwaihn give at a college in Manchester.

Bernadette did live wid a community organizer who work fi di rulin party at di time. Both a dem was Twelve Tribes people and like all good Rasta uman, Bernadette was a *Proverbs torti-wan* kain a uman. She was industrious to a fault. She have a mint garden at di front a di yaad and roun di back, she raise chickens fi eggs. She sell di mint and egg dem fi mek money fi feed her pikni dem because her man have outside pikni.

When me ask her fi keep di biebi, she readily agree but on condition dat me pump mi bres-milk and leave it fi him. Me remember her standin in a di doorway wid her back to me dat Friday evenin as me *put-aan* di bres-pump fi what feel like di thousand time. When me complain bout di discomfort, she look pahn me over her shoulder and seh, "So Jah earth run, daata. Woman always ha fi deal wid pain."

She seh it like she know all bout it and she wasn lyin. She raisin chrii beautiful black babies dat look like cherubs but dat duoh stap her man from raisin him han to her.

When we get back into Kingston after di workshop, we stap at a roadside shop fi buy soup and hardough bread fi supper and den we drive roun to Hermitage. To dis day, me ha fi conclude dat di gunman dem did a fala we but we jos never see dem.

When me go in a Bernadette yaad, me realize dat me waahn *pii-pi*, so me go behain di *tambrin* tree dat shade her mint garden. Me kud even remember a laugh at miself and feelin glad dat it was daak and nobadi kuda see me. Jos as me pull up mi panty, me hear di wol-heap a gunshot and me jrap flat. Me kyan still remember di smell a di crush-up mint a full-up mi nose. To dis day, me *kyaahn* drink mint tea.

Right dere weh me lie-dong pahn mi belly, wid mi haat a trip-hammer in a mi yez dem, me see di chrii gunman dem rush chuu di gate and staat fi kick-dong Bernadette door. Me hear when she scream out and wan a di man dem hala, "Shet up yu mout gyal and tell we weh di *blood-klaat* coolie gyal deh!"

Me know right *aweh* dat is me dem a *look-fa*, so, me smaal-up miself in a di mint-patch and A never move a muscle. Dat was when me remember dat me was wearin black and tank mi lucky stars.

By dis time, me no know weh some ada gunman come from and staat fire shot like di Wild West. Di fors set a man dem run out chuu di back door and jump over di fence.

Me still lie-dong in a di mint and dat was when me realize dat Bernadette man was in a di yaad and him a hala out, "Dem kill Junior! Jah Rastafari, dem kill Junior!"

Is like after dat, me no know miself. Me hear police kyaar wid siren come dong di road and me remember watchin dem pull Junior lifeless body out a di kyaar but is like me was in a dream. Bernadette kyari me inside and me remember wantin to wipe di blood aaf her face but me han dem was heavy like lead and me si-dong pahn a chair and to dis day, me kyaahn remember notn more bout dat night.

Two leaders from Junior political party come fi me di next *maanin* and mek me pack whatever me kuda fit in a wan suitcase. We drive chuu back road until we reach a Brown's Town. Me hide out at Uncle Nathan yaad fi chrii week and him kudn tell nobadi dat me was dere, not even mi mada. Dem leave mi biebi wid Bernadette and her man and to dis day, mi yai dem no bless him again. Later on, Uncle Nathan tek Jimmy to Miss Birdie and him granfaada. In his words, Jimmy save Miss Birdie sanity because is di biebi dat mek her come to life again.

Uncle Nathan send me some pitcha after a few years and me tank him but a pitcha kyaahn mek up fi all di milestones dat me miss. Me never see mi biebi buss him *fos* tiit dem. Me no see when him tek him fors step and me no see him ton from a bwai to a man. Mi mada and faada dead and me no see dem grave. Mi sister married and have four pikni wa me no even know.

On top a all dat, me tink back all di time to how dem bury mi beloved and A kudn go to di funeral. Me had was to *sekl* fi wod-a-mout from Uncle Nathan. When him get word dat me wasn safe because certain very powerful people a ask bout me, him kaal in some favors from very influential friends and dem smuggle me out a Jamaica by night.

Me kyaahn tell nobadi a straight story bout how me come to America. Me know me handlers dress me in a man clothes and a ongl nighttime we travel. In later years, when me ketch mi bearins, me conclude dat dem tek me to Cuba fors, because me remember di boat ride, hearin plenty Spanish and days upon days of eatin pork. Me also remember di peelin paint in a di room weh me did a stay and di 1950's lookin kyaar wa me travel in.

Is durin dat journey dat me find out dat Uncle Nathan is not a man fi tek slight. Is chrii ada uman travel wid me and di man dem no stap rape dem a nighttime, but dem never lay a finger pahn me. Me did see wan *kak-yai* wan a eyes me but di leader seh somting to him in a Spanish, kaal Uncle Nathan name and wipe him han *kraas* him *chruot.* Me assume seh him tell di ugly man wa Uncle Nathan wuda do wid him if him touch me.

My suspicion is dat me travel from Cuba to somweh in Central America. Me fairly certain dat we kraas over into di U.S. from Mexico but it was a lang time ago and A was crazy wid grief and fear. Me do what mi handlers tell me, eat what A was given and waak when dem shove me.

Me come to mi senses in a The Bronx and di people A was stayin wid keep me fi a year before dem sen me go a Larchmont fi do live-iin wok wid a wealthy couple. Di Bronx people dem was kain to me but di badness me see in a dat deh house a Larchmont kuda *patch hell an lef.* Di uman and her fren dem a run a whorehouse when di husband dem gaan a wok. Me ha fi watch all a di pikni dem and act as look-out fi mek sure dat dem husband no ketch dem.

Me did grow up wid di *andastandin* dat a haad life mek uman sink dong to di shame of sellin dem skin. Dem ya uman sell dem *badi* because dem bored. Yu live and learn. Me leave from dere and go to a shelter when a customer declare dat him did always waahn fi taste black pussy, and attempt fi rape mi.

When him waak up pahn me in a di kitchen and grab me from behain, me ton roun, look in a him two yai dem weh *fieva glaasi-maabl* and me never see so much as a *waam* hello a look back pahn me. Me kuda tell dat as far as him was *kansern*, me was as functional as a piece a *tailit* paper and him was about fi wipe him *batty* wid me.

Me feel him *hood* gainst mi *batam* and me hear him a *blow shaat* and a piece a primal rage tek-huol a me. Me pull weh from him and run toward di stove and him still a fala me. *Masi mi Gaad!* A who tell him fi dwiit? A lower mi head like any mad ram goat and leap up pahn him and *len him Katy.* Him jrap flat pahn him back wid blood a spew out a him nose. Di likl pikni dem did si-dong at di kitchen table a wait fi dem food and di four a dem staat fi scream and hala.

Di *muma* dem run out a dem room, naked as di day dem *baan* and wan a dem *gat-aan* a *helleva* red mask wid a black *feda* at her *yez-kaana* dem. When di pickney dem see her, a dat time dem hala.

Mi never wait fi kaal Uncle Nathan contact dis time. Mi run in a mi room, grab a week-end bag and stuff in mi passport and a few piece a clothes and *tek-aaf* chuu di back. Mi no *tap gyanda* till mi reach di highway and as Gaad wud have it, di *chok* driver weh tap fi me was a Indian man from Trinidad. Him deliver me to a church in The Bronx and di pastor put me in a shelter fi abused women. Dem send me to school till me get mi GED and mi associate degree in Nursing.

Is dere me stap cry and is dere me get di fors letter from Uncle Nathan wid mi biebi pitcha. Him send me wan every year after dat and me staat fi send tings to him fi mi son. Needless to seh, him kudn mek Miss Birdie know dat it was me sendin all di nice clothes and toys.

Me get mi green *kyaad* chuu Reagan laas immigration amnesty and me teng Gaad every day dat me never ha fi to do no business marriage fi get mi stay. Me hear too much horror story bout wa people give up fi get American green kyaad. Me kaal to mind a lovely half-Indian girl from Clarendon who tell me how she give up her virginity to wan *doti jankro* and him promise fi married to her and get her straight. Him no ongl nyam out her money, but him lef her wid a dose a herpes and no green kyaad.

SO MYRNA GO wid me to di airport fi meet mi son and as we stan-up outside a arrival and a wait fi him, mi knee dem weak and mi haat a dance in a mi ches. A kudn control mi feelins. Wan minute, me excited and di next, me fraid. Me was tinkin how a no me raise him and what if Birdie Whitehead ruin him and me no like him?

All mi *kansidaraishan* come to a halt when him ton roun di kaana, and him a pull wahn suitcase behain him. Me know him right aweh. Him taala dan Junior by a good six inches and him lighter, but even widout di dreadlocks, me see di same high farid and narrow face and, my Gaad, di same kaina glasses.

Me watch him a look roun and a lick him batam-lip like him well nervous. Me kaal out, "Jimmy!" and wi yai dem kanek. Him smile and show him tiit and me remember di day aanda di clothesline. Myrna feel when mi staat fi *chrimbl* and she grab mi han a likl tighter but dat kudn stap me from faalin apaat, and same place weh me stan-up in a Kennedy Airport, me pii-pi up miself.

yu-you

wan-one

gwaihn buss-going to burst; about to explode

run weh-run away

bex-vex; vexed

muos-most

sombadi-somebody

behain-behind

A-I

niida-neither

si-dong-sit down

tan-up; stan-up-stand up

kaal-call

fi-for; to

tek-take; took; tolerate

staam-storm

swala-swallow

yai-waata-eye-water; tears

duohn-don't

wid-with

granfaada-grandfather

dem-them; they; plural forming particle

biebi-baby

ton-turn; become

bwai-boy

jrap-out-drop out

grii-agree

aaf-off

kuda-could have

shud-should

jos-just

chuu-through

taak-talk

uman-woman

wahn-a; an

run weh-run away

uol-old

prapati-property

aredi-already
pahn-upon; on
choswordi-trustworthy
eniweh-anywhere
tu-moch-too much; too many
ongl-only
wol-whole
worl-world
waata paas aanda di bridge-water has passed under the bridge; much time has passed
wa-what
Laad Gaad-Lord God
kyari hebi haat-carrying a heavy heart
laas-last; lost
wol-heap; huol-heap-whole heap; many; much
farin palisi-foreign policy
aye sa-aye sir/yes sir; expression of dismay or anger that implies the intent to retaliate
kansida-consider
lef-leave; left (also as in left and right)
pikni/pikini-child
kuoko head-head like a root tuber; slow witted
Teng Gaad-Thank God
fors-first
sinting-something; thing
demself-themselves
waanin-warning
baal-head-baldheaded

tiit-teeth

rang-wrong

kil-aaf-kill-off; killed

smadi-somebody

tek huol-take/took hold

daaknis-darkness

doti-deed-dirty deed

jankro did nyam out him kanshan and tof dry chrash in deh-a turkey buzzard ate his conscience and stuffed the space left behind with trash; unconscionable

governor washing-tub-the washing tub that belonged to the chief slave on a plantation; likely larger than the others

mos a-must be; must have

wanda-wonder

breda-brother

coolie gyal-East Indian; term regarded as derogatory in some cultures

dischrik-district

gaan paas di worse-gone past the worst; the worst is behind; grown

stap-stop

naana-nanny, grandmother, midwife

bax-dong-hit someone in the face and with so much force that the victim falls

bwaifren-boyfriend

chrii-three

nyam him out-exploit; nyam also means to eat in a crude manner

maaga-meager; emaciated

alduoh-although

back-weh-back away

bag-wire-barbed wire

ha fi-have to

shaata-shorter

daaka-darker

St. Elizabeth German-people of German ancestry who hail from St. Elizabeth Parish

git-up- get up

grong-ground

dos-aaf-dust(ed) off

belang-belong

han-migl-hand-middle; palm

ada-other

gylop/gelop/gilop-gallop

swala mi spit-swallow my spit (saliva)

fala-follow

daata-daughter; young lady

kimbo-akimbo; hands on hips

bada-bother; badder (worse)

hat-wod-hot words; saucy retort

aafa-offer; after

shub-shove

lang-long

snook-*Centropomus undecimalis;* bony fish known for its protruding jaw

yaad-yard; home

hala-holler; yell; cry

out-a-aada-out of order; vulgar; improper

buss-bres-burst breasts; early stage of puberty when the breast buds become visible

uol-fashan-old-fashioned

niega-nigger

spwail-spoil

klaas-class

spwailin di chail-spoiling the child

drive-out-car ride; excursion

dep-depth

Patwa-patois; Jamaican Creole Language

backgrong-background

biebi-faada-baby's father

wotliss-worthless

go-iin-go in

huol-dong-an-tek-hold down and take; forcible rape

raw-crude; uncouth; loud; indiscreet

faas-fast; nosy; insolent

tieli/tiili-penis

farid-forehead

ches-chest

yez/ yaiz-ear(s)

naa-not

pitcha winda-picture window

almuos-almost

taala-taller

kainness-kindness

kanek-connect

li-dong-lie/lay down

aneda-another

kyaar-car

dwiit-do it; did it

hat-hurt

Twelve Tribes Rastafarian Movement-sect of Rastafarians named for the twelve sons of Jacob

tiif-thief; steal

Proverbs torti-wan kain a uman-Proverbs thirty-one kind of woman; industrious

put-aan-put on; puttin on; perform

pii-pi-pee; urinate

tambrin-tamarind

kyaahn-can't

blood-klaat-blood cloth; expletive that refers to menstruation

aweh-away

look-fa-look for

maanin-morning

fos-first

sekl-settle

kak-yai-cockeyed

kraas-cross; across

chruot-throat

patch hell an lef-fill a patch in hell with material left over; hyperbole that expresses excess or enormity

andastandin-understanding

badi-body

fieva-favor; resemble

glaasi-maabl-glass marble

waam-warm

kansern-concern

tailit-toilet

batty-bottom; derrière

hood-manhood; penis

batam-bottom

blow-shaat-blow short; breathless from rage, passion or fear

Massy mi Gaad-Have mercy God

len him Katy-loaned him Katy; loaned him a head butt (the forehead is Katy)

muma-mother (impolite)

baan-born

gat-aan-has/had on

helleva-hell of a

feda-feather

yez kaana-corner of the ear

tek-aaf-take off; run at great speed

tap-stop; top

gyanda-gander; run quickly

kyaad-card

doti jankro-dirty John crow; John crow is the local name for the turkey buzzard

kansidaraishan-consideration

chrimbl-tremble; shake

CHAPTER 2

Good fren better dan pakit moni
A good friend is worth more than money in the pocket
If mout kudn gront, belly wuda buss
If we could not groan, our bellies would burst

What a fren me have in a Myrna. If it was not fi her, me wudn mek it chuu dis crisis in a mi life. Is like di uman have a sixth sense about evriting. Fors of all, she arrange it so dat me kud get a week aaf work, wid pay. She kaal it mi lang delayed maternity leave and she was more right dan she realize. But I am sure dat if she did know what was gwaihn happen to me, she wudn did mek di joke.

Di maanin after Jimmy come, me wake up wid mi bres dem a hat me and mi clothes and bed soak wid bresmilk.

Myrna rush me aaf to di doctor and him tell me dat me have a rare case of what dem kaal spontaneous lactation and him give me medicine fi dry up di milk and sen me fi get some blood work.

Dat wol week, me kudn face Jimmy. A feel sorry fi di poor soul but me feel more sorry fi miself. A swear A was gwaihn dead. A kain a daaknis sekl over mi soul and afterwards me come fi realize what King David mean when him taak bout di valley of di shadow of death.

Jimmy comin open up wan hell of an abscess in a mi soul and nobadi know if me was gwaihn survive it. Me tek to mi bed in travail like a uman in *chailbert* wid a biebi dat dead inside. A had was to push out all a di necrosis of mind and spirit dat huol me in a *bandij* since dat night in 1980 when daakni*s* and evil pay me a personal visit.

Me ha fi seh dis duoh, Jimmy is him faada son. Him stan-up and him never run. Him see dat di ship was aanda *chret a sinkin* and him help fi bail waata. Best of all, him stay out a mi way and mek me keep what likl dignity me did have lef.

Di prescription pill never dry-up di milk immediately and pahn tap a all a dat, mi period come in di form of a hemorrhage. Myrna had was to cover mi bed wid pad and me bleed fi six days straight. Di wol time, Myrna ongl leave mi side fi go a work.

On di seventh day, me open mi yai dem and look pahn di *klak* weh deh pahn mi dresser. It was six-thirty-five in a di maanin and me hear di train a rumble into di Baychester

Station dong di hill from mi townhouse. When me look over pahn di lounge chair weh Myrna pull-up beside me bed, it empty and me hear voices a come from di far side a di house.

Di kitchen on dat side and it open to mi likl square of a backyaad. Me realize dat di two a dem hit it aaf when me hear Jimmy a laugh. Me kak me yez fi hear a wa Jimmy and Myrna a taak bout, when an unfamiliar voice ask Myrna if she waahn milk in her coffee. Me immediately guess dat di voice belang to Jimmy fiancée because him did promise fi bring her to meet me.

By di time me crawl out a di bed, shuffle to di *baatroom* fi clean up miself and mek it back to di bedroom, Myrna a si-dong pahn mi bed-foot and a sip her coffee. She look me up and dong clinically and declare, "At least a little of yu color come back and yu beginning to look like yuself again. How di bleeding?

"It dry up but me feel weak."

"But of course, Audrie. Yours is one of the worst cases of post-traumatic stress reaction I ever see. And poor Jimmy turn basket case inside here. Di boy *pu-dong* one piece a cryin and seh how he shudn come disturb yu life and dredge up bad memories. I had was to send call he girlfriend to comfort he, because I couldn't look after yu and pay mind to he at the same time. Poor soul. He still threatening to cut he stay short and go back to Jamaica."

When Myrna seh dis, me snap to mi senses and decide fi get dressed. Me kudn afford fi lose mi son wan more time and A wasn about to be aneda Birdie Whitehead to mi new found *daata-in-laa*. A put-aan a red housedress, slide mi foot dem into house slippers and wid Myrna han roun mi waist fi support, A begin di waak from di bedroom to di kitchen.

Di girl had her back to di door, but Jimmy was sittin at di head a di table and him stan-up as soon as him see me. Me kud tell from di wildness in a him yai dem dat him did well fraid.

Me hurry over as best as mi weak leg dem kuda kyari me and tell him fi si-dong. Me see di staam in him yai quiet itself and me ton roun fi greet him fiancée. When mi *bihuol* di girl, me buss out a laugh and all chrii a dem look pahn me as if me crazy. Me si-dong and ask di girl her name. She tell me dat she is Genevieve and dat she jos finish her nursing degree at di College of New Rochelle.

She look uncertain and me hurry up and put her at ease. Me squeeze her likl han and tell her dat me laugh because me kudn believe how much she resemble Miss Birdie. She give a likl nervous titter and tell me dat evribadi who duohn know di Whitehead family tink she is di gran-daata and Jimmy a di in-laa.

Jimmy stan-up and interrupt Genevieve but she ongl smile and move roun to di ada side a di kitchen table. Him staat bustle roun and ask me if him kyan mek me somting to drink. Me tell him dat me will tek a cup of whatever him a drink.

Him a spin roun and him so anxious dat me mad fi tell him fi si-dong but me leave him be and ton mi attention to Genevieve. Me kyan see why Jimmy sweet pahn her. She pretty kyaahn done. She is di kain a black uman dat keep dem good looks fi a lang time. Her iris black like raisins and glow wid light. Dat is real sparkle me see in her yai dem and yu kyan tell dat her nature sweet fi true. She have two dimples dat set so deep, yu kuda ketch waata in a dem. Her skin is di color of unsweetened cocoa and her complexion cool like she produce a natural foundation. And she shaat, jos like Miss Birdie, wid di same likl waist and big *bam-bam.* Her bres dem not as big but she not flat either. Is a girl dat grow up wid plenty love and life duohn grab her by di *chruot* yet. Wid all a dat, duoh, me see a likl shadow in a her yai dem, a touch a sadness at di corner of her glance.

Me also see how her gaze faal pahn mi son and she no mek no effort fi hide how she feel bout him. She tug pahn mi *haat-string, kaa* a same so me did love Junior. Me beg Gaad fi give she and Jimmy lang life and plenty joy. Me even allow miself fi hope fi grandchildren and a chance fi enjoy dem.

Jimmy bring me a mug a coffee and me learn dat mi son duohn know a dyam ting bout mekin coffee. Nevertheless, me drink it up like is nectar because me never know dat me wuda did live fi see mi pikni again.

Myrna reach fi mi han aanda di table and she squeeze it as if to assure me dat somhow all dis madness wud come out alright. A hitch mi *haas* to di caravan weh dem kaal hope, tek a deep breath and survey mi family gathered at mi kitchen table. If anybody did tell me a mont before dat me wuda have mi son back in a mi life after so much years, me wuda did seh dat was wishful tinkin, but in dat moment, me andastan what Ezekiel experience in di valley of dry bones. Mi bones comin alive again and fi di fors time in twenty-chrii years, me smile and dere was no cryin hidin behain mi happiness.

chailbert-childbirth
bandij-bondage
chret a sinkin-threat of sinking
klak-clock
baatroom-bathroom
pu-dong; put down; start
daata-in-laa-daughter-in-law
behuol-behold
bam-bam-bottom
haat-string-heart-string; emotions
kaa-because
haas-horse

CHAPTER 3

Nuoz huol kyan huol fambili
Your nosehole/nostril can hold your family
When it comes to our loved ones, we find a way to accommodate them
Chicken merry, haak deh near
When the chickens are making merry, the hawk is nearby
Happiness does not last; danger is always near
Kaka wash wall and daab wakl
You can whitewash your walls and hold wattle together with dung
Many unsavory objects have practical uses; in desperate times, we make do with what we have

I am sure dat to dis blessed day, nobadi kud convince certain people dat me never put di young people dem up to di wedn. anyhow, mi conscience set me free and me feel dat fi all me lose, if mi son come back into mi life of his own will and choose fi get married in front a me, fi whatever reason, me seh, "Teng Gaad," and ask him what me kyan do to help. Yes, me know dat some people wuda seh dat me encourage Jimmy and Genevieve fi behave rang, but me kudn see Birdie Whitehead a share di role of mada of di groom wid me. Dat uman hate mi guts fi wa happen to Junior and is not wan time me try fi reach out to dem and Uncle Nathan tell me fi leave dem alone. If it was not fi Uncle Nathan, me wudn even did get mi *wedn pitcha* dem and a few things dat did belang to mi husband.

A duohn know when Jimmy and Genevieve decide di matter but di two a dem meet me at di breakfast table wan maanin and tell me dat dem waahn fi taak wid me. Dem look so serious dat at fors, me swear seh dem have bad news.

Genevieve tek di lead. She seh dat she and Jimmy waahn fi get married before me and den him tek over di discussion. Me mek him taak fi a while and A duohn seh a wod until him finish. Me look pahn dem and all me see is two a di muos lovely young people me ever encounter. Me know dat duoh Junior dead before Jimmy kuda know him, him seed tek root in dis bwai and him spring up to be di kaina man dat wuda did mek him faada proud.

Me not gwaihn lie, me cry again, but dis time is because a happiness. And me grii wid dem before dem change dem mind.

Dem have evriting work out. Dem waahn fi married right in a mi livinroom and dem ask me if me know a minister who wuda perform di ceremony fi dem. Me ask why dem no go to City Hall and dem look pahn me like me cuss a bad wod. Fi tell di *chuut*, me ongl seh dat fi test dem. Me really a try fi find out if dem a rush di wedn because dem waahn license fi have sex. Dem spendin a lot a time alone when me gaan a wok, so, me no know wa dem do when me no deh bout. Mark yu, dem always behave *prapa* when dem deh in front a me but Jimmy is Junior Whitehead son. If him is anyting like him faada, is not likely dat Genevieve will mek it to her honeymoon wid her cherry *intak*. Dat a if him no pick it aredi.

Me tell dem dat Myrna livinroom wud be better because a di size. Me also waan dem dat alduoh mi pastor is a marriage officer, me no so sure dem wuda want him fi preside over dem wedn. Wa me no tell dem is dat me go to di kain a church dat dem probably not accustom to. Me avoid established churches. Too many learned men who have a direct line to God. My problem wid *nof* a dem is dat dem mistake dem private musings fi inspiration. Me worship wid a bunch a *Shouters* pahn White Plains Road. Is jos a likl storefront but di people no fraid fi hala and knock over a few chairs. In dat church, if sombadi get happy and dance till dem undies show, is no big deal. After all, David in a di Bible did dance till all a him clothes jrap aaf a him.

Dat church save mi sanity because wa mi psychiatrist and Myrna kudn untangle, me whoop and hala out in deh and nobadi no look pahn me funny. When me kansida wa black people ha fi face on a daily basis, me conclude dat if we no whoop and hala, we either kill smadi or kill wiself, or both.

Di ada reason me welcome di wedn is dat me feel dat it will give me a chance fi play mi paat as a mada. Me hope it will sekl mi brain and help me fi have di right feelins fi mi son. Dis is not somting dat me kyan bring miself to discuss wid even Myrna, and Gaad know dat me no do anyting fi encourage di feelins. Me no know if di bwai notice dat me avoid touchin him, but me no chos miself wid mi own son. Mi badi no know di difference between Junior wa dead in a Kingston and mi son dat me leave behain in a 1980. Me leave a *bres-fiidin* biebi behain, and is a grown-ass man show up a di airport. A never see him grow from toddler, to a bwai, to teens and into a young man. A few pitcha sent chuu di mail was no preparation fi di raw reality a dis good-lookin man dat waak and taak jos like Junior. When me look pahn him, hear him taak or hear him laugh, is mi unfinish love life dat wake up. A wuda prefer fi dead dan to mek anybody know dis and me will never paas mi place wid him, but chuut is chuut.

Mi psychiatrist is a Jew man whose parents survive di Holocaust so him know human nature and him know bout sufferin. Laas week, me go taak to him bout mi feelins and him seh dat wid time, me will come to respond differently. Me ha fi give me brain time fi do di new learnin and so lang as A duohn find miself a plot ways in which me kyan get wid mi son, me deh pahn *salid* grong. As me seh before, A wuda dead before me paas mi place wid him and yesterday maanin me staat fi get a likl ease.

Him did a si-dong a di kitchen table and him a wait fi di breakfast weh me a cook fi di two a we. Me paas him a cup a coffee and when di bwai reach fi it, me notice dat him han no look notn like him faada own. Jimmy have mi finger dem and when me tek a quick glance pahn him face, me realize seh him have mi mout as well. Dis might sound like a smaal ting, but dese are di likl tings weh a help mi brain fi register dat dis is mi son, and not mi dead husband, come back to life.

We had a nice likl taak yesterday, too, and me ask him how him tink him grandparents will feel bout him gettin married. Him assure me dat they will still get to have di big church wedn when him and Genevieve go home but him will inform Miss Birdie and The Reverend, as well as Genevieve parents, dat dem legally married aredi. Him tell mi dat him plan fi kaal dem after di New York wedn.

Me a wanda a wa mek him plan fi tell dem after di *fak* and me a hope him right dat dem will tek it in good grace, but me not so sure. Is at dat point me *vencha* into deep waata and ask him if him and di bride-to-be figure out contraception matters aredi. Me know dat Genevieve is a nurse but me also know dat somtime church teachin get in a di way a good science. Me tink him wuda get *bringle* but it turn out dat di bwai easygoin jos like him faada and him not a prude. Him mek me know dat him and Genevieve figure out dat dem wudn practice any contraception till after dem have di fors pikni. *Azkaadn* to him, "We will not prevent until we know what is possible."

Me no tink dat is di best approach because dem need time together before biebi come into di pitcha, but as mi mada use to seh, *"Ef di bikl a no fi yu, no dip spoon deh."* I not about to dip into anybody food.

All a we go shoppin dat week-end. Myrna know a boutique in Manhattan dat a Jamaican Chinese man and him wife own. Dem supply evriting dat yu kuda tink of, from di bridal dress to di wedn cake. Taak about wan-stap shoppin and we spen money. Is like me and Myrna get crazy but we decide fi give di children di best we kud afford.

Di Chinese man breda is a caterer and a decorator and him operate next door to di boutique. We pay-dong pahn a full-scale Jamaican wedn breakfast fi twenty and we aada black cake, curry goat and jerk chicken wid a tossed salad, white rice, fruit punch and dessert, fi di wedn lunch.

Di man wife breda own di travel agency on di ada side a di bridal shop and we book di couple a five day honeymoon to The Bahamas. When we waak out deh, between me and Myrna, we spen chrii thousand dollars but, as Gaad liveth, me no *kya*! Mi son wort every penny dat me have and me and Myrna decide fi give dem a wedn to remember. We even go as far as to hire a musician.

ME NO HAVE words fi describe how mi haat feel when wan week later me si-dong in a Myrna livinroom wid mi son and look dong di *waakway* and see Genevieve a come up pahn Myrna arm. Di gyal look so radiant dat mi yai dem full-up wid waata and me had to wipe dem quick so dat me no miss notn. When she smile, di two dimple dem go deep into her cheeks, her two yai dem disappear and her tiit dem sparkle like good quality chinaware. Mi naw lie, as mi faada wuda seh, di gyal pretty like money and di prettiness no stap at her face.

Meantime me a watch di bride, me hear Jimmy sniffle. Me git-up and waak over to where him was standin by himself wid him back to di fireplace. Me put me han roun him waist and praise Gaad, mi body behave right.

Myrna waak inside wid Genevieve and we both tek wi seat at di front, ahead a five a Genevieve klaasmate dem, Myrna two son dem and a half-dozen people from mi church.

Mi pastor prove dat him know how fi tone dong fi fit di occasion and to tell di chuut, we never ha fi shame. After di exchange of vows, him ongl preach fi five minutes and him ongl seh, "Praise di Laad" chrii time and him never shout. What him had to huol back in a di preachin him mek up in a di eatin, but A never mind. Dere was more dan enough food and as mi aunt used to seh, *before good food wies, mek belly buss.*

wedn pitcha-wedding picture
chuut-truth
prapa-proper
intak-intact
nof-enough; many

Shouters-Spiritual Baptists, a group with origins in Trinidad. They practice a syncretism of African religions and Christianity.

bres-fiidin-breastfeeding

salid-solid

fak-fact

vencha-venture

bringle-brindle; an expression indicating anger; to respond like an angry, brindled dog

azkaadn-according

Ef di bikl a no fi yu, no dip spoon deh-If the victuals are not yours, do not dip a spoon in; mind your own business.

kya-care

waakway-walkway

Before good food wies, mek belly buss-Before you allow good food to go to waste, eat until your belly bursts.

CHAPTER 4

Wa no kill, fatten
What does not kill you makes you stronger
Faiya de a mus-mus tiel but him tink a cool breeze
There is a fire blazing directly behind the mouse but it mistakes the flame for a cool breeze
There is danger at hand but the fool does not recognize the looming threat
When fool ketch koni, koni lib haad
When a fool outwits a cunning man, his life becomes very hard
When two jinal meet, all head wok stap
When two tricksters clash, neither one will outwit the other

Di kaal come-iin Monday maanin but me was at work. When me walk chuu di front door and look into di livinroom, me see di message button pahn di phone a flash but me ignore it. Me figure is a damn telemarketer. Instead, me *kik-aaf* mi nursin shoes in a di hallway and head straight fi di baatroom.

When me come home from work, me never feel like me shuda touch anyting in a mi house until me wash miself from head to toe. A hospital kyan be a more deadly place fi wok dan a garbage dump. Some a di sickness dem dat me see people get, cause pure bafflement in a me, because me kyaahn andastan some a dese people. Wan time, a likl bwai come a di hospital wid a bad sickness dat him get from him pet iguana. Why di hell any parent wud allow a pikni fi keep a reptile as a pet?

Is after me tek mi dinner tray to di livinroom dat me remember di message button again, but me still never check di machine. Me was too busy gettin into mi curry goat leftovers and tinkin bout di young people. Dem kaal when dem arrive in a Nassau and tell me dat Myrna breda who live over dere, meet dem at di airport and tek dem to di hotel. Me feel good fi know dat dem not all by demself in a strange place.

After me watch a likl television, me decide fi play mi message and me hear Uncle Nathan voice pahn di machine and him was soundin weary and sad. Him tell me dat me need fi kaal him and dat di matter was urgent.

A never bada waste no time fi go up a Boston Road. Dere is a sprawlin West Indian store at di intersection a Boston Road and Baychester Avenue and me know me kuda get a ten *dala* phonecard in deh but me too tired fi go back out. Me hasten to di kitchen and pu-dong di tray and di dirty plate. Me never even stap fi scrape di bone dem in a di chrash. By di time me get back to di livinroom me lightheaded and mi haat a hammer. From ever since gunman murder mi husband, me easy fi frighten. Dat is why me no work in a di emergency room pahn mi job.

Mi han dem did a chrimbl so bad and mi yai dem get daak but me manage fi find mi phone book and find Uncle Nathan number. Me a wanda all kaina tings. Mama and Dada dead lang time but mi sister still alive. She married and move to Grand Cayman and ten years ago, me *riikanek* wid her. Me never tink dat Uncle Nathan wud be kaalin bout her.

Uncle Nathan was probably sittin next to di phone because him answer pahn di fors ring but him never bada wid any pleasantries.

"Jimmy dere wid yu?"

Me tek offense at him gruffness but me swala mi feelins.

"Good evenin, Uncle Nathan. Him not here right now. What happen? Sombadi dead?"

"Maybe dat would have been better, Audrie. Jimmy mek big trouble out ya and me kyaahn believe him do a ting like dat and run weh. Di bwai break mi heart wid shame."

By dis time, me feel like mi belly gwaihn give way. Good ting is a cordless phone and better yet dat Uncle Nathan kudn see me. By di time me manage fi seh anyting else, me a si-dong pahn di tailit.

"Sister Birdie tek di wol ting very hard and get a hell of a stroke. She in di University Hospital and nobody know if she gwaihn mek it."

Me staat fi tink dat maybe dere wud be a couple a people who wudn mind if dat happen but me ketch miself. A duohn wish anybody fi suffer di way me suffer when Junior dead. Me also know dat Jimmy love him granmada and dat is why A never let on to him dat A kudn stand her when A was married to Junior. What Uncle Nathan seh next leave me nauseous.

"Maudie granddaughter just deliver a baby girl and she name Jimmy as di father. To mek matters worse, look like di girl gettin off her head. She will not even touch di baby. She just lie down wid her face to di wall. Me went over dere yesterday and ended up holding and feeding di baby so dat poor Maudie could get a likl rest. Audrie, wherever Jimmy is, find him and tell him to come and take up his responsibilities. He cannot behave like my father did. My father was a hit-and-run parson and I never see him one day of my life. If it was not for Parson Webster and James grampa, Maas Raphael, me wuda did eat grass. Jimmy kyaahn disgrace we like dis. We have traveled too far to go back to that! Him have to come home and own the baby. Genevieve might lef him but him ha fi come home and give this child his name!"

Uncle Nathan a taak so faas, him run out a bret. Is when him pause fi swala dat me *chruo* di stick a dynamite in a di fire and tell him dat Jimmy and Genevieve married. Uncle Nathan staat fi cuss so much bad-wod dat mi yez dem staat fi ring. Him kaal mi son every name but Jimmy. Me did waahn fi rude to him a few times but A duohn seh notn. Me kyaahn bring miself fi believe seh Jimmy kud be dat callous but me also begin fi wanda if dat is why him run-weh come to me and why him married before him go back home. Me staat fi regret seh me tell Uncle Nathan dat him and Genevieve married but me kyaahn tek it back. Me tell him dat di couple gaan to The Bahamas pahn dem honeymoon and as soon as me seh it, me begin fi feel sorry fi Genevieve.

By di time me get aaf a di phone wid di still livid Uncle Nathan, me know dat is time to go home. Me feel bad fi evribadi but more dan anyting, me feel dat me shudn did run-weh and leave mi son in di fors place. A feel responsible fi di mess dat suddenly show up pahn mi doorstep and me know dat whatever di chuut is, Jimmy not likely to find no fren when him go home. Me know ongl too well how church people kyan get once di story involve smadi else sex sin. Me also decide dat me not goin to interrupt dem honeymoon. A figure dem wud need dat likl respite because up ahead, all me kyan see is billows and me a wanda what kaina craft my son gwaihn need fi ride out di go-to-hell staam dat me see a come pahn di horizon.

All dat night A kudn sleep. Me *taas* roun in a mi bed until me catch a likl doze wid me yez bend over rang. Is di pain in a di lobe dat mek me wake up. Me sit up in a di daak, pull up mi knee dem to mi chin and hala like when Junior dead. Me hala and me never huol notn back because me know dat dis is di laas time me kyan afford fi faal apaat. A wol lot a ada people gwaihn baal and fling *rak-stuon* and I will have to be referee, guard and policeman all in wan. As mi mada used to seh, dis a *punkuss pahn pankass* and by di time dem church people deh finish squeeze, him bound fi shit snow. Me a wanda if mi son have di stomach fi wa a wait fi him back in a Jamaica. Is twenty-chrii years since me run weh from deh but A duohn tink di people dem change dat much. Dere is notn some people enjoy more dan fi see dem betters faal dong.

Me staat fi tink bout som a di *kwaaril* dem dat Junior used to have wid him parents. Wan time, me remember him go up to di manse after him jrap me aaf at mi uncle house. Dis was jos after we married. When him come back, all di way to Kingston, Junior cry and cuss. Me remember dat him was particularly angry bout wa him kaal class division and how di church uphold and reinforce di privilege a certain people in a di society. Him seh dat Reverend and Miss Birdie jos kudn see how dem was perpetuatin di enslavement a di people.

Dem was some crazy days in a Jamaica and people did even staat fi *bon-dong* church. Me never andastan what Junior was taakin bout den because Reverend Whitehead was a very kain and nice man and me did like fi hear him preach. Him had a way of mekin di message simple and him did care bout people. Dat man use to regularly visit di sick and me hear dat is plenty people him help. Is jos Miss Birdie me kudn quite figure out. Is like she live behain a wall dat yu kudn breech. Junior use to tell me dat when she fors go to di church, di people dem treat her like notn because of her daak skin. Me no find dat haad fi believe because I did not know anybody who did hate black people like mi granny and she was di exact color a *faiyakuol.* Di way my granny did hate herself, she have six pikni fi six different man and none a di man dem never black.

Me si-dong in a di daak and me do some more cryin and me do some more tinkin. Me know dat muos Jamaica people sow dem wild oats and den dem go and hug up church. Di problem wid dat, duoh, is dat di same people who duohn tink twice bout lyin dong because nature kaal, duohn grant dat same humanity to dem leaders, especially dem parson. Dem no readily accept dat a minister is a human being fors and subject to di same tings dat dem struggle wid.

Is den me decide dat if Jimmy agree, me will mek him stay and apply fi a green kyaad fi him and Genevieve. After all, weh him have fi go back to? Condemnation and badmoutin fi di res a him days?

ALL DI WAY to work dat maanin, me a taak to Gaad and a taak to miself. When me waak on to di floor, Myrna tan-up a di nurses' station a wait pahn me. She tek wan look pahn me and pull me dong di hall to her office.

When me finish tellin her about di situation and mi plans fi rescue Jimmy, she interrupt fi di fors time and tell me fi stap chat shit.

"He have to go home, Audrie. Yu forget dat dere is a child involved and it might be his?"

"But what about poor Genevieve? She not gwaihn able fi stand dis. Di marriage mash-up right after di honeymoon."

"Not so fast, honey. Dat girl look like she have backbone to me and yu never know what a woman will forgive when she love a man."

"But is how Jimmy kuda do a ting like dat?"

"Ain't he a good looking man wid a *tea pot*? When di tea pot boil, steam go fly yu know, sister. We have a tough situation here but he go have to man up. Don't allow yu heart to rule yu head. Jimmy got to go home to face di music. Ain't yu di one dat always say *wa di han commit, di badi bear?"*

Myrna get all businesslike and staat mek phone kaal. Before me know what happen, she have me shift covered and she send me home. A never go home fi feel sorry fi miself, duoh. Me go back to di yellow pages and kaal a travel agent. She find me a flight goin to Jamaica in a week and di price wasn too bad. Me book chrii open tickets. Dem cost more dan me did waahn fi pay but I needed di kain a tickets dat wud allow we fi high-tail it out a Jamaica at shaat notice, if necessary. Me hear all dat Myrna have fi seh, but wan time before, when chrobl tek me, A run weh from mi son, but as mi migl name is Agette, A swear dat A done wid running. I will do whatever I have to do, to protect what is mine.

dala-dollar
kik-aaf-kick(ed) off
riikanek-reconnect
chruo-throw
taas-toss
rak-stuon-rock-stone; stones

punkuss pahn pankass-nonsense expression that suggests that a tragedy has collided with a disaster

kwaaril-quarrel

faiyakuol-fire coal; charcoal

bon-dong-burn down

teapot-euphemism for penis

wa di han commit, di badi bear-what your hand has committed, your body will bear; karma

CHAPTER 5

When yu go a tompa-foot dance yu ha fi laan fi dance tompa foot dance
If you go to a dance held by those who have only stumps for feet, you have to dance as if you have stumps for feet
You sometimes have to adjust to circumstances

Dis time me go to di airport alone fi pick up Jimmy and Genevieve. A needed di time to tink and A wasn sure Myrna kud keep a poker face until me taak to Jimmy. A wasn gwaihn tell him anyting in front a Genevieve. Him wuda ha fi *sagl dat deh haas* all by himself and Gaad go wid him. After me was sure dat him break di news to her, me wuda try fi *get a bore by* dem and see if dere was anyting me kuda do fi ease a likl a di hurtin. Me try fi step into Genevieve shoes and imagine di pain a di disappointment and di sense a betrayal. Me still no andastan how Jimmy get himself into dis mess. What is it about dis girl back home dat cause him fi *bon* Genevieve?

Me had a haad time fi find a *paak* near to di arrival gate. Me had to paak more dan a block aweh and it was wan a those sticky late August days when di air feel like yu a breathe steam. Me no like fi go outside when it so hot, kaa mi leg dem chafe if me waak more dan half-a-mile and me get a rash aanda mi bres dem dat no clear up easy. I am what Jamaica people kaal a red uman and it duohn tek notn fi me bon-up in a sun.

When me get to di arrival lounge, di two lovebirds a wait fi me but dem so caught up wid each ada dat me had to clear mi chruot chrii time before dem ton roun. Dem a si-dong so close dat not even breeze kuda paas between dem and jos before dem hear me, me see Jimmy run him finger dem chuu Genevieve hair and she ton roun and kiss him.

Mi haat jrap but mi smooth out mi face and show mi tiit before me announce mi presence. When me see how di two a dem full-up a love, me feel fi ton tail and run but me know dat dis time, me kyaahn afford to be a coward.

All di way from Queens to The Bronx, me mek smaal taak but di two a dem barely a pay me no mind. Dem in a di back seat and when Jimmy naa kiss Genevieve neck, him a tickle and stroke her. Me see dem chuu di mirror but me no mek dem see dat me a watch dem. Me a tink dat dem deserve dis brief moment a peace cause ongl Gaad know if dem young marriage will survive di bombshell dat me have fi jrap.

When we get home is about five in di afternoon and me allow dem fi clean up while me gettin di dinner ready. When we finish eatin, me tell Jimmy dat me need him help fi get a heavy piece a garbage dong to di dumpster. Me tell him dat it is a table me have in di garage and dat if me no get it out dat day, me was gwaihn miss di garbage chok. Him readily agree fi help me and Genevieve git-up fi clear di table. When we reach down di stairs to di garage, we go in chuu di side door and me close it behain me.

sagl dat deh haas-saddle that horse
get a bore by-squeeze into a tight spot; subtly get up close
bon-burn; cheat on
paak-park

CHAPTER 6

Wa woodpecker seh in a him belly haad fi answer
It is hard to give an answer to what the woodpecker says in its belly
If we do not share our thoughts, they cannot be used against us
Daag a sweat but lang hair kiba it
The dog's sweat is hidden by its hair
The suffering of others is not always evident

Me si-dong between Jimmy and Genevieve all di way from New York to somweh over North Carolina. Niida wan a dem a taak to me and dem certainly not taakin to each ada. Me a worry bout wa gwaihn happen when we get to Jamaica because is like all chrii a ride in a separate and enclosed compartments.

Over North Carolina, me git-up fi go use di res-room and when me come back, Jimmy sittin in mi winda seat and Genevieve up aanda him ribs wid her two han dem wrap roun him waist. Him cheek restin pahn her head and di two a dem a cry like pikni weh laas and kyaahn find di paas fi go home. Me tek Jimmy seat and stretch out mi han as far as it kuda reach and me huol dem. Me no cry, duoh. Me screw-up mi face pahn anybody who look like dem a get ready fi interfere and dem get di message real quick. Dis here is family business and we duohn need di law.

Me never cry until di plane line up fi mek di final descent. Me look chuu di winda pahn di ada side a di aisle and realize dat Jamaica a really wahn crocodile a li-dong in a di sun. Di plane lean right and it a swoop dong and me lean over fi look out a Jimmy winda and me see di clear outline a di crocodile lower back and tail. Dis is di fors time dat di map from Social Studies klaas mek sense and a feelin tek me dat me kudn explain. Is like me did laas from mi mada fi a wol lifetime and suddenly recognize her face in a crowd a strangers.

Di plane a faal out a di sky and a get lower and lower over Donald Sangster International Airport and me see people pahn di tarmac dat look like action figures. A man hala out behain me, *"Dis is Jumaika! Yaad tu raas!"*

Me look roun fi see di speaker and evribadi back a me a grin or a wipe dem yai or both. Di plane hit di runway, bump two or chrii time and begin fi taxi to a stap.

Me remain in a mi seat and watch di people a faal over demself and over each ada fi get to dem han-luggage. Me almuos laugh as me a watch dem. Dis much no change bout mi people dem. Dem still aggressive and lawless. Yu wuda tink di plane deh pahn fire and all a dem a run fi dem life. Di chrii a we and a few ada people si-dong and wait until di rush over.

On aneda day, di folk singer dem in a dem bandana at di arrival gate wuda been a welcome sight, but today, dem was more like wahn irritant. When me paas by, me hear two a dem seh somting bout how di shit cleaner dem a come. Me kiss mi tiit loud and seh to no wan in particular, "Better fi clean shit dan to be full a shit! Unu a chat bout shit cleaner an unu same wan wuda beg di shit cleaner dem fi dem haad-earn money."

Me kiss mi tiit again and waak paas dem widout a backward glance.

Me mek mi way to arrival and di *renkin* immigration officer got close to tastin mi *wraat* when she tell me dat me have two weeks in a di country. Me cut mi yai and grab mi American passport from her. She look me up and dong like she is di new sheriff in town and me know right aweh a wa a nyam her. She have a problem wid mi American passport because she no have wan. A roll out mi two yai dem pahn her and tell her in mi flattest Westmoreland accent, "Me tan ya fi as lang as mi waahn and if yu no like it, yu and yu ugly muma kyan come look fi me."

Me see di consternation dawn pahn her face and she staat fi back-pedal and me buss-out a laugh. Me know dat she look pahn mi pale skin and mi semi-straight hair and conclude dat me a *tapanaaris.* She look pahn Jimmy and she look pahn

Genevieve and me tell her, "Is mi son and me daata-in-laa and we tired, so, no badda huol we up wid di lang interrogation."

Jimmy waak up to di desk, put wan han pahn mi shoulder and staat fi taak in him pastoral voice, "Take it easy, Mommy. She is just doing her job."

Him ton to di officer and him tone was so cajolin dat di uman all but bow and curtsy. Him tell her, "My mother has been away from Jamaica for over twenty years and this is her first trip home."

Di dyam *fiesti* immigration officer was not about to let it go, even duoh she a simper fi Jimmy. Di way she staat smile and show her dyam yellow tiit dem, mi figure seh her *naara* behain aanda di desk a go *twep-twep* fi him. All di same, she decide fi tek a laas shot aanda her bret and me hear when she mumble dat if me live so long a *farin,* a how come me chat so bad.

Me wheel mi behain paas her widout aneda wod. Me no have time fi self-hatin people who tink is a disgrace fi chat dem own a language. A Jamaica taak keep me from gettin aaf mi head a farin. In di early years when A kudn live and didn know how to die, is di familiar patwa voices in a Di Bronx dat keep me hangin on to di real world. If it was not fi patwa-taakin people, me wuda did a *waak and tear up paper* a road or me wuda did jump aaf a George Washington Bridge.

Me lef di immigration line wid di thought dat maybe mi people not as progressive as dem like fi tink. We have so much dat we duohn appreciate and we no *gladi-gladi* over wi own a sinting until people from farin tell we seh it good.

Den me memba seh Jimmy kaal me *Mommy* and me ton roun fi look pahn him because it dawn on me dat him seh it so naturally. Is den me know fi sure dat all dese years him never *figet* me. Di wod flow out wid such ease dat me know seh a long time him a practice in a him mind fi seh it.

Me staat fi feel sorry dat me did *hangl* di immigration officer so bad but when me mek fi apologize, me see her a look pahn Genevieve wid open contempt. Me no gaan from Jamaica so lang dat me no know what dat all about, and me begin fi hope dat Genevieve strong enough fi deal wid what up ahead fi her.

Me push mi passport into mi handbag and waak over to baggage claim fi find mi bag dem. A waahn cuss bad-wod because A sick a color. Is like in dis worl, color is evriting and it mek all a we crazy. Here yu have dis dyam immigration officer a look pahn mi daata-in-laa like she is a pile a shit, and fi wa? What give her di right? She black and Genevieve black. Di two a dem a uman but she is a likl paler, and fi dat reason, dis dyam uman wid her face fieva *pimenta-haas,* tink she have a right fi look dong pahn Genevieve. She jealous of a black uman who have di love of a brown man. A kuda see di scorn in a her yai dem. Dem kuol and haad and she a huol her snout in a snarl like a bad *daag* weh a *chospas* in yu yaad.

Where I live in America is more of di same nonsense, ongl over dere, plenty white people and even some a di black wan dem see color as a contaminant dat ruin di purity of whiteness. Dat is why dem seh Percy Sutton and Thurgood Marshall black but Eleanor Roosevelt wid her big, fat, African *mout-lip* dem, white. So by some kaina crazy rule, di evidence of yu own two yai dem unreliable and, therefore, Halle Berry and Lena Horne black, but Abraham Lincoln white. Me look pahn Abraham Lincoln face and me see di Native American ancestry a baal out in a him, but I am required to lie to miself about di chuut dat mi yai dem show me. Me also memba wahn Jewish uman wa me use to wok wid and wan day she tek-aaf her wig an me see seh her hair have more kink in a it dan mine, yet she seh she white. Dat, as far as I am kansern, is di perfect recipe fi insanity. Den yu have some white people who fraid a black people and no see notn rang wid policeman a shoot dong black man like dem a wild game. And some black people desire whiteness so much dat dem a *ratn* dem skin wid bleach. *Du Maasa Gaad! Tek di case!*

Me begin fi tink bout di Jamaican black man dem who go a America and frighten fi di wol-heap a light-skin uman who will lay-dong wid dem fi wa in a dem *pakit.* Plenty a dem lef dem good-good black uman fi trailer-trash and is when di uman dem kaal police pahn dem *aas* di fos time dem lick dem, dat dem realize what time it is.

Me remember how mi husband use to seh dat is Chalky Hill people ruin Miss Birdie. Back den, A didn really andastan wa Junior mean, but when me went to Nursing school, me tek a couple a Psychology klaas and a couple a Race and Gender klaas. Since den, mi yai open to a lotta tings. After dat, me was able fi forgive Miss Birdie. We duohn hurt ada people unless we ourselves hurtin bad. Di older di hurt, di more haad it is to cure.

Is not until after we rent di minivan and Jimmy drive up di hill from di airport dat me remember again dat him did kaal me *Mommy.* A waahn fi cry but me no waahn fi distress him or Genevieve. Dem have enough chobl as it is.

Me look out di winda, instead, and had to admit dat di airport nice fi true. When I was small, yu kuda go up to di wavin gallery and watch di passenger dem a waak kraas di tarmac fi board di plane. Now we arrivin and departin from sheltered waitin room and enclosed corridors. Wavin gallery is a ting a di paas.

Me so glad fi di air conditioning in di minivan because di heat steamin outside like we in di Amazon. Di Caribbean sea-waata bluer dan me remember and A realize dat it was di land me did miss more dan anyting. So me a drink it all in because me use to tink fi a long time dat A wuda never see Jamaica again. Me probably know every Jamaican page pahn di internet but a pitcha is a poor substitute fi di real ting.

When we ketch a Falmouth, me ask Jimmy fi mek a detour to di courthouse. A wahn uol buildin dat always mek me tink of plantations and dungeons. When A was likl, me did read a book bout di white witch, Annie Palmer, who used to chain her slave dem in a dungeon. Dat uol courthouse, fi some reason, did always remind me of dem lang ago, wicked days of slavery and A wanted Jimmy to drive by dere to see di buildin.

Di buildin still standin, jos like me remember it-gray stone façade and thick Palladian columns. Yes, me know big wod because me tek Art Appreciation when me go a community college. Dat dere is history and wid all di terrible hurricane dem weh rise up out a di blue Caribbean and assault dis man-made edifice, it tan-up *chrang*.

Me waak up di stone steps to di portico and a young man who look like a newly qualified lawyer, waak out di door and tell me a cheery howdy-do before bouncin down di steps to him kyaar. Is a spankin, midnight blue *Lexus* him get into and me wanda if him had was to tek out big student loan and if him finish pay aredi.

Me lean over di stone wall at di front a di porch and look out to sea. Di wave dem a crash forcefully gainst di shore and me kyan smell di rawness and di salt in a di air. Me see people a waak up and dong in front a di buildin. A wol-heap a kyaar paak *chaka-chaka* in di side street dem to me mi right. A special constable a argue wid a driver and a tell him fi move him kyaar. When me hear how much doti bad-wod di constable a chip up give di man, me begin fi *ekspek* di worse. In mi mind, me kyan see di outcome aredi and me imagine dat di argument gwaihn en-up wid wan a dem dead and di ada a run fi him life. A was rang duoh, because as me staat mek mi way dong di step dem, me see di taxi driver pull a fat wad a bills from him side-pakit and han it to di policeman. Now, me a ekspek di people dem weh stan-up nearby fi do or seh somting but dem all jos waak weh like dem no jos see an open case a bribery and corruption.

Me hurry back into di minivan and begin fi tell Jimmy bout di incident but him barely a pay me any mind. Him a try fi mek a reverse widout hittin any a di ada kyaar dem weh paak near di street. Me tellin him dat di policeman tek money from di driver but him dryly tell me, "That is the least of your worries, Mommy. You need to worry about the people who will want to take the very shoes from off your feet because you come from foreign. Welcome home."

dis is Jumaika, yaad tu raas-this is Jamaica, my ass, this is home.
renkin-rank as in smelly; a common term used to indicate that someone's behavior is offensive.
wraat-wrath
fiesti-insolent
naara-narrow; gassy
twep-twep trembling in fear or excitement
farin-foreign; overseas
waak and tear-up paper-analogy and image of insanity
gladi-gladi-glad; excited
figet-forget
hangl-handle
pimenta haas-pimento horse; praying mantis; cricket-insects that use the pimento tree as camouflage
daag-dog
chospas-trespass
mout-lip-lips
ratn-rot; rotten
Du Maasa Gaad- Do Lord
tek di case-take the case
pakit-pocket
aas-ass
chrang-strong
chaka-chaka-disordered; checkered
ekspek-expect

CHAPTER 7

***Ratta ma-ahn-laa* cut wahn weskot, Ratta laugh, "Ha-ha."**
Ratta *pa-ahn-laa* cut wahn night-shot, Ratta
laugh, "Ha-ha."
Ratta *bra-ahn-laa* buss him big got, Ratta
laugh, "Ha-haaa."
Ratta laugh, him laugh, him laugh, him
tumble dong, so dead.
Mongoose, hoi! Ratta tumble dong, dead!
Mongoose hoi! Ratta tumble dong, dead!

Jamaican Folk Song

The rat has laughed himself to death while laughing at the escapades of others. Now the news has been noised to the predatory and scavenging mongoose.

When Jimmy ton chuu di two iron gate at di entrance a di church prapati, me ask him fi stap and let me out a di van. Him look pahn me wid a question in him yai but him stap anyway. Me step out and tell him fi drive aan. Him never argue wid me and Genevieve reach into her handbag and give me a small, floral umbrella. Me was grateful for it because di sun hotter dan *nine day love*.

Me waahn fi waak up dat hill by miself because me have a stap fi mek. Me have a date wid di dead and dis meetin lang overdue. Me tan-up a di gate in di shade a wahn *ackee* tree to mi right and a *flame of the forest* to mi lef. Me standin behain di minivan and me kyan feel di heat from di exhaust but me no move until Jimmy drive aaf.

When di van disappear over di hill, me waak from aanda di ackee tree and look up di hill to mi lef, for me know dat is where di church cemetery lay out. Today, it look like a forgotten village. Di tombstone dem staat from di batam, near to di gate and a few a dem well tended and di ada wan dem look like nobadi no memba bout dem. Me not interested in any a dese, duoh. Mi yai dem zero in pahn di marble tomb dat stand out like a mini *Taj Mahal* pahn di hillside. It is below di manse dat is further up di hill and me ask miself how Reverend and Miss Birdie kuda si-dong pahn dem verandah when di fos ting fi greet dem yai is dis daily reminder of dem unbearable loss.

Plenty times me see Coretta Scott King pahn television and she always look put together and strong but me always wanda what lay behain dat strength. Me not strong like dat.

Myrna tell me all di time dat me is di *strangis* uman she know but me no chrang at all. Me jos stubborn and dere is a big difference between di two.

Is over twenty years since mi foot dem waak dis path and mi see di greenness of Chalky Hill. Me no know where mi mada and faada was put to res, nor mi uncle and him wife. But me know fi sure dat me kyaahn stay forever on dis gravel driveway. Mi foot dem will of necessity command mi weary body and tek me to Junior grave.

By di time me reach di hillside, me wish me did choose fi wear a pair a pants. *Cow-itch* bite up me foot and mi han dem and me a sweat so much dat mi clothes soak. Anyhow, A duohn stap waak till A get to di tomb. Is when me get to it dat me realize dat di goin was so tough because me tek di rang way. Di track-paas lead from di top a di hill, dong to di tomb and it is well trodden. If me did waak from di house dong to di tomb, me wuda did have a much easier time of it.

Dere is a vase restin pahn di tomb and a creepin waata-plant in it dat a *swizl-up* because di waata in a di vase dry out. Me tell miself dat A mos see bout it before di day done.

Where me stand pahn di hillside between di uppermuos lay a di land and di lowermuos reaches, me kyan see pastureland on both sides, and me look aroun. Di sun a beat dong pahn mi head so me open Genevieve floral umbrella and den me si-dong pahn di batam section a di tomb. Di marble hot aanda mi batty and di heat beginnin fi mek me feel like me gwaihn faint. All a mi trainin tell me dat me overexpose to di sun and much too sudden but me ha fi sit *Shiva* fi a while. I am twenty-chrii years late but me whisper to Junior dat kudn come before now.

Me a aafa dis imaginary apology to Junior in a mi mind and at di same time, me a examine di plaque at di head a di tomb. It is white limestone dat polish to smoothness and it is invisibly attached to di daak-gray, blue-seamed marble a di surface. Me read di words engraved dere in black:

JAMES JOHN WHITEHEAD II
BELOVED SON, FATHER AND NEPHEW
GONE TOO SOON

Dere was no mention of a wife on mi husband tombstone and me know dat was brought about by di hand of Birdie Whitehead. Even in di mournin of her son, di uman kudn let go enough fi have mercy pahn aneda who was nursin di same injury. Me shake mi head aanda di umbrella and hope to Gaad dat no experience wud ever teach me fi hate like dat.

Is when me decide fi git-up and get out a di hot sun dat di bird come swoopin in. Me catch a glimpse of it from mi *side-yai* but it was flyin so faas dat me had to swivel mi neck real quick and me hear and feel mi neck bone crick. By dis time, mi haat a race and mi mout dry, because di bird pitch right pahn top a di headstone, fluff di feda dem wan time and commence fi look up pahn me out a two points a light dat was like diamond fire.

Is a green bird wid red ches-feda and it wasn until later dat me learn dat it is a type of green tody, native only to Jamaica.

When me was likl, me use to see dem in a di pimento chrii dem and me use to kaal dem robin red bres.

A kyaahn explain why me huol out mi han but me decide fi remain sittin and when me stretch out mi han, di bird fly over and lan right at di joinin a mi han and wrist. Di claw dem feel dry and scratchy against mi skin and di bird so light, me judge di weight to be less dan a quarter ounce.

Me si-dong deh in a di hot sun, wid di ineffectual umbrella over mi head and me a look dong pahn dis bird pahn mi han and dis bird a look back up pahn me. Den di funniest ting happen. Di likl bird let go a jrap a waam shit pahn mi han, hop two time and den sail aaf and disappear into di molten sky.

Me look dong pahn mi han and come to di realization dat Junior send me a message and me staat fi laugh. Fors di laugh come out in a som likl explosions a air from mi nose but as me reach into mi pakit fi a tissue and begin fi wipe di jrap a gray and white shit aaf mi han, me feel di laugh buss outa me and me git-up aaf a di tomb and waak roun to di track dat lead up to di manse.

To di unknowin, me was a mad uman come back from farin and me sure dat if dere was any unseen witness a hide nearby, it wudn be lang before wod wuda get roun Chalky Hill dat Jimmy mada come back from farin, mad as hell. But wa really deh pahn mi mind is di mystery of what we kaal life and det and di encounters dat we kyaahn explain wid words. Mi mada used to seh dat is *not evriting good fi nyam, good fi chat.* Me also know dat what me experience is mine alone. Di mysterious encounter wid di green bird wid di red bres duohn tek weh di pain in a mi haat, but it tell me dat wherever Junior is, I am still known to him.

WHEN A MEK mi way to di batam step a di manse, me hear a loud voice a cuss inside a di house. Me know dat di voice was not Birdie Whitehead but di anger was jos like hers. Di uman voice harsh wid condemnation and dere was a man a try fi edge-iin. Me kuda tell right aweh dat him wasn a brave man and di voice no belang to Jimmy.

Me sigh to miself and decide dat thirsty as A was, A wud sit dis staam out because me too tired fi referee any wod war. Instead, me go over to di easy chair in a wan kaana a di verandah and ease-aaf mi sandal dem.

Di uman inside di house mos be Genevieve mada because she a taak well loud when she seh, "Genny, mi seh, tek yuh tings and *kum huom*! Mi no business if yu and Jimmy get married before di Pope in Rome! Him have woman and pikini pahn him han and dat is nasty livin! Dat woman and her pikini will be a thorn in a yu flesh fi as long as yu live!"

Di uman stap taak, probably fi ketch her bret and Genevieve chose di pause fi *chruo a helleva stone in a di pig pen.* Me kudn believe di steel dat creep into her voice but me kuda tell dat dere was no movin her when she quietly declare, "Mommy, you of all persons should know what that is like."

Me hear like a piece a furniture faal over and me git-up and hurry to di front door. Di sight dat meet mi two yai dem cause me fi rush into di house.

Genevieve spread out flat pahn her back and a uman dat me assume is her mada, a kneel dong in her stomach. Di poor girl leg dem a flail like a stunned chicken and di uman a choke di poor pikni. Me no know weh me find di strength but A reach her and grab her aaf a Genevieve and taas her. She land gainst a couple a chair leg wid so much force dat di big mahogany dining-table slide at least a foot kraas di room.

Di uman staat fi hala and clutch her haat but me no pay her no mind. Me ton mi attention to Genevieve and pull her up into a sittin position and look up fi see Jimmy a tan-up over me. Him two yai dem behain di glasses wild like animal weh about fi bolt weh go a bush. Meantime, Genevieve faada a stan-aaf to wan side and him look like him kyaahn mek-up him mind whether fi touch di daata or fi attend to di wife.

Me and Jimmy lif Genevieve into a standin position and wid him leadin di way, we enter a large bedroom dat me assume belang to di grandparents. While we easin Genevieve into di mahogany, four-poster bed, me tek a quick glance roun di room and mi yai dem lan pahn a large pitcha a mi husband a look dong from above a wide mahogany dresser. It deh gainst di wall closest to di foot a di bed. Me remember di bird and me smile back at him but me ha fi attend to di crisis at hand. In mi mind, me tell Junior dat A will deal wid him later but mi haat pick up a beat.

Me pull open Genevieve blouse and jos as me ekspek, two helleva purple bruise maak di spot weh her mada kneel dong in a her ches. Me feel fi broken ribs and she no cry out, so, me conclude seh she no sustain any internal injuries. Me sigh and tell Jimmy fi bring ice in a towel or a plastic bag.

When Jimmy leave, me hear di uman footstep dem a come towards di room. Me look pahn Genevieve and den glance at di doorway. Me no plan fi tan-up wan-side and allow dis uman fi kill mi daata-in-laa. To my surprise, she come-iin a di room and stan-up in front a di dresser. Me look pahn her face and see naked fear in her yai dem but before me kud seh a wod, Genevieve jump-aaf a di bed and staat fi address her mada.

"Mommy, Jimmy have a baby and that is a hard thing for me to take, but I am not leaving him! He is my husband and I love him and nothing is going to change dat! Get used to the idea!"

Me look kraas di room and see a door dat look like it lead to a baatroom. Me mek straight fi it and leave di two a dem alone. Pii-pi a come dong pahn me and me not about to wet miself. Me also have a strong feelin dat a skunk pissin contest about to staat and me no waahn none a di renkin spray fi ketch me. Moreover, me feel certain dat if Ms. Swearing try fi attack Genevieve again, dis time she will fight back.

Inside di bathroom clean and smell good. It smell feminine, like lavender, mint and apple blossoms. Di dominance of pinks and greens in di décor tell me dat dis is Miss Birdie domain. Me see a likl pair a house slippers pahn di floor in front a di shower curtain, and me suddenly staat fi feel bad fi Miss Birdie and fi evribadi.

Me kyan feel mi yai dem a full-up a waata again and suddenly me kyan barely see fi mek mi way to di wash basin.

Me squeeze out a likl bit a scented soap and begin fi rub it up pahn mi han dem. When me tek dem from aanda di kuol waata, me try fi break aaf a piece a tailit paper fi dry mi han dem but me realize dat me kudn do it widout wettin up di roll. Me kiss mi tiit and look roun fi a fresh towel. Me en-up a use di decorative guest towel even duoh me know dat guest is di laas person it hangin dere for.

Genevieve and her mada still a kwaaril and Jimmy in deh a try him bes fi quiet dem. Dere is no sound a di faada and right aweh, me know seh dat man a live aanda *panty govament.* Di man tan-up and watch him wife abuse him grown, married daata and him jos hitch-up in a di kaana, wid him yai dem a dart from side to side like a *cane-piece rat* weh ketch in a *calaban*. Mi mada wuda did kaal him a *woklis* brute.

Me si-dong pahn di kuol tailit and pii-pi and dat is when me really begin fi feel di hunger and thirst. Me decide fi go back to di face basin and drink from mi han. Di act remind me a mi days at primary school and di waata still taste like chlorine and sunshine.

When mi dry mi han dem and mi mout, me close di tailit and tek a seat fi lisn to wa a gwaan in a di bedroom. Genevieve was not backin dong and me realize dat a boil buss and plenty pus a run out. All dem tings me hear dat girl a seh to her mada mos a did a hat her fi a lang time. Genevieve *taak-up di tings dem* and her wod dem was like a hurricane when it ton back.

She tell her mada dat she is a hypocrite because she was di ada uman who brok up her faada fors marriage. Mek me tell yu, not even Jimmy kuda stap her from taakin and di mada kudn get a wod in.

"You think I don't know that Daddy was your teacher! You think I don't know about mi three brothers and four sisters in May Pen! You think I don't know that you believe that Daddy first wife *obeah* you and make you couldn't have children?"

Den di girl voice get deadly and she seh very quietly, "You think I don't know that you are not mi real mother? You think I don't know that mi real mother was a grade nine girl that Daddy knock-up and *unu* tek me away from her and send her to England?"

Me hear Ms. Swearing begin a piece a wailin and den she seh, "A lie! A lie! Noting no go so!" But di cryin and di shoutin a move weh from di bedroom and soon, me no hear her no more.

When me open di baatroom door, Genevieve a si-dong in a di migl a di bed wid her leg dem kraas like di Buddha and she a huol a towel over her ches. She still a cry and Jimmy a try him bes fi hush her. Me leave dem and go back to di livinroom but dere was no sign a di parents. Me kraas di livinroom and ton right and en-up in a di kitchen.

Me see chrii pot pahn di stove and when me check dem, dem was still waam. Me kudn bow to good manners and ask permission because mi light-headed feelin was enough waanin dat A had to eat. A wud get back to Genevieve wod dem soon enough but me had enough sense to know dat if A didn find food and drink, me wud be soon *facin mi own Waterloo.*

Me tek a large white dinner plate from di dish rack, run it aanda di pipe and shake-aaf di excess waata. Me do di same wid di servin spoon dat me tek out a di cutlery drawer and den me open di pot dem, wan by wan. Di *dutchie* have brown stew snapper and *okro.* Di second pot have rice and peas cook in a coconut milk and di rice grain dem cook up fluffy, jos di way me like it. Di laas pot have steam *calaloo.*

Me help miself wid kansidaraishan dat di ada two wud be jos as hungry as me was feelin and den me open di fridge and find a large glass jug a brown sugar lemonade.

A finish eatin di good food and git-up fi wash di dishes but jos as me go over to di sink and ton on di pipe, me feel like smadi tan-up back a me. Me ton roun but me no see nobadi. Me ton back to di sink and hear smadi seh, "*Who deh ya?*" Me recognize di voice of Uncle Nathan and me jrap di dish-klaat and run go in a di livinroom.

Him stan-up a di back door and him so broad dat him almuos black-out all a di light from outside. Uncle Nathan bigger dan when laas me see him in Connecticut some seven years before, and him voice still strong. Me kyan tell dat him a come from bush by di wide-brim straw hat him a wear and di graas stain dem pahn him clothes. Me run go hug him up all di same and him smell sour wid sweat but A never care.

Uncle Nathan hug me haad, lif me up aaf a di grong and plant a wet wan smack pahn mi mout-lip, but me never care at all. Him put me dong, laugh out loud and tell me, "Gyal pikini, yu is di bes ting I see since maanin. From cock put-aan him *jraaz* befo day, I been in dat dyam cow pasture looking after James cow dem. Di *blaasid* bwai him hire duohn *wot* a dyam and all him been doing is *tiifin* James cow dem and selling to butcher dong a Falmouth. A threaten him wid prosecution and A tell him dat if him bring gunman come shoot me, my gunman dem will wipe out him wol blaasid generation. Is so yu have to handle matters here in Jamaica, my dear. Dis not America and yu remember dat while yu here and duohn drop yu guard. Dis is one rough country, baby. All we have is modern day pirate and buccaneer and di biggest wan dem is di dyam politicians and dem business cronies. Dem in cahoots wid foreigners again fi chop up Jamaica assets and sell to di highest bidder. Foreigner tek over Jamaica again, mi love."

By di time Uncle Nathan finish taak, him in a di kitchen wid me a skip behain him like a puppy. Me happy fi see Uncle Nathan till me feel like me *glad bag buss*. Me yai dem full-up a waata again. Me wipe dem wid mi sleeve and ask Uncle Nathan if him want to eat. Him answer me after him tek-aaf him hat and put it pahn top a di fridge, right pahn top a di bread bin. A waahn fi laugh because me kyan imagine di ruckus dat wuda did brok out if Miss Birdie did *deh-deh.*

Him go over to di sink and staa*t* fi wash him han dem like a surgeon. Him lather-up from finger tips to elbow and him wash wid care. It please me fi see wan uol man dat still so clean. After him dry him han dem pahn wan a Miss Birdie white dishklaat, him si-dong at di table and ask me fi a glass a cool waata. Den him seh, "A have to check mi blood sugar before me eat anyting. Pass dat pouch dat yu see over dere pahn di deep freeze."

When me come back wid it, Uncle Nathan open a well stocked diabetes kit and in two two's, him stick him finger, check him sugar and sigh. "It not too-too bad but A want to go easy pahn di starch."

"All right," me tell him and head straight to di fridge fi see what me kuda find. In no time, me whip up a fresh salad of lettuce, tomatoes and carrots. Den me get a large dinner plate and serve him a wol fish and a small scoop a rice and peas and tek it over to di table where me place it in front of him.

It give me a strange, confusin feelin to be standin in Birdie Whitehead kitchen but at di same time, me feel like me have every right to be dere. Me no dwell pahn mi feelin, duoh, because Uncle Nathan look roun suddenly and declare, "But tell me somting, weh di pikini dem deh and wa happen to Deacon and Sister Swearing? Don't yu did send to say dat Jimmy and Genevieve traveling wid yu?"

"Deacon and Sister Swearing gaan home because Sister Swearing fight-aaf Genevieve because di poor pikni tell her she not leavin Jimmy. Jimmy and Genevieve roun by Reverend bedroom and me tink dem need to come in here and eat somting. Is some very terrible tings happen since we come home and me have a feelin dat tings gwaihn get much worse before dem get better."

"I tink yu dyam right bout dat," Uncle Nathan mutter between a moutful a fish and rice. "What Jimmy carry out will affect generations to come and him cannot fix dis. What is done cannot be undone and even if Joanie baby should die, the memory of her will live on."

Me begin fi get kraas but outa rispek fi Uncle Nathan and all dat him do fi me over di years, me try fi keep mi tone neutral when me answer him.

"Uncle Nate, what so terrible bout what Jimmy do? Is jos a biebi and biebi baan every day. Why we kyaahn jos focus on how we kyan keep Jimmy and Genevieve together and mek a place in all a dis fi di innocent likl infant?"

Uncle Nathan tek him time fi swala him food. Him tek a swig a waata and wipe him mout wid a paper napkin from di holder in a di migl a di table. Him rub di top a him belly and belch den him seh, "Pardon me," and den him fix me wid him sea-waata yai dem and seh, "Tell me somting, Audrie, how old are you?"

"*Faati.* Me soon ton faati-wan."

"Yu a still baby. Yu a young bod and *young bod no know staam*. Yu listen to me good fa *yai-lash uola dan beard.* Yu still have a lot to learn bout people and dem ways. First of all, dere is Joanie. According to what di granny tell me in confidence, she have it on good authority dat Joanie set up Jimmy fi breed her. Apparently she was trying to stop him from marrying Genevieve. Yu tink a woman who will go dat far will stop at anything? Yu know what kind a mind it tek to do a ting like dat? As a man, yu don't want to entangle yuself wid a woman who have a ketch-man mindset, especially if she pretty. Dem kinda woman deh is like death. When dem sink dem claw into yu, dem no leggo."

Me pull out a chair directly across from uncle Nathan and me si-dong but me no seh notn, so, him continue fi taak.

"Yu know how many promising young man me see tie up demself because a *pum-pum*? Me tired fi caution young men bout the importance of teapot governance. A man who refuse to govern him cock gwaihn live in a fowl pen, and despite what *The Mighty Sparrow* say bout *Rooster*, is not a good place fi any man find himself. Because of dis baby, Joanie will always have a gateway of entry to Jimmy and Genevieve life and depending on what Joanie choose to tell dis child, dere is the possibility dat dere will be bitterness between dis child and every pikini dat Jimmy and Genny produce.

Genevieve will have to live close to The Master if she want her marriage. Dere are days when she will be bitter and she will have to find a way to swallow it. Jimmy will have to deal wid di shame of letting her down and he will have to be man enough to embrace an unwanted child. Dis will be di true test of him manhood and him will have to find a way to keep Joanie from being a thorn in Genevieve side. If him love di child and not the mother, him stand accused by both child and mother. If him love the mother, him create a divided heart and a divided house.

I don't even begin to address what his standing will be in a Chalky Hill. Perhaps him cannot even enter di ministry, because church people very contradictory. Some a dem hold di cross in one hand and a machete in di other. Dese people who commit every sin imaginable under di sun, expect dem pastor to be a saint. Yu ever wonder why some Jamaican Christian people believe in a Jesus dat dem put up pahn wall? If yu waahn some Jamaican Christian fi chop yu up, yu tell dem dat Jesus was a man who wake up wid an erection every maanin just like any other normal man. Dem kill yu for it! Dem don't want a Jesus who was human like demself.

Jimmy action totally destroy James and Birdie! Dem and Maudie *ketch-up* over di girl pregnancy and James tell me dat Maudie come over to dis house wid her head wrap up like she a wok obeah and demand fi Jimmy married to her granddaughter. Is di quarrel dat cause Sister Birdie fi get di helleva stroke."

Uncle Nathan put him head in a him han dem and me see di big-big man shoulder dem staat fi quake and before me know it, him a sniffle and wipe him yai dem. It brok mi haat fi true and fi try fi tek him mind aaf a Jimmy and Joanie, mi ton di conversation to Genevieve and her mada.

"Uncle Nathan, do, no cry and sen-up yu blood pressure. We ha fi find a way fi go forward because bigger chobl deh ya."

Uncle Nathan lif up him head and look pahn me outa two bloodshot yai and seh, "Is wa now, Audrie?"

"When Genevieve and her mada ketch a fight, she tell Ms. Swearing seh she not her mada and how she know dat her real mada deh a England."

"*Waak ya Laad if yu no busy*! Yu think is only one time me tell James and Birdie dat one fine day dat secret was going to fly outa di box. Umph. Aye sa. So wa Dawn and Deacon have to say bout it?"

"She cry and seh is lie."

"Wa bout Deacon? Wa him say bout it?

"*Never said a mumbling word.*"

"Just hung his head and died, uh? I swear to God dat is *pimento seed* dat man have in a him jraaz. Never could stan-up when things falling down roun him. Yu know dat alduoh is him did have di title of principal at Chalky Hill School, him wife was runnin di school all dese years?"

"What you sayin to me? Den, is really true dat she not Genevieve mada?"

"Is true, yes. Dawn Swearing sterile like any *man-guinep* tree and Deacon breed-aaf a grade nine girl-pikini. Yes mi child; dem try fi *kiba* it up. Dawn persuade Deacon fi mek dem tek di baby and ship off di mother to England. Dis happen when dem was working at a bush school up in di hills and since di people dem did fraid Dawn Swearing sue dem, dem only whisper behain dem hand. Dat is why him and Dawn run come back to Chalky Hill."

Before me kuda ask any more question, me hear footstep and soon Jimmy was standin in di kitchen doorway. Him greet Uncle Nathan but him was stiff and distant. Me know right aweh dat mi son no plan fi bend before Uncle Nathan. In mi head, me hear Myrna a seh, "Di boy wrong *and* strong," but it was soon clear dat Uncle Nathan was not about to let him aaf a di hook.

Him look right up pahn Jimmy and taak *saaf* but firm at di same time when him seh, "Get a plate, Jimmy and get some food from di stove. Mi and yu going to have a long talk today and we might have to go far back into some history. If yu have to grow two big jackass yez to listen, so be it. But when yu done fixing dat plate, yu come and tek yu place at di head a dis uol family table and mek me tell yu how far we coming from and how far yu drag dis family back to, by yu careless actions."

Me wait fi Jimmy fix him plate and den me fix wan fi Genevieve. Di laas ting me hear as me a waak weh from di kitchen was di soun a him chair harshly scrapin di kitchen floor when him pull it out fi si-dong."

nine day love-the heat of young love; intense infatuation
ackee tree-*Blighia sapida*; tree that bears fruit that is a part of Jamaica's national dish
flame of the forest-*Butea monosperma*; tree that blooms bright red petals
strangis-strongest
cow itch-stinging nettles
swizl-up-shriveled up
Shiva-Jewish week-long mourning period for first-degree relative
side-yai-side or peripheral vision
not evriting good fi nyam good fi chat-Some things should remain unsaid.
kum huom-come home
chruo a helleva stone in a di pig pen-This is an expression that indicates that an offense has been caused; this alludes to the saying that when a stone is thrown into a pig pen and a pig squeals, it has been hit.
panty govament-panty government; female dominance

cane-piece rat-wild rat that lives in cane fields and reputed to have been used in the past, in soup, as a cure for asthma and whooping cough

calaban-wooden trap used for catching ground-walking birds and small animals

woklis-worthless; cowardly

taak up di tings dem-to talk from deep feelings and without customary restraint

obeah-witchcraft; the act of working witchcraft

unu-you (plural)

facing mi own Waterloo-meeting my own crisis-an allusion to Napoleon's defeat at Waterloo

dutchie-Dutch pot; Dutch oven

calaloo-green, leafy, spinach-like vegetable that is steamed and eaten, sometimes with salted fish

Who deh ya?-Who's here?

jraaz-drawers

blaasid-blasted

wot-worth

tiifin-thieving

glad bag buss-bag of gladness has burst; fullness of joy

deh-deh-there

faati-forty

Young bod no know staam-A young bird does not know what a storm is; inexperience

Yai-lash uola dan beard-The lashes are older than the beard; older folks have more wisdom

pum-pum-female genitalia (vulgar)

The Mighty Sparrow-Slinger Francisco, world famous calypsonian

Rooster-reference to a Sparrow calypso, *Cockeyed Rooster*

ketch-up-to get caught up in an altercation

waak ya Laad if yu no bizi-walk by here Lord if you are not too busy

never said a mumbling word/ just hung his head and died-quote from the song, *Didn't They Crucify My Lord*

pimento seed-*Pimenta dioica*; allspice seed

man-guinep-guinep tree that does not bear fruit

kiba-cover

wrong and strong-in the wrong and arrogant

saaf-soft

CHAPTER 8

Raphael Caine

1910-1930

Uol groj mek patu lay hegg
An old grudge will cause an owl to lay an egg
An old hurt will lead to retaliation

He left the hill country of Darling Spring, Hanover parish, as Raphael Caine and returned calling himself Carlos Jimenez Riviera. The year he departed Jamaica was 1910 and he returned from digging the Panama Canal in 1914, the year of The Great War. Nobody in Darling Spring knew what to make of him and the people of the village soon concluded that he was crazy. Some even said that grudgeful people had worked obeah on him and turned him fool-fool because of the money he had made in Panama. After all, what could make a man wear a suit while tilling his field? And only a mad man would refuse to answer to his given name.

The first time he dressed in his three-piece broadcloth, donned his good felt hat with his water boots and appeared for breakfast, his wife, Miss Adlyn, began to beat her breast and cry. He cut his eye at her, swallowed down his breakfast and marched out the door to his mule.

As he mounted the sturdy beast, a young man walked into the yard and said, "Maanin Maas Raphael."

His response was, "Mi dyam blaasid name is Carlos Jimenez Riviera! Show rispek or I will open yu head wid mi blaasid *cutlis*!"

The youngster stepped hastily away from man and beast and stood watching them until they disappeared from sight.

He made enemies for this behavior and worse because parents did not take kindly to a grown man using such big bad words to children, but few dared to confront him because of the fire in his eyes and the long gun strapped to the back of his mule.

In 1925, he left for Cuba and when he returned in 1929, he was worse. After Panama, he had been terse and foul-mouthed but now he was often violent and dangerous. One morning, he opened a four-inch gash in the leg of his field-hand with his machete. He had to pay for medical care and compensation to prevent the young man's parents from going to the police. His excuse for the act was that the boy was lazy and moved too slowly.

Maas Raphael worried Miss Adlyn even more when he started spending lavishly to improve their lives. Who ever heard of a black man riding around in a horse-drawn buggy and buying prime bottom land by the acre? He paid good money too, solid gold coins which the white land owners viewed with suspicion until the testing bite of metal revealed gold beneath gold.

His willingness to spend his money caused secret derision in some, but money was money. If he was prepared to pay in gold for their overpriced land, he could damn well have it.

He soon built a long, low, *Spanish-walled* house on top of a low, grassy hill. It became his testament of achievement and from his expansive verandah, he could see the village spread out below. He could even see the steeple of the Moravian church, visible between the royal palms that lined both sides of the sloping driveway. His wife and daughter Nerissa went often, but he kept his distance from the corpulent Scotchman who was both preacher and head teacher of the elementary school that was held in the church building. The last time he had been near a church had been to bury his mother and much to the horror of Darling Spring, he had stood outside in the pouring rain rather than step into the sanctuary for the service. His uncles, who were staunch churchgoers, had warned him that God was going to kill him for his wickedness but in his customary fashion, he had spit on the ground and walked away without saying a word.

From the sides of his house, he could see his cattle in the far and near pastures. When standing at his kitchen window, his eyes often followed the course of the stream snaking its way below the footbridge at his gate, past his property and down the bottom of the hill. There it disappeared underground until it joined up with the river a few miles away.

Sometimes when Miss Adlyn and Nerissa were done with the evening chores, they joined him on the verandah to enjoy the evening breeze and Maas Raphael would talk to them if his mood was right. He rarely looked at them as he spoke but from the stiffness of his shoulders and the rigid line of his jaw, Miss Adlyn knew that the anger was still in him. He almost always went back to the subject of the Caribbean men who dug out the Isthmus jungle to make way for the Panama Canal. He talked about the fever, the drownings in mud, the men left to rot where they perished and the open prejudice of the American bosses.

"We wok like *brute-biis*, Adlyn, but dem pay fi wi man dem in a silver and fi dem man in a *guol.* Yet we face more *dienja*, especially in dat Culebra Pass. Yu know *hu-moch* man me see dead in deh; blowup straight to Maasa Gaad *hebn* by *dandimait*? Me personally si *semtiin* West Indian man perish in di Cucaracha Slide dat kill hundreds. Yu ever hear dat any a we get any special *ana* fi killin wiself? Di ongl reason me get mi pay in guol is because me was di ongl West Indian man who did know how fi operate di steam shovel and A had was to raise hell to get mi pay!"

They felt his pain but they did not know how to comfort him. In fact, Miss Adlyn was terrified of him, especially since the day he gave her the side of his hand. After that, she nursed real fear for their future. What if one of the local planters got tired of his bluster and knocked him over on one of the lonely local roads? He often carried a shotgun openly and he had a license for it. But truth be told, a gun could not protect from bad mind or envy. Furthermore, Raphael did not have eyes in the back of his head.

Both Miss Adlyn and Nerissa enjoyed the comforts that Maas Raphael's money provided but they missed the camaraderie they had enjoyed with the other women of the village when they were poor. They no longer made the trek to the river to wash their clothes as the other women did because Maas Raphael had built a large water tank in the backyard. He had even provided indoor plumbing, unheard of even in the homes of most of the well-to-do brown and white people of Hanover parish.

Despite all the luxuries that Maas Raphael provided, however, Miss Adlyn felt like she was always walking around on splinters because she no longer felt at ease with this man. She did not know what had happened to him in the swamps of Central America and the streets of Havana but he was not the man she had married in girlish innocence at sixteen. Then, he had been lanky, diffident and full of laughter. Now, his hands danced when they were not actively engaged and he sometimes stared off into the distance for hours, without speaking.

One evening just as the fowls settled upon their roosts at the far corner of the backyard, Maas Raphael's brother, Uncle Ralston, appeared. Adlyn saw him before her husband did and hurried down the front steps to meet him, her face full of concern.

Like Maas Raphael, he was tall and lanky but there the similarities ended. Where Maas Raphael was jittery, he was easy like an evening breeze and when he smiled his gold teeth glinted like starlight in a friendly night sky.

He had come about money because after Maas Raphael came around the corner of the house to speak to Ralston, he patted his side pockets and pulled out a handful of notes. Before he handed over the money, Miss Adlyn heard him say, "Rally a len mi a len yu di money, fa me kyaahn afford fi *gi weh mi aas an shit chuu mi ribs.*"

Miss Adlyn hurried back into the house as both men made their way up to the verandah and sat down to talk.

She soon brought out lemonade sweetened with the dark wet sugar that she had milled herself and *toto* that was still warm from her *hell-a-tap-hell-a-batam,* fireside oven. She then retreated to the sitting room where she could listen without being seen. She pretended to be busy with her sewing but she strained to catch her husband's words.

Nerissa emerged from her bedroom to see the visitor but Miss Adlyn shooed her back and pulled her chair a little closer to the front window.

Maas Raphael's voice soon rose with passion and carried clearly into the room where she sat and as she listened, she sighed.

The subject was as always his days in Panama and Cuba. This time he was talking again about a St. Elizabeth man he saw murdered in Cuba. The pain in his voice was as fresh as if the event were current.

"Di ting dat hurt me di muos, Rally bwai, is dat is nat wan a dem Cuban outlaa dat kill him. Is wan a wi own Jumaika man dem dwiit. Him watch di man win di money in a di casino, and lay in wait outside and put a knife in a him back. A tek mi own two yai dem and see him when him dwiit, for A was in a daak kaana tekin a piss. Me was gwaihn run go fight him, but me neba hab no *wepan,* and when mi si di twelve-inch knife blade, me know him wuda did kill me too. And dat son-of-a-bitch come back a Jumaika wid di man winnins, and buil big house a Darliston. But Gaad duohn wear *pijaama.* Me *yer seh* dat wan night, him *kersiin* lamp *ton oba*, and bon di house to ashes. Him barely *ekskaip* wid him life, but two a di small wans wasn so lucky. Rally, yu si how *parents suck di sour grape and set di pikni dem tiit pahn edge*? *Wa jrap aafa pupa head, jrap pahn pikni shoula*."

Miss Adlyn heard Uncle Ralston grunt in assent and she soon became lost in her own thoughts. She worried that her husband would not be able to survive if he could not belch out the bitterness that had taken hold of him like a bad case of colic. She once dared to broach the subject to him and that was when he hit her across the face and bloodied her nose. As she lay whimpering on the floor, he stood above her and snarled, "Me wok miself almuos to det a Panama, me and wol-heap a West Indian man, an me no *yer seh* any book write bout we. An all di blaasid bad-mind people roun here do, is sing bout *Colon*

Man when dem si we in a wi good clothes. Duohn provoke me, Adlyn. A will murder yu and go a *gyalas* fi it!"

After that incident, she never criticized him but still feared that he would not live long enough to see their daughter safely tucked away under the protective wrap of early matrimony.

A few days after Uncle Ralston's visit, Nerissa made the breakfast as she often did. This time as she walked to the table with a pot of lime leaf tea, Maas Raphael spat out his stewed beef and boiled green bananas. He then jumped to his feet, glowering at his daughter and demanded, "Why di hell yu cook mi food like yu *fiidin hag*! Eh, Nerissa? Why di backside yu never season mi food!"

Miss Adlyn heard the commotion from where she stood feeding the chickens at the fenced fowl run that separated her vegetable garden from the side yard. She dropped the wide-mouthed pudding pan and the shelled corn scattered on the ground at her feet, making a crazy mosaic that she did not have time to see.

When Miss Adlyn hurried in through the back door, she found Nerissa standing with her head bowed while her father stood at the head of the table, glaring at her.

Nerissa, her voice trembling, spoke barely above a whisper, "Me kyaahn stan di smell a di seasonin, *sa*. It mek me want to *chruo-up*, bad-bad, sa."

Miss Adlyn's heart leapt within her and her worst fears were confirmed when Nerissa rushed out to the verandah and vomited copiously into the red and yellow hibiscus bushes below.

Maas Raphael had spent enough time around women to suspect the meaning of these events and he went crazy. He knocked over his chair and reached for the buggy whip that hung behind the dining-room door. He darted out after his daughter and his hand was arching downward with the first lash when Miss Adlyn charged, ramming her forehead into his back, just below the shoulders. Maas Raphael fell forward and she grabbed the whip.

She had never stood up to him before and the shock of her transformation made him weaken. She pulled the whip from him and ran to the low wall of the verandah. Miss Adlyn flung the stringed rawhide into the blooming rose bushes below her bedroom window. She then ran down the steps and made for the side of the house where she found Nerissa stooping against the water tank. The girl hugged herself as she wept.

Her mother took her by the hand and led her through the back door of the house and into her narrow bedroom. She sat her on the edge of the hard bed and wiped her streaming eyes and nose with the hem of her dress. Then Miss Adlyn began to rock Nerissa and blow air onto her face just like she did when she was a toddler and threw a tantrum.

That was how she got the story out of her daughter. With halting words and through her tears, Nerissa told her mother how her teacher, The Reverend Angus Whitehead, had held her down and raped her at the back of the church office.

Miss Adlyn stretched Nerissa out upon the coir mattress, covered her with a light cotton blanket and walked out of the room. She was about to call to her husband when he emerged from their bedroom. He was clad in black from his felt hat to his high leather boots and his shotgun was across his shoulder. Without saying a word he looked back at Miss Adlyn. His thin lips were pursed but his eyes were unreadable as he turned to walk through the front door, his steps brisk and purposeful.

UP AT THE Moravian church house, The Reverend Angus Whitehead, also known to his staff and pupils as Teacher Whitehead, was getting ready for morning prayers which would take place in the church building, next door.

As was his custom, he was dressed in a tropical linen suit. This one was charcoal gray and tailored to a perfect fit. His pristine white cotton shirt was starched and his sober gray necktie was knotted correctly.

He stood in front of the full-length mirror in his mahogany wardrobe and studied himself from head to toe. The Reverend Angus Whitehead had no complaints about the figure that he cut because though his hair was streaked and thinning on top, his face was still smooth and his blue eyes were still sharp.

He reached forward to his bedside table for a silver-backed boar's hair brush and made a few strokes across his balding pate to make sure that the vanishing silver strands covered the spots where his pink scalp was beginning to show through. He whistled through his teeth as he fastidiously attended to his grooming. By the time he finally replaced the brush, he had changed his whistling to humming. He made one final turn in front of the mirror and left the bedroom that he did not share with his wife.

Teacher Whitehead had just emerged from the front door of the manse when the man on the mule cantered up the driveway, rounded the corner of the church building and brought the prancing beast up short in front of him. He frowned with annoyance and was about to order Raphael Caine from his mule when his eyes caught the glint of metal as Maas Raphael lifted his shotgun. Instinct told him to run and the first explosion blasted out the front window of the manse.

The noise brought Mrs. Whitehead, the other teachers and the pupils running from the church and on to the quadrangle.

Teacher Whitehead was by then running westward for the stone-packed wall that separated the church property from the pasture land on the other side. He had one sturdy leg upon the wall and was scrambling to bring the other up behind him when a bullet tore into the right cheek of his buttocks. He pitched headlong over the wall and fell into a bleeding heap on to the prickly grass below.

By the time Miss Adlyn got to the churchyard, the deed was done and Maas Raphael and his mule had trotted off onto the narrow track that led to the main road of the village.

IT WAS PERHAPS a full week before the people of Darling Spring could talk of anything else but the postmortem among the villagers was by no means unanimous. Some voiced stern reproach against Raphael Caine for disturbing the social order. Not all of the Blacks sided with him because if he could fire shots at the white Scottish parson, what would he do to them? The white and brown people condemned him wholesale and some even suggested that a public flogging would be appropriate to his crime.

Others stated openly that the village had looked away from Teacher Whitehead's abuse for too long and it took a man with real balls to stand up to him. It was not as though they did not know that although he had fathered no offspring with his wife, he had been littering the village with his progeny for more than twenty years. Others were too frightened to speak publicly and kept to their small cottages and hedged fields while they waited for the outcome of the outrageous event.

When four other village girls sprouted pregnancies and dared to name The Reverend Angus Whitehead as the expectant father, the Moravian Church hierarchy saw it fit to step in. Mrs. Whitehead was spirited away by night as her husband lay in his recovery bed. He later joined her in Barbados where he assumed new duties.

Raphael Caine hired a prominent barrister to defend him but he was neither arrested nor imprisoned. The Moravian Church saw sudden virtue in Christian forbearance and forgiveness. Raphael Caine saved his Spanish gold for future use.

Miss Adlyn nursed Nerissa through a difficult and dangerous pregnancy and at the time of her delivery, Panama gold paved the way, once more. An English doctor from the parish capital attended her.

The baby was born on May 3, 1930. Raphael Caine named him James John Whitehead. This was against custom because the mother was not married to the father, but the registrar of births and deaths knew better than to argue with the dictate of Raphael Caine, a.k.a. Carlos Jimenez Riviera.

cutlis-cutlass

Spanish-wall-adobe wall

brute-biis-brute-beast; animal

guol-gold

dienja-danger

hu-moch-how much; how many

hebn-heaven

dandimait-dynamite

semtiin-seventeen

ana-honor

gi weh mi aas an shit chuu mi ribs-give away my ass and shit through my ribs; to be unwisely generous

toto-dense pastry made from flour, sugar, coconut, ginger, nutmeg and butter or lard

hell a tap, hell a batam, hallelujah in di migl-literally-hell on the top (fire); hell on the bottom (fire) and hallelujah (the baked goods) in the middle. This is a rudimentary oven made with fire wood or charcoal placed on a metal sheet. The sheet is placed on top of the container of batter and fire is also placed under the container.

wepan-weapon

pijaama-pajamas

yer seh-heard

kersiin lamp-kerosene lamp

ton oba-turn(ed) over

ekskaip-escape

Parents suck di sour grape and set di pikni dem tiit pahn edge-The parents sucked the sour grapes and set the children's teeth on edge (Ezekiel 18:2).

Wa jrap aaf a pupa head, jrap pahn pikni shoula-What has fallen from the father's head has landed on the children's shoulders; the descendants reap the ancestors' karma.

Colon Man-popular folk song which was made to jeer returnees who had gone to Panama to help to build the canal. They often returned with money, jewelry and ostentatious clothes.

gyalas-gallows

fiidin hag-feeding a hog

sa-sir

chruo-up-throw up; vomit

CHAPTER 9

Raphael Caine and Cyrano Thaddeus Webster

1931-1951

If yu fraid a yai yu kyaahn nyam head
If you are afraid of eyes you cannot eat the head of an animal
One needs to be brave in the face of adversity, aggression or opposition
Frog seh, "What is joke to yu is det to me."
The frog says that what you consider a joke is a matter of life and death to him

Maas Raphael saw the car coming in the distance and shaded his eyes with his hand to see more clearly. He was not expecting any important visitor and as he stood on the bottom front step of his house, he debated with himself. Should he go to the gate? What was a car doing on this narrow, country road? Was this more trouble for him?

He hurried up the steps to the house and entered his bedroom which opened to one side of the verandah. He returned carrying his shotgun across his shoulder and walked toward the little white car that was now parked in front of the gate.

He had experienced enough trouble in the past year and if it was the police coming to bother him again about taking his gun license, he would just plug them full of holes and be done with it.

The man emerging from the car was white, delicate and very small. Maas Raphael looked at him and almost sniggered. His eyes hardened, however, when the diminutive man greeted him by name. His piercing eyes seemed enormous behind his heavy, hyperopic lenses.

Maas Raphael stood where he was and studied the man but he did not return his greeting. He was of a mind to drive him off his property but something in the man's demeanor made him hesitate as he walked toward him.

When he stood in front of Maas Raphael, he held out his hand in greeting. The gesture took him by surprise but he kept one hand on his gun across his shoulder and the other behind his back. If the gentleman was intimidated by the gun sitting across Maas Raphael's shoulder, however, his steady gaze betrayed none of that fear. He dropped the proffered hand to his side but his eyes remained unblinking. Maas Raphael was the first to look away.

"My name is Reverend Cyrano Webster and I am the new parson at the Moravian church."

His Scottish tenor was very pleasing and mild but Maas Raphael bristled, nonetheless. He turned away from the parson and sent a stream of saliva splashing against the root of the breadfruit tree that shaded the gateway.

"And what yuh waahn wid me, sa? *Me no plaahn gungu a line* wid no *paasn*, yu know, sa!"

"Pardon me," the man said, very politely. "You will have to excuse me, but I do not understand."

"Me duohn waahn notn fi do wid no bloody parson!"

With that said, Maas Raphael turned abruptly and began to walk away from The Reverend Mr. Webster but the little man followed him with determination.

When they got to the bottom of the front steps of the house, Maas Raphael looked up to see Miss Adlyn standing in the doorway. She was wiping her hands over and over in her floral apron and pushing her glasses up on her nose. He saw the fear and uncertainty in her round face and was moved to anger. He turned again to the stranger just as a baby began to wail from somewhere within the house. Miss Adlyn disappeared into the house just as Maas Raphael began to hurry up the remaining steps.

Reverend Webster continued after him but Maas Raphael lengthened his steps and marched into his house. Reverend Webster started to follow him but changed his mind. He turned, instead, and walked over to one of the support columns of the verandah. He leaned his open left palm against the warm wood and looked out over the expanse of green pastureland that rolled away downhill.

He stood silently, looking around him and seeming to note everything that his owlish eyes took in. After a while, he removed his hat and placed it on the wooden chair that was nearest to him.

It was Miss Adlyn who first returned to the verandah, bearing a hand-carved tray of refreshments which she placed carefully upon a low mahogany side table.

"Come dis way, sa," she said very gently. "Res yu foot dem a likl. Maas Raphael soon come"

She said the last more like a wish than an affirmation and disappeared into the house once more.

Maas Raphael kept the gentleman waiting for many minutes before he emerged with a squirming baby bundle in his arms. He pulled a chair with one hand and brought it to the wall outside of his bedroom. He sat in silence, his head bowed and a frown etched in his forehead.

Reverend Webster took his time with his refreshment and did not look at Maas Raphael until he had finished his lemonade and dabbed at his lips with a very clean handkerchief.

When he had placed the glass very carefully upon the starched napkin that lined the tray, he reached for the baby and to his surprise, Maas Raphael handed him over.

He looked at the child and the child looked right back at him. The baby began to drool, then broke into a wide, toothless grin and tried to pull his glasses off his nose.

Maas Raphael almost laughed too but caught himself. Reverend Webster smiled and handed the baby back to the grandfather who began to rock him from side to side on his knee.

After another lengthy silence broken only by the contented gurgle of the baby, Reverend Webster stated very dryly, "That is Angus Whitehead's child, alright, and that's the rub."

"Uumm," was Maas Raphael's pained response as the baby leaned against his chest and sucked his thumb.

When Maas Raphael added nothing more, he continued to speak.

"Those are Angus' eyes and his brow is unmistakable. I have been on my rounds this past week and this is the fifth child I have linked to Brother Angus."

"And what yu plan to do bout it, sa?"

"I plan to take the matter to the very head of the denomination."

Maas Raphael sat up straighter and began to regard the tiny man sitting in front of him with new found respect. "Yu mean to tell me, sa, dat yu as a white man, intend to stan-up fi black people against aneda white man?"

The gentleman nodded and Maas Raphael said in quiet wonderment, "Dere is a Gaad in Israel."

He leapt to his feet, startling the baby who began to sputter and whimper but Maas Raphael paying no attention, shouted instead, "Adlyn! Nerissa! Adlyn! Nerissa!"

His wife and daughter ran to the verandah to see what was afoot and both stood open-mouthed as Maas Raphael began to pummel the little man's shoulder. Still clutching the baby to one hip, he pulled the startled man to his feet, flung one arm around his shoulder and stuttered, "*Dis-ya* is-is-is a man-a-a-among men. Yuh hear me! Dis-ya-a-man!"

Reverend Webster turned scarlet to the roots of his hair but his eyes glowed from behind the thick lenses. This time when the baby laughed out loud, Maas Raphael did not suppress the same urge. He handed the baby over to the bewildered women and turned back to Reverend Webster.

"Waak wid me a likl, sa. We have business to taak, man-to-man."

Reverend Webster stood hastily, picked up his hat and followed Maas Raphael down the steps to the front yard. This time, Maas Raphael left his shotgun behind.

Me no plant gungu a line-I do not plant gungu (pigeon peas) to mark our property boundary; We do not share a common property boundary; we do not have friendly relations.

paasn-parson

dis ya a man-This here is a man; he is the real deal.

CHAPTER 10

If yu waahn fi know yu fren dem, li-dong a roadside and play jonk
If you want to know who your real friends are, lie by the roadside and pretend to be drunk

The friendship between Raphael Caine and The Reverend Cyrano Thaddeus Webster became the stuff of legend in the northwest of the island. Even today, there are hoary-headed oldsters who recall the odd pair that folks called *Psyche and Trim* behind their backs. Others, who were less polite, referred to them as *batty and chimmy.*

Miss Adlyn washed Reverend Webster's clothes, cleaned his house and prepared his food. Maas Raphael provided much of what he ate. He, in turn, took responsibility for the education of young James John as well as all of the other children of The Reverend Angus Whitehead.

As the years went by, James and Nathan, another of Angus Whitehead's sons, became particularly close. The Reverend Mr. Webster made it possible for them to attend the exclusive Moravian boys' boarding school tucked away in the hills of St. Elizabeth parish. He also assumed guardianship of the two boys so as to allay questions about their parents' marital status.

As the friendship between Maas Raphael and Reverend Cyrano Webster solidified, people grew to accept their strange bond. Never in the history of Hanover parish had such a thing ever been witnessed. The devotion of black slave to white master or servant to master had been seen many a time. But this was a friendship between equals-the one tall and quick to anger, the other, small, spare and thoughtful. They became Raph and Cyrri to each other and Maas Raphael no longer bristled and cursed when called by his given name.

Cyrri taught Raph to drive his car and Raph, in turn, often handed over his prized mule so that his friend could make home visitations where roadways were not passable by car.

As was to be expected, Cyrri tried to convert Raph to his Christian faith but, here, Raph remained unyielding. He told his dear friend that although he believed in the existence of a Creator God, he had trouble with the concept of a white Jesus whose representatives lorded it over the people. He hated that many of the local parsons broke bread with the landowners and merchants who never paid a fair day's wage and deprived the locals of education and opportunities to better themselves.

Cyrri chose not to press him on this but reminded him of the sterling work of abolitionists such as *William Knibb* and *Charles Buxton*, men who did right by the poor. Raph conceded that there were the occasional good ones in the lot, but insisted that their work was often canceled by the wickedness of the majority.

When the occasion seemed right, Cyrri began to discuss scriptures and history with him. It was he who taught Raph about ancient Egyptian culture and the robust contributions of Africans to the development of civilization. He also told him about Moses' black wife and the ancient Cushites mentioned in the Bible and how these were black people.

What really shocked Raph, however, was when Cyrri told him that he did not for a moment believe that Jesus took human form as a white male. He slowly and carefully explained the geography and history of early Palestine and the various ethnic groups which peopled the area. At first, Raph remained skeptical but Cyrri finally was able to convince him of this when he showed him early Catholic renditions of the Madonna and Child and Raph saw that they appeared even darker than his own grandson, James.

It was none of these talks that converted Raph, however. What brought his change was the day that he finally talked to Cyrri about the rape of Nerissa.

As was often common with the two, Cyrri joined Raph for lunch under a breadfruit tree near the bank of the stream that ran through the yam field. The two men ate stewed beef, yams and okra, from broad tin plates. They washed the food down with rum and coconut water. Raph had taught Cyrri to drink rum but he never gave him the local undistilled liquor that he favored. Once when Cyrri asked to sample it, Raph laughingly declared, "Dis a *jankro batty,* sa. Yuh kyaahn drink dis. It will mek yu taak rudeness in a di pulpit."

Cyrri understood enough of what was said to let the matter drop.

When they were done eating, Raph leaned back against the trunk of the food tree, pulled a strand of grass and began to chew meditatively. Cyrri unlaced his boots, removed his cotton socks and lowered his tired feet into the clear running water. He sighed with relief and began to massage his insteps over the smooth river stones under his feet.

At first when Raph spoke, Cyrri did not respond but when the silence stretched for a while, he turned to look at him. Raph had said, "Yu ever have somting dat yu value more dan life itself and sombadi spwail it?"

Cyrri pondered for a while before answering.

"I was married once, for a wee bit."

"A didn know dat."

"Long time ago. Water under the bridge but I know a little about people spoiling your valuables. If I hadn't forgot an important letter and returned home unexpectedly, I would not have found out that my much younger brother was tasting the favors of my wife."

He had spoken very dryly but the knuckles of the fingers clutching his knees were white.

"Sorry to hear dat Cyrri but my wan daata, Nerissa, spwail fi life. Yu know what dat do to me, Cyrri? Yu know what it feel like to know dat no man will ever waak up my front steps to ask fi mi daata? No *black cake* gwaihn to bake fi my daata and Adlyn will neba sew a bridal *frak* fi har."

When he said those words, it was as if dammed waters had suddenly breeched a restraining wall and Raphael Caine, for the first time in his adult life, began to weep. He made to stand up but fell to his knees under the lofty green canopy of the breadfruit tree.

Down on his knees, in his field, Raphael wept for his raped daughter, his grandson marked by bastardy, his broken-hearted wife and for his dashed dreams. And though he could not put words to the feeling, he wept for his ancestors, driven out of their homes at the sword's edge, and under the flare of bullets and the whip's lash, forced into ships' holds and carried with less care than sheep and oxen to be auctioned to the greed of empire builders.

His friend held him by his heaving shoulders and their knees made deep dents into the humid earth at the root of the shade tree. There, Raphael Caine wept until the knot that had tied him to hatred began to unwind.

Cyrri held him hard, his bony fingers kneading Raph's trembling shoulders. He spoke not a word to Raph but wept too, until his nose clogged and his breath ran short. And there for the first time in his life, the love of God was born into the heart of a formerly hard man, carried to him by the servant of Christ who broke bread with him and cried with him.

They lived the biblical friendship of David and Jonathan and when The Reverend Cyrano Webster breathed his last on Christmas day, 1951, it was his aged friend, Raphael Caine, who closed his eyes and straightened his frail limbs. It therefore came as no surprise to the people of Darling Spring, that Raphael made his departure within a week of the burial of his one true friend.

Psyche and Trim-folk expression for two extremely close friends (source unknown)
batty and chimmy-behind or bottom and chamber pot
William Knibb-abolitionist
Thomas Buxton-philanthropist and abolitionist
jankro batty-John crow's behind; stink like a turkey buzzard's behind; extremely strong, pungent and flammable. This term is used in reference to undistilled rum. In some parts of Jamaica, this rum is called kulu-kulu. It is also called rude-to-parents.
black cake- traditional Jamaican wedding cake
frak-frock; dress

CHAPTER 11

Hugh Arthur Reid

1938-1940

Ram goat seh, "Fi a peaceful life, me deh wid mi muma."
The ram goat says that for the sake of a peaceful life, he is conducting an affair with his own mother
We sometimes make distasteful decisions in order to keep the peace

Hugh Arthur Reid was going home from college and he was in a big hurry, so much so that he almost skipped the final morning prayers but thought better of it. He knew his principal to be a mercurial man who could resort to spite if he sensed insubordination in a student. Just the day before he had graduated at the top of his class, besting the scions of Kingston families that carried names like Henriques and Vendryes and he was not about to risk his teacher's certificate by angering "His Lordship."

He boarded the open-sided tram car at Cross Roads after walking all the way from Marescеaux Road with his grip in his hand. It was crammed so tight that he had to bind it with a piece of sisal rope. This was the only way that he could guarantee that the lock would not give way on the long, bumpy train ride to St. Elizabeth.

Some of the students had sniggered when he walked into the chapel with his old grip and he heard one or two of them mention country bumpkin. Hugh, however, did not much care what they thought of him. He considered most of them *pissn tail* boys. That's exactly what his father would call them. He, on the other hand, was a man with responsibilities. He had five acres under cultivation that his father and brothers were taking care of for him, and his wife, Celeste, had, only the week before, given birth to their first child.

Hugh Arthur was therefore anxious to get home to see Celeste and the baby, Birdielee Adassa. If it had been a boy, he would have been named for Hugh Arthur. They had named the baby before birth, an affront in the eyes of the elderly but Hugh did not think that they had tempted fate by doing this. He did not believe in evil spirits and obeah and had done everything possible to free his unschooled wife from fear and superstition. He had not broken completely with the ways of his people but he saw himself as a man of science and reason and felt very strongly that he was called to free his people through education.

Although Hugh Arthur had never made any public declarations of support, he admired the work of Marcus Garvey and saw himself as a man of similar mind. He had also considered the work of the late *Alexander Bedward*, the famous Revivalist preacher from August Town, but changed his mind about him when he learned that he had tried to ascend to heaven.

Hugh Arthur first started to admire Mr. Bedward when he heard from his father how he had stood up to the colonial police. The man was so well loved that he had a following of more than a thousand people. Only God knows what had got into the shepherd to make him believe that he could fly up to heaven. When his father got to that part of the story, Hugh Arthur became sorely disappointed that a man who had started out so well, ended as such a figure of ridicule.

The tram car stopped and Hugh Arthur emerged from his reverie to find a large, middle-aged market woman sitting directly across from him. She was watching him with a mixture of curiosity and concern. He smiled politely at her and removed his hat. She had an open, friendly face and when she smiled back at him, she showed gap-toothed, tobacco stained teeth.

"A kuda swear dat yu is wan a Klaadiin Jessop bwai dem but yu wud be far-far fram yu yaad."

He was surprised by the observation and frowned a little before answering in the affirmative, but she was an elder so he said, "She is my mother and I am her youngest."

"Eh, yu fieva har kyaahn done. Yu is di dead stamp a yu Uncle Aaata an yu look refine an taak so nice."

She looked at the grip resting on the floor between his knees and continued, "So yu a come fram kalij?"

"Yes, ma'am."

"Well, I never. Dat's nice. So yu goin back to country an yu goin to railway? So why yu never stay in town weh yu kuda get more *apachuuniti?*

Before Hugh Arthur could respond, a fox-faced higgler sitting two seats away from the fat higgler screamed, "Cho laad! Yu too dyam faas, Diney. Imagine, yu si di young man a go bout him business an yu a kwestian him like yu a him muma. Maasa, duohn tell har yu affairs!"

Miss Diney folded her muscled arms across her bosom and declared, "Yu kyan kiss me yu-know-what, Ethel. Ef it was not fi mi rispek fi dis *anarebl* young *jenklman*, I wuda *tear-up kopl yaad a klaat gi yu ya tideh.* I am taakin to mi faambli. Is mi dischrik him come fram. Him granny and mi pappy used to *pick straa*, so fi all I know, is me nephew me taakin to."

This was met by a chorus of guffaws and harsh laughter and Ethel of the sly eyes and narrow face announced sarcastically to the interested car load of passengers, "Diney buying cousins by the dozens. Anybody else up fi a quick sale?"

The car halted at Parade, named for the British Red Coats. This spot had been their parade ground but, today, it was the tumultuous meeting place of city and countryside-a place for horse-drawn buggies, cars, carts and drays, foot-walkers and the tramcar. The already bustling Jubilee Market was out of

Hugh's direct line of sight but he could hear the noise of buyers and sellers trying to outdo each other in volume and stridency.

The higglers, some still laughing, hastened to leave the car. To Hugh Arthur's relief, Miss Diney was among the first to leave, instructing him as she placed her *bankra* basket upon her head, "Seh howdy to yu mami an papi fi me. Tell dem is Diney Clarke seh so an you tek good care a yuself, yu hear? And duohn nyam notn from dem dyam grudgeful country people, yu hear?"

Hugh Arthur doffed his hat once more and breathed a sigh of relief that there would be no further attention from this nosey woman and her raucous companions. He knew why she had advised him not to eat from his neighbors but he did not believe that anyone wanted to poison him.

When Hugh Arthur got to Barry Street, he was pleased to see that the passengers waiting at the train station were orderly and businesslike. A few of them waited alongside handcart men who watched over their goods. These were sellers of small items of haberdashery and they were waiting to transport their goods to the hinterland of the island. Many of them were sellers of cloth and other sewing material and some of them would stay at a chosen boarding house and travel daily on foot to supply their customers.

Hugh Arthur did not mind traveling with such, especially after his encounter with the higglers. These men were higglers of a kind, also, but most of them were Jewish or Chinese and of a more quiet disposition than the food sellers of Kingston.

He stood for a while and absently studied the Georgian façade of the station building. He thought to himself that the early investors must have expected much from their foray into the railroad business. The wrought iron brackets supporting the high arch of the roof must have cost a pretty penny and the brick façade must have drawn blood and money. He found himself wondering how much the laborers would have earned in 1845 when the building went under construction. Not much, he supposed, because this would have been less than ten years after the abolition of the quasi-slavery system of apprenticeship that followed slavery.

Hugh Arthur glanced up into the ceiling and saw gray and white pigeons hopping and flying from beam to beam. They cooed and perched often on the iron supports that were all white-streaked with bird droppings. He moved himself and his grip closer to the edge of the low platform and looked eastward, inclining his ear to listen for the rumble of the train.

The train would make twenty-seven stops before pulling into his home station of Maggoty, St. Elizabeth parish. After Hugh Arthur bought his second class ticket and settled into a corner seat, he wedged his grip between his knees, pulled his hat down over his brow and prepared to doze. Sometimes there were pickpockets on the train but this morning there were two constables in his train carriage and so he doubted that any of those rascals would be plying their trade today. In any case, his three pounds and ten were safely wrapped in a small handkerchief and tucked into his inner breast-pocket.

THE SHOUTING INTRUDED into his doze and Hugh Arthur awoke to find the train idling at the Porus Station in the middle parish of Manchester. As he had been sleeping for more than an hour, he straightened his form and looked outside his window. There were about thirty men milling about on the platform and arguing with the ticket master. Hugh Arthur heard him address a stout, bewhiskered and very black man who seemed to be the leader if the group. The man in response bellowed in a hoarse baritone and shook his index finger under the ticket master's nose.

"We want to *trabl* to Montego Bay and yu hab no right fi prevent we! Where it write dong in His Majesty law dat we kyaahn ride di train in a wi bush clothes!"

Hugh Arthur sighed to himself and looked around his near empty carriage. His heart sank when the ticket master backed down and the men began to enter the train.

About fifteen of them entered his carriage and they carried the odor of the bush, sweat and *jackass rope tobacco* with them. It was not the odor of their sweat that bothered Hugh Arthur, though. The men seemed edgy and angry and as they marched into the car, they looked around them as if they expected trouble.

He suspected that they were cane workers and that they were headed to Montego Bay on their way to Westmoreland. He had been following the newspaper reports of the labor unrest that was running like a wildfire not only through the island but all over the Caribbean to as far as British Guiana and British Honduras. These men were no doubt on their way to lend support to the striking cane workers of the large Frome sugar estate in Westmoreland.

To his surprise, not one of the men took a seat and as the train pulled out of the station, the leader cleared his throat loudly and pulled a rum flask from the back pocket of his stained drill pants. He took a swig and passed the bottle to the man nearest to him.

When the bottle had made its way to the last man, the leader puffed out his chest like a wood pigeon and began to sing in the same harsh baritone:

Mi muma me waahn fi wok
Mi muma me waahn fi wok
Mi muma me waahn fi wok
Look how mi muscle deh jump

Each time he sang a line, the assembled men answered the refrain and soon the car rang with their thunderous singing. As the men sang the raucous work song, it became what sounded to Hugh Arthur like a lament, despite their laughter. In between the notes, their breathing was ragged as if they were catching and swallowing their sobs before they escaped.

By the second go round, a younger man took the lead and sang to the same tune but in a mellow tenor:

Uman a hebi load
Uman a hebi load
Uman a hebi load
When Satideh maanin come

When di money no nof
When di money no nof
When di money no nof
Dem kaal yu doti bwai

But when di money nof
When di money nof
When di money nof
Dem kaal yu sweetie-pie
Dem kaal yu sugar plum

When the men got to the end of each line, they grunted in unison, mimicking the hefting of a heavy load. Soon, a good-looking, brown woman in the corner of the car sucked her teeth and cut her eyes at the men.

She was the color of a fully ripened *Jew plum* and the kind of woman that many Jamaican men found irresistible. She was tall, too, and Hugh noticed as she rose to her feet, holding on to the back of a seat as she walked away from the group, that her hips were wide and pleasing and her waist was tiny and well defined. A few others soon followed his gaze and the singing came to a stop. The leader of the group of men addressed the woman's retreating back, "So yu duohn like di song or we singin not up to di maak?"

The woman glanced over her shoulder and continued down the carriage to the farthest seat. When she got to the seat, she arranged her ample hips by twisting once to the left and then to the right and then she addressed the group of men.

"Unu is all too dyam faas, a sing bout uman is hebi load. Me is none a unu dyam hebi load."

The leader of the group separated himself from the others and made two steps in her direction before turning back to the men. Hugh Arthur looked from the woman to the man, trying to read the air between them. He was preparing to go to her aid when the group leader bent his knees in an exaggerated bow; his behind pointed directly at her and began to sing:

Dere is a brown girl in da ring
Chra-la-la-la-laa
Dere is a brown girl in da ring
Chra-la-la-la-laa
Dere is a brown girl in da ring
Chra-la-la-la-laa
For she love sugar, and I love plum

The other men quickly caught his mood and to Hugh Arthur's surprise, the recently surly group of men joined in the ditty with all the abandon of girls in a schoolyard ring game.

By the time they had their hands upon their hips and were bellowing "A beg yuh show me yuh motion," the brown woman was wiping away tears of laughter and Hugh Arthur himself, was laughing along. He was relieved that the mood had shifted and he hoped that the men would remain merry until both he and the woman got off the train.

When the train pulled into the Mile Gully Station, the singing had subsided and the group leader was sitting next to the brown woman and putting in a word for himself. Hugh

Arthur noted with wry amusement that she was flushed and her eyes did not leave his face as he spoke in an urgent undertone.

When he turned away from them and looked out of the window on to a passing hillside, he saw a crouching crowd of crows tearing into the bloated carcass of a donkey. The train rumbled past and the smell of carrion filled his nose. Hugh Arthur silently covered his mouth and nose with his handkerchief. One of the cane men sitting further down in the car let go a vulgar expletive and the other men burst out laughing. When Hugh looked back at the tall lady, he saw that she was deep in conversation with her new suitor.

THE STEAM-POWERED TRAIN chugged into the Maggoty Station late in the afternoon when the sun was heading west in its evening descent. Hugh Arthur alighted quickly with his grip in one hand and his jacket slung over the opposite shoulder. He worked the kinks out of his knees before setting off toward the town square.

The little town had the quiet feel of a household settling down to rest for the night. There were not too many people about. He glanced over at the parochial market that ran parallel to the train track. The sellers were mostly absent and the stalls were bare. Things would be vastly different, come Friday. Then, the hum of voices would float across the small savannah and from the hillsides to the east and south, the sound would be like numberless bees in a giant gourd.

He had walked only a few steps when he saw his father, Matthias Reid, walk out of the Chinese bakery, ahead. His father had not seen him and he smiled as he crossed the dusty road, his steps suddenly brisk.

Brother Matthias saw Hugh Arthur when he was but a few feet away from him and hastily stuffed the croker sack of freshly baked bread into the back of the dray cart. He then grabbed his youngest son in a bear hug.

Hugh Arthur smelt his sweat and the strong odor of the bush that clung to him like his particular essence. He smiled and returned his father's embrace.

By then, a small crowd had gathered on the piazza of the haberdashery that adjoined the bakery and Brother Matthias announced, "Mi bwai come home safe and soun and Maasa Gaad be praised."

A woman who was even darker than Brother Matthias, separated herself from the crowd of onlookers. Hugh Arthur recognized his aunt who sold boiled shrimps between St. Elizabeth and Manchester parish. She often rode the train to do her trade and her earnings had already sent one son off to England to study. A daughter had also been sent to Montego Bay to learn catering and fine dressmaking.

She smiled shyly at her nephew and handed him a slightly crumpled paper bag that was filled with crayfish. His nose took in the spice of pimento and the sharper overriding aroma of home-brewed vinegar and *Scotch bonnet peppers.* He thanked his aunt by clasping her into a warm embrace.

The two of them turned back to his father's dray cart and Hugh Arthur stowed his grip between the sacks of freshly baked breads, buns and *bulla cakes* that Brother Matthias came into town to purchase at least once per week.

He started to climb up to the passenger side of the cart but his father urged him instead into the Chinese bakery to show him off to the owners. A small group of five or six stragglers followed them into the shop. These were the vagrants that seemed to have nowhere else to call home and were always ready to beg for a few pennies. Hugh Arthur began to feel a sense of unease because of the attention that he had drawn.

He was considering turning around and exiting the shop when he saw the elderly Chinese man who had founded the business in 1886. He was stooped and gray-headed but he recognized Hugh Arthur and walked toward him.

The little man took Hugh Arthur's proffered hand and then removed a five- shilling note from his apron pocket and handed it to him. He was very surprised by the man's gesture because Mr. Ah-Ping was legendary for his stinginess but when he began to express his pride in Hugh Arthur's achievement, he accepted the cash with gracious thanks.

His pleasure was short-lived, however, because no sooner had he put the money into his breast pocket than Mrs. Ah-Ping or Madam, as she was called by the locals, walked over to him and declared, "So yu getti big *edikaishan,* yes, but what good dat do? Yu kyan nyam dis edikaishan? It no better yu did stay wid yu faada and dig few yam hill?"

As she asked the questions she looked up at him from her height of under five feet and the disdain on her face was unfeigned.

Hugh Arthur pulled the five-shilling note from his jacket pocket and handed it to her. He was not surprised when she grasped it and stuffed it between her sagging breasts.

Without another word, he turned on his heels and walked out of the shop with his father and aunt following closely behind.

When they got to the dray cart, they could hear clamoring voices cursing at the elderly couple but he jumped up onto the cart and waited for his father to join him. Brother Matthias leapt up to the board with much agility for a man of over seventy years and they waved to his aunt who stood watching them as they pulled away for home.

The mule knew its way and headed west in the downhill direction of Paradise District. When they had passed a tall stand of mahogany and cedars, Matthias Reid finally found his voice and made a quiet declaration, "Is di laas time I buy anyting fram Missa Ah-Ping. Fram now *aan*, me buyin mi bread a Balaclava fram Missa Lee."

pissn tail-immature

Alexander Bedward-Revivalist preacher from August Town, St. Andrew. He had a great following but was arrested by the colonial police for sedition.

apachuuniti-opportunity

anarebl-honorable

I wuda tear up kopl yaad a klaat gi yu ya tideh-I would tear up a couple yards of cloth and give them to you here today; I would tell you a couple of expletives; most Jamaican curse words end with klaat.

faambli; fambili-family; relatives

pick straa-pick straw; court; In earlier times when a young man started a conversation with a shy young lady, she would often fidget with a bit of stick or straw while the young man spoke to her. These fidgets were often picked from a nearby shrub.

bankra-large, square straw basket popular in previous generations for transporting fruits, vegetables and ground provisions such as yams

jackass rope tobacco-tobacco leaves rolled to resemble sisal rope that is used to tether animals such as donkeys

Jew plum-*Spondias dulcis;* fruit with strong citric taste; green skinned before it is ripe; yellow when ripe; more commonly called June plum

Scotch bonnet pepper-*Capsicum chinense;* very hot pepper so named because it resembles a Scottish tam o'shanter or Scottish bonnet

bulla cake-dense cake made from wheat flour, sugar, lard and baking soda; sometimes nutmeg, ginger, cinnamon or vanilla are added

edikaishan-education

aan-on

CHAPTER 12

A no fi want a tongue mek cow no taak
The cow's inability to talk is not the result of not having a tongue
We often remain silent because wisdom dictates this; relationships of cause and effect are not always what they appear to be
Rain a faal but di *doti* tough
The rain is falling but the earth remains hard
The circumstances should bring prosperity but they do not

Madam Ah-Ping's bad mind did not in any way dampen the celebration that took place in Paradise, a month after Hugh Arthur returned from college. They had waited this long to celebrate because a young baby was not allowed strange visitors until it was at least twenty-one days old. Everyone who could stand up showed up for the feast spread by Hugh Arthur's parents, Miss Claudine and Brother Matthias.

By near sundown, the yard was teeming with a crowd of friends and relatives and the Mento band from Appleton was in full swing. The band members commandeered the barbecue area next to the wattle and daub storage shed and the leader asked Miss Claudine for three bottles half-filled with kerosene oil and stuffed with dried banana bark. These would be lit with several others and placed on stands around the yard to provide light once the sun disappeared.

One of Hugh Arthur's brothers soon handed the band leader a small gourd filled with undistilled rum and coconut water. The man took a deep swallow, wiped his lips in his sleeve and then he laughed, showing a mouth filled with broken and missing teeth. The other four musicians stood nearby, holding fife, cornet, rumba box and banjo. At a slight gesture from the leader's right index finger, the cornet player blasted a sharp note and all attention turned to the music men.

They were soon playing *Huol Him Joe* and the men, women and children needed no further encouragement. Soon shoes were set aside and the dust rose into the fading light of the setting sun as they danced and laughed with abandon.

Hugh Arthur and Celeste sat at a small table on the verandah of their cottage and they took turns holding the baby until somehow she fell asleep despite the sounds of merriment in the yard. As a newly minted college graduate and a church man, he was not expected to dance and Celeste as his partner was expected to be equally circumspect. Nonetheless, Celeste enjoyed watching the crowd that spilled from their yard, out onto the tracks that led from their property to the various other cottages nearby. Hugh Arthur had no doubt that some of the young people were glad to escape the watchful eyes of their parents and elders and he could well imagine the number of unplanned births that would result from this one night of merriment.

After watching the crowd for a while longer, Hugh Arthur sighed aloud and Celeste looked at him, her own eyes filled with concern. He patted her hand and smiled at her but remained pensive. She looked at him for a bit longer and then picked up the sleeping baby and went into the cottage.

He continued to watch and listen, feeling strangely detached from the events swirling around him. From what seemed a great distance he heard his father laugh and heard his mother issue instructions to his best friend, Stanley Payne. Stanley and his aunt were manning the bubbling pots of curried goat meat, *powa-waata* and *cow cod soup.* Other women in the family turned out large pots of white yam, boiled green bananas, rice and cow peas, fried fish, stewed beef and *cassava bammies.*

Hugh Arthur was fully aware that the able-bodied people of Paradise District had come out to celebrate what to them was a stellar achievement. One of their own, and a dark-skinned one at that, had entered the domain of the privileged and had not only held his own but had graduated at the top of his class. What made them even more satisfied was that he had not removed himself from among them in order to do so. Not only had he married a local girl but he continued to work his fields when he came home for the holidays. Moreover, despite the important knowledge that he held in his handsome head, he had remained humble, accessible and respectful.

Hugh Arthur knew that he was loved but his exposure to the life of Kingston and his perusal of Jamaica's **Gleaner** newspaper made him only too aware that the island was teetering upon the edge of something momentous and potentially disastrous. However, here were his people dancing mindlessly between the fading rays of the setting sun, sans all awareness that Frome was burning and Aggie Bernard and St. William Grant were leading marches in the streets of Kingston. Alexander Bustamante and Norman Washington Manley were working tirelessly to prevent another Morant Bay Rebellion but the people of Paradise were sitting down to meat and rising up to play.

He had his head down with his forehead resting on the heel of his open palm when Stanley Payne tapped him upon his shoulder and then sat in the chair recently vacated by Celeste.

Hugh Arthur looked up to see his best friend peering at him closely, his eyes puzzled. He quickly relaxed his face into a warm smile, rose to his feet and told Stanley that he was going to check on Celeste and Birdie and then join the crowd in the yard. Stanley nodded in approval, told him that he was going to put together a tray of food for him and then hurried down the front steps of the cottage and disappeared into the dancing crowd.

After Hugh Arthur looked in on Celeste and the baby and saw that they were sleeping, he made his way down the wooden steps into the yard and was soon at the center of a dancing group. The musicians were playing *Sly Mongoose* and the rum punch was flowing freely but Hugh refused the hard liquor. He chose instead, to walk over to a table holding enamel pots of ginger beer.

The woman must have been standing nearby in the shadows because she seemed to appear out of nowhere. She came up so close behind Hugh Arthur that when he turned around, he was so near to her that he could smell her sweat.

She laughed into his face, her pupils wide and her warm breath smelling of strong rum and citrus. Hugh instinctively backed away from her but she grabbed his arm and started to gyrate wildly just when the musicians broke into *Rukumbine.* He felt her breasts against his chest just as she grabbed his hips and began a frantic grind against his pelvis.

Hugh Arthur felt his temper come to the surface and raised his hand to slap her across the face when one of his brothers walked over and grabbed the woman from behind. His brother laughed and tried to make light of the moment but Hugh Arthur became even more angry when the woman sneered, "Him wife jos have biebi an if him no hungry fi uman, sinting rang wid him."

Hugh's brother continued to pull the woman away but she struggled against him and hurled more insults at Hugh Arthur. He put down the tumbler of ginger beer and walked back to the steps of the cottage. A few people greeted him warmly as he passed through the milling crowds and he was too polite to tell them to go home. He had lost all taste for merrymaking but if anyone was surprised to see him go into his house and shut the door, no one attempted to stop him.

doti-earth (Twi retention)

Mento-early Jamaican popular music

barbecue-flat, stone or concrete surface used for drying coffee, cocoa beans, pimento etc.

wattle and daub-building material used for making walls, in which a woven lattice of wooden strips called wattle, is daubed with material usually made of some combination of wet soil, clay, sand and in some parts of the world, animal dung and straw

Huol Him Joe*, *Sly Mongoose* and *Ruckumbine-popular mento songs of the era

powa waata-power water; soup made from the head, feet and entrails of the goat; also called mannish waata and commonly held to be an aphrodisiac

cow cod soup-soup featuring the penis and scrotum of a bull

cassava bammies-flat cassava cakes often used as a substitute for bread; usually served with fish

CHAPTER 13

Hag a man and pig a bwai, so him mos shuffle and find him place
The hog is grown but the piglet is still a child and so it should shuffle and find its place in the litter
We should know our place in the pecking order
For paas mek okro spwail
A far journey causes the okra to rot
A delay can lead to an unfortunate outcome

The year that followed Hugh Arthur's return from college was filled with disappointment and bitterness. But for the love of his wife and family and the fierce attachment of his baby girl, his life seemed under a cloud that followed him everywhere.

Miss Claudine watched her *wash-belly* with deep concern but could not bring herself to speak her mind to him. This education that he had gained seemed to her to have brought endless discontentment to Hugh Arthur and she was beginning to wonder if it had been worth the investment. She had sold three of her cows and Brother Matthias had slaughtered and sold a third of his goat-herd to pay for it, but it was beginning to seem that theirs had been a useless sacrifice.

The stumbling block in Hugh Arthur's way was the half-black Englishman who was the principal of Paradise All Age School. This Reverend Johnston Hawthorne was as wicked as his wife Jane was good. How these two had become one was beyond the ordinary person's ability to comprehend.

This man was the offspring of a white English school teacher and a black groundskeeper who had worked for her parents. Reverend Hawthorne's mother had brought disgrace to her family by giving birth to him outside of marriage and compounding the shame by refusing to give up her child. His mother went native, set up house with her lover and her child and lived in shameless concubinage until the sudden death of her common-law husband.

By then she had produced three other children and they all lived in various states of dysfunction after she seemed to suddenly lose her taste for rebellion and returned to England. She left her children in the care of a housekeeper.

Reverend Hawthorne's wife, Miss Jane, as the locals called her, was the proverbial do-gooder and she was earnest in her efforts. She had come from Scotland with her father who had been a Methodist minister. She fell in love with The Reverend Hawthorne when she met him at a Sunday school teachers' conference and he wasted no time in marrying her.

She ran classes for the local girls in the church basement. She taught them sewing, embroidery, crocheting, knitting, tatting, cookery and food preservation. All of the women who attended her classes learned the fine art of pastry and jam making and every year, their creations took home coveted trophies from the parish agricultural fair.

The Reverend Hawthorne was another animal altogether. He hated anyone darker than himself and spoke with pride of his children who were near white. He liked to stand in the pulpit and preach the threat of hell and damnation to the parishioners and he and the local deacons were always at odds. He was remote, cruel, sneering and detached. Not even Miss Jane was spared his acid tongue and he did not think twice about bullying her in public.

He was the de jure principal of the elementary school but it was his henchwoman, Peola Farmingham, who ran the school and carried out his wishes.

This Miss Peola was the least attractive of the five daughters of a local landowner and, at thirty-five, she was yet to snare a husband. She wanted a brown man like herself, no less, but had even considered Hugh Arthur when she saw the years creeping upon her and her jowls beginning to set in like an Indian water buffalo's.

The trouble was that Hugh Arthur, having seen the favor in her eyes, had hardened his gaze into polite rejection. He had seen and heard enough to know that the rumors circulating in the district that she and Reverend Hawthorne had more than a passing acquaintance, were more fact than fiction. Worse yet, he had once overheard his aunt telling his mother that the village naana had been called early one Sunday to Peola's family homestead. She got there just in time to deliver one very robust and very white baby that the dear Miss Peola birthed in a back bedroom. The naana was paid handsomely for her silence but reneged on her promise when the said Peola walked past her a few weeks later and failed to greet her.

According to Mama Jessop, as Peola's birth pangs made her scream loudly enough to disturb a flock of feeding yellow billed parakeets, The Reverend Mr. Hawthorne could be heard a little less than a mile away, thundering the wrath of God over the heads of his cowed and fearful parishioners.

The new baby was spirited away to poor relatives in the south of the parish where he blended in perfectly with the German immigrants who had made that corner their home.

Miss Peola returned to her desk in the ninth grade and continued her efforts to teach the little that she knew about Math, Spelling and Grammar. She was fully aware that people were talking about what had happened but she held her head a little higher, spoke a little more scornfully and lashed the children under her tutelage, with impunity.

A WEEK AFTER Hugh Arthur's graduation and with his new college certificate in a large brown envelope, he went to see Reverend Hawthorne. As he walked up the front steps of the cut-stone church building, he found his heart beating fast. When he opened the door, he heard the buzz of children's voices but he did not go in the direction of the open sanctuary where the six grades were housed. He walked, instead, to a side door at the back of the church and knocked.

"Come in," a male voice answered and Hugh Arthur pushed the door inward.

The Reverend Johnston Hawthorne was seated behind an imposing mahogany desk that took up most of the space in the cramped office. Peola Farmingham was seated on a delicate looking cane chair in one corner of the room and Hugh immediately wondered how the flimsy looking chair held up under her weight. Spread out on the desk were the remnants of a cooked lunch and from the two soiled dinner plates and the two crumpled linen napkins, Hugh Arthur knew that the gentleman had not dined alone.

He greeted them both and looked directly at Peola. Reverend Hawthorne spoke before Hugh Arthur could say anything to her.

"Miss Farmingham is my assistant and, as such, can be privy to any discussion that we hold in this room."

Hugh Arthur wanted to express his disapproval but held himself in check and handed the brown envelope to Reverend Hawthorne. He had not been offered a seat and so he remained standing.

From behind the large desk, the gentleman seemed very small especially with his head bent and the crown of his head picking up the light that fell through the high window behind his desk.

Peola Farmingham remained seated on her fragile chair and Hugh Arthur knew that she was getting very uncomfortable because from his side view, he could see her fidgeting with her hair. He looked directly at her once and saw the color creeping up her neck and into her plump cheeks.

Reverend Hawthorne rose to his feet while stuffing the document back into the envelope. He handed it over, unceremoniously, without looking directly at Hugh Arthur and spoke to some point behind his right shoulder.

"I wish I could be of help to you but we do not have a place for you at the school at this time."

Hugh Arthur was so shocked that his mouth fell open but before he could voice his protest, Reverend Hawthorne stepped from behind his desk, squeezed his way past the bewildered young man and reached for his hat behind the door. He gave a parting shot over his shoulder as he hastened through the door.

"I suggest that you go back to Kingston where they can find more use for your credentials."

Peola Farmingham choose to look directly at him at that point and Hugh saw that her eyes were filled with triumph and her mouth was stretched into a cold smile that did not show her teeth.

The following week, Reverend Hawthorne hired a pre-trained teacher to fill the position that had remained vacant after Hugh Arthur left the post to attend college. The man was semi-literate and unwashed, having bought his first pair of shoes just the week before but Peola lost no time in taking him under her wings.

Reverend Hawthorne's injustice was not lost on the village and several prominent members of his church transferred to the Moravian church but no one had the pluck to challenge him to his face. Miss Claudine threatened to show him her bloomers but Celeste hastened to talk her out of the idea by reminding her that Hugh Arthur would not appreciate her gesture.

Hugh Arthur went back to farming his five acres and selling produce to the higglers who traded in the Maggoty and Black River markets. He also gave private lessons to the school leavers who wanted to enter the civil service.

ON CHRISTMAS EVE, nineteen-thirty-nine, Hugh Arthur went to see Miss Jane. His mother had begged him not to go but she could not stop him. Miss Claudine knew that he would be wasting his time because Reverend Hawthorne was legendary for blocking the progress of anyone who was not his kin. He had once written a derogatory letter of reference for a young man seeking work at the Appleton Sugar Factory. Had the young man's mother not used her clothes iron to steam open the sealed envelope, her son would have presented a letter that would have been a certain disqualification.

Miss Claudine was of the firm opinion that Hugh Arthur needed a bush bath to get rid of the curse of failure that had settled upon him. However, she dared not speak frankly to him because he hated all mention of such things. If Celeste could be persuaded to take the journey with her to Portland, they would be sure to meet with success. The *Mada* in Manchioneal was well reputed because she did not *mix her work.* She was a strict *right hand* woman who relied on divine revelation and strong herbal baths to break the power of obeah that people frequently used to stop the progress of others.

When Miss Claudine raised the subject cautiously the week before, Celeste was firm in her refusal but Miss Claudine was surprised when she said, "Me sure dat Hugh Arthur wuda beat me or put me out, or both. Miss Claudine, yu know dat you son hate those tings so how yu going to put me married life in *jepati?*"

Celeste then looked at her hard, shook her head slowly and declared, "Is lef yu want him fi lef me."

It was Miss Claudine's turn to be alarmed when she realized that she had gone too far by suggesting that Celeste should go against her husband. She hastened to put her daughter-in-law's fears to rest.

"Ax *paadn*, mi dear daata-in-laa. Gaad shud punish me if me have any such ting in mind. Is di peace and security of yu *houshuol* me kansidarin. Yu no si dat a *rak of stumblin* pu-dong in a mi son way? Gaad up above know dat me no have no evil in mi haat and if, perchance, mi haat not clean enough to please Him, may di fors work of *Kyalvari* be done again in me. Me want to clear di hindrance from mi son *paatway* an all me was axin for was yu helpin han, for two head better dan wan."

"Gaad see and know, mi dear Miss Claudine, dat me wuda do anyting else to help him but not dat, ma'am. Hugh taak it plain dat bush doctor is evil and if him had him way, him wuda mek every wan a dem march in a straight line into di rolling sea. I not able, Miss Claudine. From I know yu son, him neba so much as raise him voice to me, but me know seh if me fala yu go a Mada, him boun fi put me out and me not gwaihn able fi stan di punishment."

Miss Claudine grunted and walked away.

On this Christmas Eve, Celeste was still filled with concern for her husband as she packed a basket of goods for Miss Jane. Once more she was thinking about the talk with Miss Claudine the week prior and she was beginning to wonder if she had made the right choice. She knew her husband to be a kind and gentle man but she had also seen the cloud upon his brow that stayed longer and longer each day. There were times of late when not even the presence of his toddler, Birdie, could cheer him for any sustained period.

Two days before that, Miss Claudine had pointedly informed her that she and Brother Matthias would be leaving the day after Boxing Day for the long trip to Portland. Celeste was surprised that Miss Claudine had succeed in persuading her normally skeptical husband to take her to Mada to find out what had gone wrong in Hugh Arthur's life. When she asked Brother Matthias how Miss Claudine persuaded him to go, his terse response had been, *"Any puot in a staam."*

HUGH ARTHUR SET out on his mule at about ten in the morning. He did not have far to go but he wanted to get to the manse at a time when Reverend Hawthorne was less likely to be at home. In the hampers of the mule he had a small croker sack of *sorrel*. He had picked the flowers from his own patch and removed them from the seeds so that Miss Jane would not have to encounter the cruel thistles that could lodge between fingers and in the creases of the inner elbows, for days. Next to the sorrel were a plum pudding that Celeste had baked and a bottle of pimento wine that he had cured under the cool cellar of their cottage.

When he got to the church house, Mrs. Jane Hawthorne was entertaining her son and daughter-in-law who were visiting from England but she introduced Hugh Arthur and then excused herself to speak with him.

They talked for about a half-an-hour and she told him that she could not change her husband's mind. Her exact words were, "Hugh Arthur, you are a good man and I know that those students would be better off with you as the headmaster of that school. I do not, however, have the power to change customs and practices. The Lord knows that I have tried. My advice to you is to try for the London External Examinations. In fact, I can get my son to send you the application and the relevant books. Go after your B.A. degree and then apply for a teaching position at the college in Malvern."

Hugh Arthur thanked her for her kind suggestion and shook hands with her before picking up his hat from the ledge between the kitchen and the pantry where he had placed it earlier.

Mrs. Hawthorne, her eyes clouded with sadness, watched him walk to the kitchen door. When he got to the top step, he turned and looked at her for a brief moment. She saw the grief and despair in his eyes and he saw the tears that were on the brink of spilling down her weathered cheeks. Much remained unsaid between them but he could not embarrass her by speaking of what they knew to be true about The Reverend Mr. Hawthorne.

He turned away from her and walked down the remaining steps to the mule. The animal stood with its head close to the ground, chomping contentedly on the avocados that littered the ground where it was tethered to the tree.

Hugh Arthur untied the mule, climbed onto the saddle, glanced at the pimento and coffee being dried on the barbecue, before leading the animal downhill.

Mrs. Hawthorne stood at her kitchen door and watched Hugh Arthur ride away. He sat ramrod straight on the back of his mule. She did not move until both man and beast made the bend in the downward path and disappeared from view.

ON TUESDAY MORNING, January second, 1940, Hugh Arthur arose early to go to his field. The sun was not yet lit in the sky and Celeste watched from her bed as he dressed in the dim lamplight. She wanted to say something to him but she was afraid that she would awaken the baby. Birdie was nestled against her breast and sucking contentedly on her thumb. Celeste knew from her intermittent sucking that her toddler was not sleeping deeply. She wanted to rest for as long as she could before the baby awakened and sent her into her usual whirl of cleaning, washing, feeding and cooking.

The mule was tied to an ackee tree and soon Hugh Arthur mounted the animal and reached over to the tree trunk to loosen the rope. As the animal clopped its way carefully along the stone-strewn track that would take Hugh Arthur away from his house to his farm, he saw little of the natural beauty surrounding him. There was a snake in paradise and it had coiled its way around his ambition. He felt that his very life was being choked out of him.

The sun had risen before he rode out of his yard but it was not in full strength. The grass was still wet from the dew and the birds were hopping overhead in the thick leaves and climbing foliage that sheltered the track from the coming heat.

Many in his village would gladly exchange places with him because he had a least three good suits. He also had field shoes, house shoes and dress shoes. Unlike many of the men in his village, he had one woman in his life, his lawfully wedded wife. His child had been conceived in wedlock and his life was ordered but Hugh Arthur had dreamed of more, much more for himself. He was close to thirty years old and at this rate, he would never become a principal if he could not even begin his career.

He made up his mind that morning that he would move. He would take a bush school in some remote corner of the island and he would teach the unlettered mass of children that through education, they could better themselves. Celeste would not be happy to leave her familiar environs but her love for him would make her obey.

IT WAS ABOUT five that evening and Celeste sat on a straight-backed mahogany chair in her sitting-room. Her toddler sat across her lap, her head cushioned by the crook of her mother's arm. She was spooning cornmeal porridge into Birdie's mouth and the happy child smiled at her after each mouthful. She had a full view of the lower front yard because her window was flung wide to welcome the little puffs of evening breeze that flirted with the ends of her floral curtain.

Celeste saw the riderless mule and her heart registered alarm before her mind fully understood what the picture meant. The animal stood between the wooden gate posts at the entrance to her yard and pawed the ground. Celeste sat with Birdie tugging at her hand, not yet knowing what to do. Knowledge came to her in a sudden small flare of revelation and she was certain that something terrible and final had met Hugh Arthur. She could feel his hold upon her slipping away. Without being told, Celeste knew that wherever Hugh Arthur lay, his life's blood was seeping into the earth and she would not see the warmth in his eyes nor feel the power of his body again.

STANLEY PAYNE DID Hugh Arthur Reid one final act of friendship by leading the party of men who went in search of him. They found him where the spooked mule had thrown him, his neck broken and his head frozen at an angle as if surprised by an unexpected event. His eyes were still open but there was no knowledge in them. Stanley felt for a pulse knowing that he would find none. He then straightened his friend and sent one of the men to his wife for a white sheet to wrap the body before taking it home to Celeste.

Miss Claudine and Brother Matthias returned home that night and the people could hear Miss Claudine wailing from a mile away from Paradise District. Her two remaining sons had met the dray cart in Maggotty and given the parents the sad news. Brother Matthias willingly handed over the reins of the mule to his oldest son and climbed into the back of the cart to lie on his side.

By the time they got to their village, he was comatose. His sons washed him and put him to bed and Miss Claudine continued to cry.

They buried Hugh Arthur Reid the next day and although Birdielee Adassa was less than two years old, that was her one, indelible memory of her father. Till the day she died, she could recall the sensation of floating in midair as the family elders passed her across the open coffin and she looked down upon the strangely remote face of her father. She cried because he did not smile at her as he normally did.

Brother Matthias Reid did not recover from the stroke and Miss Claudine, for the rest of her life, blamed Celeste for not standing in the gap with her to protect her beloved last born son. Birdie grew up to know her as a woman of frowning countenance who never smiled but loved her fiercely and protectively. She was never given an explanation for the coldness that existed between her mother and grandmother.

wash-belly-last born child
Mada-female seer or healer who often heads a balmyard where people go for healing from spiritual and physical maladies
mix her work-did not dabble in obeah
right hand-the clean hand; obeah is not involved
jepati-jeopardy
paadn-pardon
houshuol-household
rak of stumblin-rock of stumbling; hindrance
paatway-pathway
Kyalvari-Calvary
any puot in a staam-any port in a storm; desperate times call for desperate measures
sorrel-*Hibiscus sabdariffa*; also known as roselle hibiscus; native to West Africa and used as an infusion to make teas and drinks; also fermented to make wine

CHAPTER 14

Birdielee Adassa Reid and James John Whitehead 1

1956-1957

What is fi yu kyaahn be an-fi-yu
What is meant to be yours will be yours

It was getting up to six o'clock and Birdielee Adassa Reid was in a great hurry. She did not want to be late for the evening service because it was her turn to play the piano. She had to get to the college chapel in time to collect the hymn sheets from The Reverend Warmington, the principal. She would not have to practice the songs because of her photographic memory and her excellent sight reading skills. Nevertheless, she liked to get to the chapel before the other students. Birdie, however, was detained by her uncooperative girdle and garters. How she hated the hot, confining undergarment, but her mother insisted that she should always wear a girdle to keep her generous bottom under control.

Every time Mama Celeste sewed a new dress for Birdie she would complain, "Yu certainly did not get dis big batty from my side a di family. Dis is Claudine Jessop all over. She cause a driver fi run a *maakit chok* aaf a di road wan time. Di *iijit* driver so busy a watch her behain, him all but drive di chok over precipice. Right a Maggoty it happen."

Mama Celeste had laughed when she said it then, but after the *kas-kas* with her neighbor and friend Stanley Payne, she didn't joke about Birdie's behind anymore.

Birdie finally got her stockings hitched to her garters and so she slid into her full under-slip and reached for her white blouse. Thank God that it buttoned at the front and her mother had sewed it with a peplum that covered her bottom. She slipped into her straight black skirt and put on black pumps.

The hinges of the front door needed to be oiled and she heard them creak in resistance when she pulled up the door of her aunt's cottage behind her. Birdie was soon hurrying across a small patch of grass that separated the building from the identical one that stood next door. She walked briskly up the hill while continuing to think of her mother.

Birdie knew Mama Celeste was looking forward to the occasion of her graduation and she had every right to be satisfied. It was sixteen years since that awful day that Birdie vaguely remembered but her mother had rehearsed the painful details to her so many times that she knew the sequence by heart. She still talked from time to time about how she was feeding dinner to the two year old Birdie when her husband's mule ran riderless into the front yard and stood snorting and pawing the ground under the sugar mango tree, near the gate. She told Birdie that she dropped the plate and spattered the floor with food as she ran screaming into the yard.

His friends, the men who found her dead husband, brought him home, wrapped in a white sheet. They buried him the next evening, and Birdie still carried a small spot of sadness within her that represented her missing parent. Her uncles and her father's best friend, Stanley Payne, had stepped in to do for her what they believed her father would have wanted them to do, but at an untouchable spot inside her, she carried his absence, always. It was a long time later before she understood death but she was to marry and give birth before she came to know its personal sting.

This Sunday evening would be the last time that Birdie would play the piano for the evening service. The following Sunday would be her graduation and her mother would be coming all the way from Paradise District, a distance of more than twenty miles, to see her only child step out at the head of her class. Her aunt, Reece Hinton, would be sitting among the lecturers on the platform and in deference to the occasion, she would wear a skirt suit instead of her customary trousers.

Birdie took the uphill footpath to the chapel and passed three other cottages that were shielded by high shrubbery.

These were the homes of the expatriate teachers. The locals lived at the bottom of the hill near to the games field and tennis court. Aunt Reece was one of them and Birdie lived with her rather than on the large dormitory that housed the fifty young ladies of good character who made up the student body. If there was any among them who had been scarred by past moral failure, the facts had been carefully disguised and as far as Birdie knew, every girl was as innocent as she.

Birdie's innocence had been preserved at a great price, however, and her own mother lived outside of church and village approval for a long time, because of the drastic steps she took to protect her.

She frowned briefly at the memory of the events that had caused her to come under the care of Aunt Reece. She still recalled her sorrow at having to leave her friends behind, so suddenly, and her initial fear of Aunt Reece.

Aunt Reece often wore men's trousers, smoked and drove her own car. All of this was bold for the times in which they lived but coming from a black woman, this caused open scorn and rebuke from the upholders of public virtue. Aunt Reece did not care, though. She drove her car, smoked her rolled cigarettes and drank when it suited her.

The principal of the college, The Reverend Samuel Warmington, was very modern, however, and welcomed Reece Hinton to the faculty when she returned from her studies in England. She possessed a master's degree in Mathematics and Science and she played all the ladylike sports that were allowed at the college. The fact that she had talked her way into a local cricket club and bowled a mean off spin, earned her the dislike of many of the local women but the respect of the male cricketers. She was known to drink more than a few of them under the table after a match, but no man had succeeded in taking advantage of her. She was stronger than many of them as they discovered when she had a disagreement with the pace bowler.

The young man stood six inches above Reece and he was younger by at least five years. They had a disagreement about the quality of the umpiring after they lost a match to an inferior team. The brash young man shoved her when she told him that the quality of his bowling had contributed to the team's loss.

Had the poor soul known anything about Reece Hinton, he would not have done such a foolish thing. She knocked him unconscious, got into her car and drove away without a backward glance.

When Reece turned up for practice a few days later, she found out that the captain of the team had dismissed the young pace bowler and the others had voted, as one, to name her their new vice-captain.

Birdie's mother did not much approve of the ways of her younger half-sister, but when Stanley Payne made his intentions known, she was more than happy to call upon Reece to defend Birdie and remove her from the lustful gaze of her godfather.

Matters boiled over in 1953 after Stanley finally returned from England. He had gone over in 1943 and had served in the Second World War. After the war, he had decided to stay in England but changed his mind because of the cold and because his wife refused to join him there. His property bordered the Reid family land and with Hugh Arthur gone, Celeste welcomed his company.

After the untimely death of Birdie's father, Celeste rented out most of the farmland to tenants and focused her attention upon dressmaking and the upbringing of her only child. Stanley was supportive and caring but with a wife and family of his own, he could not help her as much as she needed. Mama Jessop and Hugh Arthur's brothers helped out too, but they were not always available when she needed them.

When Stanley went to war, his wife moved the family to Westmoreland to stay with her mother but soon found comfort in the arms of another man. She did not return to her husband when he came back to his neglected homestead. Stanley's heart was broken but he soon took to visiting Celeste after his long days on the farm. In short order, Celeste became the subject of crude speculations but paid little attention when rumors were circulated around the district that Stanley Payne was getting much more than a hot dinner from her. Birdie heard her tell one of her neighbors that when she buried her husband, she did not bury her life and so she was free to do whatever she wanted. She said this in a tone that made it clear that she was throwing word at the neighbor as well.

The Thursday evening when Stanley Payne turned Celeste's ordered world off its axis began ordinarily enough. He had just come in from tending to his farm and stopped by

Celeste's kitchen before he went home. He sat at the back door, as he often did, and pulled out his pipe for a smoke.

Mama Celeste told Birdie all the details as she packed her belongings to send her away. She was still seething and after she folded one of Birdie's nightdresses, she put it on the growing pile of clothing and turned to her daughter.

"Di man si-dong deh as cool a cucumber, a look dong di hill pahn mi goat dem a come home from pasture. Me have mi puddn-pan pahn mi lap, and me a roll mi dumplin fi put in a di pea soup. Mi mind did a wanda so when him taak me neba pay him no mind. Stanley clear him chruot and seh it again. Him seh, 'Celeste, I tinkin bout buyin some more lan.'

Me ax him wa dat fa and him seh him gwaihn buil a four-room house. So, me ax him wa him need four-room house fa when di wan dat him have is chrii room and it mek out a good-good Spanish wall. Dat is when di man open him doti mout and spit out di indecency. Di ting dat hurt me is dat him seh it like me and him have a long-standin agreement. Di man jos seh it dry-dry, 'I tink is time I married to Birdie.'

Jos like dat, di man come put it in a mi way fi kill him. If chobl did set like rain, we wuda all see it comin and get out a di way, but di man tek me by surprise and discombobulate mi cogitation! Di nasty, doti *rang-goat*, dangle yu pahn him knee, rock yu like a daddy, and now di same man waahn fi li-dong wid yu! A come chat bout how yu too delicate fi di big foot, yam-head young man dem roun here, and it better me allow him fi married to yu because him wuda tek good care a yu. Him gone to hospital and me ekspek corporal fi come *ares* me any minute now, but me no kya! Yu hear me Birdie? Me no care a *blaas*!"

Startled, Birdie sat down quickly upon the trunk at the foot of her bed and began to cry. She had never heard Mama Celeste say even the word "damn" before and to hear her godly mother spit out the harsh swear word was very frightening. Moreover, the idea of marrying Uncle Stanley left her queasy. She did not want to marry anyone, for that matter.

Celeste looked at her but seemed strangely remote as she continued, "A never know dat A wuda ha fi tell yu dese tings so soon, Birdie, but yu growin-up and every kain and quality a ram-goat Sammy ready fi jump pahn yu. But A dead fos before A *low* any a dem fi *faal* Hugh Arthur Reid wan *dead-lef* pikini! Yu gwaihn married good and prapa before any man know bout yu and *ef* a ha fi *chap* di *Debl* himself, A gwaihn to dwiit!"

"Oh God, Mama Celeste, no taak like dat. Yu wi go a hell."

Mama Celeste barely glanced at Birdie before continuing her tirade.

"A sen telegram fi yu Aunt Reece to come and tek yu. A may go a *wok-house* before too long, for A bon-up Stanley Payne wid me pot a soup. Yu hear me? A bon him from him yez to him aas. A cook him from him put-upon to him sit-upon. Di police gwaihn lock me up but A duohn care. Yu hear me? Di man whe gwaihn mek me sell yu out to bidder no baan yet and him muma dead! Stanley Payne lucky seh me neba hab me *wampara* side a me, fa a wuda did *lim him up!*"

In the middle of her rant, Celeste declared with sudden concern, "Yu gwaihn ha fi eat somting light fi yu supper because all a mi good-good soup dash weh. All because a dat dyam jankro, Stanley Payne."

She seemed genuinely alarmed when Birdie began to giggle hysterically.

Mama Celeste did not permit Birdie to go to school the next day. She finished packing her belongings and waited for Aunt Reece. While she awaited her sister's arrival, she cautioned Birdie to stay indoors.

The following evening, Aunt Reece arrived in a cloud of dust, driving a tan *Austin Cambridge*, and wearing dark glasses and a pair of men's corduroys. She listened to Celeste's tale of woe and laughed heartily when she heard that her normally circumspect sister had all but cooked Stanley Payne in his clothes. Aunt Reece readily agreed to take charge of her niece and Birdie went back to Malvern with her.

There, she finished her secondary education and went straight to the teachers' college for further studies. Birdie never returned home to live and her mother stood trial at church and was disfellowshipped for a full twelve months.

Later that year, Mama Celeste paid forty pounds in criminal court for grievous bodily harm. She narrowly escaped going to prison and doing hard time. The judge showed clemency when her attorney explained that Stanley Payne was Birdie's godfather and had stood in the gap when her father died in her infancy. The judge did an about-face upon hearing this and cried shame upon him. According to His Honor, Stanley

Payne was a village ram and should be ashamed of lusting after his godchild. He made it clear that he fined Celeste only because he was duty bound to uphold the law.

WHEN BIRDIE ARRIVED at the chapel, the first and second year students were already seated and the principal was standing at the main entrance of the chapel. He was waiting for Birdie to give her the program notes for the evening service. Standing next to The Reverend Warmington was a very tall, light-skinned young man who looked straight at Birdie as she approached. She glanced at him and as quickly, looked away. His eyes, she noted, were gray-green and of that piercing quality that made her very self-conscious. She had also noticed that his nose was straight and his hair, though close cut, covered his scalp in thick waves. She concluded that he was more than half-white and as quickly, decided that he was not her type.

As soon as Birdie took the sheets of paper from her principal, the young man stepped forward and bowed politely to her. In a voice soft and resonant, he declared, "Good evening. I am James John Whitehead and it is a pleasure to meet you, Miss Reid."

Birdie was suddenly flustered and surprised that he knew her name but had enough presence of mind to offer her hand. Her hand was briefly wrapped in the warm clasp of his palm and she felt the strength in his grip and saw the appreciation in his eyes. She blushed and hurried up to the platform to take her seat at the piano.

Throughout the service, Birdie could feel his eyes upon her but she kept her gaze averted. However, in between the hymns, she found herself remembering the warmth of his long fingers, the angle of his very arrogant nose and his very dark lips which were caught between thick and thin. Her Mama Celeste would say he was a fine, *bunununus* bwai. It did no harm that he was also a fine speaker who impressed her with his knowledge of scripture and the balance and control of his delivery. His voice was a slightly husky baritone and he could sing, too.

Birdie stopped her thoughts from straying with the reminder that men of his coloring and background were not normally interested in women like her. She felt more than a twinge of bitterness at the thought that despite her education, most black men who were her equal, would pass her over because of her dark skin. Some of them thought nothing of choosing a light or near white dunce to stand by their side rather than an intelligent and polished black woman. Birdie had heard Aunt Reece speak of a male colleague who often reminded his near white wife to do nothing more than nod and smile politely whenever he took her into social situations. Behind his back, some of his co-workers referred to her as *pretty dunce.*

At the end of the service, James John Whitehead was waiting at the bottom of the chapel steps. There were many young ladies milling around and looking at him with curiosity but he showed not the slightest interest in the excitement that his presence had generated. Birdie saw him as she came to the door and although she could not see the color of his eyes in the waning evening light, she felt the sudden heat of his gaze as he looked directly at her.

Birdie turned to walk back into the building but the young Reverend Whitehead moved very quickly up the steps and was soon standing next to her. He gently asked to walk her home and she told him that she was waiting for her aunt. To her surprise, he immediately went up to the platform where Aunt Reece was speaking to the vice principal, introduced himself and asked for permission to walk Birdie home.

Aunt Reece cut her conversation short and turned her attention to the bold young man who seemed to have no interest in anyone but Birdie. Even while he was speaking to Aunt Reese, he kept glancing back at the suddenly self-conscious young lady. Birdie herself was wondering why he was so adamant about walking her home but she could not deny the pleasure that his attention brought her.

A smile entered Aunt Reece's eyes and she said, "You may walk us both home. It has been a long time since a handsome young man walked me anywhere."

When they left the chapel, the three made an odd party that had all eyes following them. The young Reverend James John Whitehead walked just a little behind the two significantly darker women. He had his ear leaning toward the older woman but his left palm gently steered Birdie by the shoulder toward the exit of the chapel. He passed a cluster of young ladies on his way out and they all looked up and smiled at him but he was oblivious to their admiration. It was clear to anyone who cared to observe that the young minister had found the object of his desire.

maakit chok-market truck
iijit-idiot
kas-kas-quarrel or fuss
puddn-pan-pudding pan
rang-goat-ram goat
ares-arrest
blaas-blast
low-allow
faal-impregnate outside of marriage; to take a woman's virginity
dead-lef-a child left behind by a dead parent; any person who has lost a next of kin
ef-if
chap-chop
debl-devil
wok-house-work house or prison
wampara-short machete that has a broad blade
lim him up-severed his limbs
bunununus-handsome, beautiful, pleasing
pretty dunce-a beautiful dunce

CHAPTER 15

Ebri hoe hab him tik a bush
Every hoe has a stick in the bush that is a perfect fit
Everyone, no matter how odd, has someone who considers him or her lovable

In some ways, Birdie later felt like the wedding happened to someone else. She was so nervous and unprepared that she let her mother and Aunt Reece take over the event. They went with her to Hanover to meet James' mother and grandmother and Miss Adlyn welcomed them warmly into the family. Nerissa only smiled absently at them when they were introduced and showed them hairpin lace that she was making to decorate a satin slip.

After a late afternoon dinner, Miss Adlyn took Birdie for a walk over the property and showed her the grave of her husband, Raphael. She then walked her down to the bridge at the gate and with the water flowing beneath their feet, she told Birdie the story of Nerissa's rape.

She closed the final chapter of that book by putting her arm around Birdie and declaring, "A kyan see dat yu love mi granson and me kyan tell dat him faal fi yu. Be happy no matter what life have in store fi yu. *Choch-wok* a no easy business but if yu *laan* fi pray, Gaad will do di res. Di wan thing me gwaihn to beg yu to promise me is dat if me dead before Nerissa, yu will tek care of her."

She said the last words with a tremor in her voice and Birdie hugged her hard in silent assurance.

ON THE MORNING of her wedding day, Birdie came suddenly awake in a sweat. She had a sense that some momentous event was about to explode upon her and then remembered that it was her wedding day.

She sat up and swung her legs to the floor. She could hear her mother and Aunt Reece talking quietly in the bedroom next to hers. Birdie wanted to go into the room and talk to Mama Celeste but she did not know how to talk about what was troubling her. Instead, she sat down upon the edge of her bed and stared hard at her feet.

Aunt Reece found her thus and started to laugh until she realized that Birdie was crying.

"Why are you crying, child, and on your wedding day at that?"

Birdie made no answer but cried a little harder. Her sniffles brought Mama Celeste rushing into the room and over to where Birdie sat on the edge of her bed. She pulled her daughter into her arms and told her to hush.

"Me know yu frighten mi love, but duohn fret. Yu get a good man fi true and him will tek good care a yu. No need to cry. Today yu will be di envy of even some a di married uman dem. A sew yu frock real pretty and yu satin shoes and yu headpiece kuda mek di society page in a di newspaper."

Birdie cried even harder and Aunt Reece grew suddenly aware of what could be troubling her niece. While Mama Celeste continued to hug her, Aunt Reece sat down on the other side of her and asked softly, "Is it your wedding night that you are frightened about?"

Birdie nodded silently and the two women burst out laughing. Mama Celeste was the first to get a hold of herself when she realized that Birdie had stopped sniffling and was looking at them with hurt and annoyance.

Mama Celeste wiped her eyes with the back of her hand, patted Birdie's thigh and sought to reassure her daughter. "Do what yu husband ask yu to do and yu will be fine. A wife mos obey her husband and if yu do dat, him will be kind to yu and peace will reign in yu life. Remember dat yu husband is a parson and yu want to live good wid him so dat di church people dem no tek him fi *prekkeh*."

Aunt Reece got up from beside Birdie and went back into her room. When she returned, she had a mid-sized book with her. It was covered in plain brown paper and she handed it to Birdie. She then took a small upholstered stool that was in front of a cedar wood dresser, directly across from the bed. She sat with her back to the mirror and watched Birdie's face as she timidly opened the book.

When Birdie started leafing through the pages without once looking at her aunt, she in turn, beckoned to Mama Celeste to leave the room with her. When they got to the door that separated the two rooms, Aunt Reece said very softly but very firmly to Birdie, "When the Bible says that marriage is honorable and the bed undefiled, it means just that. There is no shame in the feelings that you and James have for each other and sex is a gift from God. The marriage bed is a place for enjoyment and you have the same right to pleasure that your husband sees as his. James is a kind man and the Bible also says, 'Ask and it shall be given unto you, and seek and you shall find.' Ask James for what pleases you and he will be kind to you. I can see it in his eyes that he will not just take his pleasure but he will grant you yours. Ask baby girl, ask."

Mama Celeste gave a scandalized cry and started to speak but Aunt Reece pushed her not so gently out of the room, followed her and closed the door firmly behind her.

After Birdie managed to overcome her confusion and embarrassment she sat thinking about what her aunt had said, and decided that she would not be afraid because in their almost one year of courtship, James had been everything that she could have desired. He listened to her when she talked to him and he willingly shared his passion for the ministry with her. He even told her once that he had prayed for the right woman to be his wife and that the evening when he saw her coming up the hill, he had known right away that she was the one. Just the week prior, he had dreamt of a woman he had seen walking away from him and she was dressed exactly as she had been attired on that evening. In the dream, he had run after the woman but he had come awake just as he caught up to her.

Birdie unpeeled the brown cover of the book her aunt had given her and realized that it was a sex manual. She began to turn the pages and realized that it was not a filthy magazine but a very scientific manual, illustrated with drawings of both the male and female sexual organs with straightforward explanations of how they were meant to work.

Curiosity got the better of her and she soon forgot about her fear and began to read in earnest. When her aunt knocked on her door an hour later to call her to the breakfast table, she had read the manual from cover to cover and though she was still nervous about her wedding night, she was more excited than afraid.

LATER THAT SAME afternoon, Mama Celeste, Aunt Reece and two of Birdie's uncles sat in the front pew of the college chapel and waited for the wedding to begin. Behind them sat Miss Adlyn who, at the age of seventy, could still fill out a hobble-tailed dress that had a cinched waistline. Her dress was peach-colored, handkerchief linen with a satin bow stitched across the bodice. Nerissa sat close to her and she too was well turned out in a gold, silk sheath with a matching pillbox hat. If her eyes seemed a little glassy and her timid smile even more vacant than usual, it was because Miss Adlyn had talked the family doctor into providing a mild tranquilizer for her. Nerissa did not like to travel or to be around strangers.

Mama Celeste and Aunt Reece for once looked like sisters. They were dressed in identical peacock blue skirt suits that Aunt Reece had arranged for a friend to ship from England. Aunt Reece had offered to buy Birdie's bridal dress but Mama Celeste would have none of it. Instead, for three straight weeks, she sat up late into the night, hand-stitching her daughter's ivory satin and silk gown.

Every imitation pearl sewn into the bodice and around the hem had been placed with great care and attention by a mother who was bursting with pride that her beloved only child had been so favored. She had wept quietly as she cut and ruched the lace that was a part of Birdie's headpiece and veil. She did not doubt that her daughter was pure and untouched, so she did not feel like a fraud as she lovingly prepared her daughter's bridal outfit.

Mama Celeste was duly proud that her daughter had a profession and she was very optimistic that unlike her late father, she would be allowed to find employment in Trelawny and to reach the heights of her career, if she wanted to. Nothing pleased her more, though, than the sight of the fine, young man that Birdie-lee had snagged for herself.

At first, when Reece had written to her about Birdie's suitor, she had been afraid for her daughter but once she met James and saw the way he doted on Birdie, she had no more doubts about his intentions. She was not surprised when, within six months of his first visit, he took the long trip from his internship in New Market to ask for her permission to marry Birdie.

After Mama Celeste gave James her blessing, she wrote to Birdie and told her that she would be visiting her in two weeks. This was the Christmas of 1956 and Birdie was to be married in January of 1957.

When Birdie got home from work two Fridays later, she found her mother had arrived and had made dinner. Birdie kissed her cheek and noted that Mama Celeste seemed pensive and troubled. She quickly grew alarmed but her mother assured her that she was well.

"Me in good health, mi chail, but is yu me worryin about."

"Why, Mama? I am doing well at the school and the principal says that I have a good chance of being made permanent."

"Is not yu job I am worryin about, Birdie. Is yu future dat concern me."

"Why, ma'am? What's wrong with mi future?"

By now Birdie was feeling even more troubled and it could be heard in the tremor in her voice.

"Birdie, not a ting rang wid yu future and A want to keep it dat way, but yu young and unexpose and yu duohn know how people stay. Look pahn how Stanley stan-up wid me when yu faada dead and dat is di same Stanley wa me ha fi bon-up fi keep him aaf a yu."

"Cho lawd, Mama. Do, no start talk bout dat again because I can't stand it. The other day I saw him in Malvern and when he recognized me, him hurry up go into a shop. Him never even stop to tell me howdy."

"Tell yu howdy fi wa! After wa me do Stanley Payne, him kudn *bright* enough fi waahn taak to yu! Yu tink Stanley a drink *mad puss piss*?"

Birdie started to laugh but felt duty bound to scold her mother.

"Mama, you not getting nice with age, you know? You getting from bad to worse."

Without waiting for her mother to respond, Birdie went into her bedroom to remove her work clothes and to clean up for dinner. Aunt Reece was not expected until late.

Over dinner, Mama Celeste once more brought up the subject of her pressing concern.

"When yu married, yu movin all di way to Trelawny and A hear dat Trelawny people is not people fi joke wid. Dem is hell fi wok obeah and dem no like strangers. Dem will welcome yu husband because him is a brown man, but yu know seh black no love black. Yu ha fi careful of yuself and be on yu guard, Birdie. Duohn eat from nobadi and no leave yu clothes outside at night. Jamaica people too bad, mi dear, and me no able dem ton mi wan pikini in a *wa-fi-du*."

With these pronouncements, Mama Celeste started to cry and Birdie realized what was bothering her mother.

"Mama, don't worry. God is able to take care of me and He will. As soon as James and I settle down, we will send for you,

Miss Adlyn and Nerissa to spend some time with us. James says that the church house is quite spacious and we won't get in each other's way. Furthermore, I will be happy to have some of my family around me because I am aware that some people take a while to accept strangers."

Mama Celeste was mollified that Birdie planned to make room for her in her new life and so she swallowed her remaining tears and proceeded to eat her meal with gusto.

And here she was now, waiting for her daughter to walk up the aisle of the college chapel. She could not prevent herself from feeling pride and joy that were close to overflowing. She wanted so much to sing out loud and clap her hands that she barely managed to restrain herself.

Up ahead of Mama Celeste stood Reverend Warmington who was so pleased with his part in the matchmaking that he could not stop smiling as he stood waiting to perform the ceremony. Mrs. Warmington sat at the piano, having come out of retirement for the occasion. She had hobbled on a cane to get to the platform but the twinkle in her eyes left no doubt that she did not resent any discomfort that she might be experiencing. She had suffered a mild stroke the year before but was making steady progress in her recovery.

When Mrs. Warmington played the first chord of the bridal march, there was no uncertainty in the notes. And when she nodded to the congregation, everyone rose as if rehearsed. All heads turned to look down the wide aisle to where Birdie stood waiting in the doorway. She was clutching the arm of her mother's uncle who, at ninety, still walked with the firmness of the West India Regiment soldier that he had been as a young man.

The Reverend James John Whitehead stood with his back facing the altar and next to him was his slightly taller brother, Nathan. On the other side of Nathan was one of Birdie's cousins who was dressed in a soft, blush, silk, mid-calf gown.

Birdie felt like she was floating up the aisle and she was grateful for the strength of her great-uncle's arm. James met them at the first pew and much to the amusement of everyone, he grasped Birdie's arm as if the old man had stolen his treasure and he had come to reclaim it.

Most of what happened afterwards passed over Birdie as if she was in a dream but she managed to say her vows, kneel for the prayers, sing along with the congregation and sign the register.

One of the moments of her wedding that she remembered with some embarrassment was when they emerged from the chapel and stood on the stone steps. She recalled that she could feel the tension in her new husband's body and she could also feel the heat of his flesh through her gloved fingers that clutched his arm. She also remembered that as she squinted in the glare of the afternoon sun, she realized that James was looking down at her, and the crowd of family and friends gathered on the walkway below the steps was egging him on about something.

She felt suddenly flustered when his head made a swift descent and before she realized what he was up to, he had kissed her full upon the lips. Birdie felt the heat begin to crawl up from her neck into her cheeks and she wanted to let go of her husband's arm and hide her face. The crowd cheered and the flash of a camera went off and almost blinded her.

Upon the direction of the photographer, the small bridal party and the immediate family on both sides, repaired to the chapel garden for the wedding pictures.

The photographer was a professional who had traveled all the way from Kingston. His fees were being paid by Nathan. Both Birdie and James found him very amusing. He fussed like a woman and nothing seemed to please him. He, however, did not need to remind them to smile because it took all of the self-restraint that they could muster to keep from laughing out loud each time he gave them instructions. He kept referring to them as the married culprits and when Birdie realized that he meant couple, she had to turn her head away in order to regain her self-control.

Their picture taking complete, the party moved in the direction of the dining hall where the wedding reception was to be held. For the special occasion, the folding doors had been fully opened and the wide entryway was framed by a bamboo bridal arch that had been decorated by the ground staff. It was completely covered in intricately woven palm leaves and it was festooned with red and pink ginger lilies and yellow and red roses.

The fussy little photographer hastened to join them at the arch and instructed them to pose for one more family picture.

When they entered the college dining room, Birdie gave a small gasp. The tables were all covered with blinding white tablecloths and each had a centerpiece of red and yellow roses. She knew immediately that the flowers had cost a significant amount of money and she had no idea who had footed such an expense. Birdie made a mental note to find the donor and express her thanks.

The bridal table was another kind of exquisite. Both her mother and aunt had provided their best china, stemware and cutlery and there were places set for the four members of the bridal party. The tablecloth was antique crochet, bordered with handmade lace. It needed no further ornamentation but the large crystal bowl filled with lilies and roses gave the perfect finishing touch.

On a small linen covered round table at the foot of the bridal table, the wedding cake sat covered under white lace. It would be unveiled by Miss Adlyn and Mama Celeste. The cake had been baked by three young ladies of the college under the supervision of Mrs. Warmington and one of the maids. It was made from heavy stewed fruit, wheat flour, dark sugar and freshly churned butter. The young ladies had hand-creamed the butter and the sugar in a large wooden bowl until it was light and translucent. They had added a dozen fresh farm eggs with great care and then folded in the sifted flour, nutmeg, salt, baking powder, candied orange peel, chopped raisins, prunes and currants. The batter was then enhanced with generous dollops of Appleton rum, port wine, vanilla, cinnamon, nutmeg and rosewater. The final touch was the burnt sugar syrup that was added very carefully to give the cake its rich, dark color. Two days after the cake was baked, it was covered with royal icing and sprinkled with edible pearls.

The top was then decorated with three wedding bells made from spun sugar and food coloring.

Birdie looked up quickly at her husband and saw that he was very pleased with the decorations. Unlike her, he was yet to see the bridal cake but his eyes did not linger long over these niceties. From the way he kept patting his breast pocket, she knew that he was somewhat anxious about his upcoming speech. The bride was not expected to speak and for that, she was relieved.

Once the grace had been said by The Reverend Warmington, the guests and bridal party set about demolishing generous servings of rice and peas, shredded carrots with lettuce and tomatoes, curried goat meat, peppered steak and roasted pork. They quenched their thirst with ginger beer, sorrel drink and aerated water.

Birdie was surprised that she was actually hungry and once she started to eat, she began to feel more like herself. She even began to look around the room and noted that there were people present that she did not know.

When The Reverend Warmington cleared his throat to begin the toasts, Birdie prepared herself to be bored. She figured that her elders would speak the traditional pleasantries and go on for too long.

The toasts were first opened to the close family members and to everyone's surprise, the normally reticent Miss Adlyn took the floor and before long, had everyone in tears.

"Dis is a day I wish my husband, Raphael Caine did live to see. It wuda did do him haat good to see di *prapanis* wid which all tings proceed here today. God see and know dat mi haat full and mi soul tek much delight in seeing di kain and quality young miss dat mi granson tek unto himself as a wife. She come aaf a good table fi true and me have no doubt dat mi reveren granson will eat well, and sleep well and live well aanda har care. Gaad bless unu, mi pikni, and may you see lang life and have plenty pikni fi run roun unu foot dem."

When she came to the end of her toast, she did not lift her wine glass. Instead, she turned to face the platform where the bridal party sat and made as deep a curtsy as her hobble skirt would permit. She was not the only one wiping away tears by the time she had finished speaking.

When James was finally called to give the groom's response, he strode to the edge of the platform with perhaps more confidence than he felt. He clutched his wine glass so tightly that Birdie feared that the stem would snap. She was greatly surprised when he stepped off the platform and stood directly in front of the guests and relatives. When he launched into his speech, Birdie ducked her head and stared hard at the remnants of her dinner.

"Reverend and Mrs. Warmington, distinguished ladies and gentlemen, my beloved friends and relatives, I wish to tell you that he that findeth a wife, findeth a good thing."

Before the groom could go further, the audience was on its feet and cheering him on with shouts of encouragement and handclapping. Even the Warmingtons dropped their customary reserve and allowed themselves to be caught up in the moment. When the cheering finally subsided, he continued.

"I wish to publicly thank The Reverend Mr. Warmington for inviting me to speak at this college on a special Sunday and that I accepted his invitation. Had I done otherwise, I would not have met my lovely wife and I am sure that someone else would have snatched her up before I had a chance."

His speech was interrupted again and a few times more by cheers and shouts of encouragement. Like any other Jamaican gathering, the only thing that the audience loved more than good speechifying was a good feed. In that one occasion, they had an opportunity for both.

It was late at night before Birdie and James had a chance to make their departure. They had a journey of over forty miles ahead of them but they would not be traveling alone. Nathan had arranged to drive them to their new home and their luggage had already been stowed in the trunk of his station wagon by one of the workers. He sat waiting for Birdie and James to say their last goodbyes.

choch-wok-church work
laan-learn
prekkeh-laughing stock
bright-forward; insolent; daring
mad puss piss-urine of a demented cat; meant to imply that one had lost one's mind, ostensibly from imbibing said urine.
wa-fi-du-idiot; literally, someone who does not know what to do
prapanis-properness

CHAPTER 16

If yu shub me, show me weh fi faal dong
Before you shove me, show me where I should fall
Do not set me up to fail
Married man shillin hab tortiin penny
A married man's shilling has thirteen pennies
A married man can be particularly attractive or appealing

Birdie could not hurry up the hill and so she was going to be late for church. James would be annoyed because he liked to start the service at exactly eleven a.m. He would have to wait, though, because she could not make her pregnant body hurry.

James should have asked Dawn Swearing to play for the service. She had been after him for more than a month to relieve her of her duties to the choir but her husband could be stubborn, sometimes. He claimed that he and Dawn Swearing just could not work well together because she was too young and too opinionated.

Birdie hissed her teeth and stopped to catch her breath. Sweat was pouring from under her hat and trickling in itchy rivulets down to the small of her back. It was pooling in the seat of her panties and her bottom would be soaked by the time she got to the piano bench.

Just then, a male voice called out to her from across a field on the far side of the manse. She looked behind her and caught sight of a Rastaman in the distance. Three fat bad words rolled together across the top of Birdie's brain, just beneath the constricted area covered by her half hat and she stopped suddenly and began to pray. She couldn't go into the holy sanctuary in such mental disarray. It just wouldn't be right. Since this baby began growing inside her, she hardly knew herself and she was beginning to be afraid. Just last week she had yelled and screamed so loudly at her husband, that the housekeeper, Miss Maudie, had reprimanded her. And now here was this damn *Nyahman*, as he liked to call himself, bothering her peace.

She was no longer afraid of him because he was one of the kindest souls she knew, but she did not have time for him and his circuitous arguments this morning. She did not like his religion one bit and she hated the knotty coils of his hair and his churlish beard even more. But in her first weeks at the manse, he had been one of the few who said anything kind to her. In fact, he had been more than kind that day when the postmistress insulted her and she had walked home from the post office with the hot tears spilling down her cheeks and soaking the bosom of her dress.

That long ago afternoon, just as she passed under a flame of the forest tree and entered the church gates, he had appeared as if from nowhere and stopped her in her tracks. When she looked up and saw his white teeth and his fiery eyes, she stood frozen in fear but he quickly put her at her ease by offering to take her bag. He had said it more like a command and so overcome had she been by hurt and shock that she had handed over her shopping bag with childlike docility.

On the way up the hill, he told her that he had heard about the incident at the post office and had hastened through the *short-cut* to meet up with her. She had turned to look up at him quizzically, her tears undried and her soft lashes sticking together.

The unknown Rastaman stopped in his tracks and looked at her with such tenderness that she almost started to weep again. He spoke to her with understanding and said, "I and I don't deal wid your religion but di I know a wrong ting when it is done to a *sistren*. Dese people around here abide in darkness and dem hate dem very shadow if dem is black. I and I have tried to teach dem di great truths from di man Garvey but it falleth upon deaf ears. Garvey say dat if a man doth not believe in himself, him is twice defeated in di race of life. Dese people around here don't believe any teaching unless it falleth from di lips of a white man. Dat yellow-tail postmistress treat di I scornfully today, mi sistren, but I come upon dis land of Babylon to tell you dat *dow* art a princess of exquisite beauty and you tell dat brown-skin husband of yours dat him better cherish di damsel right or him will answer to I and I."

Having said his piece, the Rastaman remained in silence for the rest of the walk to the front steps of the church house. He departed quickly as if knowing that his presence was forbidden but from that day, whenever Birdie saw him, she made sure to greet him warmly, much to James' annoyance.

Today, however, she had no time to talk to her friend, so, she waved at him and hastened her steps.

It had not taken Birdie long to lose her innocence once she married The Reverend and moved into the church house at Chalky Hill in Trelawny. First, there were the whispers that she had used obeah to tie the half-white man. Then, there were the sly glances at her middle and she knew that the lookers were searching for proof that hers had been a necessary marriage. When it became evident that theirs was a love match, some of the women started making complaints to The Reverend about the ways in which his wife had slighted or offended them. When that didn't work, one of the more vicious among them started a rumor that she was a *mule* and couldn't breed.

The Reverend was a forgiving man but when the postmistress of the district referred to Birdie as a *blaki tutuss,* and in her hearing at that, he took the opportunity to address the issue from the pulpit. Had he given Birdie the slightest hint of his intentions, she would have found a reason to stay home. However, when Reverend Whitehead launched his very pointed response from the pulpit, she could do no more than bow her head and try to take herself, in her mind, off to distant places.

Years later, when the poet Louise Bennett performed her poem *Uriah Preach*, Birdie often thought of her husband and the fire in his words that Sunday morning. He put the church on notice that he was fully aware of all the steps that had been taken against his wife and he demanded that an end be put to the trespass. He warned them that if anyone made his wife cry again, he would pack his belongings and depart from the church circuit. He would also put it in writing to the Baptist Union that the church was under the influence of Satan and they should think twice before sending another minister there to be savaged by a wicked congregation.

He did not stop there but called the postmistress by name and told her from the pulpit that if she did not have such a wicked tongue, her intended might have sent for her from England instead of her rival who had lived in the adjoining district.

The offender rose from her pew, sniffed loudly, wheeled her broad, plaid-skirted behind through the side door and left the church for good.

By this time, Reverend Whitehead was in such a pucker that there was no stopping him. He launched into a sermon, the likes of which Chalky Hill Baptist Church had not heard before. He was like John the Baptist of old and the fire in his eye made many tremble. He warned them of the judgment of

God against those who spoke in malice and envy. He talked about their self-hatred and Birdie sat up in wonder when he said, "Many of you would have been happy if I had brought you a church mother who knew neither cleanliness nor godliness, so long as she possessed the light-brown skin that you so worship! Your hearts are warped by the leftovers of slavery and I warn you that there will be no help for you until you accept that all humans are made in the image of the Almighty God! Not just the brown ones and the white ones, but all humanity. Christ died for all. And to think that you love my skin that was created because a white man violated my mother."

He said the last softly and with much pain before walking off the pulpit into the congregation. He stopped at the front pew where Birdie was seated with her head still bowed. He took her gently by the hand, walked through the side door of the church and went home. Deacon Swearing had to bring the service to a close.

On the morning following the tongue lashing and the aborted church service, all kinds of visitors brought gifts to the manse. The Reverend turned them away, every last one with each gift. They all left with his words ringing in their ears.

JUST AS BIRDIE arrived at the side door of the sanctuary, the door was pushed open and The Reverend peered out, obviously looking anxiously for her. When he saw the perspiration pouring down her face, he pulled his handkerchief from his breast pocket and mopped her brow. The cloth came away with dark streaks from her face powder. He smiled, shook his head and wiped her face again.

Birdie stood impatiently under her husband's ministrations and noted the attention that his action had begun to draw from three little Sunday schoolers who stood in the now open doorway. One curious little round faced boy sidled up to the pair, looked up at them and asked, "You feeling sick, Teacher? You waahn me fi go fi mi mada?"

Reverend Whitehead took Birdie's handbag from her, handed it to the earnest little fellow and said very gently, "You are a good little boy. Take this and put it on the little table next to the piano stool."

The little boy looked at them for another second and then stepped off with such an air of importance that they both began to laugh. As Birdie watched him disappear into the sanctuary, she wondered if any of the church folks who had shown her such unkindness had ever been like that little boy.

Reverend Whitehead turned to re-enter the church and Birdie followed closely behind him. As soon as they walked in, the adults ceased whispering and shuffling around and all eyes fastened upon the pair as they made their way to the platform.

This church service marked Communion Sunday and the people had dressed for the occasion. All the communicant women were dressed in white and the men wore black and white. The visitors stood out because few of them wore the sober colors of the regular members. Birdie herself was dressed in a white maternity smock blouse and a dark skirt that had elastic at the waist.

She was soon seated at the piano, waiting for her husband to give her the signal for the opening hymn. As she waited, her eyes took in the pipe organ on the other side of the platform. It was old and in need of repairs. In her condition, she could not manage the strenuous pumping of her legs that the instrument demanded. She was grateful for the baby grand piano that had been donated to the church by a wealthy benefactor.

It was a sunny morning but the church was cooler than the outside temperature, thanks to the stone walls and the very high ceilings. The windows directly behind the platform were stained glass. The two on either side of the platform showed what looked like the rays of the morning sun against a background of blue and red. The long windows lining both sides of the building were made of plain glass and wood and the two large ones at the front opened on either side of the twin doors that were the main entry to the sanctuary. The church had been built in celebration of Emancipation and rumor had it that The Reverend William Knibb, the great abolitionist, had laid the first cut stone that started the foundation.

People were still coming in, so, The Reverend sat with his head bowed in silent prayer. Birdie wasn't praying, though. She was leafing through the hymns selected by her husband and keeping track of who was coming in and going out. She heard a little murmur and a sudden shuffle of excitement go through the sanctuary and looked around to see Old Dr. Prichard shambling down the aisle of the church. The pervert was holding the hand of his latest trollop and Birdie looked away in disgust.

The nerve of this old pagan to walk into the sanctuary after divorcing the helpless Mrs. Prichard whose sole crime was old age. Birdie thought of the poor, legless soul, moldering in her diabetic sick bed and she wanted to scream at the shameless pair. No doubt he expected to partake in the Holy Communion and for once, Birdie wished that she was the deacon of the church. Lord knows, she would humiliate them both by passing the bread and the grape juice over their heads so that they would be shamed into repentance.

The Reverend rose to his feet and Birdie played the chord for the opening hymn. The choir seated behind her rose in a rustle and at a signal from her, they broke into a fulsome rendition of *Amazing Grace*.

All was going well until an elderly sister standing at the back of the choir, decided to break off into a discordant descant. Birdie scowled and looked fiercely across at her but the old lady pretended not to see her. She would have her moment and that was that. The hymn came to its designated end and the woman managed to make her quavering last note extend until just after Birdie lifted her fingers from the piano keys.

Birdie gave a disgusted sigh, closed the hymnal and straightened her back. She did know why this old lady had decided to defy her every instruction and she was thinking seriously of dismissing her from the choir. She knew instinctively, however, that the whole choir would revolt if she did any such thing. The mystery of the source of their quiet uncooperation was yet to be definitively explained but she remembered what her mother had told her about Trelawny people, so, she was not surprised that the church folks had not embraced her.

Armed with the unwavering love and encouragement of her husband, Birdie was determined that she would not be broken by these stubborn and hard-hearted people. Moreover, she was not alone. Dawn Swearing, the teenaged bride of Principal Swearing, was firmly on her side. She, too, was an outsider, hailing as she did from the neighboring parish of St. Ann. She was disliked because her husband was more than twice her age and it was commonly held that it was his affair with her that led his first wife to an early grave.

Their common status as outcasts had soon led to friendship and further hostility on the part of the felines of the church. That was exactly how Birdie saw most of the choir members. The men were not so bad, especially when they were not in the company of their women. Birdie, however, had soon hardened her attitude to indifference. She had no intention of trying to win anyone over. She had searched her heart and finished the inventory without finding a single fault with herself. She was a godly woman who dressed modestly, played the piano dutifully for all church services, trained the choir and diligently taught second grade at the primary school. What more could she do to please these people? Why were they so willing to love her husband without question and yet they were not prepared to extend that same affection to her?

Seated upon the mid-high piano stool, Birdie crossed her legs at the ankles and swung them back and forth. She was soon lost in the memory of her first Sunday at Chalky Hill

Baptist Church. She remembered the rousing applause that had met the introduction of her husband and the polite spatter of handclaps that had greeted her introduction.

When her husband finished his first sermon, a murmur of appreciation rumbled across the congregation and a few of the less restrained shouted amens and hallelujahs.

At the invitation of the retiring pastor's wife, Birdie played the closing hymn. She took the seat in front of the piano with whispers rustling across the pews but she did not look around to read the faces. Instead, she focused her tear-filled eyes upon the hymn book that was against the reading stand and sighed with relief when she recognized the familiar *Stand Up, Stand Up For Jesus.*

Birdie played the opening notes with authority and waited for just a hair's breadth of a second for the congregation to fall in line. Then she took the hymn for a strenuous workout, her fingers rolling the notes crisply, one into the other, while she sang harmony in a clear alto. She soon heard her husband's self-assured baritone break out from the hesitant male voices on the choir and Birdie switched to soprano to accompany him. Soon, she lost track of the congregation as her husband lifted her swelling notes in support and her sweet voice rang out so clearly that it cut into the hearts of even the most resistant.

When the hymn came to its end, Birdie bowed her head in silence and remained at the piano stool. Reverend Whitehead brought the service to a close and Birdie walked over to join him. He took her by the hand and walked to one of the side doors of the chapel so that he could greet the departing congregation.

But for Teacher and Dawn Swearing, everyone who chose that exit, kept to the right and made sure to shake Reverend Whitehead's hand. A few of the older men smiled politely at Birdie but no one lingered to make small talk with them.

On their way to the manse, James tried to reassure her that the people would get used to her in time, but they both knew that Birdie was in for trying times. It was roughly a month later that the postmistress called her blaki tutuss.

While Birdie sat deep in thought, she was unaware that her husband was watching her. Dawn Swearing was reading the announcements and Reverend Whitehead was watching Birdie's back, but he was thinking of the picture she had made the day before as he sat waiting in the car to take her to her doctor's visit.

When she walked out the front door of the manse, she stood briefly in the sunlight and hesitated before descending the first steps. She looked so beautiful and now that she was pregnant, her skin glowed and her lips had darkened to a deep, lush shade.

He watched her make her way gingerly down the remaining steps and by the time she got to the car he was waiting by the passenger side. Before he helped her into the car, Reverend Whitehead wrapped both arms around her and kissed her.

Birdie, though her back was toward her husband, sensed that he was watching her and she too was remembering how her customarily private husband had kissed her in the yard for anyone passing by to see. She blushed with remembered pleasure when she recalled the passion with which he had made love to her the night before. She just could not figure out this husband of hers, because the larger she got, the more he seemed to desire her. And, stranger yet, he no longer allowed her to take a bath by herself. He insisted that he was afraid that she would slip and fall while in the tub.

At first, she was embarrassed for him to view her swollen body but she had quickly grown used to the constant attention. Small wonder that he had even allowed her to walk down the front steps by herself the day before but he had needed to check the oil and did not want her sitting in the car while he did it. He was afraid that she would get too hot while she waited.

BIRDIE FELT THE sharp pain just after she played the first chord of the closing hymn. It felt like a strong hand had pressed hard upon her belly. The next sharp constriction ran down her back and circled to her belly. She did not need anyone to tell her that she was in labor and she began to pray that her water would not break. The pain faded away and Birdie continued to play but by the time she got to the close of the hymn, she was in a cold sweat and her worse fear had been fulfilled.

She remained seated at the piano and in between the small ripples of discomfort that she continued to feel, she tidied up her music sheets and hymn books. She was determined that none of the church members would see her shame for, by now, she knew that her skirt was soaked with amniotic fluid.

When Dawn Swearing walked up to the platform to greet Birdie, she grabbed her by the arm and pulled her down to the piano bench, snug by her. After she told her what had happened, Dawn hurried to the front of the church to get Reverend Whitehead.

No one standing at the church door had ever seen the normally staid gentleman walk with more than his customary deliberate gait. However, as soon as Dawn asked to be excused and whispered in his ear, he sprinted away from the group at the door and was soon bending over Birdie.

Dawn lost no time in finding her husband where he was standing and engaged in earnest conversation with the mother of one of his students. She took him aside and Deacon Swearing was soon running off to get his car.

nyahman-rastaman
short cut/shaat-cut-a shorter way
sistren-sister; sister-friend; term of endearment
mule-infertile woman
blaki tutuss-black darling or black pet (derogatory)
Uriah Preach-a poem by Louise Bennett in which a character of the same name uses his time in the pulpit to get back at several people who had offended him.
Stand Up, Stand Up for Jesus-Christian hymn with words by George Duffield and music by George J. Webb

CHAPTER 17

Somtime yu ha fi laan fi tek butter nyam fat
Sometimes you have to use butter to eat fat
In difficult situations, we sometimes have to make decisions that seem nonsensical; sometimes we have to accept suffering on top of distress
Jackass seh di wol no lebl
The jackass says that the earth under its feet is not level
There is much unfairness in life
Somtime yu ha fi tek kin tiit kiba haat-bon
Sometimes you have to show your teeth in laughter even when your heart is breaking.

When Birdie had told her husband that she did not want to be cared for by Nurse Headley, the village midwife, he had thought her unwise. He now knew that she had made the right decision.

All the way to the hospital, Birdie moaned and ground her teeth. By the time they got to the bridge that bordered the Martha Brae River and Caribbean Sea, she was bleeding profusely and drifting in and out of consciousness. Deacon Swearing floored the gas pedal and got to the front of the hospital in record time.

Dawn ran into the building and soon had a porter with a stretcher following swiftly behind her. In short order, the porter was wheeling the now fully unconscious into the hospital.

Dawn and Deacon Swearing waited at the hospital for more than an hour and then decided to go back home to call the church to an emergency prayer meeting. They knew that Birdie was not well loved so they decided to hand-pick the comers and to hold the meeting at their house. The Reverend asked them to stop at the Chalky Hill police station and place a call to his brother Nathan who lived in Brown's Town.

Later that Sunday afternoon, the surgeon met The Reverend outside of the maternity ward at the Falmouth Hospital. The doctor, a Canadian immigrant, was wearing a dark scowl and Reverend Whitehead's hands tightened in his side pockets when he saw his expression. He continued to watch the man's face, searching the doctor's eyes for signs of what lay behind his gaze.

The corners of his eyes were cobwebbed with fatigue but the brown eyes behind horn-rimmed glasses were kind. He put a gentle but firm hand upon Reverend Whitehead's shoulder and pushed him toward a window at the end of a long corridor.

The late afternoon sun gave everything inside a reddish glow but through the window, both men could see the blue-green waves smashing against the coral sand on the beach bordering the eastern side of the hospital. There against the window where the evening sun rays made daguerreotypes of the two tall men, the doctor told James the bitter truth.

"Your wife will live and the baby is a healthy boy."

He paused for a long moment as if awaiting a response but Reverend Whitehead remained silent. The doctor looked at him once more and then continued to speak. The words that followed were slowly, carefully and bluntly spoken.

"Your wife will not have more children and she is lucky to be alive."

Reverend Whitehead swallowed and the only sign of his pain could be seen in the veins that seemed to pop up suddenly on both sides of his temple. He then bowed his head and murmured, "It is the will of the Lord."

The doctor sighed and then continued to speak. "Your wife suffered a ruptured placenta and we had to remove her womb to prevent her from bleeding to death."

He continued to watch Reverend Whitehead but when he remained silent, he patted his shoulder and spoke once more before turning back to the ward. "Enjoy your wife and your baby boy. They are both lucky to be alive."

James did not go into the hospital ward when the doctor left. He could not let Birdie see him in his weakness, not when he needed to be strong for her. Even as he wiped his silent tears with the back of his hand, he was wondering if she was awake and if she had any idea about what had happened to her. So much had changed and so suddenly, too. He was relieved that his son had survived the surgery but in that moment, his mind and heart remained fixated on the horror of what had happened to his young bride.

So many times in his ministry, even as a trainee, he had been faced with the unspeakable and had been called upon to give comfort to people who had been bowled over by sudden loss. Somehow, he had always managed to find fitting words from the scriptures. Now, in his hour of grief, he found himself alone and staring through the dusty panes of a window upon a small garden below.

Someone had taken time to tend the garden. He saw this attention in the whitewashed stones that circled a lush bed of Joseph's coat and the climbing rose bushes that encircled the trunk of a dwarf cherry tree. The little garden was bordered on all sides by ferns and lace plants.

Reverend Whitehead took in all of the details yet he did not really absorb the picture. His mind was on Birdie and now he was also thinking about the baby. He was James John, also, but they would call him Junior. He and Birdie had planned to have a large family because they had both known the loneliness of being an only child. He had at least six half-siblings that he knew of but apart from Nathan, the others were strangers to him. As a small child, he had mostly been in the company of adults because with the exception of his brother, Nathan,

Maas Raphael never allowed any of the neighborhood children into his yard and he had known better than to disobey his grandfather's rules.

How could he break this bitter news to Birdie? Just as his eyes began welling with fresh tears, he sensed a presence behind him. James turned around and saw Mama Celeste walking in his direction. She had her head wrapped in white and she was wearing a multicolored smock and a white underblouse. In her left hand, she clutched a small grip and in her right she carried a cane on which she leaned as she scrambled toward him.

When she got up close to The Reverend, he saw that she was out of breath and her eyes were bloodshot. She looked as if she had not slept in a long time. He wondered why she was walking with a cane and he wanted to ask how she had got the news so quickly but she preempted him.

"Is two night in a row me dream bout wedn and is Birdie a di bride. Me know me pikni in a chobl, so me tek di train to Montego Bay and me jos get aaf a di big bus outa Falmouth Square. Me was gwaihn go up a Chalky Hill but me see some church people out deh and dem tell me dat Birdie in di hospital."

Someone else might have elicited shock or disbelief, but Mama Celeste was known in the family circle as one whose dreams walked straight. Reverend Whitehead put one arm around her shoulder and, with the other, he gently removed the grip that she was carrying. Holding on to each other, they walked into the maternity ward.

CHAPTER 18

Maudie Elfreda Collins and Joan Marie Jackman

1991

Nof maaga cow a fence side a bull muma
Many a scrawny cow you see leaning against the fence is actually the mother of bulls
Do not be fooled by appearance
Seben year no nof fi wash frekle aaf a guinea-hen back
Seven years are not long enough to wash the speckles off a guinea hen's feathers
Some injuries are never forgotten

Dis was what The Reverend wuda kaal a harvest moon but to Miss Maudie, it was a bad sign. She did not like full moons. People liable fi do dyam foolishness when di moon full-up di night sky and a spread a watery glow into every kaana weh normally daak.

Miss Maudie grunt to harself but she duohn seh notn to di eleven-yer-uol girl weh a waak behain har. Instead, she *shaatn* har step dem so dat har grandaata kyan keep up wid har. Is not dat she waahn fi waak weh lef di pikni, but di full moon have har nervous and she focus har fear until she get well bex. Because a dat, She taak more harshly dan usual to di girl. "*Waak shaap*, yu hear me, Joanie! A waahn get home before Byron get into di house. Yu know dat if him reach home before we get deh, him gwaihn nyam all a di dinner and we will have to go to bed hungry."

Joanie hasten har step dem and shoot ahead of har granmada. Miss Maudie force har fi slow dong. "Hi, no bada run in front a me so go brok yu neck. Me seh waak faas. Me neba seh run."

Joanie faal a step behain har granmada and almuos kiss har tiit in a *bexsaishan* but she stap harself jos in time. If she ever do such a *umanish* and *force-ripe* ting, Miss Maudie wuda *help-dong* har basket from aaf a har head, brok a switch and beat har right deh pahn di spot. Miss Maudie a no smadi fi joke wid and alduoh Joanie know dat har granmada love har, she also know dat Miss Maudie wudn hesitate fi *kaan har romp* if she paas har place wid har. Is not wan time Miss Maudie tell har dat *bod weh fly too faas, fly way paas dem nes.*

And is not dat Joanie duohn love and rispek har granmada. Is jos dat she duohn waahn live wid har. She waahn go a Spanish Town go live wid har mada and har breda dem. Joanie have a feeling duoh, dat har mada duohn love har. Why else she wuda tek di bwai dem and go weh wid har new husband? If she did love har she no wuda did tek har, too? Is dis kwestian she been asking harself ever since har mada ton big Pentecostal Christian and married aaf to har new husband. Di two a dem set up house in a Spanish Town and tek har breda dem and leave har behain wid Miss Maudie.

Joanie a waak as faas as she kyan fi keep up wid Miss Maudie, and she a try har bes fi no glance sideways in a di bush weh she imagine a dozen *duppy* a si-dong over a big, smokeless cook fire and a cook *duppy pat-waata.* Miss Maudie tell har more dan wan time dat duppy prefer fi waak when di sun hat and dat when yu smell a certain pungent bush odor a waft pahn di barely movin midday wind current, a di duppy dem a put-aan a helleva cookin.

Joanie never really see a duppy yet, but from di way Miss Maudie and ada people taak bout dem, she have no doubt dat duppy a real sinting. Miss Birdie and The Reverend seh dat such talk is nonsense and downright ungodly, but dat duohn stap Joanie from tellin Jimmy every duppy story dat she know. Jimmy always ask har fi tell him di wan bout di *chrii-foot haas* at di *kraasroad.*

When she feel sinting brush har han, she almuos scream-out but she soon realize dat dem reach di *bomp* in a di paas. Di paas is di track dat will tek dem from di shaat-cut to di main road. *Guinea graas* grow pahn both side a di track and is a *staak* a graas dat brush har upper arm. She know because she kuda feel di burnin pahn har skin weh di graas cut har slightly. She always wanda how di cow and goat dem nyam di graas when di edge so blaasid shaap.

Fi such a likl girl, Joanie have much fi kansida. Fi wan ting, she know dat di children at har school duohn like har. Dem kaal har some terrible names and if it was not fi Jimmy Whitehead, she wudn have a single fren a school. She share a bench wid two likl, *dry head* gyal, but dem always a whisper and cut dem yai after har. Is not like she do dem anyting bad, but, from di day she *lan-up* in a Chalky Hill, is pure bad treatment she encounter.

But Joanie know why dem duohn like har. Dem grudge har fi har pretty hair and har fair skin. Dat is why dem kaal har red nigger, red Ibo, *malatta daag, dundus gyal and* puss yai. Dem duohn dare kaal Jimmy any a dese awful names and him is exactly di same color as she. Miss Birdie a Jimmy granmada and not only is she di principal a di school but she have a *leda* strap name "Tom Jones" and she no fraid fi use it.

Joanie know well di sting a "Tom Jones" for, di fors day dat she attend Chalky Hill Primary School, Miss Birdie beat har till she and Miss Maudie almuos ketch a kwaaril over it. And di chuut is, Miss Birdie had no cause to beat har because she was di victim.

It duohn tek notn fi Joanie remember di day when Miss Birdie beat har and likl as she was, she mek up har mind dat if she ever see Miss Birdie *jrap-dong* a road and a she fi give har kuol waata fi save har life, she wuda mek di bitch dead.

She remember dat it was recess when she waak weh from di teemin, tumblin, bad-taakin horde a pikni weh in a har klaas. She duohn like dem because young as she was, she know dat dere was somting dat mek har different from almuos evribadi dat she know. Yes, she have two yai, nose and mout like evribadi else, but while muos a di pikni dem have flat nose and *tik* lip, fi har nose staat from jos below di migl of har *yai-brow* dem. Azkaadn to Miss Maudie, it straighter dan an arrow. Har mout duohn spread out from wan yez kaana to di nex, like so much a di *ada* pikni dem. Fi har mout-lip dem small and pert, and dem is di color of di inside of a well-ripe *naseberry.* As to har hair, no need to taak bout it because it lang, way paas har shoulder dem. Is not wan time some grudgeful, *piki-piki head* pikni grab har hair and try fi pull it out by di very root. In fak, when she was in grade wan, a bwai did cut-aaf a wol plait a it and put it in a him pakit. Miss Maudie go over di schoolyaad and gwaan bad bout it. She never satisfy till Miss Birdie beat di bwai senseless and afta dat, she go to di bwai granny and tell har seh if is plan dem plan fi use Joanie hair fi wok obeah pahn har, dem fi remember a which paat she, Maudie Elfreda Collins, come fram, and if har granpikni head hat har, she wipe out di granny and every wan a har *faambli* dem. Di poor uol lady did so frighten dat she faal dong pan har uol knee dem and beg Miss Maudie humble paadn.

Miss Maudie mada and faada a did *wrap-head* people and because a dat, nof people believe seh Miss Maudie have powers and she no mind dat dem tink so.

A taal, wide, leafy *guango* tree give plenty shade to di grade wan klaasroom. It is di domain a di likl-wan dem and Miss Birdie paas law dat none a di big bwai or gyal dem mos come dong deh fi shelter from di sun or to play wid di likl pikni dem. Joanie know why because Jimmy tell har. A grade eight bwai did come dong deh and lure weh a likl grade wan girl. Is after him done rape har aaf behain di school tailit dat di teacher dem realize dat him did always have a likin fi playin wid di likl pikini dem.

Miss Birdie beat di bwai to sickness and den she kaal police fi lock him up. Azkaadn to how Jimmy tell it, di bwai foot dem kuda barely touch di grong di way di police dem drape him in a him pants waist fi fling him in a di jeep. To dis day, di bwai people dem hate Miss Birdie because him spend twelve months a juvenile prison. Dem never sorry fi di poor likl girl, duoh. Har mada had to send har go a farin go live wid relatives, because even some a di big-big man dem a Chalky Hill dischrik mek joke and song bout wa happen to di likl gyal-pikini.

Joanie a stan-up aanda di said guango tree and she have har back a rub gainst di rough bark a di *chonk*. She naa tink bout how she might get stain pahn di back of har white blouse. Joanie naa tink bout how Miss Maudie wuda beat har fi mess up har clothes. She jos glad fi di distance between she and di wol-heap a black pikni dem weh a *bada-bada* har head. It never help matters dat Miss Maudie always a seh dat *notn black no good.* She even a wanda if dis is why Miss Maudie duohn like a bone in a Miss Birdie but fi har, it seem like Reverend kyan do no wrong.

Joanie get so laas in har thought dem dat she never realize dat di bwai creep up pahn har till she smell him. Di bwai kyari a smell like rust and Joanie open har yai dem and see a mout full a yellow tiit jos before di bwai grab wan of har lang plait and tug it like him a pull graas. She shove him weh from har and him jrap pahn him batam. To har shock, di bwai git-up and begin wan piece a *cow baalin.* Before Joanie kuda seh, *"Joe Reid,"* is him wol tribe come dong pahn har fi beat har up.

Di fos wan fi lik har was a big, crufty wan, wid a spider head. A di rang smadi him lik, duoh. Joanie grow wid bwai pikni and she know how fi defen harself. She crouch-dong jos like how Uncle Byron teach har, and she rush him and lan a fis right a di top a him big gut. Two more a dem rush har and Joanie bite har batam lip, roll up her fis, and mek up har mind fi dead fightin. And it look like she was gwaihn dead too, because is about five a dem faal dong pahn har and begin fi bite and kick har. By dis time, she in a real panic but dat is when Jimmy Whitehead come roun di kaana from Miss Birdie office and realize dat is Joanie a get di *merdaraishan.*

Lucky fi Joanie dat Jimmy have a heavy eighteen inch ruler wid a metal edge. Di bwai paat di waata and staat fi slash lef and right. Evribadi back weh from di wepan and nobadi dare touch him. Dem no foolish enough fi lick Miss Birdie granson for dem know him is har wan son, dead-lef pikni, and if anybody lay a finger pahn him, is apocalypse in a Chalky Hill.

Smadi run go kaal Miss Birdie from har office and when she get to di scene, she tek wan look pahn Joanie and Jimmy and see how di two fair skin pikni dem a huol each ada by di han and di two a dem a cry.

She run Jimmy to har office and she never even ask Joanie what happen. She jos pull di leda strap from roun har neck and staat lay it into di pikini.

When Joanie realize dat aneda slash from dat whistlin ribbon of rage was gwaihn mek har wet harself, she staat fi run and she never stap till she reach di batam a di hill at di Baptist manse and Miss Maudie look chuu di kitchen winda and see har a come.

Dat evening when Miss Birdie come from wok, har food kuol, and di washin was still on di clothesline. Di back door a di house stand silent and open to di settin sun and dere was no sound a Miss Maudie radio a broadcast di soothin voice of Henry Stennett on *The Evening People's Show*.

Reverend Whitehead had to taak saaf to Miss Maudie fi a few days well and while Miss Birdie never apologize to Joanie or har granmada, she pay fi medical treatment fi Joanie cut-up skin and bruises. Joanie hear Miss Maudie tell The Reverend dat it was har rispek fi him dat buy clearance fi Miss Birdie. If it was any wan else did brutalize har granpikni like dat, dem wud bound fi sekl it before di law.

Poor Reverend. Him was in a difficult position, for, him had was to *saaf-saada* Miss Maudie and at di same time, him kudn *ben kochi* too low because Miss Birdie a blow shaat like a *pan turkl* everytime she look pahn Miss Maudie. Fi weeks, di two a dem no taak to each ada and di unfortunate Reverend had was to act as go-between.

But dis not di end a Joanie chobl, for, is not wan time big people see har a come and dem staat fi taak bout har like she deaf and kyaahn hear di tings dat dem a seh bout she and har mada. Wan time she go home and ask Miss Maudie what is a whore and a sailor pikini and Miss Maudie ask har where she hear dem deh *outlaa* wod deh. When Joanie tell har dat is di shoemaker seh so when she paas him on di way home from school, Miss Maudie cover di cook pot, ton-aaf Miss Birdie *gyas* stove and grab har straw hat from behain di kitchen door. She never even stap fi tek-aaf har apron before she march aaf dong di hill from di manse.

To dis blessed day, Joanie duohn know what Miss Maudie seh to di shoemaker out in Chalky Hill square. All she know is dat Reverend ban har from tekin communion fi a full chrii mont.

MISS MAUDIE AND Joanie reach near di street light and Joanie breathe a sigh. Ahead she see di gate weh wide enough fi a kyaar. Di waakway outline on both sides wid conch shell because Joanie grampa a did fisherman before him dead suddenly, lang before she baan.

Joanie run up di step dem ahead a Miss Maudie and reach di high verandah and feel aanda di verandah chair fi di likl slat a wood weh dem always hide di key. Di house in total daaknis, so, dat mean dat Byron still at work. Him trainin to be a sugar boiler at di sugar factory a Clark's Town and him work late some days, especially during di crop time when dem process cane fi mek sugar and rum.

When dem get into di house, Miss Maudie sniff and begin fi grumble aanda har bret bout Byron. "Me *taiyad* fi tell dat blastid bwai fi tek him shoes dem outside and air dem out. Him know him dyam foot dem *cheesy* and not fi anyting will dat nasty brute leave him stinkin boot dem outside. Joanie, opin di back door quick before me *pyuk-up*."

While Miss Maudie still a fuss, Joanie pick up di offendin shoes and tek dem from di livinroom to di back step dem. After she put dem dong, she smell har finger dem and wipe dem in di tail of har cotton school uniform.

Di light dat Miss Maudie ton-aan in a di kitchen, mingle wid di cooler glow a di moon and brighten di backyaad. Joanie stan-up in a di kitchen doorway and a tek-iin di distorted vista of tree tops, shrubs, di fowl coop gainst di fence and di outside latrine dat was a likl farther from di house. Di waata-tank stand in di foreground and di concrete barbecue was a wide patch a gray, bordered by di back step dem, di waata-tank and di dirt and di patch a graas dat mek up di res a di backyaad.

Miss Maudie voice brok di silence. "Joanie, kyari up some waata from di tank and come wash yu skin before it get any later."

"Yes, ma'am."

Joanie answer har granmada absently because har mind deh pahn Jimmy. Him a tek private lessons fi di Common Entrance Examination so him stay late after school dese days. She miss waakin home wid him from school to di church house on di hill where she spend all har afternoon and evenin dem a wait fi Miss Maudie fi finish har work.

Of late, The Reverend did allow har into di library and give har permission fi read di illustrated Bible dat deh pahn a smaal table near di door. Di book so big dat Joanie kyaahn lif it up. She kneel-dong pahn di hassock in front a di table and turn di pages.

She look pahn di pitcha dem and di wan dat she kyaahn stap look pahn, is di wan wid Abel lay-dong kraas him mada lap wid di helleva knife-cut in a him belly-side and di blood a gush out and a pool pahn di grong. More dan anyting, is di look pahn Eve face dat terrify Joanie and she know to God chuut dat if she ever feel pain like dat, she wuda mos jrap-dong and dead.

One evening, The Reverend come in quietly and see Joanie a look pahn di pitcha. To har surprise, him waak over and put him han pahn har shoulder and staat fi tell har how Abel was an innocent victim and a precursor to Jesus, a sacrificial lamb. She kudn quite andastan what him was taakin bout but she feel good all di same. But di good feelin wasn to laas lang, because di followin evenin, Miss Birdie come home early and ketch Joanie in a di library. She run har out and tell har fi go a di kitchen go help har granny.

When di chail go into di kitchen, Miss Maudie a frown-up har face and a taak to harself. She ton roun from di stove and ask Joanie wa she want in a di kitchen and Joanie tell har wa Miss Birdie seh. Miss Maudie kiss har tiit and tell Joanie, "Tek out yu school book dem and study yu work. Yu no need fi laan dis kaina wok yet. Study fi yu exam and Gaad will tek care a di res."

Joanie gwaihn tek di exam same time in a January wid Jimmy but she kyaahn go a di private lesson dem weh Jimmy a tek because Miss Maudie kyaahn afford di fee. She did well waahn fi sen har but when she kansida har gran-pikni dem weh har son dem run lef pahn dem mada, Miss Maudie kudn very well mek di pikni dem dead fi hungry.

More dan wan time, Miss Maudie tell Joanie dat she plan fi sen har go a junior secondary school because she no have money fi sen har go a high school. But Joanie no have no intention of going to no underrated school. She plan fi paas di exam in wan go and Jimmy a share evriting dat him learn in a di lesson-klaas wid har.

So Joanie a study haad but she no plan fi go back in a The Reverend office for is not ongl di children at school dat duohn like har. She know fi sure dat Miss Birdie duohn like har niida. She see it in har yai dem, how dem get kuol and haad when she look pahn har.

Joanie always a wanda a wa she do Miss Birdie why di lady jos tek-up wid dis dislike fi har. Di way Miss Birdie treat har is like she vex har jos by existin. None a di saaf wod dem dat she reserve fi addressin Jimmy was ever directed at har. When Miss

Birdie taak to har, is always, "Joanie do dis and Joanie do dat!" And never a commendation when she kyari out har aada dem.

Teng Gaad, The Reverend kain to har. Is not dat him hug har up or anyting like dat, but when him taak to Joanie, him eye dem warm and tender and him even pat har head from time to time. The Reverend not touchy-feely but him kain. *Krismos* gaan, him give Miss Maudie a wol ten dala bill fi Joanie present. "Buy the child something nice," him tell Miss Maudie and har granmada all but curtsy to him, much to Miss Birdie annoyance.

Joanie waak over to di waata tank and pick-up di bucket dat tie to a lang piece a rope and jrap it dong into di likl door dat cut into di top a di tank. She lisn till she hear di splash and di bucket begin fi get heavy as it full-up wid waata. She pull it up slowly and reach fi it wid her ada han. Joanie empty di waata into a larger plastic bucket at har foot dem and jrap di bucket into di tank again. Wid har two han dem, she lug di full container up di step dem and sigh wid relief when she get to di kitchen doorway. She glad seh none a di waata no dash weh.

Miss Maudie a wear aneda apron and she change har straw hat fi a red bandana. She glance at di bucket pahn di floor and push out har mout and tell Joanie, "Pikni, me taiyad fi tell yu dat yu mos not full-up di bucket. Yu will strain yuself and get *badi-come-dong.*"

Joanie staat fi get kraas and almuos kiss har tiit but stap harself in time. Miss Maudie know damn well dat she can manage di bucket. She a eleven and Miss Maudie same wan always a seh how she healthy and strong.

She waak weh from har granmada while she a grumble to harself but she mek sure fi keep har saucy wod dem to harself as she head fi di baatroom. Teng Gaad, she did leave enough waata in di bucket in dere dat maanin. She never waahn fi go back go a di tank. If Byron baid in di inside baatroom dis maanin, she sure him use out har waata, but him prefer fi baid in a di shed behain di tank. In fak, is a wol-heap a tings Byron prefer to do in dat shed.

Joanie see a girl a sneak out dere wan maanin when Miss Maudie sen har fi go feed di fowl dem. She did a wanda weh a girl a do in a di shed until she see Byron come out behain har while him a zip up him pants and di girl a giggle and pull-dong har skirt tail.

Joanie *tup-dong* and hide and dem waak right paas har and never even see har. She did kansida fi tell Miss Maudie wa she see but change har mind and decide fi keep di information fi bribe Byron when she go beg him money.

She pour out di waata into an enamel tub and note wid *satisfakshan* dat di water not too kuol. Is when she staat fi tek-aaf har clothes dat she feel a strange sensation in har *belly-batam.* It was a slight crampin ripple and den she feel somting warm flood di space between har leg dem. She hastily pull aaf har panty and scream-out when she see di thick, daak smear a blood weh stain up har panty seat.

Joanie run go si-dong pahn di tailit and look up fi see Miss Maudie stan-up in a di doorway to di baatroom. She glance from di stain-up panty in a Joanie han to di chail weh she si-dong pahn di tailit and a chrimbl.

Miss Maudie tek di panty from Joanie and ask har in a very haad voice, "Any bwai chrobl yu a school tideh?"

Joanie still a chrimbl while har yai dem lock wid har granmada who all pahn a sudden look like wahn avenging angel weh a come dong pahn har.

Miss Maudie reach fi Joanie and yank har aaf di tailit seat. Joanie feel di sticky warmth a di blood a trickle dong har leg dem and she instinctively try fi pull weh her han from di iron grip of har granmada.

Miss Maudie drag Joanie out a di baatroom and into di livinroom weh she kuda get a full view of har aanda di ceilin light weh no gat no shade.

"Joanie, I want to know if anybody do anyting bad to yu a school, tideh. Any bwai push dem tea-pot in a yu pum-pum?"

"No ma'am. Nobadi no chrobl me at all."

Joanie see relief battle wid lingerin suspicion in har granmada yai dem before Miss Maudie release har han and staat fi grumble to harself.

"Laad, *gi me a bearin haat.* Yu duohn even buss bres good yet and yu staat yu menses aredi. A duohn know what rang wid dis *jinaraishan. Unu waak before unu creep."*

She was suddenly all business. "Go back inside di baatroom and wash-up yuself real good and when yu finish, come in a mi room."

When Joanie reach har granmada bedroom, Miss Maudie have some strange tings put out fi har. She see a black panty and a red wan, but dese were no ordinary panties. Both a dem have somting rig up in di seat dat look like Miss Birdie girdle garters when dem a hang pahn di clothesline. Den she notice what look like a belt but it make out a elastic wid two more a di garter tings a hang dong from it.

While Joanie stand afar and a stare pahn di bed, Miss Maudie tek up what look like a wad a covered cotton wid a tail at di tap and batam.

Miss Maudie kaal Joanie fi come over and while she stan up deh and a feel *fuba* and frighten, Miss Maudie show har how fi faasn di pad to di panty seat and den she tell har fi put it aan.

Wid di pad snug between har leg dem, Joanie pull dong har dress and Miss Maudie motion fi har fi tek a seat a di bed-front. She jraa up close to Joanie and staat fi taak to har in a low voice, like di two a dem a taak big secret.

"Yu a si yu blood now so dis mean dat is uman yu ton. Yu too young fi dis but is di signs a di times. Di Bible seh dat in di laas days, children will be havin children and is dat we a si now. Dis neba happen to me til me ton fifteen. Now lisn to me careful. Wa happen here tideh mean to seh dat a uman yu ton."

Joanie si-dong quiet-quiet. She a watch har granmada face and she duohn blink even wan time. She a wanda how dat maanin she wake up a gyal-pikni and before she lie dong fi sleep, she ton uman. She duohn seh notn, duoh, because Miss Maudie still a taak in a di same low-pitch voice and dat mean dat she dead serious.

"Fram tideh aan, yu ha fi careful roun bwai pikni and yu ha fi laan fi keep and care yuself so dat people no ha fi know yu business. Dis is uman affairs and no man not suppose fi know bout it, not even yu husband. Is a shameful ting when a uman so *slobin* dat people know har *montli* business. And yu ha fi andastan yuself because yu kyan breed now. Don't yu let any bwai come near yu, not even Jimmy, because yu too young fi have biebi!"

Miss Maudie git-up and waak to di foot of har bed and open di chonk dat mek up di footboard. Is like she did know dat dis day was bound to come, even if not so soon. She reach dong and come up wid a flour bag dat tie wid string. Miss Maudie pull di string and staat fi empty it out. About two dozen square a white klaat faal out pahn di bed. Miss Maudie tek up wan piece a di white klaat and Joanie see dat is a baby *nappy*. Now she really a feel frighten but Miss Maudie soon set har haat to res.

"Dis here is *bird-eye*," she tell Joanie. "Before we had all dis *madan* day foolishness dat unu kaal sanitary pad, we had dis and every gyal-pikni had was to laan fi wash bird-eye. Dis a wa yu use if money not available fi buy pad."

Den she point to an enamel pail in a di kaana, between di wardrobe and har blue mahoe dresser. "Yu full dat up wid waata and soak dem. Den yu wash dem out wid *blue soap* and put dem out back pahn mi *bleachin zinc sheet*. Yu cover dem wid plastic and mek di sun bleach dem till dem white. In my day, you wasn kansida a prapa uman until yu laan fi wash bird-eye. All a di mada dem who hab dem son who no married yet, waak by di young gyal dem clothesline. If when di gyal dem put out dem bird-eye, dem no white like *pilikin shit*, dem deh bwai-pikni get waanin fi paas over dem deh kain a uman. Di sayin was, *'Ef yu kyaahn wash white, yu shudn wear white'*. Dat simply mean seh yu no ready fi be a bride yet."

All dis time Joanie duohn seh a single wod. She jos a watch har granmada a put back di nappy dem into di flour-bag and she a tink bout how she gwaihn go back to school wid dis misery between har leg dem and all di hateful condition weh she ha fi put up wid at school. She certainly not gwaihn pii-pi in a di pit latrine dem weh a stink up di far kaana a di schoolyaad. But is like Miss Maudie read har mind.

"Yu need not worry bout school tomorrow. Yu stayin home until me sure yu kyan hangl yuself. Come we go roun di kitchen and eat somting. Yu kyaahn go to yu bed hungry becausen *wom* wi piss pahn yu *tumok* and kill yu in a yu sleep."

ABOUT A MONT later, Joanie staat di bleedin again but dis time, she know wa fi do. She still hate di process, especially as Miss Maudie forbid har to climb tree or fi run at dat time a di mont. In fak, Miss Maudie forbid har fi do any climbin at all. She tell Joanie dat she will kill di bearin fruit tree dem or ton di fruit sour if she climb dem during har montli. She also tell Joanie dat she shudn baid at dat time of di mont, because she wud get a bad chill. Miss Maudie have so much rule bout dis blasted bleedin dat Joanie beginnin fi wish dat she was baan a bwai. She waahn Joanie fi sponge-dong in a *waam waata* mix wid *Dettol* and when a uol lady dead and Miss Maudie was plannin fi go to di funeral, she mek sure dat Joanie wasn seeing har period before she allow har fi go wid har. Miss Maudie tell di poor pikni dat if she look pahn a dead body at dat time a di mont, she will bleed to death.

At fors, di bwai Jimmy *ton-out* to be a problem too, because him begin fi ask all kaina funny kwestian bout why she duohn waahn fi climb tree and jump over walls. Joanie feel plain fed up and more dan wan time, she feel fi tell him a bad-wod but she duohn waahn no chrobl wid Miss Maudie, not to mention Miss Birdie. But dat bwai more dan a friend because him soon figure out what was going on wid har. Joanie break Miss Maudie rule and tell him how much har period mek har belly hat har and how she hate di pad dem. Jimmy never do a better ting dan go a di Chinese supermarket and use him own pakit moni buy tampon fi Joanie. She ketch har fraid dat Miss Maudie wuda find out and she kudn fi di life of har figure out how fi use dem, so, she hide di bax aanda her bed, but she love him all di more for it.

PLENTY TIMES WHEN Miss Birdie and Reverend Whitehead go out, dem leave Jimmy wid Miss Maudie. Dis is no different from di days when Jimmy faada was a likl bwai. Is true dat dere is no great love between Miss Birdie and Miss Maudie but Miss Maudie tek pride in har job and true to Gaad, she did love Junior and is many a day she still kwestian Gaad as to why di nice-nice bwai dead so bad.

So on dis day, Jimmy a bada-bada Joanie fi climb di star-apple tree fi him. Miss Birdie no low Jimmy fi climb tree. She fraid him jrap-aaf and brok him neck. Jimmy did defy har wan time and climb di tambrin tree in a di cow pasture. Miss Birdie see him up in a di *tree-tap* and she pu-dong wan piece a baalin and tell Jimmy how him wicked because him waahn fi gi har stroke, and is not bad enough dat him pupa dead and gaan lef har, but him waahn fi dead lef har too. From dat, Jimmy no bada climb no more tree because him kyaahn stand fi see him granny cry.

Di tree lean right over di waata-tank, next to di kitchen. Di Leaf dem pahn di tree green pahn wan side and gold pahn di ada and is green skin star-apple di tree bear. Dem grow as big as tennis balls but Miss Maudie always seh di tree mean and if yu want to eat di fruit, you will have to pick it. Di star-apple dem wuda never faal dong pahn di grong di way a ripe mango or a ripe pear wuda jrap. Di tree *tan* jos like some *tight-han* people. It jos tan-up deh a suck up all a di nutrients from di soil, but it naahn leggo notn.

Miss Birdie and The Reverend gaan to Ulster Spring in di Cockpit Country. Dem not expected back until in di afternoon. Joanie well glad because when Miss Birdie not aroun, she breathe freer and even Miss Maudie more easygoing. She usually jos leave di two pikni dem fi roam di prapati. Har wan stipulation was dat dem mos not go beyond di sound of har voice. To mek sure dat dem obey, she come out to di back door a di kitchen, from time to time, and whoop, "Joanieee! Jimiiiiiy!" and so long as di two a dem answer, she was content.

Jimmy staat fling rak-stone pahn di star-apple tree after Joanie refuse fi climb it. She declare in a temper dat she was not about fi tan-up aanda di tree so dat him kuda brok har skull. Him naa pay har no mind, duoh. Him jos a fling stone wid reckless abandon, so Joanie flounce-aaf go lean against di stone wall a di waata tank.

It seem to Joanie dat Jimmy get bored very quickly wid him stone-flingin because him was soon standin in front of har and him a look pahn har funny.

Joanie stare right back pahn him and she see somting in a him yai dem dat mek har self-conscious. Jimmy, in turn, suddenly staat fi laugh and declare even as him waak up closer to har, "Joanie, your eyes are crossed."

She cut har yai dem and seh, "Jos like fi yu two big wan dem."

Him mek fi grab har as him do plenty time before, but as him reach fi har, him han brush har pahn har bres. Joanie freeze and she see Jimmy staat fi ton red from him neck, all di way up to him hairline and when she look in a him yai dem, she see seh him ton fool. Joanie a wanda a wa him a go do nex and she look dong pahn him han weh it still de pahn har ches. When she glance back pahn him, Jimmy put di ada han roun har waist and staat fi kiss har.

Joanie head staat fi spin and suddenly har ches feel like when she run up di hill and duohn stap and she get *shaat a bret*. Jos as she staat fi shove him weh from har, she hear Miss Birdie voice and when she look toward di back door, is none ada dan di lady harself she see tan-up deh, and Miss Birdie staat fi cuss Joanie.

Meantime, Jimmy run to di side a di tank and tup-dong so dat him granny kudn see him. Him haat a race and him blood a bwail in a him head, but him a lisn fi hear wa a go happen. Him hear di hot-wod dem weh Miss Birdie staat fling pahn Joanie and Jimmy cringe from di harshness dat him hear in a him granny voice. Him did waahn jump-up and reprimand har but him did fraid. Instead, him go dong pahn all fours and staat fi crawl weh from di scene, but him no get weh before him hear some a wa Miss Birdie seh to Joanie.

"You are a nasty li'l whore! Just like your mother! Look at the size of you and you already trying to lure Jimmy into sin! Delilah, I rebuke you in the name of Jesus! You will not destroy Jimmy, not as long as I live!"

Jimmy never hear any more a wa Miss Birdie have fi seh to Joanie because him jump-up and tek-aaf at wan speed and him never tap run till him reach him granfaada cow pasture, all di way to the far boundary a di prapati. Him out a bret, him confuse and shame a kill him. Poor soul, him en-up aanda a guinep tree and him hala till him weak because him realize dat him relationship wid Joanie change, fi ever.

shaatn-shorten
waak shaap-walk sharply; walk briskly
bexsaishan-vexation
umanish and force ripe-precocious
help-dong-take down
kaan har rump-corn her rump; beat her bottom
bod weh fly too faas, fly way paas di nes-A bird that flies too fast flies past its nest.
duppy-ghost
duppy pat waata-duppy pot-water; pot-liquor; duppy soup

chrii-foot haas-three-footed horse; legendary three-legged ghost horse known to chase and harm night wanderers. It was believed to be very dangerous because it chased night travelers until they fell down and died of exhaustion. Jamaican legend has it that the only way of escape was to get to a cross-road before it did. The legend may have developed from the cloak or covering used by riders to cover a horse's legs. This cloak could give a horse three-legged appearance.

kraasroad-crossroad

bomp-bump; a rise in the land

Guinea graas-Guinea grass; *Panicum maximum*; clumping type of grass with sharp edges that grows very tall; common fodder for cattle and goats

staak-stalk

dry-head-short, dry, dull-looking hair

lan-up-land(ed) up

malatta daag-mulatto dog

dundus-albino

leda-leather

jrap-dong-drop down; collapse

tik-lip-thick lip

yai-brow-eye brow

naseberry-*Manilkara zapota;* brown colored fruit that looks somewhat like a kiwi fruit but without the hairs on the outside. The fruit is sweet and creamy or grainy when ripe.

piki-piki head-short, dull or very dry hair

faambli-family
wrap-head-religious sects in which both men and women wrap their heads in cloth
guango tree-*Pithicolobium saman*-large, leafy tropical shade tree that grows seed pods that are used in some places as cattle fodder
chonk-trunk
bada-bada-bother-bother (duplication for emphasis)
notn black no good-nothing black is good
cow-baalin-cow bawling; loud unrestrained crying reminiscent of a cow mooing
Joe Reid-A way of indicating how quickly an event occurs
merdaraishan-fierce beating
Henry Stennett-popular Jamaican broadcaster known for his soothing voice
Evening People Show-popular evening program hosted by Stennett
saaf-saada-soft-solder; method of soldering that uses a lower temperature depending on metals being soldered i.e., The Reverend had to cool things down
ben kochi-bend in curtsy; show humility
pan-turkl-pond turtle
outlaa-outlaw
gyas-gas
taiyad-tired
cheesy-smelly like stinky cheese
pyuk-up-puke up; vomit
Krismos-Christmas

badi-come-dong-body come down; hernia; prolapse
tup-dong-stoop down
baid-bathe
belly-batam-belly-bottom; lower abdomen; pelvis
Any bwai chrobl yu a school tideh?-Did any boy trouble (interfere with or molest) you at school today?
gi me a bearin haat-give me a bearing heart; give me strength
jinaraishan-generation
unu waak before unu creep-you walk before you creep; events do not occur in the natural order
fuba-foolish
slobin-slovenly
montli-monthly
nappy-cloth diaper
bird-eye-soft, white cotton cloth with a distinctive pattern used for making diapers
madan-modern
blue soap-blue washing cake soap used for tough laundry jobs
bleachin zinc sheet-a surface, usually made from galvanized zinc sheets, used for bleaching white clothes in the sun
pilikin shit-a pelican's shit which is very white in color
If yu kyaahn wash white, yu shudn wear white-if you can't wash white, you shouldn't wear white
wom-worm
tumok-stomach
waam waata-warm water
Dettol-brand of disinfectant often used in personal hygiene
tree-tap-tree top

tan-stand(s); is; are

tight-han-tight hand; stingy

shaat-a-bret-short of breath

bwail-boil

en-up-ended up

guinep tree-*Melicoccus bijugatus*; tropical fruit bearing tree; the fruit appears in bunches and each fruit has a large seed that is covered by an edible pulp that might be sweet or sour.

CHAPTER 19

Haas deh gyalop but him no know wa him back foot a seh
When the horse is galloping it does not know what its hind legs are doing
We cannot control every outcome and we are sometimes blind to our own weaknesses; we sometimes set an action in motion and lose control of the consequences

Joanie always looked forward to Palm Sunday because of the pageantry. The Reverend often invited one of his brother pastors to be the guest preacher and that meant a special dinner after church. Sunday was Miss Maudie's day off, but on Palm and Easter Sunday, she helped Miss Birdie to entertain.

The men of the church would go deep into the bushes where the exotic palms grew near to running water. Not for them the ordinary coconut palm leaves. Palm Sunday called for the best fan-shaped palms trees that could be pulled through narrow tracks to arrive at the sanctuary, still green and damp with dew. The little fronds were given to the children for waving during that part of the service when they enacted Jesus' arrival upon the borrowed colt. The larger leaves and some of the plants were used to decorate the aisles, doorways and windows of the church.

For Joanie, Palm Sunday seemed exotic in a way that made Jesus foreign and fascinating. He gave orders and got people to obey and to pay homage. This seemed heady stuff to her.

One year, against Miss Birdie's advice, The Reverend agreed with Deacon Swearing to let one of the farmers bring a young donkey's colt to the Palm Sunday service. The colt got away, bolted through the church gate, made off down the graveled road and bound across the main road, into the bushes. The animal all but caused a major accident on the main road and Miss Birdie could not see the humor that had some of the good Baptist church members rolling on the church lawn and laughing themselves away from all sense of the holiness and solemnity.

The green fronds and sorrel-red ginger lilies that decorated the doorways, aisles and windows, plus the rousing sermon brought by the preacher from Ulster Spring, made it possible for Miss Birdie to overcome her anger. However, she did not mince her words that night when she finally had her husband to herself.

On this Palm Sunday, the youth choir sang but Joanie had missed rehearsals and was not allowed to participate. Dawn Swearing trained the youth choir and she was even harder on her charges than Miss Birdie was on the senior choir. Joanie did not regret that she was not sitting with the young people that Sunday, though. Since the Friday before, she had been feeling soiled and unacceptable. Her grandmother's attempt to comfort her on the walk home had only prevented a wound from suppurating but it had not provided the balm of healing that her young heart needed.

It was last Friday afternoon that she had been accused of being a whore. That was the second time that this awful and mysterious word had been hurled at her. It had lacerated her soul like hot oil sizzling on bare skin and, on the walk home, she finally gathered the strands of her courage and asked her grandmother what the word meant.

Miss Maudie chupsed her teeth loudly and answered, "A whore is di *dotiess* kaina uman dere is. A whore is dem kaina gyal yu si dress up pahn pay-day and go a *Ochi Raiyas* go ketch sailor man. Dem pretty like money but hab no *kyarakta*. Yu will neba be a whore, mi chail, and Birdie Whitehead better tank har lucky stars dat I am saved. Ef it was in days when me a *chok badnis*, A bax har dong same place weh she tan-up!"

Joanie thought she heard tears in her grandmother's voice as the two of them continued to descend the hill from the church house toward the gate. When they got to the graveyard, Miss Maudie pointed to her right at the marble tomb that stood like a frozen sentinel, above the other graves.

"Dat bwai dat bury aanda di dirt was di nicest pikni anybody kuda have, bar none. Me often wanda if Maasa Gaad tek him becausen Birdie so dyam wicked. Him ton Rasta and wud not go into dat church if you pay him. Me oftintimes ax miself, how dem a preach Jesus and di pikini ton gainst *ebriting* wa dem stan fa. But me tellin yu mi chail, is dat dyam, black, *kuru-kuru* Birdie."

Joanie was too overwhelmed to respond to her grandmother and in the torrent of her passionate discourse, Miss Maudie did not seem to require a response. By this time, Joanie knew from the increasing tremor in Miss Maudie's voice, that she was crying. She turned slightly and pushed Joanie ahead of her and they crossed the main road to the track pass.

They were walking in darkness now and Miss Maudie pulled a flashlight from the basket that she held without support on her head. The basket contained Joanie's school uniforms that Miss Maudie had ironed on Miss Birdie's time and with her electricity. In her left hand, she carried a *shut-pan* that contained the leavings of the dinner table. She would throw these scraps into her fowl pen in the morning for her laying hens and the one brightly plumed hybrid Dominica cock that ruled the roost.

Miss Maudie continued to talk with bitterness about the various ways in which Birdie Whitehead had affronted her. "Dat uman yu see dere, she duohn like nobadi but har fambili and har fren dem. Nobadi to har like dem. Is same so she treat Jimmy mada bad and from di time dem kill Junior, nobadi no see har. She run weh, ongl Gaad knows where. But mek me tell yu sinting, Jimmy no better dan yu!"

Miss Maudie stopped in her tracks, took the basket off her head and put it down upon the ground. She then spun Joanie around and spoke with such force that she could feel her grandmother's spit sprinkle her face and she ducked her head.

"Mek mi tell yu sinting, none a dem no better dan yu! Yu hear me! As Gaad mek Moses, dem no mek outa flesh and yu mek outa dirt. All a we mek outa di same dirt and dat is why Christ had was to die. Yu hear me! Jimmy muma was a bare-foot, half-coolie gyal from Westmoreland. No better dan Madge who birt yu and moreover, fi yu pupa white and even duoh Madge neba tell me who him be, mi mind tell me seh him *come aaf a good table*, becausen yu hab quality in a yu. Tanks be to Gaad and Michael Manley, no *baastad* no deh again. Yu kyan grow up and ton smadi. You no whore and ef yu and Jimmy hab *pashan* fi each ada, jos wait pahn time and creep before yu waak. *Secret in a Mento but is to dance it. Jankro seh so lang as Gaad is alive, him naa nyam Guinea graas. Chikin-haak kudn wait pahn Gaad and dat is why him foot faasn.* Yu wait pahn *Big Maasa* mi pikni and di same man dat ton waata into wine, will deliver yu. A no tideh mi two *pla-plam-plam* foot dem a waak pahn doti and Gaad no let mi dong yet.

Me notice lang time seh Birdie Whitehead no *lob* yu and me know yu no do har notn. Is Dawn Swearing *es-a-spade*, Genevieve, she hab lob fa, but mek dem tan deh a *wies powder pahn black-bod*. She might a kyan *spiiki-spuoki* like Birdie, but she no better dan yu, and at least yu know a who a yu muma.

Birdie Whitehead a no nobadi. She come fram di obeah wokin parish a St. Elizabeth and a tie she and har doti muma tie Revren. Har muma was a *Maroon* uman and she did hab wolheap a hair pahn har head and har two yai dem did red like blood. A kudn bear fi look pahn har."

Joanie was shocked and confused by Miss Maudie's pronouncements but knew that she was not expected to respond. In fact, had she dared to interject a comment, Miss Maudie would have lost no time in beating her for getting into big people argument.

Miss Maudie picked up her basket and placed it upon her head. Next, she picked up her shut-pan and Joanie marveled that she was able to do this without the basket slipping from off her head. Miss Maudie then turned her flashlight in front of her and Joanie saw the track open up ahead. They started to walk again and to her shock and horror, her grandmother started to cry in earnest. She sounded like how Joanie felt whenever she got a beating that was undeserved.

JOANIE SAT THROUGH that Palm Sunday service but experienced none of her customary joy. Too many things had changed since her first period. She no longer felt comfortable in her own skin and now she was in big trouble with Miss Birdie and it was not she who had kissed Jimmy. Jimmy was the one who lost his head and all but assaulted her with his tongue. She hadn't even liked the encounter that much but she was still curious about what madness had taken hold of him and caused him to look at her as he had never done before.

She did not want to go back up to that house on the hill but she could not yet choose. Miss Maudie would not allow her to stay home alone after school and when she begged to stay with Uncle Byron, Miss Maudie's face tightened and her voice hardened when she responded. "Yu young and yu duohn know a dyam ting bout mankain. Yu tink me gwaihn leave yu in di house wid Byron?" Miss Maudie hissed her teeth and became silent.

Joanie wanted to argue with Miss Maudie but she held her tongue. She knew that Uncle Byron did not much care for her and suspected that it had something do with Miss Maudie and her mother, Madge. However, she would have preferred Byron's indifference to Miss Birdie's dislike.

Joanie went through the motions of participating in the Sunday service but her mind quickly shifted back to the brewing storm that had settled over the household since Miss Birdie called her out of her name. Miss Maudie had obviously heard when Miss Birdie used the derogatory words and quickly ran out of the kitchen into the backyard where Miss Birdie stood with her arms akimbo on a little rise above the water tank. Joanie was leaning against the tank with her arms folded behind her. Jimmy was nowhere in sight.

Miss Maudie yelled, "Come Joanie! Me waahn di likl wok but me naa tan ya aada dem ya *libati* ya!"

Miss Birdie turned on her heel, strode past Miss Maudie and marched back into the kitchen. What followed was a slamming of cupboard doors and Joanie soon heard raised voices. Miss Maudie then marched back out of the kitchen door and gestured to Joanie to follow her.

Her grandmother gripped her hand so hard as the two of them went sailing off the hill that Joanie had trouble keeping her feet on the ground. By the time they got to the gate, The Reverend had caught up to them in the car. He began to plead with Miss Maudie to get in but it was not until he reminded her that they were brother and sister in the Lord and should not bring the church into disrepute, that Miss Maudie opened the back door of the car. She shoved Joanie in with such force that she almost crashed into the opposite door. When Miss Maudie got in, she slammed the car door with equal force and Joanie saw The Reverend wince. He did not speak, however, and reversed the car and drove them back up the hill.

When they got to the manse, Reverend Whitehead took both Joanie and Miss Maudie to his study and offered heartfelt apology for his wife's behavior. Miss Birdie remained out of sight for the rest of the afternoon but the household was treated to an unsolicited piano recital from the living room. The lady of the house played the piano keys as if she wanted to throw blows. She never apologized to Joanie or to Miss Maudie.

WHEN THE CHURCH service ended, Joanie remained in her seat and watched the teenagers file down the aisle from the platform and out the front door of the church. The day was bright and warm but without the stifling heat that would arrive with summer.

Joanie sat with her shoulders hunched, chewed the tip of her right pinky finger and watched the back of Jimmy's head as he walked at the rear of the line. Genevieve Swearing marched in front of him. He had glanced briefly at her when he passed, long enough for her to see the shame in his eyes behind the wire framed prescription glasses that he had lately started to wear.

Her eyes followed him to the door where she saw Genevieve prod him to get his attention. He leaned toward her and she whispered something in his ear. When they both convulsed into giggles, Joanie jumped up and hurried through the side door that led down a passageway to a rear exit of the church.

Joanie lingered about the backyard of the church building until she was sure that Jimmy had left and then she walked downhill and turned through the side gate and into the yard of the manse. There were three cars parked on the grass below the verandah. She recognized the tan-colored *Peugeot* that belonged to Reverend Whitehead as well as the new *Honda Accord* that was owned by the Swearings. She guessed that the slightly battered station wagon belonged to the guest preacher. Joanie figured that Miss Maudie would need her help in the kitchen and headed for the back door.

In a few minutes, Miss Maudie sent her into the dining with a tray of glasses. She stood briefly in the doorway between the dining-room and the kitchen and Miss Birdie impatiently spoke from her seat at the foot of the formal dining table.

"Are you going to just stand there? Put the tray on the buffet and go back for the broth! Don't know what Maudie is going to do with you."

Joanie heard the glasses rattle as she all but dropped the tray on to the buffet. She turned and fled the room but not before she saw Genevieve Swearing sitting at the table, next to Jimmy.

Miss Maudie grabbed her arm as she ran past her but Joanie tugged it away and dashed through the open back door. She was blinded by hot tears as she made for the pasture at the back of the manse.

IT WAS AFTER Communion Sunday, one week later, and Joanie was hurrying toward the church gate. She heard Jimmy call her name but did not turn around. Instead, she walked faster and soon heard the sound of running feet behind her. She started to run down the hill toward the short-cut that would take her through the bush to her home, but Jimmy quickly caught up with her and grabbed her right arm.

She stopped in her track and he spun her around so quickly that her body came up against his. He was breathing hard and his eyes behind the glasses seemed both animated and ashamed.

"Where you runnin to so fast? You have a pot on the fire or something?"

"See here Jimmy, *no bada mi peace* because me no able fi yuh granny. She done kaal me whore aredi."

"Look here Joanie, Mama can't stop me from talking to you and furthermore, we are Christians and we not supposed to keep malice."

He said the latter slyly, his eyes never leaving her face. Joanie turned away and continued walking. Jimmy kept so close behind her that Joanie turned to face him again. The track was narrow and the green foliage surrounding them made her suddenly feel like they were alone in an enclosed world that was all their own. She wondered if he was going to kiss her again. A part of her grew excited at the prospect but she quickly grew afraid.

"I am going home wid you today and I want to see if you so mean that you wouldn't give me a likl bit a yu Sunday dinner."

"Jimmy, yu crazy? Yu waahn Miss Birdie fi run weh mi granny?"

"Mama can't fire Miss Maudie unless Daddy say so and Daddy prefer Miss Maudie Saturday soup to Mama own. Him not crazy enough to fire her and end up having to drink Mama soup. Him say it taste like cow drench."

Joanie tried to keep a straight face but she could feel the laughter rising up to her chest and before she exploded, she turned and started running again. She heard his steps behind her and started sprinting in earnest.

Jimmy did not manage to overtake her until she arrived at her gate and she stopped to see what he would do. He ran past her and dashed up the concrete steps to the verandah.

Joanie stood below in the yard and watched as Jimmy looked around him, seemingly uncertain of his next move. She sensed that he had acted impulsively and he was overtaken by bravado but she would not put him at ease. Young as she was, she knew that she was in competition with Genevieve Swearing for Jimmy's heart. He would have to choose and he had taken a step in her direction by daring to follow her home but she was sure that once he got home, he would tell neither his grandmother nor Genevieve where he had been. This thought made her suddenly very angry and for a split second she considered picking up some stones and pelting him right there where he stood on her grandmother's verandah.

Miss Maudie soon came out with a tea towel in her hand and she seemed surprised, shocked even, to see Jimmy standing at her front door. "Is what breeze blow yu here, Jimmy? Miss Birdie sen yu fi me?"

"No ma'am. A miss yu cooking so A come for a likl Sunday dinner."

Miss Maudie began to bristle with pleasure but her expression quickly changed and she asked with real concern, "Miss Birdie and Reverend know you down here?"

"No ma'am. A leave straight from church. A didn't go home or anything."

"Well, mi dear son-son, much as I would like you to stay and eat wid we, you need to go home. A duohn waahn no problems in mi uol age."

Joanie walked up the steps as he was coming down and noted with some confusion that he seemed crestfallen as he passed her. She looked up to the doorway when her grandmother spoke from inside the darkened living room.

"Huol-aan a likl, Jimmy. Joanie give him dis."

She turned back down the steps and handed Jimmy a foil wrapped package that was still warm. Joanie knew that it was toto and that Jimmy would eat it all before he got home.

He took the package from her, pinched her arm and ran off. She stood out in the yard, rubbing the spot where he had almost broken her skin and watched him as he grew smaller and smaller in the distance. That boy was a mystery and a test and she was certain that if he continued to behave in this strange fashion, she would surely hit him with a stone.

dotiess-dirtiest

Ochi Raiyas-Ocho Rios; North Coast town and tourist destination

kyarakta-character

chok badnis-behave in a disorderly, confrontational or lawless fashion

ebriting-everything

kuru-kuru-coarse; rough; bumpy

shut-pan-shuttered can such as paint can; often used as food carrier by farmers and other workers

come aaf a good table-of a good background or breeding

baastad-bastard

pashan-passion

secret in a mento but is to dance it-The Mento dance contains secrets that are known only to the dancers; there is more to a situation than meets the eye.

Jankro seh so lang as Gaad is a alive, him naa nyam Guinea graas. Chikin-haak kudn wait pahn Gaad and dat is why him foot faasn-The turkey buzzard has declared that as long as God is alive it will not be forced to eat grass (God will provide). In the past, boys would stick chicken feathers into a green calabash and hawks would mistake the gourd for a fat chicken. Once the bird flew down and sank its claws into the gourd, it would be unable to fly away and because its claws were fastened, it would be captured.

big maasa-big master; God

pla-plam-plam-sound of bare feet hitting the ground

es-a-spade-the ace of spades; derogatory term used for a person dark skin

wies powder pahn black bod-waste powder on a black bird; engage in a futile task

spiiki spuoki-speak in an exaggeratedly correct way

Maroon-descendant of runaway African slaves who fought in Jamaica and won their independence from the British colonial government

libati-liberty

no bada mi peace-do not bother or disturb my peace

CHAPTER 20

Joan Marie Jackman and James John Whitehead III

2003

Wa sweet di goat mout go sour in he
bam-bam
What is sweet in the goat's mouth will be
sour in its anus

Trinidadian Proverb

White-belly rat bite and blow
The white-bellied rat blows upon the wound
(anesthetic effect) while it is biting.
Some people are extremely deceptive

Jamaican proverb

Monkey see he seed swell and tink he a ton man, but a gourdie he got
The monkey's scrotum is swollen and he thinks it is a sign of maturity but it is a sign that he has a hernia
We often misread the signs

Guyanese proverb

James John Whitehead, the third, was on the road to Timnath and his Delilah was giving him more pleasure than he could endure. He was locked in her arms, breathing short and washed by the waves of pleasure that radiated from his loins to the tips of his curled toes. He could not think and on a distant shore, he saw fragmented images of his grandmother and his fiancée but they dissolved with each tremor of pleasure that rolled from the crown of his curly cap to the end of his spine.

He came to a sobbing crescendo and fell upon her heaving breasts. She was wet and smelled of flesh and some unknown flowery perfume. He rolled on to his back and saw sunlight wink through a tiny crack in the unsealed roof and he turned and looked at the face that was too close to his.

Joanie's gray eyes were grave and there was pain in their depths. He knew he had just taken what she had withheld from all other men and as the realization sank in, sadness washed over him.

What shamed James John Whitehead was that he had just acted like scum and he was anything but scum. The very act he had committed had been a betrayal because even as he spilled his seed into Joan Jackman's womb, his heart was already rejecting her.

His grandmother's words rang in his ears, "Licky-licky and yu wi soon bite-i."

Yes Mama, he thought, I have bitten it and the taste is bitter. As his thoughts continued to accuse him, he got up from the bed with his grandmother's voice ringing in his head.

So many times she had warned him that he had been born for better things and that when his father was killed and his life was spared, God had singled him out for a special purpose. So easily could he have been slaughtered on that night in 1980 when his father, James John, the second, had been shot to death in Kingston, but God had prevented his life from being snuffed out. Not for him, therefore, the casual couplings of the canefield or the sweaty weekend dances where men and women dubbed themselves to senseless oblivion to the tune of Reggae music and the mind bending smoke of ganja weed. He was James John Whitehead, the third, and that meant something.

As Jimmy pondered these things, he made his way to the bathroom. Once inside, he turned on the shower and opened the high window to the corridor of the student cottages. A few fellow seminarians were up and about but Jimmy had no real interest in what was taking place outside his window. He stepped under the forceful blast of the water.

Although the water was cold he did not shrink from its icy spanking. He needed its harsh castigation so that he would quickly return to the fold of fleshly restraint.

So he washed himself and as he scrubbed his body with stiffened fingers, he began to pray. The water poured over his head and he begged God to wash his guilt away, still the riot in his head and rid him of his unbearable shame.

Then as he washed his neck and armpits, he stood with upraised hands under the merciless blast of the water and whispered David's prayer, "Have mercy upon me, O God, according to thy loving-kindness: according unto the multitude of thy tender mercies, blot out my transgressions…"

Next, he washed his back, his chest, and then his feet. When there was nowhere else to wash, he brought the cloth to his loins. He wiped swiftly and examined the washcloth but there was nothing visually there to remind him of his sins. The washcloth, a light yellow, was streaked with soap suds and he thought he could smell her there. He brought the washcloth up to his nose and the odor of caustic soda, freshly killed meat and lavender oil filled his lungs.

He turned himself to the pounding water and closed his mind to the pain in his most private place. He would beat himself there and the pain would mark him deeply so that he would train himself to always remember his fall from grace as a time of agony.

Jimmy stayed in the cloistered shelter of the bathroom for a very long time. He brushed his teeth, cut his nails and even combed his eyebrows. And all the while he waited for the sound of his front door to signal that Joanie had departed.

When Jimmy finally emerged from the bathroom, Joanie was sitting at his desk and staring through the window. He glanced over at the bed and saw that she had changed the sheets. This was so like her, so casually intrusive. To her mind, there was nothing outrageous about opening his drawers and pawing through his personal belongings as if they were her own.

He knew that she was waiting for some word of affirmation but he could not give them. She wanted him to say that the sex had changed his mind about their relationship but he would not tell her what was not true. He could feel her eyes upon him but he settled into silence as he searched for his underwear.

After stirring through T-shirts and boxer shorts, he found a pair of black briefs. He thought of going back to the bathroom to put them on but then he recalled what they had done. He sucked his teeth, let his towel fall to the floor and stepped into his underwear. He knew that she was staring at him but he refused to even glance at her. He hoped that his silence would cause her to leave, but as he pulled on a pair of jeans and a scarlet T-shirt, and bent to tie the laces of his sneakers, she spoke.

"Aren't you going to say something?"

"What you want me to say, Joanie?"

He kept his eyes averted and continued to tie his laces.

"Say something, anything, cause you making me nervous."

"I am making you nervous?"

"Yes, you are."

"Is there anything you can do about it?"

"What yu mean?"

"There are many other places you could be, you know. If my presence is such a bother to you, you don't have to put up with me."

The cold, precise diction that passed between them was proof that something had changed and as if they both sensed the chasm opening between them, they reached for the language of formality to test each other.

"Are you saying that you want me to leave?'

Jimmy kept his voice very low as he responded to Joanie.

"What do you think?"

"Why you goin on so, Jimmy?

He pulled out his other chair from his desk and sat with his back turned toward her.

"I don't want to treat you bad but you are making this very hard for me."

"Me? Me making things hard for you! How do you think I feel after all of this?"

"Knowing you, you're probably very happy."

"Happy? Why you think so?

He turned to face her before replying. "Because you wanted it! But don't think that a little sex between us is going to make me leave Genevieve. I warn you all the time about coming over here so early in the morning and now look what happen! You think I feel good to know that I break a vow I made to God?"

She folded her arms across her breasts and fixed him with a gaze of such complete hatred that he was forced to look away from her. He heard her begin to sniffle and he lost his cool. Jimmy got up and walked out of the room.

He had no plans about where he would go but he had to get away from Joanie and he had to settle his turbulent emotions. She was killing him with shame and he wanted to cry and throw things.

He took long strides along the corridor outside his cottage, jumped from the concrete walkway, ducked under clotheslines and crossed the still damp lawn.

An old commuter bus rumbled past. Cars whizzed around it as it halted at the bus stop on the other side of the road. If Jimmy ran he could catch the bus at the top gate. The thought was barely settled in his mind when he realized that he had left his wallet in his room. He hissed his teeth and continued walking toward the main road that led to Papine.

As he continued up the gentle hill, he passed one block of Irvine Hall on the main campus of the University on his left and the campus residences of the seminary lecturers on his right, but he did not really see any of these things. He was thinking of Genevieve and his grandparents and he was trying not to think about Joanie.

James and Birdie Whitehead were the only parents he had ever known because his father lay buried under a marble tombstone in the Chalky Hill Baptist Church cemetery. His mother had disappeared shortly after his father was killed and he had never set eyes upon her. Through his great-uncle,

Nathan, he had recently established contact with her but this was not information he felt he could share with his grandparents. His grandfather, perhaps, but Miss Birdie had never forgiven Audrie Matthews for being the love of her son's life. She was not the kind of girl she had expected Junior to bring home and she never tired of saying that if her son had married a good Baptist girl, she would have eventually persuaded him to bow to his true calling.

He, however, had brought home the good Baptist girl. Or rather, Miss Birdie had chosen for him, but at the rate at which things were going, Joanie was about to mash-up all of his well laid plans.

Jimmy got to Papine, crossed the busy roadway and headed down Old Hope Road. When he reached the gate of the Hope Botanical Gardens, he made the right turn through the iron gates and walked into the shelter of a tall poinciana tree. The concrete seat wedged against the trunk was still damp from the dew but he sat and settled his forehead in the palm of his hand as if his head was too heavy for his neck.

His grandmother had not hidden her stick and hit him. In her words, she had not pushed him without showing him where to fall. She had told him in plain language that Joanie Jackman was not for him even though they had been playmates. She went as far as to let him know that they all would be equal in heaven but they were not equal on earth. It didn't matter that Michael Manley had preached Democratic Socialism in the 70s and turned the whole society upon its head. Joanie would never be his equal because she was born to the hired help and he was born to the manse. It did not matter that his mother, Audrie Matthews, was little more than a barefooted peasant when she gave birth to him. It did not matter that he and Joanie were both products of illegitimacy; their destinies were not identical. He was their grandson and the one chosen to take over the ministry. His wife would be specially chosen and she too would have the call of God upon her life.

Miss Birdie and Reverend Whitehead gave Jimmy the talk after he was caught kissing Joanie in the backyard.

That night after the kissing incident, Miss Birdie and The Reverend called Jimmy into the study and there among the theological tomes and Baptist journals, they gave him the talk that changed the course of his life.

They made him sit on one side of the rectangular wooden table while they sat close together on the other side. It was his grandfather who began.

"Jimmy, do you understand that you are chosen?"

He nodded solemnly and Miss Birdie corrected him sternly.

"Speak up and do not nod your head. You are not speaking to one of your playmates!"

"Yes sir."

He bowed his head again and began to chew his bottom lip.

"I want you to look at me when I am talking to you."

To Jimmy's surprise, his grandfather sounded sad rather than angry.

"You were caught kissing Joanie today."

Jimmy lowered his head and made no answer.

"This is a very serious matter and if you continue to indulge the urges of your flesh, you will throw away your whole life. I am sending you to the books of *Samuel* in the Holy Bible and I want you to learn about King David. There you will see a whole kingdom destroyed because David gave in to his flesh."

He emerged from the study tearful and ashamed but with a new awareness of his call to duty. As the grandson of the Baptist preacher, he was expected to walk circumspectly and set an example for the village to follow. After all, these people were less than two hundred years removed from slavery and too many of them were still chained by the poverty and ignorance that made it impossible for them to rise above the demands of the belly.

Not for him, therefore, the youthful rebellion of ganja weed and cigarettes. Not for him the Friday night dances held behind the zinc fence where the reggae music pulsed, the disc jockey rhymed over the tracks and young men and women danced themselves into mindless frenzy. That kind of carrying-on was for hooligans.

His grandmother told him that if people from society churches, where they held mass and said the *Apostle's Creed*, felt it was all right to dance and jig on Saturday night and then handle the holy emblems on Sunday morning, that was their business, but that was not for him. He was called to higher things and the mark was already upon him. He was a Baptist and Baptists took God at His word. They believed theology had its place but for them, holy writ held preeminence and they didn't hold with too much exegesis. Just enough to make it plain.

Jimmy knew that his grandmother was throwing words at the Anglican church members in the district because they played secular music at their fundraisers and confirmed sinners who made no pretence to repentance. He also understood that she was stating plainly that as the fatherless child of a former whore, Joanie had no place in his future. Her history and background did not make her suitable for the life of the manse. She had told him before that if he got tangled up with her, he would spend the rest of his days doling out charity to her worthless relatives.

Three weeks after that talk, his grandfather invited him to ride with him to Brown's Town. The Reverend was going to visit his favored older brother, Nathan. That drive up the winding roads of Trelawny to St. Ann was forever seared into Jimmy's memory. His grandfather talked to him for the first time as an equal and shared with him how he came into the world as a result of a sexual assault. There in the close quarters of that car, his grandfather told Jimmy about the shame of bastardy, the pain of watching his mother fade away, the saving grace of his grandparents and The Reverend Cyrano Webster.

They stopped in Stewart Town to visit with family friends and on the way back to the car, Reverend Whitehead made Jimmy promise him that he would never ever commit the sin of fornication and ruin a woman as his mother had been destroyed.

Miss Birdie soon saw to it that Genevieve Swearing became a regular guest at Sunday dinner. Jimmy knew enough about his grandmother to understand that Genevieve was the girl that she wanted for him. At first he was sullen and resentful. However, as time passed, he grew used to her presence at Sunday dinner and came to like her dancing eyes, dimpled cheeks and ready smile.

When Jimmy's mind settled upon Genevieve, his eyes filled with tears and as they splashed the gray ground, he wiped his running nose with the back of his hand. He loved her so and now he had betrayed her. He felt like he had let everyone down and a feeling of worthlessness settled on the inside of him. He had not only cheated on Genevieve. He had given in to lust, slept with Joanie and then turned on her. And it wasn't as if he did not know that she loved him.

Many of his friends at the seminary often teased him about his odd friendship with Joanie. Some were even jealous of their closeness because Joanie was the kind of woman prized by many black men. She was beautiful, shapely, educated and near-white. Together, she and Jimmy seemed like a natural fit and he was often questioned about their closeness.

They had talked about her feelings many times and he considered her his best friend on earth. They had been inseparable since grade one when he rescued her from a pack of schoolyard bullies but he was not in love with her. She was the one he would ask to be godmother to his children and witness his last will and testament, but she did not make his heart race the way Genevieve did. That was what he told himself as he sat in contemplation.

No friend would have said the words he spat at her that morning and it was not the first time that he had let her down. That time, long ago, when his grandmother had called her a whore, he had run away without defending her.

Jimmy got up from the hard bench and crossed the damp lawn back to the main road. He promised himself that he would find Joanie before the day was done and he would beg her forgiveness for taking her virginity and then abusing her. But he would also tell her that they would have to stop spending time alone. He could not afford a repeat of that morning. He should not have let her into his room when she came knocking and he should not have held her when she started crying about his upcoming wedding.

With this firmly resolved, he wiped his eyes with the back of his hand and crossed the road.

CHAPTER 21

Uol figl play new chuun
An old fiddle can play a new tune
People sometimes change their minds or act out of character
Koni better dan chrang
It is better to be cunning than to be strong
Buy beef yu buy bone, buy lan yu buy rak-stuon
When you buy beef, you also buy the bones and when you buy land, you also buy the stones
An action comes with consequence; you have to take the bitter with the sweet
Dis a ongl di *gri-gri*; di *gra-gra* deh behain
This is only the beginning; there is worse to come

Joanie lay in the middle of her bed and stared at the ceiling. She was so sad that she felt disconnected from her body. She wriggled her toes and stiffened her calves while trying to get a hold of herself. Her thoughts were rolling around in her head like loose change and her body felt beaten and bruised.

Outside her window, she could hear the sound of the traffic on Mona Road. Closer to her, she could hear the dry rattle of a branch hitting the roof each time the huge jacaranda tree outside dipped its branches as it groaned in the wind.

Joanie really hated herself sometimes because of her inability to get past Jimmy Whitehead. As far back as she could remember, he had been a constant in her life and she could not wrap her mind around the idea that someday soon, he would marry Genny Swearing and be removed from her. That was how she saw it. His marriage would mean his removal from her life. She did not like Genevieve Swearing, so, she could not imagine herself as part of a cozy threesome.

Miss Birdie had succeeded in getting Jimmy to choose Genevieve and they were to be married at the end of the year. How well she recalled the buzz in Chalky Hill when the engagement was announced. It created a stir because it was an uncommon event. Who had ever got engaged in Chalky Hill before? When Miss Birdie and The Reverend moved there, they were already married and over the years, almost all of the couples who stood at the altar, did so either out of fear of hell and damnation or to spare their children from the stigma of bastardy.

Genevieve Swearing's engagement to Jimmy had been an event of another kind and even though Joanie had not gone to the ceremony and dinner at the church hall, Miss Maudie had given her all of the details. She heard how Mrs. Swearing cried and how Deacon Swearing almost wrung Jimmy's arm from the shoulder, so overcome was he with joy that his daughter had been chosen.

Joanie continued to think about the events of the morning and shame was soon replaced by anger. Jimmy loved her. How could he not? How could he fail to be drawn to her devotion to him? After all, they had been friends since they were six years old. How could he even think of parting from her? How could he want to be held in Genevieve's pudgy, black arms when her slender, pale ones were so willing to embrace him?

She rolled over on to her stomach, buried her face in her pillow and began to sob. She did not know when she fell asleep.

The sound of a buzzing insect jerked Joanie from her troubled sleep and when she rolled on to her side, she saw the giant fly, the kind that Miss Maudie called a *maggich fly.* It was perched on the sugary crust of a half-eaten sugar bun on her desk.

Joanie watched in fascination as the creature hopped around the pastry and began to flick its vulgar proboscis beneath its red, obscene eyes. Joanie knew in an instant that she was going to kill it. She just had to remain cool, though. She had to know just when to lift a folded magazine and flatten the thieving bastard.

Mos be a dyam man-fly because only a male would be so brazen but she was gwaihn fix him business. It would be slyness against bravado and just when it felt that it was enjoying peace and safety, it would be destroyed.

The little bugger had flown into her room without so much as, “May I?” but she was gwaihn restructure him blouse and before him digest di fos bite, she was gwaihn liquidate all a him asset dem. Yes man, she was gwaihn sen him to him maker.

She cautiously raised the folded magazine and was set to bring it down in one swift stroke when she heard the rapping at her door. She knew who it was and her chest tightened and her heart began to race. She was not sure that she wanted to see him so soon after the morning’s bruising events. If he was there to apologize, she would probably let him in. However, if he was there on any other business, he could go straight to hell.

Rap! Rap! Rap!

“Who is it and what do you want?”

Joanie made her voice cold and unwelcoming with the hope that Jimmy could be shamed into contrition.

Without responding he knocked once more and she felt her anger change to the desire for revenge. She wanted him to wriggle in embarrassment while all the occupants of the rooms along the corridor heard him at her door. There were enough of them who knew Genevieve Swearing and would not mind informing her that they had heard her fiancé begging for entry to her bedroom. The son-of-a-bitch, let him squirm a little bit. Let him feel as small as he had made her feel this morning.

"It's Jimmy and I want to talk to you."

"Well me no waahn taak to yu! *Gu-weh*!"

Jimmy raised his voice and knocked upon Joanie's door, again. "Hey Joanie, I want to talk to you and I am not going anywhere!"

At least he called her by name. Earlier, he had behaved as if the very sight of her caused him pain. Mek him tan-up out deh a *mek naiz* till smadi go kaal security pahn him. Uol jankro.

Just then, the fly buzzed past her ear and she made an instinctive back-handed swipe with the magazine. She heard the semi-hard click of insect meeting glossy print and grimaced with satisfaction when the nasty little boll of black fuzz hit the curtain, fell to the floor and remained, unmoving.

Good, and would to God that all of her problems were as easily resolved. She picked up the dead fly with a bit of tissue paper and dropped it into the garbage bin. Jimmy was still knocking but she did not answer.

He adopted a cajoling tone. "Joanie, I know you are in there and I am going to stand out here for as long as it takes to get you to open the door."

Well, mek him tan-up out deh a knock till wan a Genevieve big-mout fren dem sen go tell har a farin how dem see him outa har door a beg fi she let him in. See how she wuda feel, di fat, black, nak-nii bitch.

Joanie felt very certain that Jimmy had passed her over because of Miss Birdie. If she lived to be a hundred, she would never like Birdie Whitehead. That woman acted as if her piss was champagne and for all the years that she had walked up the hill to the manse with Miss Maudie, she had never once felt her welcome.

After the incident behind the water tank, she vowed never to go back there, but Miss Maudie refused to let her stay home alone. Until she graduated from high school and started to attend university, she continued to go up to the manse after school. She mostly sat in the kitchen with her grandmother or, walked about the church property, but she took great care to avoid both The Reverend and Miss Birdie. Joanie still talked to Jimmy at school but at the manse, she stayed out of his way as much as possible. He avoided her too and no longer hung around the kitchen to tease her and chit-chat with Miss Maudie, as he used to do, before the kiss.

Joanie grew more withdrawn over the years but Miss Maudie did not mind that she chose to keep to herself rather than seek the friendship of others. She saw this as a sign of her granddaughter's superiority and often proudly told anyone who would listen that Joanie did not like to mix.

As Joanie sat on the edge of her bed and waited for Jimmy to knock again, she remembered the day when Miss Birdie gave her the stick deodorant and told her that she needed to use it every day if she wanted to come into her presence.

It was a few days after she learned that she had passed the Common Entrance Examination. She remembered it well because she was hot and achy from cramps and all too aware of the bulky pad between her legs. She felt ashamed as if she had an affliction that everybody knew about but nobody would mention.

Joanie walked by Miss Birdie as she helped her grandmother to clear the table after dinner. She was also thinking about her future and the prospect of going to high school and wondering what lay ahead. Her thoughts soon drifted to wondering how she was going to go to school if she had this bleeding coming as often as Miss Maudie had informed her. She leaned across the dining table to clutch the soup tureen and Miss Birdie recoiled and sniffed loudly. She had no idea what she had done to offend her but she was soon to know.

Later, Joanie stood at the kitchen counter drying dishes when Miss Birdie walked into the kitchen and plunked down a stick deodorant upon the counter, next to her.

"Here, take this because it is clear that Maudie does not intend to teach you these things. You are growing into a young lady and it is important for you not only to look good, but to smell good too."

Miss Maudie walked in during Miss Birdie's remarks and from the tightness of her jaw, Joanie knew that her grandmother was offended. However, she kept her voice neutral when she said, "A tank you fi yu kainness, Miss Birdie."

That night as they walked down the hill together, her grandmother told her not to pay too much attention to Miss Birdie because, thanks to Michael Manley, equality had come to Jamaican society and people like Birdie Whitehead had been unseated from their high horse. Birdie Whitehead could say anything that she wanted in the privacy of her kitchen, but free education meant that finally the children of the help could sit in the same classroom and study from the same books as the children of the haves.

Jimmy knocked once more but Joanie did not answer because her mind was still playing over that morning's events and she was beginning to be disgusted with herself. Up until then, she had believed that when she finally gave up her virginity, the moment would have been special and full of tenderness. Nothing had prepared her for the brutality of the encounter. Just that morning, Jimmy had plundered her like a ripened field. He had bulldozed his way thoughtlessly through her like she was nothing more than a hurdle to be overcome, but she had no one to blame but herself.

Now the dyam crow bait tan-up outside har door and a taak in a him parson voice. Wud to Gaad she kuda tomp him in a him blaasid face.

At that moment she hated the green-eyed bastard with such concentrated rage that her heart felt weighted. Joanie sat trembling on the edge of her bed and did not realize that she had bitten through her lip until she tasted the raw saltiness of her own blood.

"Joanie, open the door and talk to me because I am not going anywhere until you do."

Just then, Joanie heard a chorus of male laughter from the grassy center of the block of buildings. She heard one say, "Hey, wait a minute, look like parson come to preach."

She listened from behind her closed door and recognized the growling bass voice of a Trinidadian who had been pursuing her from her first year at the university.

"Hey Parson, you could just quit while you ahead cause Joan Jackman ain't kind. You could preach like Paul but you ain't getting nothing. Parson, I been down on my hands and knees and that girl kick me over."

There was more ribald laughter and she knew that they were prepared to rag Jimmy just for the fun of watching him squirm. She also knew that they were out for blood. There was nothing these men liked more than to catch a theological student chasing tail.

Inside the room, Joanie sat listening to the men and began to feel a new line of anger. Her antipathy was directed at the Trinidadian. He had told her in her first semester that because of her refusal to sleep with him, she had caused him to break his record of the past four years. He claimed that with the exception of her, he had always been the first man on the hall of residence to bed the prettiest freshwoman.

He was a graduate student on scholarship but, so far, Joanie had not managed to find out what he was studying. Someone once whispered to her that his grandfather was a powerful politician in his home country. Joanie figured that was why he was allowed to remain in a graduate program, although he attended very few classes and spent most of his time carousing and drinking at the Students' Union.

One afternoon, while she was eating lunch in the cafeteria, he walked over to her table and sat across from her. She continued eating and reading from one of her textbooks. When he realized that she was not going to acknowledge his presence, he closed her book over her downturned palm. She flung the book open again without so much as glancing at him.

After more than ten minutes of silence, he spoke in a nasty whisper, his voice husky with desire, "Yu seem to tink yu too good for man, Miss Joan Jackman, but one dark night, somebody bound to throw yu dong and pick dat cherry dat you think is such a prize. Or, maybe yu parson friend done pick it already."

Instead of responding with words, Joan mustered all of the contempt that she felt for most men, and without blinking an eye, she spat the half eaten food from her mouth onto the rest of her lunch. She then picked up her book and purse and without a backward glance, walked away from the table.

Well, today she would show the stinking billy goat that she had had her cherry picked and he had been no part of it. She got up and opened her door.

Jimmy stood, arms folded across his chest and leaning against the iron rails that bordered the walkway outside of her room. On the grassy lawn below, seven young men stood with upturned faces, eyeing Jimmy and Joanie with a mixture of amusement, cruelty and plain envy.

Joanie looked down at them and didn't know whether to spit or raise her skirt in the age-old gesture of contempt. Once more, men had lived down to her expectation.

Jimmy brushed past her to enter her room and she looked straight into the eyes of her rejected suitor and saw the feral hunger there. It took all of the restraint she could muster not to raise her middle finger.

When she turned to go back to her room, their laughter rushed up to her and she could feel her face getting hot. She was about to slam the door when a short, bow-legged, rusty-brown one hollered, "Mek a few strokes fi me but, do, no cut-up di *sappy*, yu hear, Reverend!"

JOANIE THREW HERSELF into the easy chair in her room and folded her arm defensively across her breasts. She did not speak and as she sat in silence, the afternoon sunlight filled the room and bathed her in a golden glow that startled Jimmy. Not for the first time, he was struck by her remarkable beauty but, as usual, whenever he thought of her physical perfection, he was forced to consider the imperfections of her character. He often marveled that nature could be so capricious as to couple outward beauty a flawed inward disposition.

How many times had Joanie accused him of withholding his love from her because his grandmother did not approve of her? Although there was some truth to her bitter accusation, that was not all. He and Joanie had been inseparable since childhood and to the eye of many an observer, they were so physically alike they could be assumed to be blood relatives. In spite of that, for every physical feature they had in common, they were the very opposite in temperament. Where Jimmy was usually sunny and outgoing, Joanie was often morose and suspicious. Whereas he liked most people and was willing to give even the most difficult his due, Joanie was unforgiving and unyielding, capable of holding a grudge indefinitely and dwelling upon past hurts as if they were fresh wounds.

He was often at a loss as to why he continued to befriend her but she was as much a part of his world as Mama, Daddy, Miss Maudie and Uncle Nathan were. He could no more not speak to her than he could fail to think his own thoughts within the confines of his skull. Jimmy was to Joanie what bread was to butter, and only a few hours earlier, he had come to know her in the biblical way. He could no longer pretend that he did not know what was hidden under the lumpy folds of her tattered bathrobe.

While Jimmy searched for fitting words to begin to right the great wrong he had done to Joanie, she continued to eye him with open hostility. He knew how much he had hurt her when he pushed her away after their shared intimacy, but he was out of his depth and at a complete loss for words.

She, on the other hand, knew that he wanted to make peace with her but she was not about to make it easy for him. There would be no olive branch held out to him. He would have to work for her forgiveness and she would not grant him absolution until she had made him suffer.

Joanie stood up and walked over to her standing closet. She could feel his eyes following her but she did not look back at him. For all she knew, his eyes were glued to her behind because she was learning that he was just like all other men. How many times had she walked through her village street and greeted men who did not respond to her salutation until she was several feet past them. For a long time she wondered about this but solved the riddle one Sunday morning while she stood at the bus stop in Chalky Hill square.

There were about seven men sitting on a concrete wall across from the bus stop. They were talking in low tones among themselves. Joanie could not hear their words but from their relaxed, unhurried talk, she knew that they were just passing time with social exchanges. However, all of that changed when a young woman walked past them.

She was the type of woman her grandmother called dusky and fan-tailed. The woman apparently knew a few of them and said a general, cheery good-morning as she passed on her way. No one answered her immediately. Instead, all seven heads swiveled in choreographed unison, all fourteen eyes glued to the woman's swinging hips, and it was not until she was almost out of earshot that the first to recover, stuttered a greeting in return.

That day, Joanie solved a mystery and her contempt for the opposite sex only grew stronger. She just could not comprehend the complete loss of control that she saw in the men and she did not feel empowered by it. She concluded that most men could be swept away by breasts, legs and thighs. So if Jimmy was watching her backside, she would not be surprised. He had already showed her since that morning that he was no saint.

When she turned away from the closet, she had a soap dish and washcloth in one hand and a bath towel slung around her neck. She looked briefly at him and then headed to the door. Jimmy stood up and spoke to her retreating back. "I will still be here when you return, Joan."

She slammed the door behind her and Jimmy sighed as he sat down again.

He knew what she wanted and he was prepared to give in to her desire. She wanted him to beg for her forgiveness and he would. In fact, he would go one better. He would show her that he was sorry for the cruel things that he had said to her. With this thought in mind, he left the room and hastened across the lawn to the university bookstore.

On the ledge behind the cashier, Jimmy found just what he wanted and as he paid for the bunch of flowers, he hoped that none of his classmates from the seminary would see him going to Joanie's room with a bouquet.

When he returned to the room, he saw no evidence that she had come back since his departure and he was relieved. He smoothed the top sheet, straightened her pillows and placed the bouquet gently in the middle of the bed. That done, he sat in her easy chair and waited.

THE FIRST THING that Joanie saw when she pushed open the door to her room were the flowers in the middle of her bed. She became very confused because no one had ever given her so much as a single hibiscus flower before. Her ears grew hot and she glanced quickly at Jimmy and just as quickly, looked away.

What was she supposed to do when the damn man had just swept the rug out from under her without warning? How was she going to remain angry with him with a bouquet of flowers in the middle of her bed, making mute appeal but speaking more tenderly than any plea could?

Joanie hurried to her closet, opened the door and squeezed behind it so that Jimmy could not see her confusion. After putting away her soap dish and resting her damp washcloth and bath towel over the closet door, she stood there looking down at her feet where tears were landing on her bare toes. In a surreal way, it was the physical evidence of her distress that caused Joanie to realize that she was crying. She quickly wiped her eyes with the back of her hand and swallowed her sobs so that Jimmy would not hear her.

As Joanie stood behind the door and tried to regain her composure, Jimmy walked over and pulled it toward him so that he could see her. He soon stepped around the door and stood directly in front of her. They were now confined to a space that made it possible for her to hear him breathe. She continued to look down at her feet and so he held her left arm and pulled her to his chest. When her shoulder made contact with his body, he put his free hand under her chin and forced her to look up at him. He saw so much pain in the depth of her eyes that he ached for her. If only he could take back the hard words that he had thrown at her, earlier.

While Jimmy continued to look solemnly into Joanie's pain-filled eyes, they watered and one perfectly formed teardrop slowly slid down her cheek and disappeared into the neck of her bathrobe. She did not say a single word of accusation but he stood condemned before her. While his mind searched for some way to make amends to his friend, he felt something else stir within him.

The newly washed scent of her began to fill his nostrils and the beauty of her scrubbed, upturned face soon became his whole universe. In that moment, his senses filled with her nearness and he forgot about Genevieve, his call to ministry and the wedding plans that were sealed and waiting.

He kissed her and it was as though the day of his grandmother's interruption was about to be remedied and their unfinished business was finally to be fulfilled. The taste of her was madness to his senses.

Joanie leaned into his body and the weight of her made him want nothing more than her flesh beneath his fingers. He pulled her as close as he could and in that moment, she felt precious and cherished. This Jimmy she had not met before but her intent was to bind him to her before the call of duty swept him away from her.

Jimmy walked Joanie away from the closet, his eyes closed and his lips still fastened to hers. This was her first real kiss and she felt her knees turn to jelly. He turned her around and she fell backward upon the single bed, crushing the gift of flowers he had brought.

It seemed like his hands were suddenly everywhere. She felt her nipples come alive and gasped as Jimmy's lips latched on to one while he caressed the other. Joanie opened her eyes briefly and saw that his face above hers was contorted as if he was in extreme agony and, for a moment, she was afraid. But one of his hands was peeling away her bathrobe and the other was between her thighs and stroking her clumsily. She reached for him and kissed him again while he began to remove his shirt and jeans. For a brief moment of clarity as he pushed her on to the bed and his form shadowed her, she thought of the possibility of an unplanned pregnancy but felt a sharp pain as he penetrated her recently torn flesh. She was soon weeping with agony that was shadowed by the promise of pleasure.

As Joanie began to writhe beneath Jimmy, the stems and petals of the bouquet began to bleed into the sheets. Afterwards, as the two lay trembling together, the aroma of crushed rose petals filled the room.

Joanie did not know how long they lay there but just as she shifted beneath him, Jimmy rolled out of the bed and without saying a word, he began to dress. While still tucking his shirt into his jeans, he walked to the door and for a moment, stood staring at her. She looked right back at him, her eyes bright and warm. She thought she saw tears in his eyes but he opened the door and was gone before she could say his name.

gri-gri-gris-gris, amulet used for good and bad luck
gra-gra-term probably invented to indicate something worse than gri-gri
maggich-fly-maggot fly; very large house fly
gu-weh-go away
mek naiz-make a noise
tomp-thump; hit with a closed fist
sappy-female genitalia (vulgar)

CHAPTER 22

Fowl who wuohn hear shii! will hear pam!
The chicken that won't fly away when it is chased, will be hit by a stone
Goat seh him wuda laugh but him no hab no tap tiit
The goat says that he would laugh but he has no top teeth
He is aware that he cannot make fun of others because he has his own vulnerabilities
Cloven foot kyan wear palish boot
A cloven foot can be hidden by a polished boot
Some defects are well hidden; evil can be masked as goodness

The bus ride was long and Joanie was edgy and exhausted. Her feet hurt and she was hungry but she needed to get home so that she could face the cursing and recriminations and be done with it. She knew that Miss Maudie was not going to handle her situation very well because she had invested everything in her, but nothing could be done now.

Joanie had gone over the scenario numberless times and imagined every possible outcome, so, she was not afraid. In fact, she was not even sure that she was capable of feeling afraid anymore. She had survived so many of life's disappointments by the time she was five years old that sometime soon thereafter, she told herself that she would get through whatever evils life sprinkled along her pathway, and, so far, she had.

She was eight-and-a-half months pregnant and had no place to go but home, so she was going home. Her traveling bags were tied to the top of the wildly careening minibus and her weekend bag was on the floor at her feet. She held her overstuffed purse on her lap, beneath the bulge of her pregnant belly but she was not unduly worried because she knew the treasure she carried within her.

Birdie Whitehead would hate her now more than ever but she would be unable to ignore her. Jimmy had no knowledge of her state but she would not allow worry to rule her heart. Sometimes she grew a little uncertain but then she would feel the baby moving in her and that was all the reminder she needed that he could not walk away from her now. This was what she constantly told herself whenever the thought of his fiancée entered her mind. She did not know where he was and that troubled her some, but, as soon as she got home and brought her condition to his grandparents' attention, they were bound to bring him out of hiding.

He had disappeared right after graduation and Joanie knew that he was running away from her. After their second sexual encounter, he avoided her and the next time she went over to his room, he pointedly asked her to leave. She ran into him in the cafeteria two weeks after their final exams and when she tried to make small talk with him, he was aloof and noncommittal, but she did not allow his attitude to unsettle her. By then, she was sure that she had the lure that reel him into her clutches.

She had never missed a period before and her sudden desire for salty foods told her enough. What was so strange, though, was her detached sense of relief when the young doctor at the clinic confirmed her pregnancy and looked hard at her with concern and sympathy. He lowered his voice close to a whisper and told her that she did not have to keep it because since it was so early, an abortion could be easily arranged. She thanked him for his concern but assured him that a termination would not be necessary.

Yes sir. She, Joanie, the outsider, was now within the very sanctuary of the Whiteheads' hallowed lives and if they did not know it yet, they would know soon enough. She was carrying within her, the firstborn of the future generation and she did not care that he, like her, would be a bastard. Genevieve Swearing could bear Jimmy a baker's dozen within their marriage but they would always know that she, Joan

Marie Jackman, had borne her Ishmael. They could cast her out into the desert of their disdain but they would not be able to ignore her. She would bear a young with the mark of Whitehead upon him.

What did it matter that she would bring turmoil and disorder among them? What else had she known in her lifetime? Storms she had known always. From the day that Madge pushed her from her torn body and wept at the sight of her, Joanie had been tossed about upon the choppy seas of her mother's instability. How could it have been otherwise, when the child she named for the unknown American was a daily reminder of her shame?

Madge, Joanie's mother, was the only girl of Miss Maudie's five children and she had caused her the most pain. She left home early and settled in the east coast town of Port Antonio where she produced more babies than her hand could rock or her pot could feed. Sometimes she returned to Miss Maudie's house in Trelawny and at other times, Miss Maudie would get wild and convicting dreams about Madge and go off to find her daughter and rescue her grandchildren.

One night, in a desperate search for money to feed herself and to pay her rent, Madge went with another woman from the tenement where she lived, to the harbor and accompanied a drunken American to his motel room. She had seen the man many times before and had been told that he was Peace Corps volunteer. However, they had never spoken. There, in the dank, cheap hotel room that smelled of mildew and stale sex, she let him spear her flesh and empty his seed into her in exchange for sixty green American dollars. This money paid the rent and bought food for a week. Out of this seemingly necessary exchange came a price that was higher than the soft, sweaty notes that she had prized from the wallet stolen from him, as he lay drunk and broken across the bed.

Madge named the baby Joan and attached to her the last name of the American who had planted her without knowing. When she was six months old, she deposited her upon her mother's doorstep. She had found the man's American's Peace Corps identification card in the stolen wallet but after she named the baby, she gave no more thought to him or to what it would mean for the baby to grow up without a father. Madge was more concerned about the disgrace of having a baby from whoredom. There was nothing more shameful in her world than the tag, "sailor baby." She tried to cover this fact by giving the baby the man's last name and naming him on the birth certificate as the child's father. Thereafter, whenever anyone enquired after Joanie's paternity, she would affect a wounded expression and say that the baby's father abandoned her when he found out that she was carrying his child. When the baby was about six weeks old, Madge thought she saw the man going into the market but when she caught up with him, he was someone else.

Sometimes when Madge stayed with Miss Maudie, she would drink until she became surly. At those times, she would spit cruel words at everyone, especially Joanie and Miss Maudie. Most of the time, however, she sat drinking from a squat green tumbler at her elbow. She would stare off into space and then whimper into the crook of her arm. In between crying and wiping her eyes, she would sip from her glass and talk to herself. The sight of her indulgence often elicited more harsh words from Miss Maudie.

"Ef yu kud stap drinkin dat blaasid rum, we wud all be better aaf! A had to bury yu pupa before time becausen a dis dyam rum glaas and me neba dream dat a girl-chail of mine wud be a blaasid *wine biba*!"

Then she would shoo the children outside to play. Joanie did not go too far, though. She would climb up into the verandah chair that was in front of a window, kneel in the cushioned seat and press her nose against the glass. From there she would watch this woman who hated her and her heart would pound in her chest.

Once, after Joanie's two brothers were born, Madge brought them home to Miss Maudie's after a short stay in Kingston. One morning, Joanie ran back unexpectedly into the house and came upon her mother sitting naked in a large enameled bath tub. Miss Maudie was holding an open Bible over Madge's head as she poured water out of a goblet upon her. Her mother was crying into her hands and Miss Maudie's countenance as she stood over was so transfigured that Joanie hardly knew her. As the frightened child turned to run away from what she did not understand, she heard her grandmother say, "And Almighty Gaad, if you will not deliver mi chail, please tek har home to res in peace."

That last time, Madge did not go away. She stayed in bed for more than a week and when she finally emerged from her room, she was pale and frail.

After a few more days, she started to go to church with a neighbor who was Pentecostal. Before long, Madge gave away all of her party clothes and jewelry. Within the month she started wearing very long dresses, gave up drinking and covered her head with a scarf even when she went to bed at nights. After another month, Madge talked about little else but God, the Holy Ghost and speaking in tongues.

Joanie and her little brothers grew wary of this new parent but Miss Maudie was ecstatic because her once wayward daughter was finally in the fold. If she was not in the exact corner that her mother preferred, at least she was safely enclosed.

A little over a year after her conversion, Madge met a younger man at her church summer convention. He fell in love with her and asked for her hand in marriage. He was prepared to take her with all three of her children but Miss Maudie said no. When Madge protested Miss Maudie spoke in her quiet voice which told Madge that there was no room for compromise. "Mek him tek di bwai dem, becausen him kyan grow to love dem as him own, but Joanie too big fi dat and if I was yu, I wudn pu-dong no butter fi puss."

So little Joan Jackman stayed behind in Chalky Hill with her grandmother while the rest of her siblings moved to Spanish Town with their new daddy and their almost new mommy. Joanie cried for a whole day because she was left behind when she so wanted to move to the big city.

At sundown, Miss Maudie spoke very sternly to her and told her to go and pull wild grass and *Spanish needles* for the chickens and rabbits caged in the backyard.

"Yu young and dere is a lot yu duohn andastan bout life but yu will tank me fi dis wan day. Madge happy now becausen she still have har looks, but she gwaihn to fade while dat man still in a him prime. Yu duohn want to be a temptation aanda him nose when dat happen. Better fi all kansern if when dat time come, him go outside, raada dan snatch what aanda him nose."

As Joanie stared hard at her grandmother, she continued, "Aah, me gran-pikni, yu young and yu duohn know di ways a man. Some a dem is *aligeta* self. Dem nyam dem own flesh and blood. Yu hear me? Dem *divuoa* dem own. So, dry up yu yai-waata and go feed di dumb animal dem. So lang as mi yai dem remain *wopin*, I will have to see bout yu for I is all yu hab. Yu duohn hab no faada and yu mada is spoken for, so yu stay wid Maudie and I will see dat yu go right."

And as Joanie made for the door to the front yard, her grandmother did the unexpected. She folded the child to her bosom and kissed her forehead.

Joanie scampered away from her grandmother, feeling strangely shamefaced and thrilled. For the first time in her life, she felt that she mattered exclusively to someone.

Two weeks after these tumultuous events, Miss Maudie went shopping in the open-air market behind the police station. She told Joanie that she bent over to examine the heaps of yam piled at her feet when someone tapped her on the shoulder. She looked up with some annoyance because she was in a dark mood. It did not help matters that the person standing behind her was Joanie's grade six teacher.

Miss Maudie did not like her because of her prying eyes and shrill speaking voice. She considered her a do-gooder who needed to mind her own damn business and as a consequence, she did not bother to redraw her countenance into more welcoming lines. Instead, Miss Maudie picked up a piece of yellow yam and examined it with great care.

"You seem rather preoccupied this morning, Miss Maudie. Is everything all right with the grandchildren?"

"Mi granchilvren dem is fine, ma'am."

Oh, how Miss Maudie abhorred this woman with her inquisitive eyes and overt concern. What was it that she really wanted with her?

"I have been wanting to have a word with you about Joan."

"Why? She in any kain a chrobl at school?"

"Oh no, ma'am. On the contrary, she is a very good student and so I want to encourage you to spend some money on her. She has a good head and she could go far."

At the mention of money, Miss Maudie's stomach tightened and she felt like telling the teacher a few harsh words. Where in hell dis uman come fram a taak bout money pahn a Satideh maanin? She know dat she have seven gran-pikini fi feed pahn a housemaid wages? She have di money tree in a har backyaad weh she kuda jos shake di ten dala limb? Dat was what she kudn tek bout being poor and beholden. It cause dese blaasid people fi taak shit to yu, knowin full well dat yu no have two penny fi rub pahn wan aneda. Is all good and well fi dis uman wid har montli government salary fi waak-up into har face pahn dis *Gaad-sen Satideh maanin*, and a come taak bout she fi spen money pahn dis faadaless, half-white, gyal-pikni. Weh di *kaka* dis nak-knee uman ekspek har fi find money fi spen pahn dis pikni?

In all the history of her lineage, there had never been an educated man much more a learned woman. She could no more imagine such a thing happening than she could imagine herself flying to the moon.

"Where me to get money from to spend pahn Joanie, Miss? Me is a uol lady now and me a look to mi grave. Joanie gwaihn ha fi laan a trade fi feed harself. Me no have money fi har fi go beyon *elimenchri* school."

With that said Miss Maudie excused herself and went back to her shopping. She still had to get to the butcher to collect Birdie Whitehead's pound of beef liver for there would be hell to pay if it was all sold out. For the more than thirty years that she had been working for the family, she had never bought more than a pound of liver for the Sunday breakfast. That was just enough for Miss Birdie, The Reverend and Jimmy. Sometimes Miss Maudie was tempted to ask for a half-a-pound more, but she knew Miss Birdie well and did not want to jeopardize the one job she'd had for most of her working life.

JOANIE SOLVED THE question of her future by not only passing the high school entrance examination but also gaining a full government scholarship. She would attend the co-educational academy where Jimmy was also going to be a pupil. He had also passed the exam but had not received a scholarship.

Maudie Collins was so overjoyed by Joanie's success that for a week she felt like she was walking on air. Much to Miss Birdie's annoyance, she soon developed the distracting habit of talking out loud to herself but she could not help it. After all, the unexpected had happened to her.

For the first time in her life, she saw the possibility that one from her lineage would be elevated above common toil. In Miss Birdie's words, she would now sit among the crème-de-la-crème. Her Joanie would climb the hill to the school alongside Jimmy and the children of all the tapanaaris people who attended the Church of England. Tanks to Michael Manley, fi har dishklaat ton tableklaat.

Miss Maudie took care not to gloat in front of Miss Birdie because she was yet to congratulate Joanie. Reverend Whitehead had done so and shown genuine pleasure in doing so. For all she knew, Birdie Whitehead was annoyed that her granddaughter was about to rub shoulders with her crowned prince in the school upon the hill, but to hell wid har and har dyam blaasid bad-mind. Fi har Joanie was gwaihn wear di starched blue tunic and snowy white underblouse. She too wud strut in a di well-shined leda loafers and kyari di satchel which wud be full to bursting wid di heavy book dem dat all a di high school pikni dem kyari. What did it matter dat she, Maudie Elfreda Collins, kuda barely sign har name?

As her mind leaped and tumbled over all the possibilities that lay ahead for her granddaughter, she thought of all of the other times when her own children had given her cause to hang her head low. She thought of Tyrone living undocumented in New York City and his six children who had become her responsibility. A significant portion of her paycheck went to their mother every month because she could not stand by and watch them suffer. Her mind settled briefly on George and Glen, lost to the ghettoes of Kingston. Her children had not given her much to be proud of, especially Madge who from the age of fourteen, took on the ways of the world and caused much trouble in the district because of her carnal generosity and her fondness for other women's husbands.

The nasty-minded villagers had spoken against her family on many an occasion and she had more than once been the subject of vulgar discourse in the village rum shop. There, the loose of tongue gathered and under the inspiration of undistilled estate rum, they spoke freely of all that was sordid in local life. What they knew, they embellished, and what they did not know, they invented.

Now, mek dem chat all wa dem waahn chat. She didn't much care. Har grandaata wud wan day teach in a Chalky Hill School, jos like Birdie Whitehead and Principal and Ms. Swearing. She wuda married well, too because she hab di right color. Perhaps a school principal or ebn wahn Anglican priest wuda ax fi har han.

As Miss Maudie's head swam with possibilities for her granddaughter her tears flowed often and Joanie soon grew afraid of the look in her grandmother's eyes. She often gazed upon her with such fierce pride that Joanie felt that she would be consumed if she stayed too long under her grandmother's eyes.

Her one driving ambition for Joanie translated into neglect of Byron, her own last-born and he was soon to point it out to her but what did Maudie Collins care? If there was only a little meat for dinner, Joanie ate the most of it while he had to settle for gravy. Someone told her that fish was brain food and so she bought it whenever she could. If there was only enough money to buy one good pair of shoes, then, Joanie got it and Miss Maudie wore the castoffs that came in the missionary barrels.

A few weeks after the results of the examinations were published, Miss Maudie did the unthinkable by asking Miss Birdie for the day off from work and Miss Birdie surprised her by agreeing. So, for the first time in her life, Joanie was taken on a shopping trip.

They left home before sunrise and made it to the crossroads where other people waited in the semi-darkness for the big bus called *Royal Crown.* It would take them to the town of Falmouth on the lowland coast.

When they got to the waiting spot, Miss Maudie was able to recognize many of the voices which flowed back and forth in the damp morning air but she did not speak to anyone after she said a general good morning.

She maintained silence because she did not wish to draw attention to herself or her granddaughter. As far as she was concerned, her mission was holy. She did not wish to attract any bad blessings from these envious people with their crab-in-a-barrel mentality. These were the same people who in the past had dogged her and her kin, but this time she would show them. She knew that she attracted envy because of her daily access to the parsonage and the fact that she had kept to herself from the time her husband died. She was only too aware of the vicious words spoken by these bawdy men and their low-thinking women folk, but finally God had given her something that they did not have. Her bastard granddaughter would rise above them all and they would be powerless to stop her.

Miss Maudie knew that there would be those who would be willing to employ the obeah man's potions to halt her grandchild's progress but she was prepared to fight fire with fire. She would not throw the first blow but if anything untoward happened to her Joanie, she would spend her last penny to scope it out and throw back the blow.

As Miss Maudie stood close to Joanie, she continued to mull over the disappointments of her life and the joy that had come unexpectedly to her. For all the years that had she cooked, laundered and cleaned at the manse, she had never once imagined that one of her own could have risen above common labor, and yet God had smiled upon her.

Yes sa, dem same blaasid people mek har life a livin hell, but she wud *sekl dem mesij* once and fi all. She had produced what muos a dem kudn even dream of. Her *kyaas-aaf*, sailor-sired grandaata wud soon enter di hallowed halls of learning and rub shoulders wid di likes of James Whitehead, the third, and what kud Birdie and all har fren dem do bout it?

Yes Jesus, finally har deliverance was at han and har formerly bowed head kud now be lifted high. Joanie wud have a profession. She kuda ton teacher and wear di snowy white blouse and di gray a-line skirt and matching jacket. She wuda look good in black pumps and good quality stockings. She wud teach right dere in di village school and lash di dyam *uol niega* people pikni dem wid impunity.

As Miss Maudie continued her internal musings, she sighed with satisfaction that Joanie would never need a pressing comb to straighten her hair because if that damn sailor had given her nothing else, he had given her good hair.

There was no doubt in her mind that she would marry well too, hopefully a nice brown man and den di pikni dem wuda probably be near white. If luck smile pahn Joanie, some a di pikni dem kud even paas fi white. What a wuda sinting in a Chalky Hill dischrik when di bad-mind people dem see har wid har white gran-pikni dem.

At this thought, Miss Maudie almost trembled with excitement because of the un-voiced possibility that was right within her grasp. After all, if black-skinned Birdie was able to snare The Reverend and she had no looks to speak of, what of Joanie and Jimmy?

Miss Maudie's mind was just beginning to close in upon the possibility that Jimmy would one day choose her granddaughter when the strident hoot of the *Royal Crown* shattered the morning stillness and the bus soon roared around the corner and came to a halt in a cloud of dust and flying gravel.

The sun crested Chalky Hill just as the driver brought the bus to a halt. He shouted rapid-fire instructions to the sideman and baggage boy as he scrambled from his seat, jumped from the side door and made for the shop across the road.

The owner of the shop would serve him breakfast as she did every week-day morning and as he ate, she would press him for news from up the country where most of her relatives still lived.

The sideman would supervise the loading of the market produce that would be packed on to the top of the bus and later deposited in the Falmouth Market where it would be sold. This done, the side man and baggage boy would then grab a bite and be ready to pull out by six-thirty. The people who lived along the narrow, winding roadways of the hill country knew to be ready when they heard the horn of the bus. If they missed it, they had very few other means of transportation.

As luck would have it, Miss Maudie was able to get the second seat behind the driver and she pushed Joanie into the corner of the hard bench and sat next to her. When they sat down, Joanie craned her neck to see who was on the bus but Miss Maudie sternly commanded her to keep her eyes ahead of her.

Soon after the driver put the bus into forward motion, the conductor came up the aisle to collect the fares of the newcomers. Despite her grandmother's stern warning, Joanie could not help watching the conductor. He fascinated her because she could not understand how he could walk the aisle and not topple over as the bus tore around corners, slid down inclines and labored over hills.

When the conductor got to their seat, he gave them a gap-toothed grin and said, "So where yu and dis pretty likl girl goin so early dis maanin, Mada?"

Miss Maudie bristled at his easy familiarity and answered him very coldly. "We is goin to *Falmot* and *kainli* let me know how much is di fare, bearin in mind dat she is a chail."

"Why yu goin on so miserable, lady? Is because me seh di likl girl nice? Yu duohn av to be so antsy, for me no mean har no haam. Me ongl seh di likl damsel nice."

"Maasa, *kalek* yu money and go bout yu business! Mi grandaata nice but she no nice fi yu!"

At this, the conductor let out a raucous shout of laughter, told her the fare and collected it as Miss Maudie continued to glower at him.

When he was out of earshot, Miss Maudie lowered her voice and spoke very seriously to Joanie.

"Dem is di type yu ha fi watch out *fa*, yu hear me? Dem is blaasid ram goat and dem ongl baan fi ruin people good-good gyal pikni. Man like dat wan is not your type."

Joanie nodded solemnly and thought to herself that she already knew her type. He didn't know it yet, but she had long decided in her heart that there would be no other for her. She wouldn't tell a soul but although she was only twelve years old, her passion for him was as un-movable as the North Star.

They made it safely to Falmouth and Miss Maudie suited her out for school. She got two pairs of loafers, six cotton panties, two brassieres, three pairs of navy socks, a full slip and a plastic raincoat. Miss Maudie also bought six yards, each, of navy cotton and white Dacron and cotton. These would make the tunics and underblouses that were the uniform of the academy.

They returned home on the same bus and Joanie felt that come the first Monday of September, she would enter a place that would take her away from all that was ugly and belittling in her life.

wine biba-winebibber; drunkard
Spanish needles-*Bidens bippinata*, flowering plant from the aster family; often used to feed chickens and rabbits
temtieshan-temptation
aligeta-alligator which has a reputation for eating its young; this is undeserved as the alligator carries its young in its mouth but does not habitually eat them
divuoa-devour
wopin-open
Gaad-sen Satideh-God-sent Saturday
kaka-a reference to the anus
nak-knee-knock-kneed
faadaless-fatherless
elimenchri-elementary
kyaas-aaf-cast-off

uol niega-old nigger; uncouth

Falmot-Falmouth; capital of the parish of Trelawny

kainli-kindly

kalek-collect

fa-for

CHAPTER 23

Birdie Whitehead and James John Whitehead I

2003

Tan saafli better dan beg paadn
It is better to stand quietly to the side than to have to beg pardon for rushing in
If chobl did set like rain, all a we wuda siit
If trouble presented itself like rainclouds, we would all see it coming

Birdie Whitehead was dreaming and flailing her arms so hard that she hit The Reverend across his nose. He groaned and sat up very quickly. When his head cleared, he held Birdie's arm down across her breast and shook her awake.

She struggled into a sitting position and held on to her husband. When he felt her tremble, he wrapped his arms around her and rocked her. Before too long, he felt the dampness of her tears against his chest and he gently told her to hush.

He was relieved that it was Saturday and Miss Maudie would not come in until after she had done the marketing. He was not ashamed of his wife's emotions but he hated for anyone to see her like this. Junior had been dead for almost twenty-three years but the pain had not gone away. He had simply learned to build layers and layers of forgiveness upon the insult of his son's murder, but Birdie still cried. Jimmy's disappearance had not made matters any easier and sometimes he felt genuine anger towards his grandson. The young were so damn selfish. How could Jimmy have gone to his mother so soon after his graduation and so suddenly, too? He thought he knew his grandson very well but he was learning from his own teaching. The heart of man, aah, the heart of man, indeed.

He was pulled from his own thoughts when Birdie spoke.

"A just dream bout Jimmy."

"That's why you crying?"

She nodded against his chest and wiped her eyes.

Miss Birdie spoke loosely in the dialect because Miss Maudie was not around to hear her.

"He was in the deep part of a river and the water look like it was going to wash him away. A call out to him but he did not hear me. So, A wade out in the water to get to him and the water tek him away from me. A begin to holler out his name and the boy keep washing away from me. Him come to the bend in the river and the boy do an unnatural thing."

"What?"

"He walk over to the bank and take off his head and walk away leave it. Lord, James, Jimmy leave his head and wash away in the river. A call and call but A couldn't reach him."

Birdie began to weep afresh and Reverend Whitehead soothed her as best as he could.

As she began to quiet, his eyes wandered around the room and settled upon their twin images in the mirror that stood at the foot of their four-poster bed.

The bed was the one in which his mother birthed him more than seventy years before and she had received it from her father who carved the head and foot out of solid mahogany wood after he returned from digging the Panama Canal in 1914. He thought to himself that he would like to die in the bed in which he was born but he could not die yet because his grandson and successor had cut and run without a proper explanation.

Jimmy's note sent by Nathan had offered nothing to still his disquiet. Why had he gone away to the United States without first informing them of his intention?

In her manner, to which he had grown accustomed after more than forty years of marriage, Birdie spoke his thoughts before he could voice them.

"Look like the boy don't want to take over the church so he run away. Why he would want to go to his mother after all these years? It's not like she ever did anything for him."

"Truth be told, Birdie, you wouldn't let her."

"What could she do for him after she kill off his father?"

"Birdie, after all these years you shouldn't be saying these things. Audrie did not have anything to do with our son's murder. She ran away to save her own skin."

"Why you always take up for that woman, James? You think if Junior did not get mixed up with her he wouldn't be alive today?"

"Birdie, Junior was killed by people that we don't even know about. From what Nathan told us, it may even have been a case of mistaken identity."

"Mistaken identity, my foot. You know damn well that the same people who kill Junior help Audrie to escape, so don't talk nonsense!"

From the set of her brow and the tightness of her lips, The Reverend knew that there was no arguing with Birdie. But in his heart, he believed that his son had been killed because of his close resemblance to a well known leftist and anti-American critic of the seventies. They had both taught in the same department at the university and both had waist length dreadlocks. The fact that their son was also anti-establishment and anti-government did nothing to protect him on a dark night when he was in the wrong place at the wrong time.

Birdie wriggled off the bed and padded to the adjoining bathroom. Reverend Whitehead opened the bedroom door and walked out to the verandah. The sun was climbing from behind the far hills and a few grass-quits hopped about the lawn below the verandah.

He took in the vista before him-the star apple tree that shaded the kitchen to his left, and the line of coconut palms that marked the driveway on both sides, all the way to the foot of the gentle hill upon which the house sat. And midway down the driveway, his eyes came to rest upon the marble tomb where his only child lay. His mind went reluctantly back to the Sunday in 1980 when they laid him rest.

Thank God for Nathan and the people of Chalky Hill Baptist Church. What would they have done without them in that season of clouds and uncertainty? They had shown their better side when Junior was murdered because most of them had loved him. And now everything that he and Birdie had lived for seemed to be tottering. Jimmy had gone away to his mother, claiming that he needed to make his peace with her before starting his ministry, but the good Reverend wondered if his grandson was looking for a way out of his commitment.

He heard Birdie flush the toilet and was reminded of his own aching discomfort. He knocked at the bathroom door, heard water running and walked out of his bedroom, and crossed the living room to use the bathroom that was between the two guest rooms at the back of the house.

When The Reverend returned from the bathroom, he was freshly showered and shaved. He could smell the aroma of coffee and fried breadfruit coming from the kitchen. His stomach rumbled in anticipation and he quickened his steps.

In the kitchen, Miss Birdie moved in a regular arc from the dining table to the stove, the refrigerator and the kitchen cupboards. By the time The Reverend ducked his head and entered the room, she had his breakfast laid out and she was seated and waiting for him.

He glanced at her and saw with relief that her face was smooth and there were no signs of the tears she had shed earlier. She had her short hair covered at the front by a cloth headband but her gray curls were visible at the back of her head. Her brown-rimmed spectacles sat at the tip of her upturned nose and her dimples became visible as her eyes met his.

The Reverend took his seat at the head of the table, reached for Birdie's hand and said grace. They were halfway through the meal when they heard a motor vehicle pull up at the back of the manse. They heard muffled voices and then a male voice called out a greeting. It was Danny Willis, a young member of the church. He drove a taxi and often brought Miss Maudie home with the produce on Saturdays.

They returned his greeting but neither got up from their meal. Within a few minutes, the car was heard crunching gravel as it departed and Miss Maudie soon entered the kitchen.

She greeted them both but her eyes settled on The Reverend, taking in the half eaten food on his plate and his empty coffee cup. She walked over to the sink to wash her hands and Birdie's eyes followed her without any warmth.

When she had dried her hands, she brought the coffee pot over to the table and poured more coffee for The Reverend. She walked back to the stove without offering any to Miss Birdie and she, in turn, cut her eyes at Miss Maudie before going back to her food.

Miss Maudie walked to the back door to begin bringing in the supplies and Reverend Whitehead wondered if he would ever be able to figure out the low-grade animus that fused the two women's relationship.

As far as Miss Birdie was concerned, Miss Maudie was a necessary evil and Miss Maudie considered her an affront. The thing that neither of them knew was that it was their fierce love for the light brown, long-limbed man seated at the table that connected them.

Even now, Miss Maudie had still not figured out what it was about Birdie Whitehead that had this near-white man fawning over this short-legged, tar-baby. At first, Miss Maudie felt it was obeah but in the more than forty years that she had worked at the manse, she had never once found any vials hidden in corners or seen any powders sprinkled about the locale. If it was something Birdie had put in his food to tie him, it had been a job well done. But Lord, this man loved his Birdie so much that he thought nothing of bending low to buckle her shoe.

Miss Maudie began to put away the supplies and quietly sucked her teeth while she pursued her musings. If The Reverend James Whitehead had once asked her for intimate favors, she would have complied without question and she would not have disturbed his domestic arrangement. She considered herself better looking than Birdie Whitehead by far and even though she did not have The Reverend's lightness of skin, neither was she the dense black of Miss Birdie. Furthermore, her nose was straight and her figure the envy of many half her age.

She had birthed more children than Miss Birdie but she had bound herself after each birth and regained her figure after every baby was weaned. But for all her years of attendance, Reverend James Whitehead had never once looked at her with more than pastoral concern. Not even when Junior died and Miss Birdie looked like she was going to lose her mind did that man once turn to her for comfort. She loved him the more for his decency, however, and quietly despised Birdie Whitehead for her good fortune.

By the time Miss Maudie was done in the kitchen, Miss Birdie was watering her flowers in the front garden and The Reverend was going over his sermon notes in the study. She washed the breakfast dishes, swept the floors, made the bed in the master bedroom and prepared to leave.

Miss Birdie met her at the back door, handed her the brown envelope that contained her week's pay and thanked her politely for doing the marketing. The Reverend rejoined them and offered to take Miss Maudie home but she declined his offer. She told him that she had to make a few stops along the way. Joanie was expected home for the weekend and she needed to purchase some naseberries for her.

After Miss Maudie left, they both went to sit on the verandah. The Reverend had his newspaper and Miss Birdie, her Sunday school lesson plan and Bible. They sat quietly for a while, the rustle of paper the only sound between them.

It was The Reverend who finally broke the silence. He lowered his newspaper and looked at her over the top of his glasses until Miss Birdie met his eyes.

"Birdie," he spoke very slowly, "I have a bad feeling about Jimmy. I feel that he is not going to take up the mantle."

"So where would that leave us, James?"

"I have already put the General Secretary on alert that we may need an intern, after all."

"What did he say?"

"Wanted to ask all kinds of questions about Jimmy but I cut him short. You know how nosy he is. He also said that at this late stage, he would have to send us one of the female interns because all of the males have already been assigned."

"Well, James, it's better to have an intern on standby and not need him than to need one and not have one, but I don't know about any lady intern. Chalky Hill isn't ready for that."

"I agree on both counts and I do not know what is going on with Jimmy. However, if he wants to spend time with his mother, I do not think that we should interfere."

Birdie gave him a hard look and pursed her lips, but she did not say anything more.

Reverend Whitehead continued to speak. "Do not hold it against him, Birdie and have a heart for Audrie. She has gone without knowing him for most of his life and it was not for want of trying. I have often felt that we took the wrong road, Birdie, by shutting her out."

"James, no mek me rude to you dis Saturday morning! Where was Audrie in all those days after they kill Junior? Where was she when Jimmy was small?"

"I have no answers for that, but she gave him to Nathan and asked him to take him to us. It could not have been easy for her to part with her one child, but she did and that baby gave us life again. So, it is only fair that now that he is a man he should want to go to her. He has questions that only she can answer."

"Chut! All this talk of Audrie Matthews is making mi heart hurt me. I don't want to hear any more about her. She lure mi son away from his calling and send him to his death and now she steal Jimmy away from me. Only God knows if he will come home in time for the wedding."

"But if he is gone to New York, he must be in touch with Genevieve."

The Reverend frowned and continued, "I only hope he remembers his calling and don't get familiar with her before the proper time."

"James, this is more pahn plenty and I am not able for it. This consideration will give me a stroke if I am not careful. Get the car and come drive me down to Dawn. We need to iron out a few things about the wedding.

CHAPTER 24

Joan Marie Jackman and Maudie Elfreda Collins

2003

Wan finga kyaahn kill louse and wan han kyaahn clap
A louse cannot be killed with one finger and we cannot clap with only one hand
To get good results, it is necessary to cooperate with others; we should help each other
If yu han in a hag mout, tek yu time jraa it out
If your hand gets into a hog's mouth, pull it out slowly

The necessity for wisdom and caution when situations of conflict arise

The minibus arrived at the Chalky Hill square just as Joanie's legs began to fall asleep. There were three other passengers alighting ahead of her, so, she patiently waited her turn. She did not want anyone bumping and boring against her because she was tired and hungry.

She finally got her chance to pull herself from the confines of the window seat and hefted her weekend bag to her shoulder before stepping down to the pavement. Joanie then waited at the back of the bus for her two large travel bags and did not look around her until the bus had pulled away.

Talk about a one-horse town, Joanie thought to herself. For the first time she began to wonder if coming back was the best thing for her. Very little seemed to have changed. The silent clock tower was still the center of the town. The burnt out cinema still stood roofless to the sky. The old market behind her had been converted into a used car lot and the two grocery stores still stood facing each other like habitual enemies. It even seemed to her like the same vagrants still sat on the shop piazzas.

The signs of the town's demise were everywhere and the only people who seemed prosperous were the taxi drivers who transported the people who no longer walked anywhere if they could help it.

Joanie was prepared for curious stares and so she did not make eye contact with any of the people who passed by her. Instead, she focused her attention upon finding a cab to take her up the hill and down to the valley floor where her grandmother lived. On the way home, she would pass the Baptist Church and the manse where Jimmy lived, but she was not ready to face him yet. She needed to make sure that she had her grandmother on her side.

Earlier on, she had thought of going to her mother in Spanish Town but quickly changed her mind. Their relationship had improved over the years and she had even spent a few weekends with her while she was at the university, but she did not like her stepfather and her brothers were a little too street smart for her liking. There was also the matter of her paternity standing between them like an unstated accusation and Madge had still not volunteered an answer to the unasked question.

Danny Willis saw Joanie before she saw him and he pulled up next to her. She turned in annoyance but her face soon melted in a wide smile when she saw him.

"Miss Maudie gave me strict instructions to deliver you safely, Miss Joan, so I am at your service."

He jumped from the car, opened the passenger door for her and was gone to stow her bags before she could respond. She closed the door and opened one of the back doors instead. He looked quizzically at her before he took his seat and she quickly assured him that she was more comfortable in the back seat.

"Alright den, Miss Joan. I was hoping dat yu pretty face wuda light up me taxi front, but next time."

Joanie blushed and giggled and he continued to talk.

"But Miss Maudie certainly kyan keep a secret. A tek har up to di manse dis maanin and she never even tell me dat yu was married and expectin."

"That's how life is, Danny. You don't get to know some things until you do."

"A guess so. But A hope yu husband a treat yu right, Miss Joan."

"I hope so too, Danny."

Joanie almost burst out laughing when she saw the consternation on Danny's face. The baby started to kick, however, and she figured that it was as hungry as she was. Instead, she said, "Drive as faas as yu can widout di police a come fi lock yu up, Danny. Me so hungry dat mi belly a wanda if mi chruot cut."

"Alright Miss Joan, A know how it is when you have to eat fi two. A will have yu home in a haatbeat."

He reversed into the abandoned service station, made a half-circle at the roundabout and began the steady climb past the derelict shoemaker's shop on the right. Soon, he was forced to slow down for a trio of goats that chose that moment to cross the main road. It was a mother goat with two small kids and someone threw a stone to shoo them from the middle of the road. All three animals ran down into the gully and disappeared. Danny continued on his way.

They went past a wooded hillside, turned a corner and climbed a winding road that soon left a few cottages behind.

They drove past a cut-stone Methodist church that had been constructed by slaves in the early 1800s.

When Danny began the descent to Miss Maudie's valley cottage, Joanie looked over to a far hill on their left where she could see the Baptist Church and the manse in the distance. She thought then of The Reverend and how much she was going to hurt him. She felt genuine sorrow for him but nothing but pure satisfaction for the grief that she would bring to Birdie Whitehead. That woman had called her a whore when she was still wrapped in innocence and she had never forgiven her for the insult. Well, the whore was bearing her great-grandchild and if she didn't like the idea, she could jump, head first, from her high verandah.

The car made the turn on to her grandmother's property and Danny blurted, "So when yu husband a come join yu, Miss Joan?"

She felt a twinge of annoyance but to her relief, they arrived at Miss Maudie's front steps and he was suddenly all business.

Joanie opened the door and alighted just as Miss Maudie rose from her wooden, green verandah chair. Her look of pleasure soon turned to horror, however, when she saw the full bloom of her granddaughter.

Danny brought the first of Joanie's bags up the front step and Miss Maudie collected herself. She pulled a cloth purse from her bosom and paid him the fare while Joanie stood silently at the bottom of the steps.

When Danny had stowed the last bag under the front window, he walked down the steps and over to Joanie. He reached into his pocket for a plain business card that had his name and cellphone number.

"If you need me fi anyting, jos give me a ding, Miss Joanie."

His eyes held genuine concern and he squeezed her hand before he went back to his car.

Miss Maudie's eyes followed the fast disappearing car as she struggled to collect herself. She walked like a blind woman over to her chair and sat down heavily. Joanie stood in the yard, watching her and thinking that she should have stayed in her flat and hired a helper instead of coming home. If she had known where to find Jimmy, she would have gone to him, but he had moved out of his room right after graduation and had not contacted her since. If he was at the manse, she would need her grandmother's support to confront him and force him to marry her.

She straightened the front of her dress, tucked Danny's card into her pocket and climbed wearily up the concrete steps of the verandah. She passed Miss Maudie, entered the dark living room and went straight to the back of the house where the small indoor bathroom stood behind her bedroom.

After Joanie relieved herself, she picked up a pail of water from the enamel bath tub and flushed the toilet. There was a goblet of water on the face basin and she washed her hands, one at a time.

By the time she emerged from the bathroom, she had serious second thoughts about staying to have the baby. Could she deal with the inconveniences of home?

Joanie went back to the verandah and spoke to her grandmother's back.

"Miss Maudie, yu have any food ready?

Miss Maudie turned to look at her and she hesitated before getting to her feet.

"If you can't stand to have me here, I will go back to town, ma'am."

"Hush-up yu dyam mout, Joanie. Weh yu gwaihn go?"

"I have mi apartment in Kingston and I am on paid maternity leave from mi job."

Joanie continued to talk as her grandmother entered the house. She walked behind her to the kitchen, but Miss Maudie told her to sit at the dining table. After she kicked off her shoes, Joanie placed her handbag on one of the blue mahoe chairs and stretched out her aching legs and swollen feet under the table.

Miss Maudie returned from the kitchen with a bowl of beef soup and placed it in front of Joanie. She then seated herself across from her granddaughter and watched as Joanie brought each steaming spoonful of soup up to her mouth. Neither woman spoke for a few minutes and the only sound in the room was the clink of metal against porcelain and the cuckoo clock ticking on the wall.

When Joanie swallowed the last mouthful and belched gently, Miss Maudie looked at her and then spoke. Joanie watched her face, noting the gray tendrils that had escaped her head scarf and the deep lines furrowing her brow.

"So dis is wa mi life dream amount to, Joan Marie? Dis is wa me get fi mi labor? Dis is how yu plan fi sen me to mi grave?"

With the last utterance, Miss Maudie began to weep bitterly and Joanie felt like a stone was growing in her chest.

She had prepared herself for curses and recriminations, not for brokenness. She wanted to reassure her grandmother, to make some gesture of tender regret, but she sat glued to her chair.

"Yu is mi life labor, Joanie and it look like mi labor dash-weh a sea-batam."

"Don't say that, Miss Maudie. I have a job, a place to live and maternity leave..."

Miss Maudie waved her words away like gnats.

"A duohn care how much maternity leave yu hab, yu still *disapaint* me. A didn spen all a mi money pahn yu fi yu come home wid a *anmarried* belly. When me come up to yu graduation, it was not fi dis. Yu mada tek me dong dis road over and over, but me raise yu fi better tings. Why at my age mi shuda si-dong a di back bench in a church and heng dong mi head wid shame? Me uol now and me deserve some satisfakshan. All mi life, me wok fi ada people, jos so dat tings wud be better fi me wan day. Me pour mi haat and soul into yu, and yu disgrace me. How yu tink me feel, eeh Joanie, fi si yu tan-up in a mi yaad wid yu bag dem a yu foot, a biebi in a yu belly and no man beside yu? Eeh, Joanie? Why yu choose such a haad road when yu kuda do so much better?

Joanie could not listen to any more of Miss Maudie's lament. She had come home for her support and even though she had expected anger and disappointment, she was finding that she had no real stomach for it. She could think of only one way to stem the outpouring of words.

She stood up and Miss Maudie jumped to her feet. She raised her hand as if to strike her granddaughter but when Joanie spoke, she fell backward onto the un-cushioned, wooden chair.

"This baby is not only your great-grandchild, but he is the great grand-child of Reverend and Birdie Whitehead".

Miss Maudie looked at Joanie and then bowed her head as if in prayer.

disapaint-disappoint
anmarried-unmarried

CHAPTER 25

Goat mos know di size a him behain before him swala pear seed
The goat should consider the size of its anus before swallowing an avocado seed
We should think of the possible consequences before we carry out an action
Kakroach neba so jonk dat him waak a fowl yaad
The cockroach never gets so drunk that it ventures into a fowl's yard
Levity should not cause us to become reckless
Fowl bex wid rooster, a weh him sleep?
If the hen is angry with the rooster, where will it sleep?
Do not burn your bridges

The sudden afternoon downpour had slowed to a drizzle and the sun was creeping out through the clouds. This was what Miss Maudie's mother used to describe as a sign that the Devil and his wife were fighting over a herring bone. A half-smile creased Miss Maudie's thin lips as her thoughts filled with memories of her parents, but her eyes remained cloudy.

If her mother were still alive, she would know what to do. Minnie Acquhart, had been an *Ettu* woman, a descendant of sea-rescued, slave ship occupants. She would have known how to fight this battle. Her people had been freed from illegal slave ships and settled upon Jamaica's western coast before they could have been traded for gain. This Miss Minnie had been no *pyaahn-pyaahn* woman. She had possessed the fighting spirit of a bantam hen and the courage of a lioness.

How Miss Maudie wished she could go back in time and sit in a dark corner of the Revivalist booth where her mother and father held services with the villagers who believed in their syncretism of Christianity and the remnants of their African beliefs. Their ardent followers had come from as far away as Hanover and Westmoreland in the west and Portland and St. Thomas in the east and, oh, how they used to worship.

They made the earth shake and the dust rise in the temple made of plaited coconut fronds and *crocus bags*. The lantern hanging from the center of the roof of the flimsy sanctuary created fantastic shadows on the white sheets that shaded the inside walls from prying eyes.

In those long gone days, Miss Maudie's father would become possessed by strange spirits and carry out unexplainable feats, like the time he tore out of the booth and ran up the trunk of a large *number eleven mango tree* without taking a hand or a foothold. The people of the district talked about this event for years.

She also remembered her mother falling into three-day trances and the other turbaned leaders laying her out before the altar where she remained as if dead until she returned from her spiritual journeys. She always came back with portents that never failed to be fulfilled.

In the March convention of 1944, Miss Minnie prophesied that their wells would run dry and the sheep of the flock would be scattered forever.

That was the year of the wind of a thousand horses. Miss Maudie's cousin lost his head when it was severed from his neck by a sailing sheet of zinc. The family was forced to bury him without ceremony because the land was flooded and torn up by the hurricane.

That was also the year when the Baptist pastor thundered from his pulpit that his church building had been spared the wrath of God because it was a place of true worship but the grass-thatched temple of Minnie and John Acquhart was the seat of Satan and that was why it was demolished by the hurricane.

He followed his strong words by calling the Colonial Constabulary to investigate acts of obeah and necromancy when the straggling members of the Revivalist church started meeting under a silk cotton tree that had survived the hurricane.

Matters later came to a head when the inspector of police raided their rebuilt temple of coconut fronds and thatch and forced Miss Maudie's father to consume the anointing oils that he kept for ministering to the sick among them. He collapsed and died after he reluctantly swallowed three vials of oil.

Miss Maudie stood looking out at the sodden landscape but her thoughts were turned completely inwards. She was saying one phrase over and over, "Laad, look pahn mi chobl; Laad, look pahn mi chobl."

She heard the bed in Joanie's room creak and turned away from the window, hoping that her granddaughter had plenty of money saved because they would need it. After what she was a planning to do, she did not expect to have a job come Monday morning. She was going up to Baptist Hill to confront The Reverend and Miss Birdie. She meant to let them know that Jimmy had put Joanie in the family way and he would need to right this awful wrong by putting gold upon her wedding finger.

But she was only Maudie Collins, widowed and poor. How was she going to stand up to such a wall of reproach? If it was Reverend Whitehead alone, she would stand a chance, but with Birdie and Deacon and Mrs. Swearing against her, she needed more than her failing will to fight them.

Miss Maudie walked over to her blue mahoe bed and bent her aging knees to the floor. She dipped her head and peered into the shadowy space until her eyes settled upon a dark object at the far corner. It was the mahogany cane that her father had used to chastise his errant flock. Many a transgressor had wept under its blows. The leaders of the temple had believed in flogging sin out of the iniquitous among them.

She reached for it and brought it out to the light. It was covered in dust and cobwebs but the gloss of its natural polish would return once she took a soft rag and some coconut oil to it.

Next to the cane was an old *dulcimena grip* and Miss Maudie reached back under the bed and pulled it out onto her bedside rag rug. It too was frosted with dust and cobwebs but she did not try to clean it before prizing open the rusted lock. The acrid odor of mothballs soon filled the room as she sat looking at its contents.

The items within were packed in layers of brown paper and a rumpled red turban sat on top like a giant maraschino cherry. Miss Maudie picked it up very gently and blew the dust from its creases. Next, she laid it upon her pillow and reached for some items of clothing. She unpacked her father's white shepherd's gown, his flour sack underdrawers and her mother's scarlet waist sash. Her task done, she closed the grip and pushed it back under the bed.

Miss Maudie began to dress herself in her parent's Revivalist regalia and as she did so she began to sing very softly:

Bam-bam, praise di Laad, oh
Bam-bam
Bam-bam, praise di Laad, oh

Bam-bam
Ef yu jump pokominna, yu wi ketch a faiya
Bam-bam, praise di Laad, oh
Bam-bam

She fixed the old turban on top of her graying head and turned to look at herself in the mirror at the foot of the bed. Her image did not frighten her although it was as if Minnie Acquhart was looking back at her. She felt her heart beat faster and her courage rise up within her. She was no longer afraid to face James and Birdie Whitehead because she now felt that she would not go alone.

She reached for her father's cane, whirled three times to make a complete circle of her bedroom and stepped backward through the doorway.

Miss Maudie continued to walk backward until she got to the steps of her verandah and then she did an about face, curtsied to the four cardinal points and descended the concrete steps. She struck her cane forcefully to the ground and began to walk to the main road. She would speak to no one until her mission was accomplished.

UP AT THE manse on Baptist Hill, Miss Birdie stirred from her afternoon nap and sat up in bed. But for the sound of the ticking wall clock, the hum of the refrigerator and the birds chirping in the yard, the afternoon was quiet. She had eaten her Saturday beef soup earlier in the afternoon and was feeling a little hungry.

She walked softly to the kitchen on the other side of the expansive living room and heard the murmur of male voices from her husband's study. She recognized the gravelly tenor of Deacon Swearing and continued on her way. Miss Birdie resolved within that she would talk to him later because she wanted to have a sit down with his wife, Dawn. The wedding was less than two months away and she still had not heard much from the young couple. She had tried to get James to take her down to the Swearings, earlier, but he had said that he had other matters to which to attend.

She and Dawn needed to go over the details of the wedding cake and the bridesmaids' dresses. Genevieve was bringing her dress from the United States and Miss Birdie was disappointed but she held her peace. She had wanted to make the dress but had not pushed too hard because Dawn seemed very satisfied with her daughter's decision.

Miss Birdie was reaching for a cup and saucer from a high kitchen cabinet when her eye caught the flaming red of Miss Maudie's turban as she started to climb the front steps. Her breath caught in her throat when she saw the rigid lines of Miss Maudie's face when she passed the kitchen window and moved upward. If she had seen Miss Birdie in the kitchen, she showed no sign of it.

In the second in which Maudie looked into the house before disappearing, Miss Birdie noted that the planes of her forehead and cheeks seemed carved and polished and her thin lips lay like a laceration below her imperious nose. The clicking sound of her cane came clearly into the kitchen through the open window and Miss Birdie shivered.

She wondered why Miss Maudie was wearing such a strange outfit and why she was approaching the front door when she almost always entered from the back. She was suddenly affronted by this unexpected boldness and hastily put her cup and saucer away before hurrying to the living room.

By the time Miss Birdie got to the room, Miss Maudie was standing in the doorway and the evening shadows mixed with waning sunlight made her a frightening spectacle. She stood silently, glowering at Miss Birdie and tap-tapping her cane on the tile floor.

Miss Birdie felt her hackles rise and without planning to, she raised her voice and almost screamed at Miss Maudie.

"What you come up here in this get-up for, Maudie! You have any reason to march through my front door as if you have ownership in this house? How dare you, Maudie Collins!"

Miss Maudie walked further into the room and stood directly under the ceiling light. The sight and smell of her made Birdie recoil. She smelled of age and death and her visage under the scarlet turban was chiseled and implacable.

Before Miss Birdie could speak again, The Reverend and Deacon Swearing rushed into the living and stood on either side of her. She instinctively reached for her husband and he held her tiny trembling hand in his.

Deacon Swearing looked at Miss Maudie and stepped back a little. She looked at him and said, "No move, Deekan, becausen whatever me have to seh *kansaan* yu too."

Deacon Swearing seemed very shocked but he stopped his backward shuffle and continued to look quizzically at Miss Maudie, his mouth slightly open.

Reverend Whitehead pulled Miss Birdie a little closer to him, wrapped one arm around her shoulder for a few seconds and then took charge. He led her gently to the two-seater arm chair under the wall clock. He indicated to Deacon Swearing that he should take Miss Birdie's piano bench and he gestured Miss Maudie to the single armchair that was next to a potted fern on the other side of the room.

She sat, click-clicking her ebony cane on the tiled floor and looking sternly at the three gathered across from her and then she spoke.

"Joanie come home wid a *stumok* and she identify Jimmy as the man who faal har."

The three listeners continued to stare at her without speaking and so she tapped her cane for emphasis and spoke very slowly, "Mi-gran-daata-come-home-wid-a-an-married-belly…"

Before she could go further, Miss Birdie rose to her feet and hissed through clenched teeth, "Maudie Collins, you and your whore of a granddaughter can…"

The Reverend tugged Miss Birdie's arm with such force that she fell back into the armchair. He slapped an open palm over her mouth and said urgently, "Hush, Birdie, hush. Don't say anything more. I will handle this!"

Birdie bit him so hard that he unsealed her mouth and she ran towards the kitchen, Deacon Swearing scuttling behind her like a land crab caught in daylight. In the meantime, Reverend Whitehead remained seated and rubbed his right palm over his right knee as if tending arthritic pain. His eyes never left Miss Maudie's face.

Miss Birdie could be heard sobbing in the kitchen and Deacon Swearing could be heard trying to quiet her. Miss Birdie's distress did not stop Miss Maudie from saying her piece. She stood up and said to The Reverend, "Whatever plans yu and di Swearing dem have fi wedn, unu better close it dong becausen Jimmy will have to married to Joanie. Me spen too much money pahn har fi she come *ton wotlis*. If a man spwail mi goods, me *entaikl* to compensation."

Miss Birdie started to wail in earnest as the words spilled out of Miss Maudie's mouth in a torrent. She ran back into the living room and the sound of her house slippers echoed off the tile floor as she continued to her bedroom.

Deacon Swearing returned to the piano seat and sat milking his fingers like a man condemned to death.

The Reverend James John Whitehead, the first, rose to his full angular height and looked down his aquiline nose at Miss Maudie before he spoke.

"That's the most vulgar thing I have ever heard in my life, Maudie Collins. I have no way of knowing who fathered Joan's child and my grandson is not here to defend himself. Please leave my home and do not come back here until you can prove that you have some manners."

"So dis is what me years a labor reap me? Yu a run me out a yu house like mi is a *kaman* lap-daag. Is alright, Rev."

She nodded her head as if slowly comprehending her true situation and then she stood up and whirled upon her heels as if ending a *Kumina* dance. Still mincing in that light, dancer's walk, she made her way across the room and stood in the doorway.

"*Ebri daag hab dem day and ebri puss dem four a'klak.* A live clean all mi life, Reveren. No matter di *provokaishan,* A neba dip dese two hands into evil and A want to keep it dat way. A give mi wol life to yu and Birdie. When yu son dead and Birdie all but get aaf har head, A nurse har back to *helt.* When di biebi-bwai Jimmy come to yu, A *niglek* mi own granchilvren fi help wid him…"

Reverend Whitehead sat down again but his voice was filled with reproach when he interrupted Miss Maudie.

"So, because you did acts of kindness for this family, you think that gives you the right to invade our home with your nonsense and nastiness?"

He stood again, straightened his bony shoulders and walked up to her where she stood in the doorway. Miss Maudie faced him boldly and her face remained a stark African mask.

"You come up here to the church house, dressed in your *Myal* clothes. Do you think I am afraid of you, Maudie? You make me sick; you, with your skin deep conversion and your heartfelt secrets. I will call a board meeting tomorrow and see to it that you are removed from fellowship. And to think I ate from your hands!"

Miss Maudie looked long and hard at him and then she turned with a swish of the voluminous skirt of her gown and walked to the top of the concrete steps. She paused and with her back to Reverend Whitehead, she bent and removed her shoes from her feet. Miss Maudie then wiped the soles with the hem of her gown and replaced them. When she got to the verandah, she sprayed an arch of slimy, silvery saliva over the concrete wall. The dying rays of the evening sun disappeared with it as it splattered to the earth.

Ettu-Yoruba people found in the western section of Jamaica, especially Hanover and Westmoreland. They are also called Nago.

pyaahn-pyaahn-feeble and inconsequential

crocus bags-croaker sacks

number eleven mango-type of mango known for its distinctive flavor

dulcimena grip-old fashioned suitcase; usually rectangular and made from dark material

kansaan-concern

stumok-stomach; euphemism for pregnancy

entaikl-entitled

kaman-common

Kumina-religious African retentive dance used for celebrating births, deaths and other special memorials

Ebri daag hab dem day and ebri puss dem four a'klak-Every dog has his day and every puss his four o'clock; every person has his season of triumph or downfall.

provokaishan-provocation

helt-health

niglek-neglect

CHAPTER 26

Maudie Collins and Miss Mama

2003

If yu no mash ants yu no find him got
If you do not mash an ant you will not find its guts
Sometimes you have to offend someone to learn the truth about that person
Tan an see no pwail no daance, is intafierants kaaz it
You can only spoil the dance by interfering; you do not spoil it by standing to the side and watching
If di bikl a no fi yu, no dip spoon deh, oh

If you have not provided the victuals, do not dip a spoon in, please; Mind your own business

Miss Maudie left Chalky Hill the next day, at three in the morning. Before she walked out of her house, she stood in the curtained doorway of her granddaughter's room and watched her as she slept. She considered waking her and taking her on the trip with her but thought better of it because of Joanie's advanced pregnancy.

When she got to Danny Willis' car, she was morose and barely greeted the friendly young man. She did not tell him where she wanted to go until they were outside of the district and only after warning him that she did not want Chalky Hill's uol niega people fi faas in har business. She also warned him that if she heard about her journey in the future, she would know the source of the leakage, because she had not told even Joanie about her plans.

While speaking she watched Danny's face through the rearview mirror and although she could see very little beyond the whites of his eyes and the glint of his teeth, she knew he could see her. She maintained a dark scowl until they were on the coastal road to Kingston.

Miss Maudie planned to make one stop in Spanish Town to inform Madge of Joanie's condition. She would then proceed to the easternmost point of the island to consult with Miss Mama, a powerful and respected Revivalist Mada who had been Maudie's playmate when they were children.

When Danny drove out of Yallahs in St. Thomas, it was almost eight o'clock and the car was steaming. He had unbuttoned his shirt and Miss Maudie sat sweating in the back seat. She stared out of the car window at the lush landscape flashing by but her visage remained stern.

The road soon began to climb to hill country and Danny was relieved because of the thick hanging vegetation that held off the powerful rays of the sun. They crossed over into the parish of Portland and when they arrived in Manchioneal, Miss Maudie advised Danny to park the car near the police station and wait there for her. She would take the rest of her journey on foot.

He offered to go with her but she refused, with thanks. As Danny silently watched her, she laced crepe-soled shoes on to her feet. When Miss Maudie was done changing her shoes, she placed a mid-sized, multicolored straw basket upon her head before disappearing on an uphill dirt road that entered a stand of tropical rain forest.

As Miss Maudie walked, she began to talk to herself. Her feet carried her through a coffee walk and dense vegetation shot through with violent colors of blood crimson, funerary purple and bold yellows. The wild flowers touched everything that grew, sprouting between thick shrubs and hanging from giant withes that wound around the trunks of trees that grew to magnificent heights in search of sunlight.

The tropical daylight glinted through the green to dapple the forest floor with streaks and ripples of golden light. The whistling and chirping sounds of birds carried on the wind that rustled through the vegetation.

On a better day, she would have stopped to enjoy the free bounty of nature's trappings but, today her heart was too heavy to see more than the path for her feet.

It was close to ten in the morning when Miss Maudie arrived at the river. She stepped from the bank and felt the cool water lap at her ankles. It was a good day for crossing because there were no rain clouds in the Blue Mountain. When the river came down in all its muddy vigor, it could be uncrossable for many days.

The water was so clear that she could see the pebbles and rocks at the bottom. Big-eyed mullets flashed by, hiding behind stones and logs in the gentle flow and when her shoe bumped a rock, a crayfish scuttled away.

The little creature brought back memories of her childhood when her parents would take her on the three-day cart ride to Portland for revival and Emancipation celebration. While the adults tended to their spiritual nourishment, the children frolicked in the river and in the surrounding vegetation.

That was then, but Jamaica had undergone more than a transformation since those days of *Busha* and the white mistress in the big house. Because of free education, nobody could ever tell her granddaughter where she could go and what she could become, but all the education in the world would not make Birdie Whitehead accept her. She couldn't make Birdie embrace Joanie, but, perhaps, with Miss Mama's intervention, she could make Jimmy marry her.

That was how Miss Maudie rationalized her actions as she crossed to the other bank of the river and set her feet on dry land. What did it matter that she had Jimmy's underwear into the basket that she balanced upon her turbaned head? What did it matter that she had a picture of Birdie and Reverend Whitehead in there, too, and a few strands of her granddaughter's hair? It wasn like she did a set out fi kill anybody or fi ton dem in a *tuffenkeh*. No, she wuda never put a spell pahn anybody fi ton dem in a *kunu-munu*, but she felt that her cause was just and she was therefore entitled to Divine favor. Furthermore, her friend Miss Mama worked with the right hand and would never hurt anyone.

When Miss Maudie reached the valley between two giant hillocks, she saw Miss Mama's balmyard laid out like an ancient village below. Her compound was fenced by bamboo and three flags atop a wattle and daub temple, waved in the mountain breeze.

Miss Maudie straightened her skirt, wiped the perspiration from her face and then removed the basket from her head. She pulled off the wet crepe-soled shoes and exchanged them for a pair of black pumps. After sliding the wet shoes into a plastic bag, she placed the bag in the basket and walked to the gate.

Before she could knock on the zinc and wooden gate, it swung inward and a broad, orange-brown woman scooped her into a warm embrace. Miss Maudie had last seen her ten years before when she had taken Joanie to her for a blessing after she won the government scholarship for high school. Many years before that, she had sought her help to cleanse her house after her husband's sudden death. Miss Mama, however, did not seem surprised to find Miss Maudie standing at her gate and after kissing her cheeks, she led her into the house.

Miss Mama called out to a young lady who answered from the thatched outside kitchen. She soon came in with an enamel face basin and a fresh wash cloth. Miss Maudie thanked her and gratefully washed her hands and face. The young lady deftly removed the items and returned with a steaming mug of chocolate tea, fried johnny cakes, ripe avocado and codfish fried in onions, tomatoes and sweet peppers.

While Miss Maudie ate she listened to the singing coming from the temple next door and from its subdued nature, she knew that the worshipers were in contemplation and meditation. The call was done by Miss Mama's second husband, Breda Baada, and the response followed from the congregants.

They were singing the hymn *Guide Me, O Thou Great Jehovah* and Miss Maudie soon found herself chewing her food to the slow measure of the singers. By the time they got to the last stanza, she had stopped eating and her tears were falling without restraint.

Miss Mama wiped Miss Maudie's face with a red bandana and started to fan her with a large, plaited, straw square. She spoke soothingly over her, and, soon Miss Maudie's tears subsided.

The quiet young lady returned to remove the unfinished food and Miss Mama asked her to close the door behind her. When Miss Mama was sure of their privacy, she drew her wicker chair closer to Miss Maudie and regarded her earnestly before speaking.

"Di Spirit show me more dan a mont ago dat yu was gwaihn come to me and I was given specific instructions fi yu."

Miss Maudie sat up straighter and her eyes remained glued to Miss Mama's kind, round face.

"So yu know wa me come bout, Mama?"

"Yes mi love and mi haat go out to yu, but, me answer to a higher *kaalin.*

"What yu mean? Yu a try fi tell me dat mi labor dash-weh a well batam?"

"No *daalin*, yu labor no dash-weh, but dis *sitiaishan* is bigger dan yu and yu ha fi waak into it wid *kaashan. Mek yu belly taak more* dan *yu mout. Nyam some and lef back some*, mi dear sista in Christ."

"What yu a try fi tell me, Mama? Yu a tell me dat me kyaahn get justice?"

"Wa kain a justice yu waahn from me, daalin?"

"Me waahn di bwai Jimmy fi married Joanie because him kyaahn chruo har dong a bush and waak weh lef har like she a *leggo-biis*!"

Miss Mama drew her chair a little closer and took Miss Maudie's hands into hers. When their eyes connected, Miss Mama's were bright with tears that soon spilled down her freckled cheeks. She squeezed Miss Maudie's hands and swallowed before responding.

"Maudie, mi sista, remember dat wa yu han commit, yu badi bear. Dese two hands of mine are committed to di work of Gaad. When *Big Maasa* chruo me dong in faastin fi chrii day, Him gi me a gif and Him aada me never to tek payment fi di work and never to participate in di pursuit of wickedness. Mi kaalin is healin and restoration and me mos obey. Vengeance belang to Him. *Furdamoar,* dis matter *hinvalv* more complexity dan wa yu know bout. So, duohn overshoot yu mout, because wan wod spoken in ignorance kyan staat a war dat never done."

"So what mos I do? Me fi jos sit back and watch Jimmy married to Diikan Swearing daata while mi grandaata si-dong wan-side like a doti gyal? Where is di justice in dat, Mama? Me mos watch Birdie wear di robe of proud granmada while me slink in a kaana like *maaga daag?*

Miss Mama let go of Miss Maudie's hands and pulled back her chair before interlocking her fingers over her ample middle. She closed her eyes and began to speak in a sonorous sing-song. She had moved from personal friend to Divine Emissary and Miss Maudie knew better than to interfere in the exchange.

"Di way of di transgressor is haad and he that is often reproved and stiffeneth his neck, shall be cut-aaf and widout remedy. Gaad know di secrets of every haat and whatsoever a man soweth, dat shall he also reap. Di haat of man is deceitfully wicked, who kyan know it? When a man's ways please di Laad, He makes even his enemies to be at peace wid him."

Miss Mama slowly opened her eyes and looked at Miss Maudie. There was kindness in the depths of her gaze but her tone was firm.

"*So me buy it, so me sell it*; so me get it, so me ha fi deliver it. *No better herrin, no better barrel.* Uol groj mek patu lay hegg, sister."

Miss Maudie bowed her head and began to weep quietly. She felt like a gambler who had bet all and lost. What did she have to look forward to? She found herself pleading before she could stop herself.

"Dere mos be somting yu kyan do fi ton tings to mi favor. Yu kyaahn leave me high and dry like dis, Mama. Me wok too haad and tek too much advantage from Birdie Whitehead…"

"Hush yuh mout, Maudie! Don't yu vencha dong dat road, because di way back is all up-hill!"

She rose to her feet and beckoned to Miss Maudie to stand with her. Miss Mama faced her friend and the two survivors of the colonial constabulary persecution of 1944, looked at each other, both remembering past days. Miss Mama's eyes were gentle but her tone was firm as she wrapped her arms around her sister-friend and gripped her in a tight embrace. Her lips were warm upon Miss Maudie's ear as she whispered deep counsel to her friend.

"Tan saafli better dan beg paadn, sista. Laan fi tek butter and nyam fat and *duohn buy distress put pahn pavati.* Yu do not know yu grandaata half as well as yu tink yu do. Fram di time yu tek har here when she was a likl gyal, me know she was gwaihn to brok yu haat. But when A si how yu dote pahn har, A kudn bring miself fi tell yu so early. She will waak far before she come to har senses and yu kyaahn go wid har. She will *kraas waata* and *sop wid saro* before she find har way, but tek courage, mi dear sista. *Maasa Gaad a Gaad.*

A will waak wid yu back to di *riba* and when yu ketch deh, yu mos chruo-weh di basket dat yu bring wid yu so dat yu no kyari *kandemnaishan* go back in a yu house. Di stumok dat Joanie a kyari is a *ketch man belly* but di man is far beyon har reach. Unfortunately, she will have to live wid di consequences of har doings. Memba seh uol-time people use to seh, '*A kansikwenshal mek kraab no hab no head.*' Yu mos also mek peace wid di revren jenklman and him wife, because dere is a likl-wan a come who gwaihn need a saaf place fi land."

The two women walked out of the house and climbed the path that led away from the balmyard. Neither of them spoke until they got to the bank of the river. There, Miss Mama helped Miss Maudie to take the straw basket down from off her head. Together, they walked into the shallow water and Miss Mama led Miss Maudie to a large river-bleached boulder that had been weathered into the shape of a crude altar. Miss Mamma instructed Miss Maudie to place the basket at the center of the rock. When this was done, she pulled a small rum bottle from her apron pocket and poured its content over the basket. She dropped the bottle back into her pocket, fished out a box of scarlet-tipped matches and handed them to Miss Maudie. Miss Mama instructed her to put a light to the basket. When Miss Maudie hesitated, Miss Mama's face grew stern and her voice took on the flint of a Victorian school-mistress.

"Maudie, yu mos burn dat basket and yu mos beg Big Maasa fi paadn yu! Di wan ting dat elevate man-kain over *brute-biis* is di exercise a him free will. Any time we seek fi interfere wid di freedom to choose, we waakin in daaknis. Dat is obeah. No dwiit again fa Maasa Gaad wi *tear yu aas* an yu kyaahn stan it! *Him lick hat!*

Miss Maudie lit a match to the leeward side of the basket and it caught fire immediately. As flames ran up one side of the basket and spread over the top, she began to weep afresh.

Miss Mama had stepped away from her sister-friend as she chastised her. She now closed the distance between them, wrapped both arms around Miss Maudie and folded her to her bosom. They did not speak again until the flames petered out and all that was left of the basket was a pile of black cinders.

MISS MAUDIE GOT back to the police station to find Danny dozing over the steering wheel. He had locked the doors of the car and opened the roof vent. She had to knock three times before he opened one eye and squinted owlishly at her. Under other circumstances she would have laughed at the picture he presented, but there was no merriment in her as she stood waiting for him to unlock the back door.

Danny turned to look at Miss Maudie and he grew concerned.

"Wa happen to yu, ma'am? Yu not lookin too good. Yu want me get yu a *kuokanat waata?*"

Miss Maudie declined, but Danny ignored her and hurried across the street to the bar and restaurant that abutted a grocery store.

When he returned, he had a large disposable cup of chilled coconut water and a boxed dinner of brown-stewed fish, boiled yellow yam and steamed calaloo.

Miss Maudie was so overcome with emotion that her hands trembled when she took the food and drink from Danny. She asked him how much she owed him, but he smiled and brushed her off.

"Fi how you good to me all di time, Miss Maudie, a bax dinner is a smaal ting. Enjoy."

He closed his door, told her to put on her seat belt because they would be going downhill and around tricky curves for a while.

If he was surprised by the tears trickling down her cheeks, he kept it to himself and for that, Miss Maudie was grateful.

They got back to Chalky Hill when only the vagrants were abroad and it was not until late the following morning that Miss Maudie learned that while she journeyed to Portland, Birdie Whitehead collapsed in the middle of playing a hymn and was rushed to hospital. She had suffered a massive stroke and her life yet lay in the balance.

busha-overseer; property manager; landowner
tuffenkeh-idiot, feeble-minded
kunu-munu-idiotic; ugly and simpleminded
johnny cakes-fried dough; fried dumplings
Guide Me, O, Thou Great Jehovah-Christian hymn written by William Williams, Welsh hymn writer
kaalin-calling; vocation; ministry
daalin-darling

sitiaishan-situation

kaashan-caution

mek yu belly taak more dan yu mout-keep your thoughts to yourself; be wise and reticent

Nyam some and lef back some-Eat some and leave some on the plate; do not throw caution to the wind; show some restraint; do not reveal all that you know.

leggo biis-wild beast; term used to describe an uncouth or promiscuous person

gif-gift

fordamuor-furthermore

hinvalv-involve

maaga daag-underfed and skinny (meager) dog

so me buy it, so me sell it-I have sold it in the same manner in which I bought it; I have delivered the message as I got it.

no better herrin, no better barrel-The herring is no better than its container; the message and the messenger are one and the same; I cannot give you a different message.

duohn buy distress put pahn pavati-Do not add distress to poverty; do not make a bad situation worse.

kraas waata-cross water; travel overseas

sop wid saro-sup with sorrow

riba-river

kandemnaishan-condemnation

ketch-man belly-pregnancy that is meant to entrap a man

Kansikwenshal mek kraab no hab no head-The crab lost its head as a consequence of something that it did; karma.

brute-biis-brute beast

tear yu aas-tear your ass; punish you harshly

him lick hat-he hits hard; his punishment is harsh

koukanat waata-coconut water

CHAPTER 27

Maudie Elfreda Collins and Joan Marie Jackman

2003

Haad yez pikini nyam rak-stone
The child who does not listen will eat stones
Disobedience and wrongdoing bring harsh consequences
When young bod shit, him tink him lay
When the young bird shits it thinks it has laid an egg
The young can be very ignorant and arrogant

When Joanie awakened the next morning, Miss Maudie was already up and busy in the kitchen. She heard the kettle whistle and then stop. The smell of fried plantains, sardines and eggs mingled with strong coffee, was brought into the room by her whirring fan.

Joanie sat up against her pillows and rubbed her breastbone, trying to press the heartburn reflux back to where it belonged. She wanted to put down this baby real soon because it was beginning to feel like a malicious overgrowth. It kicked at inconvenient times, pushed at her bladder and made her pee frequently. She was also always hungry but she did not want to go into the kitchen to face Miss Maudie because she did not know what was going on with her.

Miss Maudie had come in on Saturday night, looking as mad as a landed alligator and dressed weird. She had seen *Pocomania* and Revivalist people dressed like that before and keeping their *clap-han* and *jump-up* meetings at roadsides and in the market in Spanish Town. She even recalled an occasion when the Prime Minister had allowed several groups of them to spread a table and carry out their rituals at Jamaica House, his official residence. The traditional church leaders had cried shame upon him for allowing the worshipers to carry out their activities in such an important public space. However, like everything else that did not involve bellyfull and government handouts, the controversy was soon forgotten.

But for the life of her, Joanie could not understand why her grandmother had walked into the house wearing a flowing white gown, a red turban and carrying a black cane. She had even wondered if Miss Maudie was working obeah to make Jimmy marry her but had quickly dismissed the thought.

There would be no need for witchcraft to get Jimmy to the altar. He was a soon to be ordained minister and who ever heard of a minister having a *biebi mada*? He would have to marry her to take shame out of his eye and that was that. To hell wid Genevieve Swearing and Miss Birdie and, too bad fi Reverend.

Joanie had awakened the day before to find Miss Maudie gone and she had not returned until way past midnight. Yet, here she was, cooking breakfast at her usual hour. How she did it, Joanie did not know, but her grandmother was a creature of habit who often went to work even when she was ill.

Joanie coughed and Miss Maudie answered from the kitchen behind the living room.

"Yu up, Joanie? Wash yu face and come in here. A want to have a taak wid yu."

Joanie sucked her teeth quietly and pushed open the bathroom door with her foot. She held her belly-bottom with her right hand and hiked up her nightdress with the left. When her bottom made contact with the cold toilet seat, she recoiled but was soon emptying her bladder in relief. These days she did not bother with panties unless she had to leave the house. They were too tight and they got in the way when she had to go with urgency. Pregnancy was no easy business, so, Jimmy had better have something good to give her for blessing him with his first child.

She heard Miss Maudie calling her again and in a voice tight with impatience and annoyance, she responded, "A comin, ma'am!"

Her grandmother's back was toward her when she entered the kitchen but she turned around as soon as Joanie stood in the doorway.

The first thing that Joanie noted was the seriousness of Miss Maudie's face. Her lips were folded inward and there were bags under her eyes. When her grandmother looked at her, there was no warmth in her eyes, just a bottomless sadness.

Joanie quickly averted her eyes and walked over to the stove but Miss Maudie shooed her back to the table and brought over a prepared plate and a mug of coffee. She shook her head indicating that she did not want the coffee and Miss Maudie looked back at her with a puzzled frown.

"The doctor said I shouldn't drink it. It's not good for the baby."

"Dyam foolishness. I drink *kaafi* wid all a mi biebi dem and nat a ting happen to dem."

"Well, him seh A mos not drink it and I am followin orders."

"Yu lucky. So wa yu gwaihn drink fi buss di gyas weh in a yu *pazam* tumok? Yu ha fi drink somting hat becausen when yu a breed, yu duohn waahn gyas fi tek yu up. If bad gyas get aanda yu *pupu root*, aye sa, or up in a yu *paapm crease*, yu *faat faiya*."

Joanie began to laugh, helplessly, and a fleeting smile creased Miss Maudie's lips before she walked back to her storage table and removed a brown paper bag filled with dried mint.

"Yu waahn dis mint or yu waahn *cerasee*?"

Joanie began to protest in alarm and Miss Maudie shoved out her bottom lip before declaring, "Yu lucky. *When puss got full, him seh ratta seed bitter.* Cerasee good fi yu insides, especially when yu prignant. And yu shuda drink some *sinklebible* and eat nof okro fi mek di biebi slip out easy."

"Far from it, ma'am. Cerasee harden yu liver and yu shouldn't drink it at all."

"Cho, unu young people duohn know anyting."

Miss Maudie rinsed the mint, crumpled the leaves in her porcelain teapot and poured in water from a thermos before covering the brew and bringing it to the table.

"Mek it steep fi a likl bit and den yu kyan sweeten it."

She put the pot on a straw placemat and a *polly-lizard* scuttled away from the heat. The little reptile skittered along Joan's forearm which was resting on the table. She screamed and jumped up, her chair making a clatter behind her.

Miss Maudie grabbed her by the shoulders and steadied her.

"Yu kyaahn frighten so over a likl lizad! Yu will maak di biebi!"

She picked up the chair and Joan sat down gingerly while peering under the other mats to see if there were more crawlers there.

"Pikni, eat up di likl food before it get kuol. Yu no waahn frighten over every likl ting, becausen dat not good fi yu when yu a ekspek. Dat's how Chinzee bwai come fi so favor goat. Chinzee mada did a clean a goat head and belly fi mek soup and di goat head frighten Chinzee when she waak into di kitchen and *bok* it up pahn di stove. Di pikini dat she did a kyari, baan wid a livin goat face. Di ongl ting missin a di two goat *haan.* Mi no *iibn* tink him hab any tap tiit."

Joanie started to giggle again and then asked her grandmother, "Yu really believe dat Chinzee son look like a goat because a goat head frighten him mada when she pregnant wid him? Me agree seh him favor goat fi true, but a jos so him baan."

"Tan deh a laugh. *Wa yu no know uola dan yu* but A duohn have time fi fun dis maanin. A need to have a serious taak wid yu."

"What about?"

Joanie's face was suddenly somber and the mood in the room shifted from warmth to brittle suspicion. She declared with more defiance than she actually felt, "Miss Maudie, if is my staying here you worrying about, I can go back to town as soon as I talk to Jimmy."

Miss Maudie's sigh came like a half-sob and her hand trembled as she placed her breakfast plate across from Joanie and sat down. She carefully speared a piece of boiled green banana, swished it in gravy and brought it to her mouth. She chewed steadily for a few moments and Joanie busied herself with the pouring of her tea.

When she leaned back in her chair she found Miss Maudie watching her.

"Joanie, yu get a good edikaishan but yu future not lookin bright."

Joanie started to eat but remained silent, so, Miss Maudie continued to talk. "What plan yu have fi yuself and di *anbaan* chail if Jimmy refuse fi married to yu?"

"Jimmy ha fi married to me!"

Her face had closed into a mask of cold determination and Miss Maudie sighed again.

"A blame miself, becausen A neba teach yu notn bout man. A teach yu ebriting excep dat, and A was rang."

Miss Maudie stopped eating, placed her right elbow upon the table and her fork up to her cheek, like a shield. She studied her granddaughter for a while as if trying to decide something very important.

"Tell me somting, Joanie, did Jimmy *put kwestian to yu*?"

The query was so unexpected that Joanie turned bright red. She did not answer her grandmother but attacked her food and began to chew ferociously. The rapid rise and fall of her bosom and the force of her chewing were the only signs of her turbulent emotions.

"A need yu to tell me if Jimmy approach yu or if is yu approach him, becausen, if is yu aafa yuself to him, *daag nyam yu supper*. What a man hunt, him will value, but wa dash give him, him will rend to pieces. So if Jimmy neba ax yu kwestian and yu lai-dong wid him, yu *fish-pat ketch trash*." A man *piragitiv* is to ax uman kwestian and a uman piragitiv fi answer 'yes' or 'no.'"

"Miss Maudie, whether Jimmy ask me question or not, this child is his and he will have to put a ring on my finger or there will be no peace in his house. He will marry Genevieve but I will always be a *maka* in a him foot. I do not intend to be a biebi mada. I intend to be a wife."

"Eh! Yu taak chrang and mighty but memba seh goat better know di size a him *batty-wol* before him swala pear seed. Wa a man *kuotn*, him love, but wa dash give him, him trample aanda him foot. All me ha fi tell yu is dat dere is a pikni between yu and Jimmy and if him no want it, yu will burden wid it fi a lang time."

"Whether Jimmy want it or not, it will be here and when Miss Birdie see it, she will not be able to do anything about it."

"Oh, so dis pikni is about spiting Miss Birdie?"

Miss Maudie's tone was deeply reproachful as she continued, "Is nat ongl a ketch-man stumok yu a kyari, but spite in a it, too. Oh, I see. Umph, yu gwaihn *suck salt chuu udn spoon* and when Birdie Whitehead done wid yu, yu *fenneh* grease. A fraid a yu. You bad no bitch, but try memba dat dere is always a bada bitch. *Time langa dan rope and di langis liba will see di muos.*"

Miss Maudie pushed her unfinished food away from her and stared at her grandchild for a long time. Joanie glanced at her once, her eyes fierce and defiant, yet evasive. She turned back to her food and continued to eat between sips of mint tea.

Miss Maudie rose from the table and stood looking down at Joanie but this time she refused to meet her grandmother's condemning eyes. She continued to chew her food and sip her tea.

After standing over Joanie for a few moments longer, Miss Maudie walked to the steps that led down into her backyard and her body blocked the morning sunlight as she stood in the doorway. With her back turned to her beloved granddaughter, she spoke as if to herself.

"And to tink dat because a yu, A all but put mi han to evil. Me trabl far fi go see bout yu and all dis while, is a ketch-man belly yu a kyari."

She turned back into the room and picked up an aluminum pan filled with corn grains. Turning back to the door, Miss Maudie walked down the steps and began to whistle for her fowls. She threw the first handful of grains and the birds began to clamor and flap their wings as they bore down upon the feeding place.

Miss Maudie watched the fowls pecking furiously in the grass and gravel and then turned to go back into the house. That was when she saw a mongoose streak away from the chicken coop that leaned against the sturdy guinep tree, next to the fowl-coop. The thieving animal had a fresh egg clutched in its jaws and she reached for a stone to pelt the creature. By the time her hand came up, the mongoose had disappeared into the shrubbery. Miss Maudie released a long sigh, dropped the stone and threw a final handful of corn to her fowls.

It was when she heard the crunch of wheels on gravel and the quick beep! beep! of Danny's car horn that she remembered that she no longer had a job. She sighed, slapped the empty aluminum pan against her aging thigh and walked around the side of the house to greet the young man.

Pocomania-syncretism of African religions and Christianity; shares similarities with Revivalism but there are some points of difference

clap-han-religious worship that involves singing and handclapping

jump-up-derogatory reference to the jumping and dancing involved in some forms of worship

biebi mada-mother of a child; a term often used by the father of the child

kaafi-coffee

pazam-spasm

pupu-root/paapm crease-anus (vulgar)

Cerasee-*Momordica charantia*; very bitter herb used for making tea

when puss got full, him seh ratta seed bitter-When the cat has eaten enough, it says that the rat's scrotum tastes bitter; when we are full, we find fault with the meal; we are enjoying prosperous times and so we become picky and critical.

sinklebible-aloe vera

polly lizard-*Sphaerodactylus argus*; juvenile house lizard

bok-butt; butted into

haan-horn

iibn-even

tap-tiit-top teeth

Wa yu no know uola dan yu-What you don't know is older than you are; your elders possess ancient knowledge; you are not privy to all of the facts.

anbaan-unborn

put kwestian to yu-propositioned you

Daag nyam yu supper-A dog has eaten your supper; you are out of luck or you have fallen upon hard times.

Yu fish pat ketch trash-Your fish pot has collected trash; your effort is in vain ; you are out of luck.

piragitiv-prerogative

maka-thorn

batty-wol-anus (vulgar)

kuotn-court; woo

swala pear seed-swallow an avocado seed

suck salt chuu udn spoon-suck salt through a wooden spoon; an expression denoting hardship and futility

fenneh-vomit

Time langa dan rope-Time is longer than a piece of rope.

Di langis liba will see di muos-The person who lives longest will see the most.

CHAPTER 28

Ef yu no get it in di whiilin yu will get it in di jiggin
If you do not get your turn in the reel you will get it in the jig
We do not escape the consequences of our actions
Some people come-iin like cow doo-do: haad a tap and saaf a batam
Some people are like cow droppings in the pasture that seem hard at the top but are actually soft underneath.
There is a difference between appearance and reality

It was late Friday afternoon and Miss Maudie had been home for almost a week. She had cleaned the house from top to bottom, laundered the baby's clothes and sniffed in disapproval when she saw the bags of disposable diapers that Joanie had bought. In short, she had done all that there was to do in the house and was growing restless and fretful. Joanie felt sorry for her grandmother but was too preoccupied with her own concerns to pay attention to her.

Still thinking about Miss Maudie, Joanie pushed up her back bedroom window and stood watching the tops of the crowded trees in the gully behind the chicken coop. As the sun crept away from the land, the tops of the trees darkened like bruised broccoli tops. She liked this time of day when all came to rest and the chickens came to roost in the backyard. At that time of the day, she always felt a sense of relief that the escape of sleep would come with the night.

She could hear the low hum of Miss Maudie's sewing machine and she smiled. Miss Maudie, despite her bluster, was a pussycat as far as Joanie was concerned. She had glared at her and talked to herself out loud for most of Monday, especially after Danny told her what had happened to Miss Birdie and she asked him to drive her up to the manse. Miss Maudie reported that when she arrived, she found Dawn Swearing presiding coldly over affairs.

Miss Maudie also told Joanie that Mrs. Swearing would not even divulge Miss Birdie's whereabouts or her state of health. If she had not run into Nathan Whitehead on her way back home, she would not have learned that Miss Birdie had been airlifted from the St. Ann's Bay Hospital to the University Hospital at Mona and that her condition was considered grave.

He told her that his brother was distraught and staying by her side. Miss Maudie said that poor Nathan Whitehead seemed beside himself as he told her of the sad happenings and for a moment she considered not telling him about Joanie's pregnancy. However, she needed someone on her side, so, she took him into her confidence.

Miss Maudie also felt genuine regret over Miss Birdie's illness and moments of heart-sickening guilt for the part she had played in her downfall. Now that she knew that Joanie was in the wrong, she wished she had sat in stillness before her God instead of trying to twist events to her favor. God knows, she had not thrown a blow at Birdie Whitehead but she knew that Reverend Whitehead and the Swearings would never see it that way. No doubt, her name was already being savaged by the members of the church. If Miss Birdie should die, she would be blamed for it.

Joanie knew of Miss Maudie's agony of spirit because she overheard her talking to Danny on the verandah and she heard when he told her that Deacon Swearing had called a meeting of the church officers and reported that Miss Maudie was an obeah worker and should be disfellowshipped from the church.

Miss Maudie had fresh worry lines etched into her forehead and Joanie was somewhat troubled about her but she kept her misgivings to herself. As far as she was concerned, if Miss Maudie was even working obeah, she was not doing anything that most of the villagers did not do. To hell wid di lot a dem, including Birdie Whitehead. If di bitch dead, it would be fine by her because it would mean that Jimmy could more easily be persuaded to marry her. With Uncle Nathan on her side, he could talk Reverend Whitehead into seeing things from her point of view.

That Nathan, according to Miss Maudie, was good through and through, because he had driven back to the cottage with her and visited with Joanie for more than an hour. Before he left, he promised them both that he would personally contact Jimmy in New York and let him know of Joanie's condition. Joanie had felt physical pain upon learning that Jimmy was in New York but she had quickly hidden her feelings.

He also gave Joanie his telephone number and at the door he handed Miss Maudie three thousand dollars to help with Joanie's hospital bill with a promise that he would be back to see them in the near future. His voice carried clearly back to Joanie as he stood talking to Miss Maudie before leaving.

"Maudie, my dear, A feel bad to know dat Jimmy do dis kinda damage and run leave it. Your granddaughter is a lovely girl and any man who have two senses knocking together would be more than happy to marry her. You did a good job raising her. She is truly refined."

She had heard Miss Maudie thanking him again for the money and she had grown more than little annoyed. Miss Maudie had a way of simpering and acting humble in the presence of her betters which Joanie found mortifying. She did not think that the Whiteheads were better than her because they had prestige. Furthermore, the Jamaican dollar was losing value against the U.S. dollar every day and the money would not cover all of her expenses. Uncle Nathan was reputed to be loaded, so, she believed he could have let off ten thousand dollars without feeling it.

His voice faded as he made his way to his car that was parked on the road outside the gate and Joanie watched him from the living room window while he walked away. If only The Reverend could be as easygoing as Uncle Nathan. Joanie had met him only a few times over the years but was always struck by how comfortable he was with himself.

He was a brown man like Reverend Whitehead and he had plenty of land at Minard in Brown's Town but he lived as he pleased. According to Jimmy, Miss Birdie considered him a disgrace to the family because he lived openly with his concubine who had borne him eight children. He sent them all to the best schools and he did not seem to care what others thought of him. The Reverend loved him too, because according to Jimmy, they had both known what it was to grow up on the wrong side of society.

Joanie turned from the window to sit on her bed and that was when the first pain hit. She suddenly felt caught between equal demands because while fierce, gripping sheets of pain rippled down the backs of her thigh, her pelvic muscles tightened and loosened in alternate currents of agony. Without meaning to, she let out a yelp of pain and sat down on the edge of the bed.

Miss Maudie came running into the room, her voice tight with concern.

"Is wa happen? Yu feelin *biebi pien*? Lay dong pahn di bed and ketch yu bret and whatever yu do, duohn push becausen we not ready fi dat yet."

Joanie felt an urgent need to move her bowels and got up but Miss Maudie shoved her back on to the edge of the bed and instructed her once more to lie down. Joanie did as she was told.

"Yu may feel like yu waahn fi doo-do but yu kyaahn sit pahn di tailit. Di biebi kyan come sudden and faal dong in a di tailit. A will put a uol sheet aanda yu bam-bam and if yu ha fi *go out*, yu dwiit pahn di sheet. Weh yu *waaki-taaki* phone?"

Joanie started to laugh but gasped as fresh pains tore through the muscles of her lower abdomen.

She pointed with her chin to her handbag on the dresser and Miss Maudie rummaged within and withdrew Joanie's cell phone. She handed it to Joanie and instructed her, "Ketch yu bret and kaal Danny becausen yu know A duohn like fi use dem ya madan day foolishness."

Joanie sat up and dialed the number which she had memorized. When Danny answered, she asked him come and take her to the hospital.

After she handed the phone back to Miss Maudie, she stood up and rubbed her fist into the small of her back as if trying to loosen a kink. That was when her water broke and Joanie stood next to her bed and watched the liquid pool at her feet and begin to spread across the floor.

Miss Maudie's sigh was caught between annoyance and resignation and she stepped out of her old cotton skirt and dropped it onto the puddle. She bent to begin to wipe the floor while speaking over her shoulder to Joanie

"Go sit over di *piel.* Duohn si-dong pahn di tailit and when all di waata stap comin, wash-up yuself and change yu clothes."

Still clad only in her full slip and blouse, Miss Maudie retreated to her backyard and returned with a pail of soapy water and a mop. When she was done wiping the floor she went to check on Joanie.

She found her sitting gingerly over the white enameled pail that Miss Maudie normally kept for washing herself when she did not feel like taking a full bath.

The girl looked at her grandmother with hunted eyes and Miss Maudie felt her eyes moisten. She sighed deeply, cleared her throat and said with forced briskness, "Yu did pack di biebi bag as me tell yu?"

Joanie nodded, indicating compliance and Miss Maudie turned to walk away but saw her granddaughter lurch to her feet and stumble to the face basin. By the time Miss Maudie got to her, she had vomited and started to slide to the floor.

Miss Maudie grabbed Joanie from behind and wrapped her in a bear hug, just above the bulge of her vanished waistline. She soon felt the slimy wetness of saliva as Joanie began to drool over her interlaced fingers.

She ignored the spittle that covered her hands and began to drag Joanie with all her reserves of strength toward the bedroom. She got her to the front of her bed and was contemplating the next move when she heard the sound of a car pull up to the house and the churchy music of *The Grace Thrillers* blaring from the vehicle. Under normal circumstances, Miss Maudie would have ordered Danny to turn down the volume but she was so glad that she called out, "Come ya likl, Danny!"

Her grandmother's voice in her ear caused Joanie to wince and look wildly around her. She mumbled something and Miss Maudie pushed her gently off her. Joanie lowered herself to the bed and sat with her hands braced against the mattress. She was still drooling and pulled a case off one of the pillows and began to scrub at her lips and then at Miss Maudie's hands.

Danny called from the front door and Miss Maudie asked him to come all the way in.

His tall frame soon filled Joanie's bedroom doorway and if he was in any way surprised by the sight of the two half-dressed women, he hid it very well. He was soon bending over Joanie with tender concern.

Without waiting for any further instructions from Miss Maudie, he gently raised Joanie's swollen legs and feet up to the bed and pressed her against the pillows. He turned then to Miss Maudie and with eyes filled with gratitude, she said, "Run go fi Nurse Headley fi me. Tell har dat Joanie *tek-iin* fi have biebi sudden and we kyaahn mek it to di haspital."

Joanie began to protest and Miss Maudie shushed her, impatiently.

"Yu duohn want to go down to di haspital becausen yu duohn waahn uol niega in a yu business."

Danny nodded vigorously in agreement and turned to leave the room. Miss Maudie urged him as he hurried away.

"*Mikies* mi dear son-son and Gaad wi surely bless yu."

biebi-pien-baby pain; labor pains

go-out-defecate

waaki-taaki-walkie-talkie

piel-pail

Grace Thrillers-Jamaican gospel singing group

tek-iin-go into labor

mikies-make haste

CHAPTER 29

Fowl no mash har chicken hat
No mother hen will hurt her chickens by mashing them under her feet
We make excuses for our children or punish them lightly when they are wrong
Kansikwenshal mek kraab no hab no head
The crab has no head as a consequence of something that it did.
Uman luck deh a dungle heap and *senseh fowl* ha fi kratch it out gi har
A woman's lucky findings are often hidden in the refuse and she will only discover them if a chicken scratches them to the surface; our good fortune often comes from lowly and unexpected places and we will not find it on our own

Who shit a bush figet but who tep in deh,
memba
The person who defecates in the bush
quickly forgets about it, but the person who
steps in it will remember for a very long time
Those who cause harm are quick to forget
but the victim is often scarred for a life

By the time Danny returned with the querulous Nurse Headley, Miss Maudie had Joanie clean and wearing a fresh nightdress. Her bed was by then covered with an old plastic shower curtain and an even older cotton bedspread was placed over it. She lay against a pile of pillows and tried to remember what day of the week it was.

Yes, it was Friday; she was in terrible pain and she was about to deliver Jimmy's child. The thought left her feeling suddenly bereft and for the first time since she confirmed her pregnancy, Joanie was afraid. What if Miss Maudie's words of reproach had been right, after all? What if she had crossed some well defined moral boundary when she tricked Jimmy into impregnating her?

Her reverie was broken by the entry of Nurse Headley, her imposing black bag and the unmistakable odor of garlic and kerosene oil. Joanie wrinkled her nose and turned her head away.

Nurse Headley bent over her, placed a callused palm under Joanie's chin and forced her to look up at her.

"How you doin chail?"

Joanie looked right back at Nurse Headley but said nothing in response.

Nurse Headley's eyes were so dark that Joanie saw little of the iris. Her seamed face was the color of dried tamarinds but the concern in her manner was not lost upon her.

With one firm hand on Joanie's belly, the wizened little lady turned to Miss Maudie and said, "Why you didn't call me before now, Maudie?"

Miss Maudie heard the unspoken accusation that hung suspended between them and felt ashamed. Nurse Headley was not to be numbered among the small-minded inhabitants of Chalky Hill. In Miss Maudie's' book, she was the salt of the earth. She had delivered all of her offspring and perhaps more than half of the inhabitants of the district.

This woman who was her senior, was nigh onto God in her knowledge of the secret carryings-on of her people. She knew which children were calling the wrong men daddy and who had got rid of unwanted pregnancies by shady means. But, Nurse Headley knew how to see and not see. She was a staunch Methodist but she drank her rum whenever she felt like it and if she fell down drunk every once in a while, this did not prevent her from safely delivering every baby that was entrusted to her care.

If Joanie had given Miss Maudie due notice, she would have arranged for Nurse Headley way in advance. She trusted her more than those damn doctors and nurses at the hospital. After all, childbirth was not a sickness, so, she didn't see why these modern day women liked to run off to the hospital to deliver their babies.

Miss Maudie hung her head and Nurse Headley went back to attending to Joanie.

Joanie wished that it was all over and the wrinkly lady who smelled of stale cooking and wood fire was gone but Nurse Headley, who had quickly slipped into the bathroom to wash her hands, was now peering at her and telling her that she was going to have to examine her to see how far the labor had advanced.

Joanie scowled fiercely and turned her face to the wall. Nurse Headley chuckled and muttered, "Di goin-iin sweet but di comin-out bitter. Aah sista; is uman road dis. If yu do di deed, yu ha fi pay di price. Roll pahn yu back and open yu leg dem."

Joanie refused to comply and the old gnome of a woman slapped her thigh smartly and raised her voice. "Me seh open yu legs and duohn mek me ha fi slap yu again! What happen? Yu no waahn di biebi and yu plan fi kill it? Yu bex wid di daddy? By di way, a weh di daddy deh?"

Joanie glared at Nurse Headly but did not answer.

The lady was not wearing gloves and when Joanie felt Nurse Headley's callused fingers probing at her genitals, she barely prevented herself from making a violent response.

Nothing in her experience had prepared her for the raw humiliation of childbirth and she began to cry. Her tearful spasms brought on a series of cramping pains and she began to grind her teeth and roll her head from side to side.

From somewhere between her splayed thighs, the midwife spoke impatiently but not unkindly. "Stap di cryin, sista, and save yu *strent* fi later. Yu *pasij* smaal and di biebi big, so yu gwaihn ha fi wok wid me. If yu dance wid me, we will land safe, but if yu fight me, yu pretty pum-pum gwaihn tear-up and yu man wuohn want it again."

"Tek yu time wid har, Nurse Headley. She duohn grow rough and A duohn taak to har like dat. A tank yu fi di service, ma'am, but please duohn tek no step wid har. *A di right choch bot a di rang pew.*"

Joanie turned her head to look at her grandmother and saw that Miss Maudie had pushed out her lips to signal her disapproval. She felt comforted.

Nurse Headley hissed her teeth softly and got all business-like. "Get me a basin of hot water, Maudie, and give her a drink of castor oil, if you have it."

Miss Maudie walked away from the bedroom and Joanie felt alone and exposed. The baby was raging violently within her and each spasm of pain made her catch her breath.

Where was Jimmy now that she needed him? Jimmy had never abandoned her until now. When she was eleven and started her period, he comforted her. When Miss Birdie called her a whore, he defied her and continued to befriend Joanie. When the young people at church shunned her at the instigation of Genevieve Swearing, he remained her friend. His engagement to Genevieve had been the one event that had almost torn them apart but when Genevieve went off to the States to study, they restored their friendship.

She had thought that sex would have cemented their love and opened his eyes to the mistake of his engagement to Genevieve, but that was what had driven him away from her.

As Joanie lay on her back with her thighs splayed, she felt something depart from her-a loss of control over her body and a sense that some alien force had taken the lead in her life. Her eyes avoided the woman who attended her and fastened to a single thread of cobweb that floated from a corner of the ceiling.

Her body began to labor in earnest to expel the baby who no longer needed the shelter of her womb, and as the pain tore through her, she felt that she had no friend in the world. After all, no friend would send a beloved into this maelstrom of unrelenting agony without a guide book to say where the shades of respite could be found. She was learning that childbirth was a journey for one and even if there were cheerleaders alongside, they could not suffer for her.

Miss Maudie returned with a basin of hot water and the castor oil and soon came to stand next to Joanie's head. Joanie gripped her grandmother's hand and heard Nurse Headley instruct her to push.

She caught her breath, expelled it in a labored sigh and began to bear down with all of her strength. Fresh pains caused her to thrash her legs and Nurse Headley, who was stronger than she looked, forced her knees toward her chest and told her to be still.

"Di biebi crownin. Look like it don't like it in dere and it waahn come out."

Miss Maudie mopped Joanie's wet face with a washcloth but avoided meeting her eyes.

"Yu waahn me give har some a di *kyasta ail*?"

"No," answered Nurse Headley. Di biebi comin faster dan expected."

Miss Maudie hurried away and returned with a pile of snowy white, cotton, flour sack sheets and handed them to Nurse Headley.

"Yu come and huol dem, Maudie. Yu ketch di biebi when it come out."

Joanie paid little attention to the exchange because she felt the baby wrench and twist itself and then her lower quarter caught fire. She began to push and grunt even as sweat pooled behind her head and soaked her pillow. She raised her buttocks off the bed and dug her heels into the mattress as the baby broke through her birth canal and began to cry.

She did not look at it but heard when Miss Maudie said, "Teng Gaad. She arrive wol and soun."

Joanie turned her face to the wall and began to wail as if her heart would break. She felt like she had been bested by an unknown power. All along she had thought that she was carrying James John Whitehead, IV.

senseh fowl-Twi retention (asense) which refers to a fowl with ruffled and scattered feathers. This fowl was often kept for the purpose of digging up obeah paraphernalia that were sometimes planted in people's yards

strent-strength

pasij-passage

a di right choch but a di rang pew-you are in the right church but in the wrong pew; this applies generally but this case is an exception

kyasta ail-castor oil

CHAPTER 30

Miss Mama

2003

Hag pikni ax him muma why har mout so lang. She grunt and tell him, "Aah mi pikni; yu da grow; yu wi soon find out."
The piglet asked its mother to explain why she had a long snout. She told him that he was growing up and he would find out the reason for himself
If we live long enough, we will grow to understand suffering

Miss Mama got the call at three in the morning. She was in that halfway place between sleep and wakefulness when she saw the big, cut-stone church building on the hill break in two from the roof to the cellar. The two halves rolled downhill and crashed into a smoky pile of broken wood and masonry.

She came fully awake and furiously shook her husband, Breda Baada. He was snoring, not so gently beside her, and at her prodding, he curled himself into a ball and rolled away from her. She shook him harder and called him by name.

Breda Baada, who was a very devout man, groaned in a sleep muffled voice, "*Speak Laad, dai saabant hearet.*"

Miss Mama began to laugh softly to herself and called him a little more loudly, "Wiek-up Breda Baada! Wiek-up!"

Her husband sat up against his pillows, raised his left arm and began to scratch frantically at his right armpit.

Miss Mama sighed, got off the bed and disappeared into the bathroom. When she returned a few minutes later, her face was washed, her head was turbaned and she was wearing a sleeveless cotton undershirt and long underwear.

Breda Baada watched her in silence for a moment and then croaked, "A wa now, Sista?

Miss Mama did not answer but continued to dress. She pulled a black half slip from her bedside drawer and stepped into it. She then opened the wardrobe next to the dresser and pulled out a flowing red gown.

As soon as she turned away from the wardrobe and Breda Baada saw what was in her hand, he scrambled out of bed and knelt on the floor next to the bed. He began to pray softly but urgently and Miss Mama began to sing:

What a mighty Gaad we serve
What a mighty Gaad we serve
Angels bow before Him
Heaven and earth adore Him
What a mighty Gaad we serve

She was about to sing the song again when Breda Baada rose from his knees and interrupted. "Yu need me to go wid yu, Sista?"

"No dear. Dis journey is fi me alone. Me ha fi trabl far and me ha fi go by night. Me gwaihn ha fi ride di *danki* so help me wid di hamper dem. Pack waata, crackers, lime and chrii change a clothes. Get two plastic bucket, a pail a river stone and a small wash-basin. Yu and Deekan drive di *pick-up chok* come a Trelawny fi mi, Sunday. Yu wi find me dong a Maudie Collins yaad."

"Alright mi dear. Den, yu no waahn likl tea and bread before yu go?"

"Waata in a di termos and bread deh pahn di table. No worry yuself. Jos mek sure dat yu ax Deekan or wan a di ada man dem fi drive yu dong Sunday. Memba seh yu naa si so good so mek sure seh smadi drive yu. Me will ready bout chrii a'klak."

By the time Miss Mama was gowned and ready to depart, Breda Baada had her faithful donkey waiting at the back door. He had brought the animal close to the high back steps so that Miss Mama could step down rather than having to climb up to mount the donkey.

She sat straight in the saddle and looked up at Breda Baada where he stood with the light from the dining-room framing his body. He prayed over her, asking God for traveling mercies and remained standing in the doorway long after he could no longer hear the clip-clop of the shod animal against the graveled roadway. His wife's comings and goings were not strange to him. He knew the gift that was in her and unlike her first husband, did not resist God's call upon her.

Miss Mama did not take the asphalted coast road when she got down to the bottom of the hill. Instead, she turned to her left and headed uphill, once more. She would be riding parallel to the coast road for about twenty miles but she would be traveling through the rain forest and adhering to the tracks that had been carved through the undergrowth by the footprints of the Maroons who had fought the British into compromise and a formal treaty in the 1700s.

Miss Mama herself was part European and had come by her orange-brown coloring through a torrid love affair between an Irish bookkeeper from a sugar estate and a Maroon woman, twice his age.

Miss Mama had known her father and loved him. He was an angular, towheaded man who had gone completely native. Red nosed and irascible from rum drinking, he had been famous for his terrible temper and foul mouth. However, he had fallen hard for the bow-legged, African woman who caught his eye as she came down from the John Crow Mountains into the Rio Grande Valley to sell her coffee and chocolate that she had grown, parched and beaten, herself. He followed her home that Saturday night, plodding, half-drunk behind the swishing tail of her female donkey and he never left. He outlived her by twelve years and, today, lay buried under a large guinep tree and next to his beloved, as he had requested.

IT WAS GOING on four a.m. and it would take Miss Mama another two hours to get to Port Antonio. She would have made swifter time on the asphalted coast road but the bush track was kinder to the donkey.

By the time she emerged from the forest near San San beach, she had seen much and had been seen by many, but no one acknowledged her passage. Those who got the message would show up where they were needed and those who regretted that she had seen them, would come bearing gifts of many kinds in the coming days. Miss Mama was used to the ways of her fellowman and by now was no longer capable of being shocked by the revelations that would come to her at any time of the day or night that The Spirit chose.

On one of her night journeys, Miss Mama surprised two burglars in the coastal town of Buff Bay as they were breaking into a supermarket. She was on her way to St. Ann's Bay to visit a shut-in woman who was transitioning to the other side and interrupted the robbers at about three-thirty in the morning.

They were young men, both wearing hooded jackets. They were stooping in front of the metal security door of the supermarket, so intent and earnest that they did not see her or the donkey until they heard the sound of the animal's shod hooves. She knew immediately that wrong was afoot because she felt the donkey tremble beneath her and slow its walk.

The two dropped their tools and took off up the southern road with Miss Maudie's laughter ringing in their ears. The next day, local newspapers and radio stations carried a story about a duppy riding a donkey. Some even said that it was a rare appearance of the legendary chrii-foot haas and the two young men were lucky to have escaped with their lives.

When these and other such stories reached Miss Mama, she simply sighed. If her donkey was just a duppy setting out to frighten the wicked, that would be fine with her. Her night journeys showed her far more sinister truths, however. There was no doubt in her mind that if night should suddenly turn to day, many would come undone.

The donkey knew when they were near to the Port Antonio Market and picked up speed. Miss Maudie slowed it down by applying pressure to its sides with her knees. She could tell from the tremors rippling through the animal's muscles that the donkey wanted to break into a trot but Miss Mama was firmly in charge of it. She spoke to the animal as to an overly frisky child.

"Beg yu slow dong, yu hear, daalin? Me deh pahn Maasa Gaad business and me beggin yu fi no dash weh mi *kansikraitid* waata and mi *anaintin ail*."

The donkey slowed to a steady pace and Miss Mama patted its side.

The sun had not yet crested the mountains behind her but from the rose-fringed morning clouds, she knew that full light was not far away. Miss Mama wanted to be in the market before the bustle of the Saturday trade began.

Most of the traders and higglers in the market knew her well and not a few of them had consulted her with their troubles ranging from the petty to the serious. She willingly offered her prayers and ministrations but most knew better than to seek her aid in obeah. She also refused to be paid for her services but it was not uncommon for her hampers to be fully loaded with ground provisions, fruits, vegetables and cured meat when she was ready to depart from the market.

Some of the people who came to see her with complaints about how others had harmed them through witchcraft, were actually physically ill and in those instances, Miss Mama did not hesitate to refer them to doctors that she knew well. They, in turn, sent her the ones who were beyond the mere physical cures that they offered.

Sometimes when Miss Mama gave the bush baths and saw the transformation in her patients, she marveled. However, it was Breda Baada who helped her to gain insight when they discussed the changes that she observed. He was very dry as usual but she never forgot what he said. He had declared with sorrow underlying his clipped tone, "Mama, maybe a yu a di fos smadi ever touch dem and duohn hurt dem. Yu ever kansida dat fi plenty Jumaika people, di ongl time smadi touch dem is fi haam dem? Some a we no nice, yu know, Sista."

When Miss Mama and her donkey arrived at the gate of the market, she saw that the watchman was sleeping on the job. She therefore declared in her most strident tone, "Awake dou dat sleepest for di day is at han!"

The young man scrambled to his feet, looking around wildly, his eyes wide and panicked until he came to his senses. When he recognized Miss Mama, he muttered, "Is why yu av to frighten a man so, Mada? Yu know yu kuda give a man a haat attack?"

Instead of answering him directly, Miss Mama alighted from her donkey and began to sing:

Bright soul, wa mek you ton back?
Bright soul, wa mek you ton back?
Bright soul, wa mek you ton back?
Fa yu go a *Riba Jaadan* and you ton back!

When Miss Mama was done singing, the security guard was still muttering and he had begun to walk away. He seemed angry but dared not address her. Her voice followed him as he headed to the beach below the market.

"Run *galang*. How far yu tink yu kyan run? Jonah did go a whale belly and him did still ha fi obey."

The young man stopped in his track, turned back and started to walk toward Miss Mama and her donkey. When he got within touching distance of her, he humbly asked, "Yu waahn me fi *anluod* di danki fi yu, ma'am?"

Instead of responding, Miss Mama took a deep breath of the salt-laden air and looked around her before tethering her donkey to one of the metal window guards at the front of the building. The animal immediately started to chew on some sugar cane peelings that littered the ground and Miss Mama removed the two large hampers from its back. While it was being unburdened, the donkey stood stolidly and chewed and spat out the cane trash in dry, yellow clumps.

The young watchman continued to stand uncertainly and Miss Mama walked away from him with one hamper clutched to her chest. He picked up the other one from against the grilled façade where she had placed it and followed her through the wrought iron gates.

Inside, the market was stirring and multiple ribbons of food odors filled the air-coffee, coconut milk, fried dumplings, breadfruit, cornmeal porridge, corned pork and codfish. It was as if the odors embraced each other in the air above their heads.

Miss Mama made her way through the cluttered hub of the market toward the back where she knew she would find her friend. She greeted several of the higglers as she passed through but did not stop to make conversation.

When Miss Mama found her friend, the woman was still wrapped in a checkered blanket and sleeping on top of her stall. She lowered the heavy hamper to the floor next to the woman's stall but did not attempt to awaken her. The young man put down the other hamper and stood watching Miss Mama. She silently indicated to him that he should follow her and they both made their way to a back exit.

Outside, the air was crisp and sharp with the iodine smell of the sea. The land sloped gradually to the beach where the water slapped not too gently against the shoreline. The water was the gray-blue of early morning because the sun was still partly hidden behind the Blue Mountains.

A few fishing canoes were visible on the horizon and Miss Mama knew that they were further away than they seemed. It would be closer to seven o'clock before those tough, sinewy men and their flimsy boats would reach shore.

Miss Mama turned away from the shoreline vista and met the young man's still uncertain gaze with a stern countenance. He looked back at her, partially defiant but nervous.

"Yu put yu han to di plow and den you *abandan* di field. Why yu chruo weh yu good-good *salvaishan* fi pum-pum?"

The young man remained silent and the defiance melted from his eyes. He lowered his gaze and began to chew at his bottom lip. Miss Mama continued to verbally chastise him.

"Yu life no wot fly doo-do if yu decide fi live it in a disobedience. Yu know dat yu get di kaalin and yu staat out on di road to holiness but di *renkin meat* sweet yu. Try memba seh wa sweet a mout, hat a belly and memba seh when two jinal meet, all head-wok stap."

After her harsh pronouncements, Miss Mama walked up to the watchman, placed a firm hand upon his left shoulder and in a much gentler tone she said, "Mi did mek di same mistake and married to di rang man and it nearly cause mi fi lose mi gif. Obey di kaalin and yu will *praaspa.* Disobey, and yu foot dem will tie-up."

"Yes ma'am," he whispered and turned away to go back to his post at the front of the market.

"Bring mi danki come tie roun di back here," Miss Mama shouted at his retreating figure. She had no doubt that he would do exactly as she had asked.

Miss Mama reentered the market to find her friend up and dressed. She was arranging her stall for full display of the cosmetic products that she sold. The woman turned around, embraced Miss Mama and kissed her on both cheeks.

"Is wa breeze blow yu ya dis maanin, Mama?"

"Me on mi way to Trelawny. We have a big work to do a di Baptist Church in a Chalky Hill."

"So, me need fi kaal di band together, den."

This was said more as a statement than a question and Miss Mama nodded her assent.

"Yu mos well hungry, den."

Miss Mama laughed, rubbed the top of her stomach and conceded, "Sista, A so hungry, A wuda *nyam Hannah and har kyaaf.*"

Speak Laad, dai saabant hearet-speak Lord, thy servant heareth

wiek up-wake up

danki-donkey

pickup chok-pick-up truck

kansikraitid waata-consecrated water

anaintin ail-anointing oil

Riba Jaadan-River Jordan

galang-go along

anluod-unload

abandan-abandon

salvaishan-salvation
renking meat-smelly crotch
praaspa-prosper
nyam Hannah and har kyaaf-eat the cow named Hannah
and her calf as well; ravenous

CHAPTER 31

Audrie Agette Matthews

2003

One finger does not take oil to the mouth
without soiling the others
We do not hurt others without putting
ourselves at risk
Igbo Proverb
He that is without sin, cast the first stone
Jesus, the Christ

So di Day a Judgment come to paas and mi son is to be put on trial by Chalky Hill Baptist Church. Dem charge him wid fornication and di wol church a meet in lieu of Sunday service. In di absence a Reverend Whitehead, Deacon Swearing and di church board will lead di proceedings. Also, in di name of transparency, dem plan fi try mi son in front a di wol church and den dem will tek a vote among di member dem as to whether dem gwaihn low him fi tek up him ministry or dem gwaihn run him weh.

Me mek up mi mind fi go wid him to di hearin and alduoh A duohn tell him, A plan fi speak up fi him. Me taak to him about di girl and me satisfy seh a trap she trap him. When him taak to me bout it, me lisn wid mi yez as well as mi haat and me kuda tell dat it pain him fi taak bout di girl behain her back. Him tell me seh she is him bes fren from him was a likl bwai.

Me ask him if him ever did love her and him tell me seh him still love her. When him seh dat, me frighten and quick-quick, me ask him wa him mean. Him tell me dat from him likl, him know dat she wud always be special to him and him tell me dat dem grow like breda and sista. So, me ask him how him en-up a sleep wid smadi weh him kansida him sista. Di bwai get bex and shame at di same time and den him staat fi cry.

In between di tears and sniffles, him pour out him haat to me and tell me dat him did always love Joanie but Miss Birdie *mark chalk line* against any such relationship from him was eleven and she ketch him a kiss Joanie in a di backyaad. Him tell me seh him granny put such a fear into him dat him swear dat Gaad wuda strike him if him ever so much as kansida a relationship wid Joanie.

Miss Birdie tell him dat Joanie is a nobadi wid no backgrong and ask him what him wud tell him children bout her and her family when dem ask. She seh to him, "What you plan to tell them? You plan to tell them that their granny was a whore who had a child with an unknown sailorman and brought it home and threw it at her mother's feet? Is that the kind of heritage you plan to give your children?"

So mi son a taak a so di sadness a wet up mi soul. All me kuda remember is how Birdie Whitehead treat me when Junior kyari me to dem and tell dem seh him plan fi married to me. Me tink of her back den and me tink of who she is now. Mi remember how she look in a di hospital bed when Uncle Nathan tek we go a Kingston, day-before-yesterday. It did brok mi haat fi see her, gray-faced and near death. Di stroke lean her mout to wan side and she have machines helping her to breathe.

Poor Reverend Whitehead was never a fat man but him did always sinewy and strong. Me remember dat him was always waakin roun Chalky Hill and Junior use to tell me how Miss Maudie always a complain dat him kyaahn get fat because him waak too much. But Reverend Whitehead was a different man when me see him at di University Hospital. Him thin and frail and him look like smadi weh deh pahn di verge of a nervous collapse. Him look sad, laas and uol, but him allow me fi hug him and him huol me a likl langa dan mi did ekspek. Mi see di sorrow pahn him face and me feel dat him regret plenty tings.

Aanda ada circumstances, me sure him wuda did express shock fi see me, but di poor soul so laas dat at fors, A wasn even sure seh him know seh a me.

Dis maanin when me and Jimmy have di haat-to-haat, him tell me dat at twelve years uol, him never have di wod dem nor di will fi speak wa did aredi a bon in a him haat fi Joanie. Him douse it and accept him granmada choice in Genevieve. Wid di paasin a time, him come fi love Genevieve deeply but when him search di batam layer a him haat, him discover unfinish business hide weh in a di crevice and kaana dem. Him now know dat him wuda did eventually choose Joanie if him did have more courage.

Me hush him and tell him fi cut himself some slack, because at twelve, if him did decide fi put up resistance to Miss Birdie, him wuda did ha fi ton monster in aada fi win dat deh fight. A remember dat uman as being so implacable and rejectin dat Jimmy wuda did need di brain configuration of a psychopath fi win dat deh *bakl.*

Me leave mi son a si-dong in a him granfaada study and go into di guestroom where A been stayin. Me dress miself in red and black warrior colors and pull mi hair into a big topknot pahn mi head. Den me powder mi face and don mi sunshades.

DI FOUR A we mos a did mek quite a pitcha when we appear at di side door a di church. Me and Uncle Nathan leadin di way wid Jimmy and Genevieve a waak so close behain dat Genevieve shoes collide wid me heel. Me speed up mi step and waak between two row a seat. A kuda feel di people dem yai faasn pahn we and A hear di silence dat was suddenly broken by a *haad-a-yerin* uman who a taak too loud and she duohn know.

"Well Gaad bless me two yai dem. No Junior wife deh? Me tink me did yer seh she dead!"

Sombadi try fi silence di uol lady but she was havin none of it. She staat taak even louder and her tone get more insistent. On aneda day, it wuda did sweet me.

"Me seh a she! She have di same nak-knee dem and a same so har batam *kak-out!*"

Me waahn fi slow mi step dem fi hear which paat else a me kak-out but me know dat more urgent business is at han. A kyan still feel di people dem yai pahn we and me sense a charge in a di air. Dese people come out fi a spectacle and me know dat few if any a dem will show any mercy pahn mi son. Dem give him a sacred chos and him did suppose fi prove himself better dan dem. Him let dem dong and dem disappointment in a him will mek dem exact more dan a poun a flesh. Him is a brown man and him study a good school. So, dem ekspek him fi kyari di burden a fi dem sin and him wasn suppose to have none a him own. What a bitter let-dong dat dis man who look so much like di Jesus pitcha dat dem kyari in dem mind, prove himself to have feet of clay. Dem Golgotha will be di dais of dis same church and dem a plan fi put Jimmy up high and nak him dong low. If dem get fi have dem way, dem gwaihn buss him open like a piñata.

I will stand between dem and me only son dis day and if I have anyting to do wid it, him will bear only him own sin.

Dese blasted people gwaihn ha fi go somweh else go find dem sacrificial lamb.

Dem have wan chair put out front and center and me see di plan right aweh. Me son is to be a spectacle fi all eyes. A wanda whose idea it was dat dis wud be di bes way fi proceed? Well, not if me have anyting to do wid matters.

Me look up to di platform and see about eight wooden chairs up deh. Me eyeball dem fi see which wan a dem me kuda move because some a dem carve outa solid wood and look well heavy. Me jos imagine wan a dem a lik mi pahn me shin bone and me cringe in a mi mind.

As soon as me staat fi go up di step dem, Uncle Nathan read me intention and him fala back a me. Him come back dong wid two chair and me kyari wan. We put dem on either side a Jimmy chair and him tek him seat and me and Genevieve sandwich Jimmy. Uncle Nathan si-dong next to me.

Me still a wear mi sunshades and me decide fi keep dem aan. From behain di shadow, me tek-iin di congregation. Me notice dat some a dem bring likl pikni wid dem. A wanda how dem come fi tink dat di trial a di pastor is a fittin event fi a pikni witness. Me conclude dat dem waahn di likl wan dem fi staat *shaapn* dem tiit early. Me also know dat if Reverend Whitehead was here, dis kudn gwaan. Right aweh, me begin fi tink bout di scripture dat seh di Debl strike di shepherd and scatter di sheep. Dat is when me staat fi pray because me see wa out fi tek place. Dis is not di prapa way fi huol a hearin of dis nature. Jimmy shud face di church board and no wan else. Me conclude seh Deacon Swearing choose dis as a way fi shame Jimmy. When me look roun fi him, me realize dat him was nowhere in sight.

Wahn uol man who need a cane, stan-up suddenly in a di front row, clear him chruot officiously and announce, "Di Laad is in His temple; let di eart be silent before Him. It is only right dat we shud pay prapa rispek to Him. I wud like to ask di chrii people who sitting wid young Pastor Whitehead to come dong from di front and tek a seat in di congregation."

Before me kuda respond, Uncle Nathan stan-up, ease him weight on to him right foot and lower wan shoulder like a *faamyaad* cock wa ready fi fight. In a voice deep and resonant and haad as a river stone, him seh, "My grand-nephew stands accused in front of this congregation today and I have decided that he will not stand alone."

Him point to me and continue, "This lady here is Jimmy's mother and she has traveled all the way from New York to support her son. Genevieve is his newly wedded wife and I think you will all agree that she has a right to stand with her husband."

When him finish taak, him si-dong but as soon as him mention seh Jimmy married, di church erupt. A kudn believe dat A was in di house a di Laad. Wahn fat uman in a di front row staat fi scream pahn Jimmy. A waahn fi laugh because har head big like *foreman brokfos* and she have chrii descendin row a jowl. Each time she open her mout, di batam jowl brush di bow wa spread-aaf kraas her ches. But me kyaahn laugh because dis uman a get real personal and aggressive. She a taak wid so much venom dat di ada people dem allow her fi own di moment.

She *pint* straight pahn Jimmy and hala, "Yu too wikid and bad! Imagine, yu spwail-up Miss Maudie nice-nice grandaata and when yu done, yu run go married to Deekan good-good daata! Di two uman dem shuda *geng* yu and beat out yu side. Ef it was me, A beat yu out like *sea-kyat* meat! A wuda beat yu till yu mash-up saaf like *parij!*"

Me tempted fi laugh again but me keep a straight face, especially when Uncle Nathan almuos knock over him chair when him jump-up and staat fi address di walrus uman.

"But lady, dis not yu business! Yu run way paas yu gate ma'am, and A have a mind to turn yu back! Tek care A duohn come dong deh and slap yu up properly, if yu no shet-up yu *yabba* mout!"

Me grab Uncle Nathan elbow and try fi get him fi si-dong but di man was way past caring. Only Gaad himself know what was gwaihn happen nex when di front doorway a di church suddenly full-up wid a presence and me look out deh and see wahn taal, strappin, brown-skin lady stan up in a di doorway. She dress in a full red, from her turban to her uol-time smock dress, and she have two bucket in a her han dem.

Me look behain di lady and me see a band a worshipers and dem staat fi sing a song dat have no words. Two young man standing behain di lady and dem a beat two small drum dat dem each huol aanda dem armpit.

A sudden silence wash over di sanctuary and me see naked fear pahn some a di people dem face but me notice what look like relief pahn ada faces. Di lady begin fi waak up di lang aisle a Chalky Hill Baptist Church and when she reach about halfway, she close her yai dem and open her mout in song. She have a voice dat sweet in a di migl and rough roun di edges. Is a powerful alto and it come up from deep inside of her. She is a true singer of di soul.

A kyaahn fully explain how me come fi know but me recognize a kindred. She was shrouded in power and authority and her presence was clean like the newly risen sun. She send me right back to the storefront church pahn White Plains Road. Before me know it, me staat fi answer her:

Enoch waak wid Gaad
Enoch waak wid Gaad
Enoch waak wid Gaad and neba fail
He was *transilaitid*, because he was *obiidiant*
Enoch waak wid Gaad and neba fail

Di lady pick up di song again and by di time she finish, the church in a total hush, all eyes glued to the stranger who now standing right next to Uncle Nathan. She pu-dong di two blue plastic bucket dem at her foot, raise her han dem upward and do a slow circular dance and den stap. When she raise aneda song, me know dat she come fi do serious business. Dis time me no fala her wid mi voice because A sense dat A mos pray fi clearance fi her. Me know full well dat Baptist and wrap-head no mix. Inwardly, duoh, A sing every wod and every note:

Mada di great stone have to move

Mada di great stone have to move

Mada di great stone

Stone of *Babilan*

Mada di great stone have to move

An elderly uman pahn di back row to mi lef hala out, "Speak Laad!" and soon faal out into di aisle and staat fi cut a caper dat astonished all. She staat fi clap her han dem and di brown uman continue fi sing. She was soon joined by a chorus and me never know dat so much wrap-head people live a Chalky Hill. A duohn even know weh dem come from, but me see at least two dozen man and uman a stream dong di aisle and dem was singin, shoutin, clappin and dancin. Dem was all in red and white and dem head wrap-up in a some fantastic headgear.

Di people dem come into di church and dem come wid a presence dat full-up di sanctuary. Di song dat dem was singing I had never heard before but mi soul seh yes to di melody and di harmony. Dem was kyariin di *chuun* like *ketchi-shubi* and nobadi mek wan single note jrap. It was a combined sound of di flow of many streams bubblin over gravel stones and mixed in wid it, was the sound of a thousand doves cooing in harmony.

At a signal from di brown uman, di drummer dem pick up di tempo and di band staat to stomp pahn di floor and bend dem head dong to di grong and come back up. Is like dem did a try fi brok di spirit a judgment and cruelty weh in a di church. Den dem fala di leader lady up to where we sittin and dem surroun we and staat fi dance. We in a di migl a di circle and me feel somting lif me up and me hala out from mi belly. Me staat fi clap mi han dem in time to di stompin and drummin. Me kudn tell a person exactly what di feelin was like. Is like me did have a terrible case a constipation and me suddenly get a ease.

Me grab Jimmy wid wan han and grab Uncle Nathan wid di ada. Jimmy huol Genevieve and me no know how we come fi know di dance but is like wi foot dem remember. In fak, all a we seem to remember how fi dwiit and di wol church brok-out in a dancin and singin.

Me glance over pahn Jimmy and him face calm and peaceful. Him rocking backward and forward pahn him heel and toe dem and me see when him raise him two han dem, close him yai and ben-dong and come back up. Me smile and see Uncle Nathan wheel past me, do two dip like him a dance *Brukins* and den him ketch Jimmy, bring him up to him ches and gently bok him farid like when two goat kid a play pahn hill side.

When me see dat, me reach fi Genevieve, wrap her in a close embrace, let her go halfway and den spin her two time. She lif up wan han and jrap di ada wan to her waist level and dat gyal faal back pahn her heel dem and spin two time like she a dance Mento from she baan. Me spin her back to me and we mek two steps and den me paas her to Jimmy.

When di two a dem face each ada, the Mada dance over to dem, put dem fi stand side by side and pull a lang white scarf from roun her neck and wrap di two a dem roun dem waist. Dem mek fi faal dong but a wrap-head man catch dem in a him two strong arms and bring dem to dem knee.

Laad, mi soul tek flight and I was soon sailin high, over mountains, ocean water, tropical bushland, savannah and desert. Me come full circle and faal out a di present. Me staat fi travel in a mi spirit and soon reach a valley and me see wahn uol time whitewash, adobe house pahn a hillside. Me enter di house and paas an elderly lady si-dong in her kitchen. Me feel a sense of urgency and so me move paas her and find miself in a back bedroom. A girl who wearin a shaat, cotton nightdress, stan-up wid her back to me. She have somting in a her han dem. Di girl look over her shoulder pahn me and her yai dem blank and soulless. Me try fi kaal to her but she no seem to even be aware dat me a stan-up in a di room. Before me kyan get to her, she jrap somting outside. A biebi staat fi wail and di soun a come right back into di room but di girl close di sash winda and waak right paas me out a di room.

Me come back to di present to see aneda wrap head uman a come up di aisle wid a white enamel basin in her han dem. She place it a di Mada foot dem and dance back dong di aisle.

As soon as di uman get halfway down di aisle, di Mada raise her two han dem and a simmerin, semi-quiet come dong over di church. We at the front si-dong when she staat fi taak.

"*Bredjrin*, I come in di name of Jesus, our soon comin king and I have been sent to deliver a *mesij. Me no wehn waahn come ya* because I fear dat I wud not be received, but where I am bound, I mos obey. Akaadin to di word of Gaad, it is better to obey dan to sacrifice and to hearken, better dan di fat of rams."

She pause fi a few seconds and me hear sombadi clear dem chruot. Di uman ton her head and allow her yai dem fi paas over di entire congregation and den she continue fi taak.

"Di sin of disobedience is worse dan witchkraaf. And so, I mos tell yu brothers and sisters, di Laad tell me to tell unu dat di wraat of man does not work di *raichosnis* of Gaad.

Di young man faal into a snair and him foot dem tie up! Unu kyan loose him or unu kyan kill him. Brothers and sisters in Christ, which will it be today?"

Di Mada point dong at her foot dem and seh, "I have a bucket a stone and I have a bucket a kansikraitid waata. Will you stone him or will you wash him foot dem and put him back on di road to glory?"

When she ax di kwestian, a hush faal over di church and di lady use di pause to raise aneda song:

Everywhere He went, He was doing good
He's a mighty healer, He cleansed the leper
When the people saw Him, they knelt
before Him
Everywhere He went, my Laad, He was doing
good

"Di word of Gaad is sharper dan any two-edged sword, cutting dong to bone and marrow. I come to you dis day as a servant of di Laad and He has given me *aatariti* to tell unu dat he dat is widout sin, cast di fors stone.

Dis young man stan accused before unu today and nof a unu come into di house a di Laad wid blood in a unu yai dem. But mark, oh, dat not wan a unu sitting in dis chapel kyan claim to be *perfik*. Yu wasn dere when di chail was conceive. Yu do not know what tricks di Debl was playin dat day. Yu duohn know what yu wuda did do if yu was standin in him shoes dem on dat particular day. Remember dat ongl Gaad have di aatariti to condemn and Jesus never condemn anybody, except hypocrite. Him kaal sinners to repentance.

Nof a unu tek night journey come a mi balm-yaad, in pursuit of evil. Unu so bad dat unu duohn even know dat balm mean healin. Unu tief unu neighbor smaal garments aaf a dem clothesline and bring to me fi ratn out people insides. Mi ha fi meet unu a road and run unu fram mi place because a di intention wa some a unu have in a unu haat.

I ask di kwestian again dis maanin. Who will wash di young disciple foot dem and welcome him home?"

A hear a wail go up and di wrap-head people dem mek a paatway on both side a di aisle. Me look and see Genevieve mada a move up di aisle pahn her han and knee dem. She a hala and water a faal from her two yai dem. Some ada people tek up di wailin and before too lang, it seem like evribadi weh in a di church a lament.

Ms. Swearing stap in front a Jimmy and widout a single wod to him, she staat fi pull aaf him shoes dem. Before she kuda finish di job, is Deacon Swearing mi see a come. Mi think him was gwaihn put a stap to what him wife a do, but, to my surprise, him kneel dong and tek a piece a klaat dat di

Mada give him and right before all, Deacon Swearing wash Jimmy foot dem. Di Mada give him a lily white towel and him tek him time and dry Jimmy foot dem carefully, toe by toe and den each sole. But so him a dry Jimmy foot dem a so him a wet dem up wid him yai-waata.

Di miracle never stap dere. Ms. Swearing shuffle pahn her knee dem over to Genevieve, hug up her daata two knee dem and begin fi wail. Genevieve pull her up fi stand in front of her and hug up her mada so tight dat not even breeze kuda paas between dem.

Dat was when me know dat dere wud be a new beginnin between di two a dem. A waahn go over to dem but me remember di vision and me pull Uncle Nathan out into di aisle and ask him fi tek me to Miss Maudie house right aweh.

Uncle Nathan mos a did see di urgency in a mi yai dem because him no ask no kwestian. Instead, him tek mi han and lead me toward di same side door dat we enter earlier. Dis time, nobadi no pay we no mind and me was glad. We hurry over to di manse and Uncle Nathan head fi him brand new Range Rover dat paak outside di garage door. Di garage is aanda di kitchen and me see an older Volvo paak inside. Me assume dat it belang to Reverend.

Uncle Nathan open di driver side, hop-iin and reach kraas di seat and open di passenger door. Inside di kyaar hat like a furnace and him ton on di air. Me fraid fi plant mi batty-jaw fully pahn di seat because it so hat but di machine in tip-top condition and soon, me feel cool air a come up from di floor.

Uncle Nathan lock di winda dem and by di time we get to di main road, we a ride in a cool comfort.

Alduoh A been gaan fi such a lang time, di land very much like me remember. Di *never-dead* tree dem still a grow pahn both side a di road and dem form an arch over di top. Di kissin tree top dem stretch fi a good half-mile and di tree dem in a full bloom. As we drive chuu, me see di vermillion petal dem cover di bankside a di road. Is enough richness fi gladden mi haat. Di tropical beauty a di land is all aroun me but we a rush chuu so faas dat A kudn get a chance to drink it all in.

A never know dat A was gwaihn ask Uncle Nathan di kwestian, but as soon as it come out, it feel like di time was ripe.

"Uncle Nate, you ever did find out a who kill Junior?"

Him never answer right aweh and fi a while, me tink him was gwaihn ignore di kwestian, but it seem like him did a try fi frame him answer.

"Is a wol-heap a people kill Junior but di trigger-man was a bwoy who eat from my very table. Him claim dat him and him henchman dem get rang information and is when dem done shed Junior blood dat dem realize dat is di rang man dem kill. Him get-aaf a him head, clean-clean, and me hear dat him live pahn street in a Spanish Town. Mi woman say she drive through di bypass and see him a walk street, baan naked.

Some a di people who tek CIA money fi purge Jamaica of socialists, ton big philosophers and thinkers today. And some a dem ton *uol haigue* in a bakl an kyaahn dead. Plenty of us know who was involved but we pretend dat 1976 to 1980 was a time of peaceful transition in Jamaica, land we love, but I know we had a civil war. Plenty fren kill fren and nof doti waata put out faiya."

A never say anyting after Uncle Nathan finish taak and we continue in silence fi about aneda half-mile. Di landscape outside a flash by like movie scenery but me naa pay it no mind. From time to time, me glance pahn Uncle Nate and see seh it look like him a grind him tiit dem. A was sure dat like me, him was rememberin things him wuda prefer to figet. We ketch a Miss Maudie yaad widout aneda wod a paas between we.

ME NEVER NEED anybody fi tell me dat Miss Maudie house was a place weh sadness come to live. It was evident in a di yaad dat duohn sweep, di verandah furniture dem dat duohn dos fi days and when Uncle Nathan kaal out and di uol lady come to di door, A see di sadness in a di droop of her batam lip and in di deep line dem in a her farid.

When she see Uncle Nathan, her yai dem light up like when di sun peep out behain rain clouds, but when she look pahn me, di light go out and she suddenly look uncertain.

Uncle Nathan tek mi han and waak me up to di doorway weh Miss Maudie stan-up. Me know is she because me recognize di familiar contours of her face despite di changes dat time and chobl deposit. It is clear dat she duohn know dat is me and me andastan why. Di laas time she see me, A was barely eighteen and now, me close to faati-wan.

"Maudie, you remember Jimmy mother?"

Miss Maudie mout faal open and to my surprise, she staat fi cry and taak at di same time.

"Gaad bless mi two yai dem. A neba know dat A wuda *lib* fi si yu on dis eart again. A weh yu did deh mi chail?

She never give me a chance to answer before she grab me roun mi waist, pull me up to her skeletal frame and squeeze me so haad dat she almuos cut-aaf mi bret. A kud tell dat she overjoyed to see me but A was knocked off mi balance a bit and relieved when she let me go.

Jos den, me hear a biebi squeal-out and sombadi smother di sound. Me never wait to be guided but staat fi run toward di back a di house. Me paas chuu a livinroom to a shaat passageway and me see a half-closed door to mi right. Di ada two was so close behain dat we almuos a faal over each ada as we rush into di room.

Di girl a stan-up in front a di winda a wid her back to we. Di back of her cotton nightdress stain wid blood and di same dry blood cake on to di back of her leg dem. Me glance over to di bed and see dat di top sheet and blanket bloody.

Me look back toward di girl and see dat di sash winda open and when me look dong, me see dat she have a pillowcase in her han and she a clutch di top into a bunch. Di pillow case a dance in a her han and me kyan hear di biebi a cry and a sniffle. Is a sound like an oversize kitten wuda mek.

A never wait fi Uncle Nathan or Miss Maudie to intervene. Me run over and grab di pillowcase from her han. Me see Miss Maudie spin her roun and bax her kraas her mout. Me hear

Uncle Nathan a kaal her aaf a di poor pikni but me have mi attention pahn di pillowcase dat still a *stor up-stor-up* in a mi han dem. Me put it pahn di bloodstained bed and reach inside. Me feel a saaf, fat, kickin leg and me huol it firmly wid mi lef han and slide mi right han aanda di head and neck and pull di strugglin biebi free. Me checkin it over real quick to mek sure it breathing right and feelin fi swellins or any ada sign a trauma. In di meantime, Miss Maudie a hala and cuss di girl.

"Joanie! Joanie! Mi neba know seh a so yu wikid! Lawd oh, yu waahn fi kill Jimmy pikni! Yu wikid bitch yu! Maasa Gaad boun fi strike yu dong!"

Me waahn fi tell her fi tap cuss di pikni but me ha fi tend to di baby fors. Is a fat likl girl and her face screw up and red like wahn over ripe tomato. By now, she a splutter wid rage and me put her up to mi shoulder.

When me ton roun fi shush Miss Maudie, di girl tek her two han dem, brace herself against di winda ledge and pull herself up and jump chuu di winda.

We all run up to di winda and see her pahn her han and knee in a di *brush-brush* dong below. Me kyan see her a bleed from a gash pahn di side of her face and she a huol her side when she manage fi stan up. She look up wan time and me see a mad uman wid matted hair, bare feet and bloody nightclothes, limp-aaf into di gully below di border a di backyaad. Me han di baby to Miss Maudie and tek-aaf behain Uncle Nathan.

When me reach di verandah, me see a taal, nice-lookin young man a come outa wahn station wagon weh paak behain

Uncle Nathan chok. Him see we a run and him shout out, "Is wa happen? *Sopm apn* to Joanie!"

Uncle Nathan slow dong and as me run paas him and reach roun to di side a di house, me see di young man sprint paas me. Me know right aweh dat him have feelins fi di young lady.

Me look dong and me see a bloody trail in a di dirt and pahn di bush dem and me fala di trail.

When me and Uncle Nathan reach di gully batam, we out a breath and mi skin a bon me in all a di expose area dem. Me know dat both ants and cow-itch bite me. Is down dere in a smaal ganja field we find Joanie. She mash dong a wol patch a di weed where she collapse and lie dong pahn her side. She a breathe shallow and me a wanda if we a look pahn potential haat-failure. Me also a worry seh she sustain internal injuries when she jump chuu di winda.

Me feel notn but sorrow fi di poor soul because me know dat is not wicked she wicked. Me see dis kaina response to chailbert before and me know dat dis is postpartum psychosis. Me also know dat plenty people duohn know notn bout it and dis ignorance kyan have disastrous consequences.

Di American uman come to mi mind and me immediately have a flashback to di five likl casket dem line out side by side after she drown her children. Me still get bex when me remember how di husband did lang pahn college credentials but shaat pahn emotional intelligence. Imagine, yu breed yu uman two time and di two time, she get aaf her head. Dat not enough sign to yu dat she kyaahn breed good? Yu get a blasted vasectomy or somting, but not him. Him keep on a breed di uman and leave her fi home school di pikni dem. Police shuda did lockup him *blouse'n-skirt* and leggo do uman.

We lif up Joanie and di chrii a we kyari her back to di house. Me support her leg dem, Uncle Nathan support her head and shoulders and di taal young man support her back. She duohn mek a sound. She jos stretch out limp in a wi han dem, wid di sticky blood matt-up her hair and stain-up her neck and di back and front of her cotton night dress. Aanda all dis disfigurement, me see dat dis is a girl who kuda waak weh wid di Miss World Crown, easy-easy.

When we reach in a di yaad, di young man, who Uncle Nathan kaal Danny, staat fi cry and taak same time. "*Wid all juu rispek i-no,* Maas Nate, mi a beg yu waan Jimmy and tell him seh if mi bok him up, mi boun fi spill him blood. Look how him do di nice-nice girl. A mad she mad yu know, sa."

Mi surprise how Uncle Nathan calm when him respond. "If you love dis girl, don't do anything to hurt di man dat she love. She will hate you fi life."

Me still mi haat and tek a good look pahn dis Danny fi get di full measure of him. Me conclude dat is haatbreak a taak.

We tek Joanie back into her granmada house and me and Danny baid her and put clean clothes pahn her. Me watch how him tender wid her. Him even help me mek-up di bed after we tek-aaf di blood-up sheet dem and A seh to miself dat if Joanie smart, she figet bout mi son and huol-aan pahn dis wan.

After me dress and bandage Joanie head, me kwestian Uncle Nathan and him tell me dat di best psychiatrist in di island is one name Dr. Frank Higgins and him in private practice in Kingston. Him agree to tek we back into di city in a di maanin fi get Joanie into di hospital. Him tell me dat di University Hospital have a fairly decent psychiatric wing.

A DIDN GO back to di church house dat day. Late into di evenin, Jimmy and Genevieve come dong to Miss Maudie house and me see di agony pahn him face when him tek up di likl baby-girl. To my surprise, Genevieve tek di baby from him when him and Miss Maudie and Uncle Nathan go into di kitchen fi taak. Me go back into di bedroom fi check pahn Joanie. She still an a deep sleep from di tranquillizer dat she get at di Falmouth Hospital where me, Uncle Nathan and Danny tek her after we clean her up.

Me more tired dan I have ever been in mi life but me no hopeless. I am prayin dat di spirit dat di Mada bring will stay wid di church. Miss Maudie tell me dat she come to di house when we gaan to di hospital. She pray and bon frankincense and myrrh in a di house and she bless di likl baby-girl and she gaan back to Portland wid her husband.

Me truly sorry dat me never get a chance fi meet wid her but me promise miself dat me will go to see her before goin back to New York. Me gwaihn certainly need a special anointin fi wa me a plan fi do. A will aafa fi tek di likl biebi-girl if di parents will agree. Me a watch Genevieve as she si-dong aanda di bare light bulb weh a hang dong from di ceilin. Di light harsh but her face saaf wid tenderness as she a gaze pahn di face of her husband pikni but me a tink beyond dis moment and into di future. Joanie will not always be broken and somting tell me dat when she *get back pahn foot*, mi grandaata will be a convenient weapon of war.

Me decide den and dere, right weh me si-dong and a see backward and forward, dat perhaps A will get a second chance fi raise Jimmy by raisin him pikni. In di meantime, A will go back into di bedroom and sit wid dis sleepin and strangely beautiful girl who a pull pahn mi haat-string fi reasons me kyaahn yet explain. A have a knowin sense, strong upon me, duoh, dat our story jos about to begin.

mark chalk line-a method used for outlining, mainly in construction; she made matters clear to him and told him how far he could go

bakl-battle; bottle

haad-a-yerin-hard of hearing

kak-out-cocked out; protruding

shaapn-sharpen

faamyaad-farmyard

foreman brokfos-the foreman's breakfast; a very large breakfast

pint-point

geng-gang

sea-kyat meat-sea cat meat; octopus that is beaten with a hammer or mallet before it is cooked

parij-porridge

yabba mout-big mout; the yabba (Twi) is an earthenware bowl that has a wide opening

transilaited-translated

obiidiant-obedient

Babilan-Babylon

chuun-tune

ketchi-shubi-informal game played like cricket

Brukins-dance that involves stately movements and European costumes. It is performed in celebration of Jamaica's emancipation from slavery.

bredjrin-brethren

mesij-message

Me no wehn waahn come ya-I did not want to come here

raichosnis-righteousness

aatariti-authority

perfik-perfect

never-dead *Delonix regia;* poinciana; branches cut from the tree will grow again even when used as fence posts

uol haigue-blood sucking vampire that disguises itself as a young or old woman by day; known elsewhere in the Caribbean as *soucouyant*, *fire-raas* and l*oogaroo*

lib-live

stor-up-stor-up-stirring; jumping around

brush-brush-brush; shrubbery

Sopm apn?-Has something happened?

blouse'n-skirt-euphemism for a curse word

wid all juu rispek-with all due respect

I-noh-you know

get back pahn foot-get back onto her feet; recover

Acknowledgement

There are many friends and supporters who contributed to the writing of this book by their encouragement. If your name is not mentioned here it is because of my flawed memory but know that your help was invaluable.

I pay homage to my African ancestors who survived the Middle Passage and in defiance, created Jamaican Patwa to let their oppressors know that though their flesh would perish, their spirit would live in their words.

I would also like to thank Olive Todd who kept me on task by her well timed phone calls and unwavering support, over many rears. Thank you also to my editorial team: Nadine Todd, Jo-ann Richards-Goffe and Dr. Stephanie Fullerton-Cooper. A special thank you to Marcel Goffe for providing the image for the cover.

The following individuals either read the manuscript or listened patiently while I read portions out loud. Their

very constructive suggestions and critique helped me significantly: Norma Francis-Hewitt, Dotlyn-Daley-Poyser, Jenni Campbell, Jennifer Small-Graham, Rohan Dennis, Jean Goulbourne, James Walsh, Janel Charles, Anesha Smart-Fullerton, Thelma Johnson, Sonji Johnson-Anderson, Judith Jones-Nugent, Judith Allwood, Mark Jennings and Dr. Kwame Dawes.

I must also thank my elders who taught me how to speak in pictures by way of proverbs and pithy sayings. Most of you have already gone to the ancestors but I have tried to keep you alive for future generations in the pages that I have crafted. If I have not done you sufficient honor, I ask for your forgiveness.

Finally, eternal thanks to my husband, Deverton Gilphilin, who taught me to think like a man and waited patiently for 19 years for me to complete this book.

Disclaimer

The Road to Timnath is a work of fiction that references historical facts that are in the public domain. However all characters and events are fictional and any resemblance to any person or event is completely coincidental.

Praise for The Road to Timnath
Shortlisted for the Una Marson Prize: 2015

This is a novel that caused me to stay up past my bedtime. *The Road to Timnath* is gripping from start to finish. This is the kind of book that would have caused my mother to say, "Hush yu mouth. No everything good fi eat good fi chat." The author has popped the lid off circumstances and occurrences that are rife in our Jamaican culture but which so few people are willing to acknowledge. This is a must read.
Judith Allwood-author of *My God, My money*

A maelstrom of emotions is evoked in this saga as it delves into the psyche of our people, exposing deep-seated beliefs and cultural norms. Like the Caribbean landscape, there are various curves, turns and twists that present a challenge to the characters, test their mettle and affect their behavior as they journey to their Timnath.
Norma E. Francis-Hewitt-Educator

The author of *The Road to Timnath* somehow manages to irresistibly pull her readers in. She paints portraits of real, down-to-earth characters that possess a mysterious touch of magic that makes them leap from the pages and hold on to you, pulling you toward that sequel that just had better be coming soon!
Jo-Ann Richards, author of *Godincidences,* educator and ethnomusicologist/ethnodoxologist

This is a scholarly book that presents a clash of color, religion and culture. This book is a winner and I see it being studied in colleges here and overseas. Bravo!

Jean Goulbourne-Author and Educator

A compelling read that reveals the author's grasp of the intricacies and undertones of rural life. The characters are alive and real, akin to people I have met in my own life. This is a story that most Jamaicans, attuned to the fullness of our social life with its contradictions, multiple layers of meaning and deceptive surface appearances, can relate to. This is a commendable work that will hopefully be the first full flowering of an immense talent.

James Walsh-Educator

Gilfillian's Road *to Timnath* is a deep and delicious scoop up of well-seasoned soup from the rich Jamaican pot of authentic characters and traditional culture. It is a taste of the language, proverbs and sayings of the Jamaican people. It is filled with the wit, wiggles and wiles of relating and doing things. It brings together the homegrown tinged with the foreign. A great refresher of memories long past and a flavor of an exotic lifestyle set against a landscape of beauty and intrigue. A must-have for Jamaicans at home and abroad and those who have an interest in things Jamaican. Taste and see.

Jenni Campbell, Managing Editor, The Jamaica Gleaner

Made in the USA
Middletown, DE
30 January 2020